BREWER
AND
THE BARBARY PIRATES

BREWER
AND THE BARBARY PIRATES

BY
JAMES KEFFER

www.penmorepress.com

Brewer and The Barbary Pirates by James Keffer

Copyright © 2019 James Keffer

ISBN-13: 978-1-946409-82-9(Paperback)
ISBN—978-1-946409-83-6(e-book)

BISAC Subject Headings:
FIC014000FICTION / Historical
FIC032000FICTION / War & Military
FIC047000FICTION / Sea Stories

Editing: Chris Wozney
Cover Illustration by Christine Horner

Address all correspondence to:
Michael James
Penmore Press LLC
920 N Javelina Pl
Tucson, AZ 85748

DEDICATION

To Christine—For all the love and support I didn't deserve.

CHAPTER ONE

Lieutenant William Brewer stepped up on the deck of HMS *Agamemnon* an hour after sunrise. The air was crisp, but the sky was a beautiful cloudless blue. Even though he just got off watch, he was not about to miss this. Ever since the first gulls appeared during his watch, the entire ship had grown excited—it wasn't every day you came home, and Plymouth was just over the horizon.

He was thankful for a swift passage home. He was also surprised at how easily he had slid back into his role as second lieutenant after nearly a year ashore on the island of St. Helena acting as secretary to the island's governor, Lord Horatio Hornblower. It felt like coming home after a long journey to ride your favorite horse again.

"Back already, Mr. Brewer?"

Brewer turned and saw Lieutenant Gerard, first lieutenant and officer of the watch. Gerard wore his perpetual brilliant smile, which made him easy to like.

"Aye, sir," Brewer said. "I never miss the first sight of England when we're coming home, and Plymouth should be just over that horizon."

Gerard nodded. "I know what you mean. When Lord Hornblower brought *Lydia* back from the Pacific—that was when he first met the Lady Barbara—every hand was on deck. We had been at sea for nearly eighteen months."

"Land Ho!"

Brewer jumped into the mizzen shrouds to get a look ahead. The low strip of green he saw, set atop the horizon of the blue sea, was the most beautiful thing he'd ever seen. (Of course, he thought that every time he came home.) Soon, Plymouth itself would be visible. Brewer could feel his heart quicken; it would not be long now.

"Mr. Brewer," Gerard said, "please convey my respects to the captain and Lord Hornblower. Tell them England is in sight."

"Aye, aye, sir," Brewer said. He saluted and left the poop. He knocked on the door of the great cabin where Captain Bush and Lord Hornblower were having breakfast.

The marine guard came to attention as he approached. "Second *Lef*tenant, sir!" he called.

"Enter" came from within.

Brewer entered and closed the door behind him. "Begging your pardon, Captain. Mr. Gerard sends his respects. England is in sight."

"Ah, good!" Bush said. "Thank you, Mr. Brewer."

Brewer came to attention and left the room.

Hornblower turned to his old friend. "Well, Bush, looks like the end of the adventure."

"Indeed, my lord," Bush said. "Do you think we will ever see him again?"

"Boney?" Hornblower thought for a moment, and Bush noticed a sad, hard look come over his friend's face. "No, Bush, I don't. I think it will take nothing less than a letter from the King himself to get me back on that island as long as that man Lowe is the governor. I fear he will undo all the good work we accomplished while I was governor."

"A shame, my lord," Bush said.

"Yes," Hornblower looked at the deck for a moment

before seeming to assert his will and dismiss the Emperor and St. Helena from his thoughts. "Tell me, Bush, what are your plans?"

Bush stood, and his mentor followed suit. "Tomorrow I must see the Port Admiral," he said, "and I fully expect him to tell me that *Agamemnon* will be paid off." He patted the bulkhead affectionately. "No place for the old girl in the peacetime navy, it seems."

Hornblower had a thought. "Isn't Admiral Pellew still port admiral in Plymouth?"

"I believe so, my lord."

The ex-governor smiled. "In that case, if you don't mind, Captain, I will accompany you on your visit tomorrow. I find that I have a sudden desire to drop in on an old friend."

Bush smiled as well. "You'd be most welcome, my lord."

Midmorning of the following day found both Lord Hornblower and Captain Bush awaiting an appointment with Admiral Sir Edward Pellew, 1st Viscount Exmouth. They had made their way from the wharf to Hamoaze House, which recently been appointed the home for the port admiral. It was built by the Duke of Richmond in 1795 and taken over by the navy for the purpose in 1809. The tram delivered them to the front door where they were graciously greeted by a servant and asked to wait in the parlor.

The two men waited in silence until the Admiral's aide came to them and asked that they follow him. He led them to a door on the first floor where he stopped and knocked with his head near the door. He opened the door and announced the visitors.

"My lord, Lord Horatio Hornblower and Captain William Bush." The aide stepped back to allow them to enter and then closed the door behind him on his way out.

The two officers stepped into a room of what might best

be described as understated opulence. A big oak desk sat in the back corner of the room. Overstuffed, high backed leather chairs sat before the desk and also in front of a large, empty fireplace on the opposite wall of the room, a portrait of the King mounted over the hearth. Bookshelves lined the remaining walls. The room was obviously designed to impress, but its occupant was the main attraction.

"Hornblower!" Exmouth said as he rose and came around his desk. "So good to see you!" The two men shook hands warmly; their friendship went back almost to the day that Hornblower joined the navy some twenty-five years earlier. As captain and admiral, Pellew had watched over his protégé's career with great interest, helping from time to time when he was able.

"Thank you, my lord," Hornblower replied. He was pleased to see the admiral appeared to be in good health, if a little heavier due to age. Many admirals allowed their health to go bad after being assigned to the beach, thinking their service—and therefore their usefulness—was over. Apparently, Exmouth would have none of it. "May I present Captain William Bush, captain of the *Agamemnon*, who has brought me back from St. Helena?"

"You certainly may." Exmouth turned to Bush and shook his hand warmly. "I have read all of the Governor's reports, Captain. You did splendidly commanding the squadron guarding the island."

Bush nodded his thanks as Exmouth picked up a bell on his desk and rang it. A servant opened the door. From his promptness, Bush guessed he had been standing outside awaiting that very event.

"Refreshments for three, please, George," he said. The servant closed the door behind him.

Exmouth resumed his seat and said, "Do you remember Driver, my coxswain on the old *Indefatigable*? After we returned from the East Indies in 1809, Driver took over my household. Ran it every bit as well as he did the old *Indie*. He died while I was in the Mediterranean in 1811; terrible loss, I can tell you. George there is his son. I offered him a commission in the navy, but he said he would rather carry on his father's work of caring for me and my family." Exmouth shook his head, the look on his face one of compassion and gratitude. "You don't fine loyalty like that much anymore."

"No, indeed, my lord," Hornblower said.

At that moment, George came in and set a silver tray on the desk with three glasses and a decanter of port. The servant bowed to his master and withdrew, all without saying a word.

"Captain, will you do the honors?" Exmouth motioned toward the tray. Bush obediently rose and poured drinks for each of them. Exmouth rose, and Hornblower followed suit. Exmouth smiled to Hornblower and then turned to Bush.

"Well, Captain, I imagine it's been many a year since you heard these words directed at you." He raised his glass. *"Mr. Vice, the King!"*

Bush smiled and raised his glass. "Gentlemen, the King!"

The three men drank the toast, and Exmouth laughed.

"Well done, Captain!"

"Bless me, my lord," Bush said, "I feared for a moment that I'd forgotten the words!"

All three laughed and resumed their seats. "Well, Hornblower," Exmouth said, "how was our friend Boney, when last you saw him."

"Well enough, my lord," Hornblower said, "although I cannot say how long he will remain so, with Lowe and his ilk in charge now."

"Yes, well," Exmouth shifted uncomfortably, "fortunes of war, I suppose." The conversation drifted to the respective families and how they fared. Exmouth was able to report that he had kept tabs on young Richard since the lad and his mother returned to England, and at last report the boy was progressing well and was expected to fully recover from his illness.

"Thank you, my lord," Hornblower said. "That is a great relief to me."

"I daresay it is," Exmouth replied. "It's the least I can do for my favorite midshipman." The old admiral smiled and nodded.

"Now then, Captain Bush," Exmouth said, all business now. "As to your current position. I fear I must give you the unpleasant but probably not entirely unexpected news that *Agamemnon* is to be paid off."

Bush sighed. "I expected as much, my lord."

"I am sorry, Bush," Exmouth said. "I hope something will come open for you."

"Begging your pardon, my lord," Hornblower stirred and said, "but the last time I inspected HMS *Lydia* at St. Helena, she was badly in need of a refit. It is my considered opinion that, once the refit is completed, she will have at least one more good cruise in her."

Exmouth's eyes narrowed at Hornblower and he scratched his chin as he considered his friend's proposal. Suddenly, his eyes grew wide and he sat forward.

"Why, Hornblower," he said, "I think you may have something there. A report crossed my desk within the last forty-eight hours stating that those Barbary infidels were starting more trouble in the Mediterranean. I bombarded Algiers into submission when I took a fleet to the Mediterranean back in 1816, but it seems they're ready for another go-round. If there's one thing I learned fighting those pirates, it's that frigates are the best weapons we have to get the job done. I believe I can justify the refit of *Lydia* on that basis, in light of the current emergency in the Med. But who is available to command her?"

"I'm sure we could put an ad in the *Times* and see who applies, my lord," Hornblower said.

Bush just sighed loudly, crossed his legs and rested his chin in his hand, content to let his friends have some fun at his expense. Hornblower heard his friend's sigh and smiled.

"Wait, my lord!" he said. "What about Captain Bush for the *Lydia*?"

"Bush? Do you think he's up for it?" Exmouth deadpanned. His face broke into a great grin. "Of course! What do you say, Captain?"

Bush nodded. "I accept, my lord."

Exmouth and Hornblower had a laugh; Bush just smiled and let them.

"I shall issue orders to take *Lydia* into drydock for a refit. Captain, you may take your officers from *Agamemnon* with you, if you wish."

"Thank you, my lord."

"See my flag lieutenant on your way out to settle the details," Exmouth said as he rose. "I apologize that I cannot invite you to dine with me this afternoon, but the demands upon my time are beyond my control of late. Hornblower!" Exmouth took his protégé's hand again. "It's good to see you again. I must tell you, you have justified my confidence in you many times over the years, sir. And you, Captain!" he turned to Bush and shook his hand. "I can see that Hornblower has picked good men to be his officers. You are a credit to the navy, sir."

"Thank you, Sir Edward," Bush said, his voice cracking with emotion.

Exmouth nodded and turned back to Hornblower. "Give Barbara my best, won't you?"

"I will," Hornblower said. "Good-bye, my lord."

They left the Viscount in his office and went to find the

flag lieutenant. It took some time to iron out the details of *Lydia's* refit. Bush and his officers were put on leave until notified that *Lydia* was ready for them. The details having been settled to everyone's satisfaction, Bush and Hornblower were shown the door and made their way back to *Agamemnon*.

"What a wonderful turn of events, Bush," Hornblower said as they rode. "A cruise against the Barbary pirates in the Mediterranean could take up to two years or more, depending on how much they want to fight, and how permanent Whitehall wants the solution to be."

"We'll be ready for them, my lord," Bush said.

Hornblower smiled. "I have no doubt of that, Captain." The two men rode in silence for a moment, then Hornblower turned to his friend. "Say, Bush, do you have any plans while *Lydia* is undergoing her refit?"

Bush seemed embarrassed that he had nowhere to go. Hornblower already knew that his sister was visiting friends in Ireland for the next several months.

"No, my lord," Bush said.

"Then why not come and be our guest at Smallbridge?" Hornblower asked.

"Oh, I would not wish to impose, my lord."

"Nonsense!" Hornblower said. "You know Barbara would love to see you again, as would Brown, I have no doubt. No, Bush, I insist that you come to Smallbridge."

Bush surrendered gracefully. "Thank you, my lord; it would be an honor."

"Good," Hornblower said. "I shall tell Barbara to expect you within the week."

The tram came to a halt, and the two men got out and shook hands.

"Your dunnage should be on the coach, my lord," Bush said.

"Thank you again, Bush. I don't think I could have done the last year without you."

Bush blushed. "You are too kind, my lord. Begging your pardon, my lord, but I was wondering if I might invite one of my officers to Smallbridge with me. I happen to know he has nowhere to go during the refit."

"Mr. Brewer?" Hornblower asked.

"Yes, my lord."

The ex-Governor smiled. "Yes, Captain. Bring him along. Good-bye, Bush!"

The next evening, Bush invited his officers to dine with him, and he broke the news to them that, as they expected, *Agamemnon* was to be paid off. Even though the news was expected, Bush felt the disappointment that swept the room.

"But that's not all," Bush told his men. "The port admiral has authorized HMS *Lydia* to undergo a refit preparatory to being sent to the Mediterranean to fight the Barbary pirates. I am to be her captain, and I am authorized by Admiral Pellew to take any of my officers who wish to go with me. What do you say, Gerard?"

"Absolutely, sir!" Gerard beamed.

Bush nodded. "Mr. Brewer?"

"I would be honored to go, Captain," Brewer said.

"Excellent. And you, Mr. Starling?"

"I will go, Captain."

"Thank you," said Bush. "As of now, you are all on leave until *Lydia* finishes her refit. Be sure to leave me an address where you can be reached."

"Captain," Starling said. "I will be visiting my family in London. I can write down the address for you."

"Excellent, Mr. Starling." Bush found him a pen and paper, and Starling wrote the address down.

Gerard stepped up. "I shall be in London as well, Captain.

You may reach me through the Admiralty building."

"Very good, Mr. Gerard."

Bush shook hands with both men. "Thank you both for all you did for *Agamemnon*. Now, if you will excuse us, I need to speak to Mr. Brewer."

Both men made their farewells and left the cabin, leaving Bush alone with Brewer, who was looking both surprised and nervous at his captain's announcement. Bush smiled, knowing the reasons behind it.

"And you, Mr. Brewer?" he asked. "Where will you be staying while *Lydia* undergoes her refit?"

Brewer shifted uncomfortably. "I hadn't decided, Captain. I think I told you that I cannot go home."

"Yes," Bush said, "I remember that you told me."

Brewer shrugged—a sort of there-you-go gesture—and shook his head. "I imagine I will just stay in Plymouth until our new ship is ready."

Bush could barely contain himself and not spoil his surprise. "Mr. Brewer, would you be interested in spending your leave with me?"

Brewer was surprised at the invitation. "Oh, sir; I wouldn't want to intrude on your time with your sister."

Bush shook his head. "No need to worry, Mr. Brewer; my sister is visiting friends in Ireland. I am going to Smallbridge."

Brewer was confused. Bush's smile grew broader as he saw the significance dawn on the young lieutenant. Brewer looked at him with his eyes wide, and it was all Bush could do not to laugh.

"Well, Mr. Brewer? What do you say?"

Bush himself was surprised to see the younger man smile.

"When do we leave, sir?"

The coach bounced through a rut in the road, jostling young Brewer awake. He opened his eyes, trying to blink the sleep out of them, to see Bush sitting across from him, arms crossed and smiling.

"I apologize, sir," Brewer said as he sat up.

"No need, Mr. Brewer," Bush said. "I would have slept as well, if I could get comfortable, that is."

"Where are we?" Brewer asked.

"Still a couple of hours from Smallbridge."

Brewer nodded and looked out the window at the passing countryside.

"I want to thank you for inviting me, Captain," he said.

"My pleasure, Mr. Brewer. When we were on our outward voyage to St. Helena, and Lord Hornblower came to me and asked for my recommendation for an aide, I recommended you. You have more than justified my faith in you. I am pleased I could do this for you."

Brewer thanked his captain and spent the remainder of the trip looking out the window. Bush let his young lieutenant be. As good as Brewer's performance had been as Hornblower's aide and secretary, Bush had been even more impressed with how Brewer had conducted himself after his return to *Agamemnon*. Bush had known too many young lieutenants over the years who would have made a show of their position or tried to use it to curry some advantage, but Brewer never showed any inclination toward either vice. He simply put his uniform back on and resumed his duties as though St. Helena had never happened. Bush heartily approved and hoped Brewer would remain unchanged.

The coach pulled into Smallbridge, and the two officers gathered their luggage and walked the short distance to the outskirts of the hamlet where Hornblower's house lay. As they approached the house, they found Lord and Lady Hornblower outside bidding good-bye to a guest.

Hornblower saw them coming and greeted them.

"Bush! Mr. Brewer!" he hailed them. He shook both their hands and ushered them up to the house. "Barbara, my dear! Look who has arrived!"

"Captain Bush!" she greeted him warmly, kissing him on both cheeks. "Thank you for bringing my husband home to me once again. And Mr. Brewer!" Brewer bowed over her hand. "Welcome to Smallbridge."

"Thank you, your ladyship," Brewer said.

Hornblower ushered both officers forward to be presented to their departing guest.

"You gentlemen are just in time to meet my brother-in-law," Hornblower said. "Arthur, this is Captain Bush, whom I've told you about, and this is Lieutenant Brewer, who was my aide and secretary on St. Helena. Gentlemen, my brother-in-law, Arthur Wellesley, Duke of Wellington."

Brewer was awestruck by the introduction and remembered barely in time to bow along with his captain before the Duke.

"An honor, your grace," Bush said.

"An honor," Brewer echoed.

The Duke nodded a greeting to the two officers. "Captain Bush," he said, "both Horatio and Barbara have told me of your exploits at my brother-in-law's side. I will tell you that my sister considers you to be nothing less than a miracle worker, due to your ability to repeatedly get Horatio out of scrapes and bring him home to her alive."

"Thank you, your grace," Bush said.

The Duke looked at Brewer for a moment before turning to Hornblower. "Horatio, is this the young man you spoke of last night?"

"Yes."

The Duke turned back to Brewer with a more appraising eye, then a smile appeared at the corner of his mouth.

"Lieutenant, you are a member of a very small and unique club. The three of us—you, Horatio, and myself—have each in our own way stood up to Bonaparte's fury and survived."

"I have done nothing, your grace," Brewer protested.

"Not so, sir!" the Duke said. "My brother-in-law told me of coming into his office after ordering a security crackdown at Longwood to find Bonaparte standing toe-to-toe with you in your office. Did that happen?"

"Yes, your grace."

"Horatio also said that outside the office, he heard Bonaparte screaming at you. Did that happen?"

"Yes, your grace."

"Then you are indeed a member of our little club, Lieutenant. Your modesty speaks well for you. I pray it remains genuine. Listen to these two men," he motioned toward Hornblower and Bush, "and they will teach you well."

Brewer bowed. "Thank you, your grace."

Wellington kissed his sister on the cheek. "Good-bye, Barbara my dear."

"Good-bye, Arthur," she said. "Safe journey."

"Hornblower," the Duke said, "once again, you have done a great service for your country."

"Thank you, your grace," Hornblower said, "but I fear it will all be undone."

Wellington shrugged. "Beyond any of our control. You did your duty, and you did it very well. England can ask no more." He boarded the carriage and waved to them as the driver whipped up the horses. They watched him drive away and out of sight.

Hornblower offered his arm to his wife, and they ascended the steps to the house. Bush went to follow them. At the top of the stairs, he notice they were missing someone.

"My lord," he said. Hornblower turned, and Bush motioned to Brewer, still standing there, staring after the departed Duke.

"Mr. Brewer," Hornblower said, "you may come inside, if you wish." The young lieutenant's trance was broken, and he blushed in embarrassment as he hurried up the stairs. The Lady Barbara smiled at him; she had seen the same reaction from countless young men who had met her famous brother.

"My apologies, my lord," Brewer said.

Hornblower laughed. "Nonsense! Come inside!"

Inside the door, the faithful Brown waited to take their coats. He smiled when he saw Captain Bush.

"Bless my soul!" he said. "Captain Bush! A pleasure to see you again, sir!"

"And you, Brown," Bush said as he handed over his cloak. "You remember Lieutenant Brewer, don't you?"

Brown smiled and nodded at Brewer as he accepted his coat and hat. "Of course! Good to see you, sir!"

"And you, Brown," Brewer said.

Brown nodded and left to take care of his duties.

"If you gentlemen will excuse me," Lady Barbara said, "I shall go check on our son."

"Of course, my dear," Hornblower said as the others nodded their agreement. "We shall be in the study."

She went her way, and Hornblower led the way to his study in the back of the first floor of the house. Brewer was impressed by the room, the opposite and left hand walls of which were dominated by windows that let a great deal of light into the room. To the right of the door in the far corner was a large desk with a high backed leather chair behind it. In front of the windows to the left was a red settee with a low table in front of it. Hornblower headed straight for a table to the right of the door with decanters and glasses on it and poured each of them a drink. When they had drunk, Hornblower walked over to the desk.

"I don't think you've seen this, Bush," he said. Brewer saw

14

that there was something lying on the corner of the desk, still wrapped in the blanket meant to cushion it during its journey from St. Helena. Hornblower set his glass on the desk and carefully began to unwrap what appeared to be a large platter, beautifully decorated. "I don't think you were there, Mr. Brewer, when Bonaparte presented this to me. The Emperor had been given a set of Sevres china by the people of Paris on the occasion of his coronation in 1804. He had each piece painted to illustrate an event from his life." Bush and Brewer stepped up to take a good look at the plate. It depicted a panoramic view of an army camp with several campfires burning in the foreground and men cooking a meal or relaxing. In the background, troops were drilling in formation, and cavalry were practicing the charge. Both men looked to Hornblower for further explanation.

"He called it the victory that never was," Hornblower said. "The army camp at Boulogne."

"It might have been a great victory indeed, my lord," Bush said grimly, "if it weren't for the Channel Fleet blockading Brest, Rochefort, Boulogne, and the rest."

"Yes," Hornblower said. "Bonaparte thought as much, too."

Lady Barbara rejoined them, and her husband got her a glass.

"How is Richard?" he asked.

"He is sleeping," she replied. "You know how excited he gets whenever Arthur visits. He is still weak enough from his illness that it tired him out."

"Is the child recovering?" Bush asked.

"The doctor saw him this morning," Barbara said. "He was cautious in his words, but he thinks Richard is over the illness itself and now only needs to recuperate and regain his strength."

"That is good news," Brewer said.

Lady Barbara smiled. "Brown, can you please show our guests to their rooms so they can freshen up?"

"Yes, my lady."

"After you've settled in," Hornblower said, "I shall be in the library. You gentlemen are welcomed to join me."

"Thank you, my lord," Bush said, answering for them both.

The two men followed Brown upstairs and down a corridor in a wing Brewer thought was newer than the central wing they just left. Brown stopped at the last two doors on the right.

"Mr. Bush can have this one," he said, nodding to the near door, "and yours is there, Mr. Brewer. Fire should be laid in each one already."

Brown left them there, and Brewer went into his room. It was a small bedroom that would be easily warmed by the small fireplace in the wall between his room and Bush's. The furniture was sparse but comfortable, with a bed, dresser, and a wash stand in the corner complete with pitcher, bowl, and towel. Brewer unpacked his kit and stowed his bag under the bed. He walked around the bed to look out the window. The scene was one of the open countryside dominated by small local farms, and Brewer was struck by how much it reminded him of his home county of Kent. He wondered for a moment if his father knew of his service on St. Helena or that he had met and interacted with someone like Napoleon Bonaparte. He had written regularly to his mother, sisters, and brother, but they never wrote anything to him about any reaction of his father's. He leaned against the cool window glass as a wave of depression swept over him. After a few moments, he pushed himself off the window and shook the depression off him with an almost physical effort. He poured some water in the bowl and splashed it on his face. He patted it dry with the towel and hung it neatly in place before heading for the library.

He found Bush already there, speaking with Hornblower while Brown lit the fireplace against the growing cool of the evening.

"Ah!" Hornblower said, "there you are, Mr. Brewer. Pour yourself some claret. Captain Bush and I were just discussing your upcoming operations."

Brewer poured himself a glass and joined the others. Bush was speaking.

"Perfect heathens, from what I hear, my lord. They think nothing of taking prisoners as slaves and selling them if they are not ransomed by their government!"

"Yes," Hornblower said. "They bother our commerce just enough to get our attention, and then they demand tribute to cease their activities and ransom for their captives. The lunacy of it is that part of their tribute has been small warships such as brigs or schooners, which they use to attack our commerce the next time!"

Bush shook his head with a scowl on his face as he took another sip of claret. Brewer tried very hard to keep his face still and listen with as little reaction as possible.

"I'm afraid," Hornblower said, "England has underestimated these villains in the past. When Lord Exmouth was sent to shell Algiers into submission back in 1816, it was actually his second time dealing with them. The Med has been more or less quiet since then, but ships began disappearing again about six months ago."

"What about the Mediterranean Fleet, my lord?" Brewer asked.

Hornblower gave him a sad smile. "The Mediterranean Fleet is not what it was under Nelson. Like the rest of the navy, it has suffered from the drawdown from a wartime to a peacetime navy. The *fleet* is now more like a *squadron*, and can call upon no more than one or two frigates and a handful of smaller ships. You may well understand Exmouth's eagerness to add another frigate."

Bush got a serious look on his face, his eyes flashing from Hornblower to Brewer to the floor and back again. Brewer wondered what was racing through his mind. Hornblower must have noticed as well, but he did not ask Bush about it, so Brewer remained silent as well. There was a knock at the door. Brown entered and said that supper was ready.

The two officers followed their host into the dining room. Lady Barbara and Richard were there, standing behind their seats until the men found their seats and sat, Hornblower hold the chair for his wife before taking his own at the end of the table with the Lady Barbara on his right hand and Richard next to her. Bush was given the place at his former captain's left hand with Brewer next to him. The servants brought the feast, pheasant leading potatoes and carrots and beans followed by fresh bread and butter. Lady Barbara kept the dinner conversation light, describing Smallbridge for their guests and asking Brewer if he had any trouble adjusting to being a naval officer again. As the plates were being cleared, Richard came and sat on his father's lap.

"I'm glad to see the boy doing so well, my lord," Bush said.

"Yes," Hornblower said. "I took heart from Barbara's letters and those from the East India Company's doctors, but it wasn't until I saw him myself and he leapt into my arms that I knew he would be well."

"Did you know my uncle, sir?" Richard asked Bush. The captain looked to Hornblower, confused by the boy's question.

Hornblower smiled. "He wants to know if you knew Bonaparte, Bush."

"Ah," Bush said. "I met him only twice, Master Richard, once at your house when we came for supper, and then when your father brought him to my ship."

"I see," the boy said. "And did he play soldiers with you on the floor?"

Bush blushed. "Ah, no, he did not."

"He did with me," Richard said. "He showed me how he beat the Russians, Prussians, and Austrians in all his great battles.'

"Richard," Hornblower said, "Lieutenant Brewer here met your Uncle on several occasions."

"Really?" the boy asked.

"Yes," Brewer said. "My post was outside your father's office, so I saw him every time he came to see the Governor." Brewer smiled, anticipating the next question. "And no, he did not play soldiers with me, either."

"That is too bad," the boy said.

Later that night, Brewer excused himself from the conversation in the library and went to his room. He had just begun to take off his boots when he was interrupted by a knock at his door. He opened the door to find young master Richard standing there holding a box in his hands.

"Yes, Master Richard?" he asked.

"I thought you might like to play soldiers on the floor," the boy said, "since you never got a chance to play with my uncle."

Brewer just looked at the boy, trying to think of a kind way to say no, but the lad's look of earnest expectation melted his heart.

"Why, yes, I would," he said as he stepped back to allow the boy to enter. He gently closed the door. "Perhaps you can show me how your uncle always beat the Russians, Prussians, and Austrians."

So, over the next couple hours, all the major battles of the Napoleonic Wars were refought on the floor of Brewer's room. About an hour into the exercise, Bush stuck his head into the room, interrupting the battles of Jena and Auerstadt. He hastily made his apologies.

"I beg your pardon, Master Richard," he said. And to Brewer, "I shall make your excuses to his lordship."

"Thank you," Brewer said. Bush closed the door softly as Brewer listened while Richard decried what an "addle-brained lout" D'Eleron was for marching his corps back and forth between the two battlefields (due to conflicting orders received from Bonaparte and Ney) while impacting neither and allowing the main Prussian army to escape. Brewer smiled as he pictured those words coming out of Bonaparte's mouth.

The next morning, Brewer presented himself for breakfast. Hornblower greeted him even as the servants deposited a steaming plate of eggs, bacon, roasted potatoes, toast and butter before him.

"I understand you were playing soldiers with Richard," he said with a grin.

"Yes, my lord," Brewer answered. "Now I know Bonaparte's side of all his victories. I noticed the boy never refought any of Boney's defeats."

"No," Hornblower admitted. "Somehow Boney never got around to those."

"I am curious, my lord," Brewer said between mouthfuls. "The Duke—did Richard ask him about playing soldiers?"

"Yes."

"And did he?"

"No."

Brewer lowered his fork. "How did he avoid it?"

"He told Richard he had already played soldiers with his uncle."

Brewer was now thoroughly confused. "And when did he do that?"

Hornblower grinned. "At Waterloo, William."

Brewer smiled as well, and, shaking his head at his own obtuseness, dug into the excellent breakfast before him. As soon as the plate was empty, a servant whisked it away and replaced it with a steaming cup of coffee.

"It's funny about Bonaparte, my lord," he said.

"How's that?"

"Well," Brewer paused to take a drink of his coffee and order his thoughts, "his force of personality, his manner, call it what you will—*something* inside him drove him not only to the peak of power as Emperor of the French but also led him to conquer most of Europe. And yet it was also that same drive, that sense of his own superiority and perhaps invincibility that made him unable to stop and coexist with the other nations of Europe. Eventually, of course, this would lead to his downfall, and he was overwhelmed and deposed. Twice! All that ability, all that talent, and what does it get him in the end? A house on a despicable rock in the middle of the South Atlantic."

"That's because your name is not Bonaparte," Hornblower said. Seeing his protégé's confusion, he tried to explain. "William, had you given that speech to Bonaparte himself before we left, he would have listened to you quietly and then agreed with you whole-heartedly when you finished. And if you had asked him why he allowed it to fall out that way, do you know what he would have told you?"

Brewer shook his head.

"I don't know."

The look on Brewer's face told Hornblower the younger man still did not understand. He sighed and tried again.

"In my many conversations with Bonaparte, he often referred to his 'star' that guided him to his destiny. This included the French throne and his victories, but it also included St. Helena. What I'm saying is, in the overall scheme of things, Bonaparte saw himself as a *passenger* on the coach and not the *driver*. The driver was his 'star', and he could not see his star settling for anything less than total domination." He shook his head at the waste. "So, he let it happen, because he considered it his destiny. He had to take the chance, much like a gambler who feels he is powerless to resist rolling the dice one more time."

Brewer sat back with a blank look on his face as he thought over what his mentor had said. Finally, he shook his head in sad realization and said, "I think I see, my lord, but I still don't understand. Think of what he could have done for France, or even for Europe, if only he could have avoided war."

"I agree," Hornblower said, "but remember one thing, William—war was not always his choice. True, he never shied away from it, but there were times when the European Powers went to war with him. This happened in 1806 with Prussia and again in 1809 with Austria. It also happened in 1815 after his return. The Powers declared him an outlaw and declared war on him. Can you believe it, William? The European Powers declared war, not on a nation, but on a *man*."

Brewer dwelt on this for a moment, amazed at the thought. "Tell me, my lord, what was Bonaparte's opinion of all this?"

Hornblower paused to allow Brown to refill their cups. "Thank you, Brown. Bonaparte was almost of two minds on this. On the one hand, he was bitter and considered that his star had deserted him. On the other hand, he said that it was his destiny and seemed resigned to his fate. He told me he rolled the dice and now he had to live with the results."

Brewer shook his head again. "Too bad, my lord; with a different 'star', he might have ended his days as a great man."

Hornblower's face grew hard and stern, and he leaned

forward in his chair with one elbow on the table. "Mr. Brewer, you need mark one thing and never doubt it again—Napoleon Bonaparte *did* end his days as a great man."

"Of course, my lord," Brewer said. "I am sorry if I offended. I meant no disrespect, either to him or to yourself."

Hornblower blinked and sighed. "Of course, William. I suppose I am a bit sensitive on this topic. Please forgive me. I fear for Bonaparte. Lowe is determined to undo all the good work we did and all the good will we have built up. At times, I fear for his life."

"I hope you are wrong, my lord," Brewer said.

Hornblower stared at his cup. "So do I, William. He was a good friend."

Bush came in, fresh from a walk around the village with Lady Barbara. "My lord," he said, sounding slightly out of breath. "I can see now why you paced the quarterdeck all those years."

Barbara came in right behind him. "Is it some kind of navy rule, Horatio, that none of the King's officers have any idea what the word *stroll* means? I fear our dear Captain Bush is no better at it than you are, even with his peg leg."

"My apologies, my lady," Bush said, adding an apologetic half-bow. "I shall do my best to slow down."

"Perhaps Mr. Brewer, my dear?" Hornblower said. "I shall even order him to take small steps, if you like."

Barbara's eyes narrowed to a "later for you" look, then she smiled at her husband and left the room. Hornblower and Bush smiled after she left.

"Mr. Brewer," Bush said, "it is said that the Duke of Wellington fears one and only one personage on this entire planet. Do you have any idea who that might be?"

"No, sir. Who?"

"His sister," Hornblower said.

Brewer stared at the door as the two officers chuckled.

That evening, Brewer was indeed drafted to accompany Lady Barbara on her walk through the village. Hornblower and Bush were "cordially invited" as well. When they stepped outside, Barbara took Brewer's arm (much to his surprise, but a quick glance to his lordship brought a reassuring nod that it was all right), leaving Bush and Hornblower to fall in together. Soon they were deep in conversation, their natural strides taking them far ahead. For his part, Brewer tried very hard to allow his companion to dictate their pace. Everyone they met greeted Barbara as they passed by, and several time she stopped to ask after someone's health or even just to chat.

"The people love you, my lady," Brewer said as they started off again.

"It's mutual, I assure you," She said as she waved at a woman working in her garden. "They took us all into their hearts almost from the moment we arrived. They adore Horatio, even more than they do the Duke my brother." She leaned in close and whispered, "But don't tell Arthur" as she patted his hand with a coy smile on her face.

They walked a little farther, and Brewer spoke up. "A question, if I may, my lady," he said. "About your husband."

"Yes?"

"What was he like?" Brewer said slowly. He wanted to choose his words carefully now. "Your husband. When you first met him, I mean. It was in the Pacific, wasn't it? What did you think of him when you met him?"

"What did I think of him? Do you mean as an officer, or as a man?"

Brewer thought for a moment and decided on the safer course. "As an officer, my lady."

"And *why* are you asking me this?"

"My lady! I beg your pardon if I seem forward, or if I have

offended you," he said hurriedly. He tried to stop, but she kept him moving. He went on, "Your husband has been something of a mentor to me since St. Helena, and I want to model myself on him, not only as an officer but also as a man. You are an intelligent woman, and I am interested in your opinions of him—again, I apologize if I seem forward—when you, being a stranger, first encountered him."

She said nothing for a time, and Brewer had just begun to think of how to apologize again when she squeezed his arm playfully and smiled.

"Forgive me, Lieutenant," she said. "Your question caught me quite off guard. I was caught up in memories just now." They strolled on for several paces before she turned to him again. "You must remember, Mr. Brewer, that I met my husband at a dire moment in his life. We were at war, and all Horatio's orders and accomplishments, including his capture of a Spanish 60-gunner, were undone when news arrived—on the same boat as I, if you can believe it—that Napoleon's invasion had made Spain an ally and not an enemy. Now he had to go and fight the *Natividad* again. And in the midst of all this, I present myself and demand a ride back to England."

She smiled. "I'm still amazed that his only words to me were 'Ha-hm' and not orders to have me thrown overboard!" She paused, lost in the memory again. "Do you know, Mr. Brewer, I truly believe he let me stay, not because my name was Wellesley, but because to send me back to Panama would be to condemn me to death by yellow fever. He would have allowed me to stay had I been a common scullery maid. I am sure of it."

Brewer nodded as they walked.

"And so I went to war, too," she continued. Her voice was soft, and it was clear she did not intend that her words be for any ears but his. "We caught the *Natividad* and sank it at a considerable cost to the *Lydia* and her crew. We headed south, only to be told by the envoy of the Spanish Viceroy in Panama that we were not welcomed anywhere in Spanish America. Were *I* Horatio, I would have blown their miserable little boat out of the water at that! Still, Captain Hornblower accepted the decree with civility. We found a secluded inlet on a deserted isle and made our repairs to the ship.

"All this time, I was watching him, Mr. Brewer. Slowly, the walls came down, and I was afforded a look inside at the man within. What I saw was not a perfect man, but a caring one to be sure. He cared for the men under his command. He spoke to the wounded and encouraged them. He was open to suggestion; he took one from me about bringing all the wounded who could be moved up on deck for some fresh air."

She paused to consider her words. "I think, because of this, his men adored him. I remember something Arthur once told me: *'The men will follow you anywhere, as long as they know you give a damn.'* Throughout the terrible fight with the *Natividad*, the voyage south, the rejection at Panama, the hard work repairing the ship, and then the log voyage around the Cape to St. Helena where I left them, I never heard one word of sedition or rebellion."

She smiled again. "To answer your question, Mr. Brewer —your *real* question, I mean—which was, what kind of *man* was my husband when I met him, he was every inch a King's officer, which means the most important things to him were his duty and his integrity. I have never known him to fail in either."

Brewer nodded and thought as they strolled along the lane. "A tall order to aim for, my lady," he said.

She patted his arm comfortingly. "The good news for you, my dear lieutenant, is that my husband is a human being and not a god. If he can do it, so can you."

He smiled. "Thank you, my lady." She nodded, and they walked back to the house in agreeable silence.

Later that evening, Brewer joined Hornblower and Bush in the library for Madeira and cigars. Brewer gratefully accepted one of each from Brown and set about puffing life into his cigar.

"Well, Mr. Brewer," Hornblower said from his seat on the divan, "it seems you have found dutiful employment ashore."

Brewer blew a satisfying cloud of smoke toward the ceiling. "How so, my lord?"

"Why, when my wife came back from your walk this afternoon thanking the Almighty that there was at least one officer in the King's service who knew how to take a civilized stroll, I'd naturally imagined you'd resigned your commission and accepted the position."

Hornblower smiled at Brewer's momentary embarrassment while Bush laughed openly. Brewer blushed and nodded as he puffed his cigar.

"Not as yet, my lord," he said.

Hornblower and Bush chuckled, and Brewer drank of his wine before setting his glass on the table. He sat back and took a deep draught on his cigar as he ordered his thoughts.

"A question, my lord, if I may," Brewer said. Hornblower waved his cigar and granted permission. Brewer gathered his courage and said, "What is your secret for leadership?"

Bush's eyes flashed from Brewer to Hornblower and back again, and for a moment Brewer thought he had overstepped his bounds, but Hornblower silently studied the cloud he had just sent skyward, and Bush sat silently. Brewer did the same.

Finally, Hornblower looked at Brewer and said, "Simply put, Mr. Brewer? Leadership is this: Do your duty, and treat the hands as you would want to be treated in their place. I'd say that about sums it up nicely, wouldn't you, Bush?"

"I would indeed, sir."

Brewer nodded behind another cloud of smoke. "I don't suppose it's as easy to do as it is to say?"

Hornblower smiled and raised his glass in salute, and Bush followed suit.

"William," Hornblower said, "you are halfway home already."

Bush nodded, a knowing look in his eye.

Brewer picked up his glass and returned the salute, and all three men drank a healthy dose.

"I have not known you very long, Mr. Brewer," Bush said, "as most of your time under my command was spend in his lordship's service ashore. But from what I have observed of you on the voyage south to St. Helena and back, you seem to have a good foundation for leadership. You should have no trouble learning the rest."

"But how shall I learn?" Brewer asked.

"Bush?" Hornblower deferred to his friend.

"You learn by watching," Bush said. "Every officer you encounter will have good points and bad. You observe him and note everything. I say 'everything' because sometimes a bad point will be revealed by later events to have been necessary. But you observe and you note, keeping the good and discarding the bad. I began that with Captain Harvey when I was a young lieutenant in HMS *Tremeraire*, and I continued it all the time I was under his lordship's command."

Hornblower gestured with his glass. "I did the same when I was a midshipman and a young lieutenant under Captain Pellew in the old *Indefatigable*. You have a very good sense of right and wrong, William—what some would call a 'moral compass'. An apt analogy, in my opinion. Your compass is pointed in the right direction, and that gives you a tremendous advantage over officers who try to lead through fear and punishment. I urge you not to lose it."

"I am far from perfect, William," Bush said. "You watch me, keep the good and discard the bad, and make it your own. That's what I did with Captain Hornblower, and what he did with Captain Pellew. The system works, if you've got the brains to work the system. I believe you do."

Brewer looked to his lordship, who simply nodded his agreement. He mumbled his thanks and sat back to smoke his cigar and contemplate how to craft his life. *The system works,* he thought as he blew another cloud toward the rafters, *so work the system.* He felt the old uncertainty return, the same curse that had bedeviled him throughout his naval career. His eyes flew between Bush and Hornblower, but they were engrossed in reminiscing of their adventures in the Baltic. *They did it, and did it well,* Brewer reasoned with himself, *so you could as well. Just do it as they did. Prove yourself as they did. You can do this!*

Brewer leaned his head back and closed his eyes, trying to keep his demon at bay, but it was no use. He remembered once again what his father said after Brewer told him of his decision to join the Royal Navy.

"I knew you would disappoint me. You have always disappointed me, William, and you will continue to disappoint all who rely on you as I did."

Brewer drew a deep breath and let it out as unobtrusively as he could. Try as he might, his father's words still haunted him. They were the last words he ever said to him; he disappeared into his study and did not return before Brewer left home. He laughed within himself, realizing how ridiculous it was. He had proven himself in battle, risen steadily in rank and responsibility, performed with distinction as the aide and secretary to Governor Hornblower on St. Helena, and stood toe-to-toe and nose-to-nose with no less than Napoleon Bonaparte himself, and yet he was haunted by something his father said out of frustration and anger more than ten years ago.

Brewer opened his eyes calmly. Hornblower and Bush were still in deep conversation, and neither had noticed his predicament. He took a deep drag on his cigar, leaned his head back, and blew the cloud heavenward. He wondered what the Corsican would say to him if he were here.

He leaned his head back and closed his eyes again, this time picturing Bonaparte as he was when he last saw him. The Emperor looked tired, worn out, tired of fighting and ready to surrender to the verdict of life. The image looked at him, and a strange, spectral conversation took place in Brewer's mind.

"So, M. Brewer," it said, "after all our talks together and all the advice I have given you, we still find ourselves here, mon ami?"

Brewer said nothing, and the Bonaparte-image sighed and shook its head.

"M. Brewer, you appear to doubt yourself. How can you seize the opportunity when she presents herself if you are not confident you can do it? The opportunity, she will smile at you and dance away from your grasp if you play the shy schoolboy! Do you not remember, mon ami, how in your office we spoke of this, and I told you that you must play the wolf and jump on the opportunity, taking it by the throat and sinking your teeth into her and making her yours? To do this, you must have confidence—confidence in yourself, confidence in your star, which is your destiny! You seize the opportunity, conquer it, make it your own! That is what I did, both on the 18th Brumaire and on the heights of the Pratzen! Timidity will cost you, M. Brewer!"

"I know," Brewer said unconvincingly. "But seizing the opportunity can have a terrible price. I disappointed my father by running away to sea from our family farm, and he disowned me. Now, Lord Hornblower wants to become my mentor. Don't get me wrong—I know how lucky I am to have his help, and I am grateful for his confidence. I just don't want to disappoint him as well."

The Bonaparte-image looked at him. It seemed to be studying him, as though trying to decide what to make of what he said. Brewer felt vaguely grateful that he was speaking to a figment of his imagination and not the real thing.

"M. Brewer," the image finally said, "you do yourself a grave disservice. At our last meeting, I saw a young officer, fearless, trustworthy, ready to take on the world. You reminded me a great deal of another young officer I loved, my stepson Eugene. You proved yourself fearless when I pressed you after the security crackdown at Longwood."

Brewer smiled. "I was terrified, but I determined not to show it."

The Bonaparte-image nodded. "You did well. I was most impressed with you that day, and I made a point to tell that to the Governor some days later. Now, however," the image shook its head, "I see before me a man very much the opposite. You are troubled by the words of your father, a man who wanted you to deny your destiny in order to remain with him. And now you worry about something that has not happened yet—that you might disappoint M. Hornblower! Imbecile!"

Brewer flinched. A quick look told him that Hornblower and Bush hadn't noticed. He closed his eyes again, and the Bonaparte-image reappeared.

"Fool! Will you let your imagined weakness rob you of the chance of a lifetime! Do you think you will ever have the chance of mentors the likes of M. Hornblower or Captain Bush if you allow this opportunity to slip through your grasp? I know the M. Brewer I spoke to on St. Helena would not allow such a thing to come to pass!" The image gave him a chilling look, in all respects worthy of the original.

"The question is, sir," the image said, "which are you?"

"William?"

Brewer's eyes jerked open. Hornblower and Bush were looking at him.

"Sir? My Lord?"

"You gasped, William," Bush said. "Are you well?"

"Ah, yes, Captain," Brewer stammered as he sat up. "My apologies, my lord."

"Not at all, Mr. Brewer," Hornblower said. "Are you sure you're all right?"

Brewer nodded absently as he rose and walked toward the window. He pictured again in his mind the plate Bonaparte had given the Governor as his mind replayed his conversation with the Bonaparte-image. A feeling came over him, one of control and freedom. Without knowing how or why, he knew he was liberated from his fears. He smiled and nodded to himself. *Thank you, my old friend.*

He turned to look at Hornblower. "Thank you, my lord. I've never been better."

The time at Smallbridge flew by for Brewer in a flurry of strolls with Lady Barbara, fighting battles on the floor with Master Richard, and conversations with Hornblower and Bush about strategy, tactics, and making the most of a naval career. Brewer was happy.

It all ended on a calm afternoon when a knock was heard at the door. Brown brought a letter from the Admiralty addressed to Captain Bush. Bush broke the seal and read the letter quickly.

"It seems *Lydia* is ready," he said. "Mr. Brewer and I are required to report aboard at once and make all preparations for going to sea. We shall receive orders from the port admiral in Plymouth when ready for sea."

"Brown," Hornblower said, "please make arrangements for Captain Bush and Lieutenant Brewer to take passage on the Plymouth Coach."

"Aye aye, my lord," Brown said. He left immediately on his errand.

"If there are seats available," Hornblower said, "you will leave at noon tomorrow. There is a coach nearly every day."

Brown returned and announced that he was able to reserve the last two seats on tomorrow's coach. Brewer spent his last night in Smallbridge fighting the Battle of Austerlitz on the floor and packing his kit.

In the morning, after breakfast, he walked into the study to get one last look at Hornblower's Bonaparte plate, which was now hanging proudly on the study wall. He looked at the French encampment, the order, the power, and he felt confidence.

"Impressive, is it not?"

Brewer turned to find Hornblower standing beside him.

"Indeed, my lord," he said. "I'm glad he never got the chance to cross the channel."

Hornblower was silent for a moment as he studied the plate. It was several minutes before Brewer heard a sigh and saw him nod.

"As am I, William," he said softly. "As am I."

Hornblower and Barbara walked their guests to the coach and said their good-byes as they boarded. They stood arm in arm as they watched the coach pull away down the road.

Barbara looked up at her husband, who was deep in thought. "What are you thinking about, Horatio?"

Hornblower shook himself. "I'm sorry, my dear; I was just remembering how good it felt to be at sea again."

"Well, husband," the Lady Barbara said as she turned her

husband toward home, "what shall we do now?"

"I don't know about you, my dear," Hornblower said with a grin on his face, "but I was thinking about writing the Admiralty to see if they could use me one more time. What do you think of the idea?"

CHAPTER TWO

When Captain Bush and Lieutenant Brewer boarded HMS *Lydia*, they were surprised to be greeted by none other than Lieutenant Gerard.

"Good God, Gerard!" Bush cried. "Did you fly back from London?"

Gerard flashed one of his fabulous smiles. "Actually, I've been here for several days now, sir. Let's just say my plans in London fell through at the last moment."

Bush stepped up on deck and looked around, impressed at his ship's advanced state of readiness. "Probably a good thing you were here," he said. He started to walk around the deck. "So, where are we?"

Gerard fell into step beside his captain. Brewer stayed a respectful two steps behind, listening discreetly and looking around.

"We are actually in pretty good shape, sir," Gerard said. He went over the details as they walked around the deck, Bush nodding occasionally to something Gerard pointed out here or there. They arrived back at the quarterdeck.

"I estimate another three days before we're ready for sea, sir," Gerard said. "There are some lines that the bosun still is not happy with, and I agree with him. The purser's ashore now, as is your steward. The stores you ordered from

Smallbridge arrived yesterday and have been stowed below, sir."

"Powder and shot?"

"Scheduled for tomorrow, Captain," Gerard said. "Water casks to be filled the day after." Gerard chuckled. "There was a rumor as I was leaving for London that *Lydia* might be in line for one of those new metal water tanks. I've heard they keep the water fresh for far longer than the old fashioned casks. I understand the cooper was worried about keeping his job." He sighed in mock despair. "Alas, it turned out to be just a rumor, curse the luck. The cooper keeps his job for now." He shook his head and snuck a wink at Brewer. "Too bad; I was looking forward to making good topmen out of the cooper and his mates!"

The two officers laughed.

"You've done well, Mr. Gerard. Anything else I should know? What about the hands?"

"Believe it or not, Captain, but we're full up! I signed the last topman this morning. I should have the watch bill ready for your review this evening."

"Thank you, Mr. Gerard; that will be fine. If my steward gets back in time, I want to invite you and Mr. Brewer to dine with me this evening."

"Thank you, sir," Gerard said, answering for them both.

"I'll be in my cabin," Bush said. "I'll send for you when it's time."

"Aye aye, sir," Gerard said. Both lieutenants touched their hats as their captain departed.

"I tell you, William," Gerard said after the captain had disappeared below deck, "we're in for a hot time before this cruise is over with."

"How many new hands in the crew?" Brewer asked.

Gerard shrugged. "About seventy or so. I'm afraid most of them are landsmen, but I'm not worried. You'll whip them into shape soon enough, I'm sure!"

Brewer grunted. He hoped he'd be given the time to train them properly.

Gerard dismissed him, and Brewer headed below to the gunroom. Upon entering, he saw old Coles, the gunroom steward, putting the gunroom in order.

"Welcome, Mr. Brewer," Coles said warmly. Brewer smiled and clapped him on the shoulder on the way to his cabin. He had a soft spot in his heart for Coles; the man had manned cannon at St. Vincent and Trafalgar. He was too old for that now, of course, but he still wanted to serve. Brewer was glad to have him.

He entered his cabin and was pleased to see the rest of his dunnage had been transferred from the *Agamemnon*. He smiled when he noticed the shelf Coles took the liberty to build a shelf on the bulkhead to hold his library. He had a dozen or so different works, from Dafoe to Locke to the Bible his mother gave him when he turned ten. Their presence on his wall was a comfort to him. He wondered how long it would be before he was able to get a reliable biography of Bonaparte to add to his collection.

He took his coat off and laid it on his cot beside his hat. He gathered materials to write a letter and walked out to found Coles.

"What have we to drink, Coles?" he said.

"Only wine at the moment, I'm afraid, sir. Will that do?"

"Yes, please," Brewer said as he sat down at the table. He was just setting up to write his sister when Coles returned with his glass. Brewer thanked him and took a drink.

"Any idea where we're going, sir?" Coles asked.

"What have you heard?"

"Rumor is the Med, sir. Barbary pirates, I heard." Coles shook his head. "Is it true?"

Brewer nodded. "I'm afraid it is. Have you ever fought

them before?"

"Oh, no, Mr. Brewer," Coles said. "I've never sailed the Med before, I'm afraid."

"Well, I'm glad you're with us, even so," Brewer said. He took a sip of his wine and began the letter.

The next morning, Captain Bush stepped on deck wearing his best coat and breeches for his visit to Admiral Pellew.

"Mr. Gerard," he said, "I shall return as soon as I can. Carry on with provisioning and making ready for sea. Knowing the Port Admiral as we do, I suspect I may well return with orders to sail on the morning tide."

Gerard smiled. "Aye, sir."

Bush had no sooner set foot on land than he was accosted by the sound of his own name being shouted across the waterfront. He turned to see his old friend Dick Thompson.

"Dick!" Bush cried as the two shook hands. "Dick Thompson! Why, I haven't seen you since the old *Tremeraire*! How have you been?"

"Not as good as you, I'm afraid," Thompson said. He stepped back to look at his friend and pointed to Bush's peg leg. "I see your new leg hasn't slowed you down any."

Bush laughed and shook his head. "Not in the least! And I can tell you, it beats being dead!" Both men laughed again.

"Post Captain!" Bush said, noticing the two epaulettes on Thompson's coat. "What's your date of rank?"

"July, 1814," Thompson said proudly. "I know it's nowhere near you, William, but I'm proud of it. I tell you, for a while there I thought I'd never make it."

"Nonsense!" Bush said in a reassuring voice. "I always thought it was only a matter of time. Come on, let me buy you a drink to celebrate!"

"I know just the place," Thompson said, and the two set off. Fifteen minutes later they were sitting in the best coffee house Bush had ever seen. Thompson ordered for them, and Bush handed the waitress three coins when their beverages arrived.

"So, Bush, what takes you to the Med?" Thompson asked.

Bush took a drink and set it on the table. "I'm in command of the frigate *Lydia*. Lord Exmouth thought the Mediterranean Fleet could use another frigate to fight the Barbary pirates, so there we are."

Thompson gave an exaggerated nod. "That's an understatement. Frigates are worth their weight in gold out there."

"Do you have one?"

"Me?" Thompson feigned surprise. "Not bloody likely. No, sir, I command a 16 gun sloop which has been recalled to England, probably for decommissioning."

Thompson took a drink and brought up the subject of the CinC Mediterranean.

"Ever met him?"

Bush shook his head.

Thompson sat back and smiled. "Sir Thomas Fremantle. His claim to fame is that he was captain of HMS *Neptune* at Trafalgar, and it was his ship that towed HMS *Victory* to safety after she was dismasted. He rose steadily up the captain's list. By 1814, he was Commander-in-Chief, Adriatic. When Napoleon abdicated in 1814, Fremantle received the surrender of over 800 French ships from all over the Baltic coast. The prize money he was awarded was staggering!"

Bush pursed his lips and blew out a silent whistle. He could not begin to guess at the sums that went into Fremantle's pockets. Sums like that would allow a man to retire anywhere in the world and live comfortably for the rest of his life.

Bush thanked his friend and wished him luck. He rose and made his way to the street to hail a cab.

The morning was bright as Captain Bush rode to his appointment with the Port Admiral. The cab let him off at Hamoaze House, where he was shown inside by a waiting porter. Bush thought the house even more impressive than the last time he was here.

After a wait of only a few minutes, a servant came and took him to the Admiral's study. He announced the Captain and withdrew.

"Hello, Captain," Pellew said as he came around his desk to shake hands. "It's good to see you again. I believe you know my flag lieutenant." He indicated the officer sitting in the corner.

"Yes. Thank you, my lord," Bush answered.

"Lieutenant," Exmouth said, "I shall need the sailing orders for HMS *Lydia*."

"At once, my lord," the lieutenant rose and left the room.

"Sit down, Captain, sit down," Exmouth said, indicating the overstuffed chair before his desk. "The flag lieutenant will bring you your orders, but I can tell you that they are the standard ones. You are to sail at the earliest possible date and report to Commander-in-Chief, Mediterranean fleet. If you do not find him at Gibraltar, you are to proceed to Malta or any other such port where he may be found."

"Yes, my lord," Bush said.

Exmouth shook his head in disgust. "Be careful, Captain. I don't envy you your assignment. Those Barbary infidels claim to fight for their god, but only until the ransom is paid, mind you. Have you ever fought them before?"

"No, my lord," Bush said.

"A word of advice then, if I may?"

"Of course, my lord."

"There are some things you need to bear in mind when you fight them," Exmouth said, "that are true by and large, but, as they have the occasional European commander among them, cannot be universally true." Exmouth sat back and counted his points off on his fingers. "They usually attack in packs, like dogs or wolves. This is especially true for their rowed galleys that sometimes dash out from a cove or bay to fall upon an unfortunate merchant vessel that has been blown too close to shore. They have been known to feign a surrender by lowering their flag and then firing on the prize crew in their boat or attacking them with swords when they board the prize. As for tactics, their gunnery is generally not of the best quality; they very much prefer to grapple and board. Our best defense against them is to keep your distance as much as possible and blow them out of the water."

"It will be a pleasure, my lord," Bush said.

"The majority of their ships are small, fast, and highly maneuverable, Captain; your seamanship will be tested, but I am confident that you and *Lydia* will acquit yourselves honorably."

"We shall do our best, my lord," Bush said.

"I know you will. There is one thing more; I have a passenger for you to take. George!" Exmouth called loudly. The servant opened the door. "Send Ali in."

George disappeared and returned a minute later leading a youth into the room. He was of Turkish rather than African descent, nearly six feet tall and thin. Bush's first thought was that he was one of the foreign students who came to England to study at Oxford or Cambridge.

"Ali," Exmouth said, "this is Captain Bush of the frigate HMS *Lydia*."

"A pleasure to make your acquaintance, Captain," the boy said as they shook hands. Bush found the handshake firm and the voice with only a slight accent.

"Ali here is a student at Cambridge," Exmouth said, "and he has volunteered to accompany you to handle any translation that is needed. Ali, gather your kit and be ready to leave with Captain Bush."

"Yes, sir," the youth bowed and left the room.

"I know what you're thinking," Exmouth said after the door was shut, "and yes, he can be trusted. I want you to take him, because the biggest problem I had back in 1816 was that I didn't have anyone who could speak Arabic, so I had to rely on the Bey's translators. Ali reads and writes the language, which will be a great help when examining captured papers and the like."

"Agreed, my lord."

"Good. You can bunk him in with your clerk, if you like, but I will of course leave that to your discretion." Exmouth adjusted in his chair, and for a moment Bush thought the Admiral might be having a problem of some kind with his back. However, the Viscount leaned forward in his chair and continued.

"Your mission, of course, will be two fold. Primary will be the protection of His Majesty's ships and subjects. Secondarily, you will engage and destroy these Barbary pirates wherever and whenever possible. Matters of ransom must of course be referred to the commander-in-chief. You may encounter or hear word of government officials or military officers being held as captives; they may even threaten to sell them as slaves. You will naturally be inclined to attempt to rescue them. Do no attempt it if there is a chance the captives will end up dead. Better to let the government negotiate for their release. Do you understand?"

Bush shifted in his seat. "Yes, my lord."

Exmouth smiled. "I know what you're thinking, Captain; I have been there myself. It is not in our nature to sit back and do nothing in such circumstances, but that is exactly what you must do sometimes. The important thing is to keep them alive."

Bush nodded. "Aye, my lord."

Exmouth rose and walked over to a large scale map of the Mediterranean Sea and the North African coastline spread out on a table. Bush came and stood beside him.

"As I remember," Exmouth said, "there were several inlets and coves along this stretch of shoreline." He pointed to the African coast west of Tripoli. "Be careful that you are not ambushed. You may even be able to trap a pirate in one and force him to surrender. Keep your ships as far out to sea as is practical, especially at night. Pirates have been known to row a half-dozen galleys out from one of these inlets and board an unsuspecting ship at night or in bad weather."

"Yes, my lord," Bush said automatically. He studied the map and saw the wisdom of the Admiral's advice. "How sturdy are these xebecs, generally?"

Exmouth looked up from the map. "What do you mean?"

"Will a 12-pounder broadside in passing put one out of action?"

Exmouth stared at the map through narrowed eyes as he considered. Finally, he looked at Bush as nodded. "Yes, Captain, I believe it would. As long as it is well placed."

There was a knock and the door, and the flag lieutenant entered the room and handed a packet to the Admiral. Pellew took the packet to his desk and motioned for Bush to come over and sign for his orders.

"It's all official now, Captain," Exmouth said as Bush handed him the paper. "God be with you, and good hunting."

Bush accepted his orders and came to attention. "Thank you, my lord."

Bush made the entire trip back to HMS *Lydia* alone with

his thoughts. He had rarely been on a commission without his friend and mentor, but this time Hornblower would be staying behind with his wife and son in Smallbridge. Bush would miss his friend's company. Hornblower had mellowed —Bush thought that was the right word—in his old age; he was not nearly so closed and alone as he was fifteen years ago. Bush thought that, after this commission was over, he hoped to have enough prize money to purchase a small estate for himself and his sister around Smallbridge to be near Hornblower and the Lady Barbara. The coxswain's cry of *"Lydia!"* in answer to the frigate's challenge brought him back to the present. Lt. Gerard was there to meet him as he came aboard.

"Welcome aboard, sir," Gerard saluted.

Bush saluted. "Please join me in my cabin, Mr. Gerard."

"A pleasure, Captain."

Gerard followed Bush below and past the marine guard at the door. Inside, Bush surrendered his hat and coat to his servant before opening the packet he carried. Gerard held his hat under his arm and waited for his Captain to give him the word.

"It's just as the Admiral said," Bush said as he scanned the orders. "We are to sail at the earliest possible moment." He looked up at his first lieutenant.

"That would be the day after tomorrow, Captain," Gerard looked apologetic. "We were not able to get our full allowance of powder today. We are still several tons short, but the armory said they should be able to make it good tomorrow. Our water is also scheduled to be delivered tomorrow as well."

"Well, it can't be helped," Bush said. "We'll sail on the morning tide, the day after tomorrow, for Gibraltar and report to C-in-C Mediterranean."

BREWER AND THE BARBARY PIRATES

The next day brought HMS *Lydia's* final preparations for sea to completion. Brewer stood off to the side and watched the gunner as he supervised the stowing of the last of the powder barrels in the magazine. Brewer watched as the gunner—whose name was Benjamin Reilly—inspected each of the barrels of powder that was lowered into the hold to ensure it was water-tight before allowing it to proceed. In between barrels, Reilly's eyes took inventory of the adzes, drivers, and vises carefully hung up over the filling-room before the bitts, on wooden pegs to avoid any chance of a spark. He also moved to ensure that the copper funnels, shovels, and powder-measures were stowed at the ready. Brewer grew curious when he observed the gunner arranging empty cartridges—used to carry powder to the guns themselves—atop the barrels of powder and then laying tanned hides over them.

"That keeps the cartridges dry and ready to fill at a moment's notice," Reilly said when Brewer questioned him.

Brewer was at his station near the foremast when Captain Bush stepped up on deck in preparation for the *Lydia's* departure. He saw Lieutenant Gerard step up to the Captain and salute, and a few moments later Gerard stepped forward and called for hands to man the capstan. Brewer's eyes were aloft watching his topmen race skyward in answer to the orders to loosen the tops'ls, and within minutes HMS *Lydia* was crawling through the harbor toward the open sea. He sent more hands up in response to Gerard's order to set the fore-course. He motioned to one of his midshipmen, Percy Rivkins.

"You'd better follow them up, Mr. Rivkins," Brewer said. "Make sure they're doing it right. We don't want any mistakes today."

"Aye, aye, Mr. Brewer."

Once free of the land, course was set SSW, their destination the meridian known as 10 degrees west, along which they would head due south past the Iberian coast.

Brewer had the deck during the forenoon watch on clear day that promised not a hint of rain. Mr. Trench, the sailing master, was in conversation with two of his mates at the wheel. Three bells had just sounded when the lookout called.

"Deck there! Sail on the larboard bow!"

Brewer grabbed a glass and headed for the rail. "Where away?"

"Two, no, three points off the larboard bow, sir!"

Brewer quickly found the point of white on the horizon. "Lookout, can you make it out?"

The lookout studied the horizon through his telescope. He lowered it once and looked like he was about to report to the deck, but instead he brought the glass back to his eye and remained silent. Brewer waited as patiently as he could until the man finally called down from the tops.

"Looks like *two* ships, sir!"

Brewer looked at the horizon and nodded grimly to himself; this confirmed his own opinion. He looked around for the midshipman of the watch.

"Mr. Bennett! My respects to the Captain. Tell him two ships sighted, and I am about to alter course."

"Aye aye, sir."

Brewer turned to the wheel. "Straight at them, Quartermaster."

"Aye, sir. Straight at 'em."

Captain Bush appeared on deck and saluted. "Report, Mr. Brewer."

Brewer touched his hat and handed the Captain his telescope. "Lookout report a strange sail off the larboard bow. Further investigation revealed it to be two sails. Per your standing orders, I have altered course to close on the contact."

"Thank you, Mr. Brewer," Bush said, accepting the glass. He studied the strange sail for several minutes before lowering the telescope. "I have the deck! Mr. Brewer, call all hands to make sail!"

"Aye aye, sir!" Brewer grabbed a speaking trumpet. "All hands! All hands! Make sail!"

Hands sprung to the shrouds and raced skyward. Brewer watched the forest of white above his head thicken and fill with air. HMS *Lydia* leapt forward.

Brewer saw Captain Bush talking to Mr. Trench, the sailing master. He wished mightily that he could hear what was being said. He had just begun to move in that direction when a familiar voice stopped him in his tracks.

"Mr. Brewer."

Brewer turned to see Lieutenant Gerard walk up beside him. He saw the Premier's eyes were also on the Captain and Sailing Master, and he was embarrassed to have the first lieutenant catch him in a moment of weakness.

Brewer turned and touched his hat. "Mr. Gerard."

Gerard walked around Brewer to stand between him and the Captain. Brewer felt himself flush and looked at the deck to hide it. When he looked up again, Gerard was wearing his usual smile. "What's going on?"

Brewer repeated the report he had given to the Captain. Gerard listened without comment, his eyes on their quarry.

"Any further orders after make all sail?"

"No, sir."

"Thank you, Mr. Brewer." Gerard touched his hat and wandered over to join the Captain.

Captain Bush looked up as his first lieutenant

approached. "Good morning, Mr. Gerard."

Gerard saluted his captain. "Good morning, Captain, Mr. Trench."

"Deck there!"

Bush stepped out onto the deck, away from his two officers. "Let's hear you, lookout!"

"Definitely two ships, sir! One is a merchant ship, and the other is a smaller ship, looks to be chasing her, sir!"

All three officers spun around at the sound of a gun going off. They turned in time to see the smoke from a starboard gun on the chase ship. No one saw where the shot fell, but there could little doubt as to its meaning.

"Lookout!" Bush cried.

"Chase fired a warning shot, sir! Merchie is heaving to!"

Brewer had by this time wandered back to the quarterdeck and so heard the lookout's report. He snapped his eyes from the tops back to sea level to see for himself that the merchantman was indeed hauling in sail. His eyes went from the Captain to the cloud of sails overhead to the rapidly closing distance as *Lydia* approached the scene of action. He looked back to the Captain and saw at once in his eyes that he was making the same calculations. Bush took a quick look at the sails before making his decision.

"Reduce sail, Quartermaster," Bush said. "Slow us down."

"See here, Mr. Gerard, Mr. Trench," Bush explained his plan. "If we can, I want to put *Lydia* between those ships. Mr. Gerard, when we are done here, you will load the starboard battery, but do not run them out yet."

"Aye, sir."

"If we are too late, I want to rake them as we pass. You will have to load the larboard battery as well, Mr. Gerard, but do not run them out until I order it. After we rake them, we'll come around and either rake them again or go in and board. Mr. Gerard, I shall try to give you as much warning as possible as to which course I choose."

"Aye aye, sir," Gerard said. "Thank you, sir."

Bush looked to the action ahead of them, trying to estimate their arrival at their new speed. "Very well, Mr. Gerard. You may beat to quarters."

The order rang out throughout the ship, and drumming began which sent men to their stations for the coming battle. Brewer went to take command of the larboard battery.

On the quarterdeck, it soon became apparent to Bush that *Lydia* would not arrive in time to get in between the merchantman and her pursuer.

"We will be too late, Mr. Trench," Bush said. "On my command, I want you to put the wheel hard over to starboard. At the same time, we shall back the main topsail to slow us down just long enough for Mr. Brewer to put a broadside into the chase ship. Then we'll come around and see what needs to be done."

"Aye aye, sir," Mr. Trench said.

"Mr. Lee!" Bush called. The midshipman saluted. "My compliments to Mr. Brewer. Tell him I am about to turn hard to starboard. When I do, he is to run his guns out and fire as they bear. He needs not wait for the command."

"Aye aye, sir!" The midshipman disappeared to deliver his message.

Bush watched as the youngster made his way to the Second Lieutenant. The noise was such that Mr. Lee was forced to shout in Brewer's ear to make himself understood. When he was done, Brewer looked up at Bush and waved his hat to show he understood. Brewer ran to each gun captain in turn to explain the Captain's orders.

"Deck there!"

Bush looked up to the lookout.

"The chase ship is altering course, sir! Looks like she's coming at us now!"

Bush had his telescope to his eye in a flash. Sure enough, the smaller ship was making sail and altering course toward them. Bush imagined they would try to get a broadside into *Lydia* as they passed by and headed for the open sea. *Not so fast, my friend,* Bush thought.

"Mr. Trench!" he bellowed. "Hard to starboard!"

HMS *Lydia* came around smartly. Bush watched as Mr. Brewer, not knowing about the alteration in course by the enemy ship, carried out his last orders—which is exactly what Bush wanted him to do. The target would be smaller, but hopefully Brewer and his gun captains could do some damage.

The gun ports flew open and the *Lydia's* 12-pounders were run out. Brewer ran to the bow gun just as it went off, the captain taking advantage of the target. Brewer did not seem to mind; he just went to the next gun and on down the broadside. Gerard helped as well, his starboard battery standing by for their chance.

Bush turned his attention to the enemy ship. The first two splashes went wide right, but then Bush counted five balls that struck home. One lucky shot took the enemy's bowsprit, and her deck looked like a shambles. More importantly, the ship sort of staggered off to port.

"Mr. Gerard!" Bush shouted through a speaking trumpet. "Now it's your turn! Make every shot count!" Gerard waved his hat, and Bush turned to the sailing master. "Bring us about so the starboard battery can pound them!"

HMS *Lydia* swung around hard to bring her starboard battery to bear, and as soon as the ship came out of the turn, Bush could hear the ports flying open and the guns being run out. Gerard and Brewer were running from gun to gun, explaining the Captain's instructions. The Premier ran back to the bow gun and looked over the gun captain's shoulder. He patted the man on his back and went to the next gun.

Soon, the guns were going off, singly or in pairs, and Bush saw the eruptions on the deck of the enemy as each shot struck home. Eight of twelve shots from the broadside found their mark, the enemy losing their mainmast ten feet above the deck. The ship staggered to the side and smoke began to rise.

"Hard to port!" Bush bellowed.

The quartermaster and his mate leaned hard into the wheel, turning it over as quickly as they could.

"Course NNW!" Bush cried.

"NNW, aye, sir!" the quartermaster shouted as he straightened HMS *Lydia* up on the course Bush ordered.

Bush joined Trench and Gerard at the fantail. They watched the smoke billow from the hulk that was the pirate ship. Suddenly, they saw one or two tongues of flame peek through the smoke followed immediately by an explosion that left only wreckage and splinters across the surface of the sea. Bush kept his feet through the blast that swept over the *Lydia's* deck.

"Mr. Gerard," he said quietly, "Get me a damage report."

"Aye, sir," Gerard said.

"And get a boat over the side to look for survivors."

"Aye aye, sir."

"Heave to, quartermaster."

"Aye, sir."

Bush swept the sea with his telescope, but he saw no indication of movement or any other sign that anyone had survived the blast. He turned to look for the merchantman; she was hove to just where she had been, her rails lined with passengers and crew cheering HMS *Lydia* and her crew for their rescue. Bush felt distinctly uncomfortable at the attention, but he raised his hat in acknowledgement.

Brewer was almost lost in the cheering when he was

brought back to reality by the sudden arrival of the first lieutenant.

"Mr. Brewer!" Gerard said, "Take the launch and search that wreckage for survivors!"

"Aye aye, sir!" Brewer saluted the Premier's back.

"Perkins! Launch's crew!"

"Right away, Mr. Brewer!" The petty officer ran off, bellowing orders to his men.

Minutes later, Brewer was in the stern sheets of the launch listening to Perkins call out orders to the seamen at the oars. As they entered the debris field, Brewer called for quiet and ordered the men to listen for survivors. He looked around for any signs, but what few there were were hard to see. Pieces of wreckage both large and small were still burning, and the smoke was a hindrance to both seeing and breathing.

"Two points to larboard, Perkins," Brewer said.

"Aye, sir," the petty officer replied. The launch settled on its new course, and two strong pulls brought them into a clear space. Brewer and his men paused to enjoy the fresh air while he looked around to see where they might look next.

"We'll try over there next," Brewer said, pointing to where the aft part of the ship was slowly settling into the water.

"Beggin' yer pardon, Mr. Brewer," Perkins said, "but I'd be careful. That hulk is big enough to carry a good bit of unexploded powder. Not a good place to be if the fire reaches it and she goes up."

Brewer thought about that. "A good point, Mr. Perkins. Still, we need to look. One pass, quick and quiet, just to be sure."

The launch crisscrossed the debris several times before turning back for HMS *Lydia*. They found no-one alive, although they did find several body parts amongst the debris. One in particular would stay with Brewer; they found part of a mast with a yard still attached floating at the edge of the debris field. As they closed on it, a cry arose from the bows. As they passed, Brewer witnessed what the excitement was all about, a human arm was stuck in a yard arm as though it had been fired from a gun. The arm was still intact, right down to the clothing; there was even a ring with a large stone on one finger. Brewer clamped his jaws shut and turned away in a desperate effort not to vomit.

"Mr. Perkins," he said with as much control as he could muster, "set course back to the ship."

"Aye aye, sir," the petty officer said sullenly.

The ride back was made in total silence, which made Brewer wonder if the men had been as affected by the sights of the debris field as he was. Once back on board, Brewer reported to the Captain and First Lieutenant.

"No survivors, sir," he said as he touched his hat. "Lots of body parts." He shivered. Bush looked at Gerard, but the Premier shook his head; the second lieutenant was fine.

"Mr. Gerard," Bush said, "I would like to have a dinner party tonight. I would like to invite yourself, along with the second and third lieutenants, the senior midshipman, captain of marines, sailing master, and the doctor."

"Thank you, sir!" Gerard beamed.

Bush pulled his watch from his pocket and thought for a minute. "Shall we say the turn of the second dog watch? Excellent. Until then, if you will excuse me, gentlemen?"

The two officers touched their hats as their captain turned away and made his way below.

The officers were gathered around the supper table in the Captain's cabin when Bush stood from his place at the head of the table.

"Gentlemen! I want to congratulate you on you excellent performance in the recent battle."

Cheers erupted, and Bush raised his hand for quiet.

"I shall be pleased to note same in my report to the Admiralty. But first, let me offer some delicacies I had delivered before we left Plymouth. Mr. Goodnight, if you please!"

The Captain's steward led a procession of four mates into the cabin, each loaded with a bowl or platter that teased their senses to the full. Goodnight carried a huge platter of mutton chops and slices. He was followed by mates carrying a roast goose, stewed potatoes, carrots, cauliflower and pudding. Several of the officers around the table began to applaud; Captain James even began to whistle his appreciation. Brewer sat back and observed the reaction of the various officers and smiled. Starling just sat and stared as the food was placed around the table, while Mr. Hanson, the senior midshipman, was one of those who were cheering. Mr. Gerard cheered as well, while the Captain simply stood at his place and watched the proceedings with a huge grin on his face. The only one who was missing was the doctor.

"Mr. Starling," Bush said, "help yourself to the stewed potatoes. Captain James, do not allow the carrots to go to waste. Gerard, won't you see to the carving of that goose? Excellent! Mr. Brewer, help yourself to those chops and then pass them around, sir! No need to keep them all for yourself!"

The table laughed again as Brewer did as he was bidden. Soon the company settled into a comfortable silence as they did justice to the cuisine. Brewer willingly joined in; in fact, he found he had to be very careful not to overeat and make himself sick.

The steward and his mates cleared the table and poured wine for everyone before withdrawing. The Captain stood and picked up his glass.

"Mr. Vice, the King!"

They all looked to the senior midshipman, Mr. Hanson. Being the youngest at the table, the honor of drinking the King's health fell to him. He duly stood and raised his glass.

"Gentlemen, the King!"

Echoes of "The King!" were heard around the table. Hanson took a sip from his glass and sat down.

"Well done, Mr. Hanson," Bush said. "I remember the first time Mr. Gerard was called upon to drink the King's health, he was coughing his lungs up by the time he sat down!"

Gerard looked embarrassed as a few of the men at the table chuckled. "Couldn't help it, Captain," he said. "I was used to better wine."

The table erupted with laughter. Mr. Trench slapped Gerard on the back merrily, and Captain James laughed so hard he fell out of his chair. Bush sat at the head of the table and smiled. He had heard the joke before, and he thought it would get a good reception in this company. He gave silent thanks that Gerard picked up on it as quickly as he did and followed through. Now he stood, and the room slowly came to order.

"Seriously, gentlemen," the Captain said, "I am proud of you and the way you fought in the recent engagement. Very well done."

"Thank you, sir," Gerard answered for them all. "I must say, I am surprised the victory was such an easy one. I for one expected a tougher fight."

Bush resumed his seat. "I spent a good deal of time with Lord Exmouth, who, as you all know, led the fleet back in 1816 and shelled the Barbary pirates into submission. The tactics he described to me are not at all what he fought against earlier. It is my opinion we chanced upon a rogue pirate who was off on his own."

Brewer leaned forward. "So you believe he was trying to

catch us by surprise with his last change of course? Perhaps put a quick broadside into us as he dashed off the other way?"

Bush shrugged. "I suppose so. If that was indeed his plan, Mr. Brewer, he certainly reckoned without you and Mr. Gerard. Please give your crews a 'well done' for me."

Gerard was smiling again. "Thank you, sir."

Bush paused while the steward refilled glasses. "According to Lord Exmouth, we must be ready to fight multiple pirates at once. He said they usually attack in packs like wolves. This is especially true if a ship is unlucky enough to be blown too close to a shoreline; in such cases, several galleys have been known to row out quickly, hoping to overwhelm the merchantman before the escort can arrive."

"Convoy escort," Gerard lamented. "The second most enjoyable task of the Royal Navy, right after blockade duty. We'll need extra lookouts, in that case," Gerard said. "Also, communication with the ships of convoy with be vital. The sooner the pirates are spotted, the better chance we have to deal with them."

"Agreed," Bush said. "But we also have to watch out for a decoy trying to lead us away from the convoy." He stared out into space for a moment, remembering the conversation and ordering his thoughts. "His Lordship also said that the pirates are not known for their gunnery; their preferred method of attack is to close in and board. Therefore, our best defense is to stand off whenever possible and blow them from the water. Should they attempt to close with us, their decks will most likely be crammed with men ready to board. I plan to fill the tops with your best marksmen, Captain James; we are counting on you and your men to lay waste to their numbers."

"Never fear, Captain," the big marine said. "We shall be ready for them."

"Thank you," Bush said. "We may frequently have to put a broadside into one and then leave it to deal with his partners in order to keep the convoy safe. It means we cannot be too diligent in the destruction of any one pirate. We must watch our backs constantly."

"Sir," it was Mr. Starling who spoke up now. "Perhaps we could have the ships of the convoy fire a signal gun, or a rocket whenever they sight a pirate."

"An excellent idea, Mr. Starling," Bush said. "Remember, these pirates do not play by our rules of warfare. They ask for no quarter, neither do they give any. Capture by them means a life of slavery at best, torture and execution at worst."

Heads nodded all around the table. Brewer swallowed silently, a gesture designed to deal with his fear that was only partially successful. He dared not look at anyone, lest his eyes betray something he did not wish known. He kept his eyes on the captain.

"We are two days from Gibraltar," Bush said. "I suggest we all enjoy our last breath of ease by getting ready to go to war."

CHAPTER THREE

HMS *Lydia* slid into the harbor at Gibraltar. The weather was exactly what one would wish for were they going sailing on a country lake in a homemade skiff rather than guiding a frigate of His Majesty's Navy to a berth. Still, Captain Bush was not about to look over a gift like this. Honors for entering a friendly port were just being completed, and the pilot gone over the side on his way back to shore.

Brewer went to the rail to survey the traffic in the bay. Cargo ships from nearly every seafaring nation in the world were here. Brewer noted everything from the big East Indiamen to Dutch doggers, cutters, ketches, parancelles, and pinks. There were others he had never seen before; he could only assume that these made their home in the Far East.

The British Mediterranean Fleet was represented as well, depleted though it was from its wartime glory. A frigate and a brig were in drydock for what looked to be extensive refits. He saw two schooners and a cutter moored not far away, their gun ports open to get a cross breeze going. The dominant presence by far was that of HMS *Victory*, the flagship of the fleet. Famous as Nelson's flagship at Trafalgar, the ship was still serving her country. She towered above all other traffic in the bay. Only the biggest of the

Indiamen came close. The broad pennant that flew from *Victory's* mainmast informed everyone that the Admiral was on board.

Captain Bush came on deck dressed in his best coat and breeches. Fine silk stockings and polished shoes with polished gold buckles completed his wardrobe. He carried his reports in his hand on his way to report to the Commander in Chief, Mediterranean Fleet, Vice Admiral Sir Thomas Fremantle. Brewer watched as the Captain made his way over the side and down to his waiting gig, wondering how he would behave when it finally became his turn to report.

Bush was greeted at *Victory's* entry port by the captain, Sir Derek Leeds.

"Greetings, Captain," he said. "I've wanted to meet you for a long time."

"Greetings, Captain," Bush said as the two shook hands.

"If you'll follow me, Captain? The Admiral doesn't like to be kept waiting."

"At your service, sir."

Bush followed Captain Leeds through the innards of the great warship to the Admiral's day cabin. The marine guard opened the door for them, and Leeds made introductions. The Admiral did not come out from behind his desk. Bush handed over his reports.

"Thank you for coming, Captain," Fremantle said as they all sat down. "I trust you had no problems on the way here."

"Actually, sir, we had to rescue a merchantman off Portugal."

"Really?" Fremantle said. "I must say I'm surprised. There hasn't been any pirate activity that far north in the Atlantic for some time."

"I think it was a Barbary raider, sir," Bush said. "One of

my crew who has served in the Mediterranean identified the attacker as a Barbary xebec."

The look on the Admiral's face grew dark. "I shall read your report in earnest at a later time, Captain, but for now I would like to hear it from you firsthand."

Bush recounted the battle in as much detail as was possible when drawing events from memory. He noticed that Fremantle and the flag lieutenant traded a knowing look when he described the attacking craft. When he finished, he sat back with his hands folded in his lap while the Admiral digested the information. It was not long before the Admiral blinked and looked to Bush.

"The craft you describe certainly sounds like a Barbary xebec," he said. He spoke slowly as though ordering his thoughts as he went. "I wonder, however, if you happened to run into one who had gone rogue. I say that for two reasons: One, Barbary pirates rarely attack alone, and two, they rarely venture out into the Atlantic." He thought for a moment or two more before shaking his head to dismiss a line of thought. "In any case, Captain, I'm glad you are here. The Mediterranean Fleet needs every frigate she can lay her hands on, especially one of HMS *Lydia's* reputation."

"Thank you, sir," Bush said.

"Now, then, let's talk about the general situation. There has been a decided increase in the boldness of these Barbary pirates in the last year or so. Lord Exmouth pounded them into submission back in 1816, but now the serpent has reared its ugly head once more. The Americans have also had their problems with them, so it is possible you may encounter one of their ships pursuing our common enemy, as it were." The Admiral looked out *Victory's* great stern windows and shook his head in frustration. "Fighting has changed, Bush; it's not like it was at Trafalgar. A straight up fight that was, ship against ship, man against man. None of this going after merchantmen and women and children..." He suddenly turned to Bush. "Were you at Trafalgar, Captain?"

Bush sat forward in his seat. "Why, yes, sir. I was a lieutenant in the old *Tremeraire*."

Fremantle sat forward and slapped his desk with the palm of his hand. "I *knew* it! I was captain of HMS *Neptune*. One can always tell a fellow officer who's been through a battle like that."

"Yes, sir."

Fremantle sat back and thought for a moment. "There is one particular that I want you to keep in mind. Every effort to should be made to capture or kill Murad Reis. He is the Grand Admiral of the Bashaw's forces. He is of interest to us because he was born a Scotsman by the name of Peter Lisle. The story is that he shipped out on the schooner *Betsy*. He was caught stealing from his shipmates. The only thing that saved him from punishment was that his ship was captured by Barbary pirates in 1796. The crew were sentenced to death as infidels. Lisle escaped by going Turk. He converted to their heathen religion and rose through the ranks to become the Grand Admiral. Took the name Murad Reis after a famous pirate of theirs from two hundred years or more ago. He got command of the *Betsy* and converted her into a sixth rate under the name *Meshuda*. Rumor has it she carries twenty-eight 12 pounders and over 350 men."

Bush showed his surprise.

"Crowded, I agree," Fremantle continued. "Of course, they rarely stay at sea for more than a week or so, and the numbers aboard are reduced with every prize crew. At the moment, *Meshuda* is the pirates' most powerful ship in the Mediterranean. I want this man Reis taken back to England to be tried and hung."

"Aye aye, sir. Do we have a description of him?"

Fremantle shook his head. "Only a vague one. He is

reputed to be of slight build, with light hair and a blondish beard. Indifferent morals, of course. He is said to be a hard drinker and a violent drunk."

Bush raised his brows. "Not much to go on, sir."

The Admiral shrugged. "True, but I get the impression that this is a man whom you will have no trouble identifying. Bring him back alive, Captain, if at all possible, but under no circumstances should he be allowed to escape."

Bush nodded. "Understood, sir."

"Your orders are to proceed at your earliest convenience to Cagliari on the southern tip of Sardinia. There you will pick up a convoy and escort it safely to Leghorn on the Italian peninsula. From there, you escort a brig carrying the new British counsel to his post in Naples."

"Why didn't his ship just drop him at Naples?"

Fremantle sighed. "It seems he came overland from a posting in France. Someone in London got the idea that it might be more impressive if he were seen to arrive in the company of the Royal Navy. I suppose they want to remind King Ferdinand that we got rid of Bonaparte's sister and brother-in-law for them."

"Aye aye, sir."

Fremantle rose, and the meeting was over. Bush quickly rose and came to attention.

"The Flag Lieutenant will hand you your orders, Captain. Good Luck."

Bush nodded. "Thank you, sir."

Outside the great cabin, he was met by the Captain Leeds.

"Here are your orders, Captain. May God grant you victory."

Bush took the parcel. "Thank you, Captain."

Back on board HMS *Lydia*, Brewer stood on the

quarterdeck, admiring the lines of the admiral's three-decker and imagining what it must be like to serve on the flagship when he realized, much to his displeasure that he was no longer alone.

"Pretty ship, isn't she?" Mr. Starling said.

"Yes," Brewer replied.

Starling leaned on the railing and sighed. "You know, I wouldn't be surprised if the captain had secret orders to transfer you to *Victory* as soon as we arrived."

Brewer turned in disbelief. "What are you talking about?"

Starling stood and shrugged. "I don't know. I just assumed that Lord Hornblower would arrange some soft job for you as the admiral's aide or some such thing." Starling smiled and walked off.

Brewer stared at the third lieutenant's retreating back and wished for just a moment that he could thrash the man for his insolence. Instead, he closed his eyes and leaned again on the rail, trying to will his anger away. He recalled something his father once told him about dealing with people like Starling—he called them 'small people'.

"William," he had said, "getting angry at small people does about as much good as getting angry at one of those cows. There are only two ways to deal with them: one is to strike back some way that will leave them with no doubt of your displeasure at their comments. Unfortunately, this method may involve consequences for you to deal with, and sometimes they are a necessary evil. The other method is to ignore them totally. Sooner or later, they will make a mistake in a public setting, and society itself will be their judge and executioner. The second method is much harder than the first, and also much more satisfying."

He drew a deep breath and let it out slowly, willing his anger to depart with his breath. He stood and opened his eyes. A small shake of his head in frustration, then he retreats to the gunroom.

CHAPTER FOUR

Brewer stepped out of his cabin after a good night's sleep. He was in a good mood and looking for a hearty breakfast to help him stay that way. He quickly discovered it wasn't going to be that easy.

"Well! Look who's awake! The mighty Lieutenant Brewer!"

Brewer turned to look to the end of the table and saw the third lieutenant, Mr. Starling, sitting before an empty plate, a glass of wine in his hand.

"Good morning, Jonah," Brewer said out of politeness. "Isn't it a little early for the drink? Even for you?"

"Perhaps, sir, perhaps," Starling mockingly saluted him with his glass, "but I'd imagine you wouldn't mind if it was some of that good French Cognac, now, would you? Come now! I bet you and your friend Boney had a belt of two back on the island, what?"

"What are you babbling about, Jonah?" Brewer could see that Starling was drunk, and it angered him that the third lieutenant let himself go this way, even if the ship was in port.

"Come now, sir! This is no time for false modesty!" Starling slammed his glass down so hard it broke on the table. "Now see what you've made me do! Still, it shouldn't be any problem for a man of your connections to fix, should it?"

Brewer was fast becoming exasperated at this verbal jousting with a drunk and his temper slipped a bit. "What are you talking about? What connections?"

Starling rose and slammed his fist on the table. "I mean Hornblower, you fool! Not to mention old Boney hisself! That's the reason you're Captain Bush's fair haired boy now, isn't it? Let me tell you something, Mr. Captain's Darling, if Captain Tyler had taken the old *Agamemnon* to St. Helena, things would be very different! I can promise you that! *I* would have been the one to be sent ashore as the Governor's secretary, not you! *I* would be the Captain's darling, not you! Do you hear me? *Me! Not you!*"

Brewer stood there, astonished at what he had just witnessed, not knowing whether to laugh or be disgusted. He watched Starling, leaning on the table and breathing heavily, his eyes rapidly glazing over as he slid back into his chair with a plop. Brewer walked over and pulled him to his feet by the front of his shirt. Starling was up on his toes, and his eyes grew wide with fear at Brewer's anger and show of strength.

"Don't hit me," he said pitiably.

Revulsion swept over Brewer, and it was all he could do not to drop Starling where he was and leave him for Gerard to find. As it was, he drug the drunken third lieutenant back to his cabin and threw the door open. He took Starling inside and dropped him unceremoniously in his hammock.

"Drunken sot," Brewer said. "Stay in here until you sleep it off."

Back out in the gunroom, Brewer called for Coles to bring his breakfast. As he worked his way through his eggs, slab of ham, and fresh bread with marmalade, he thought about what Starling had said to him. He had purposely not mentioned Hornblower's name to anyone, hoping to avoid just this sort of reaction, and he certainly had not mentioned Bonaparte. Brewer wondered if he was going to get this kind of reaction from his fellow officers if they found out he had been on St. Helena.

Brewer swallowed his mouthful and sat back in his chair, his mind full of dark thoughts. Starling had all but called him a traitor by referring to his "friendship" with Bonaparte. True, he was drunk, but what if the wine only enabled him to say what others were thinking? Brewer stared out into space from under hooded eyes and furled brows as he considered the implications. He didn't think he had to worry about anything of the sort coming from Bush or Gerard—after all, they were at St. Helena, too, and they knew what happened. But what would happen as others put his name together with St. Helena and Bonaparte?

Brewer closed his eyes and took a deep breath to try to calm himself. He told himself he was making way too much of the ravings of a drunken lieutenant who was jealous of Brewer's good fortune. His eyes snapped open at the thought, and he knew it was much more than that. *So be it,* he said to himself. *I can't control what others think. I know the truth. That will have to be enough.*

Brewer shook his head as he rose and wondered if it would be.

HMS *Lydia* sailed the next day. Captain Bush stood on the quarterdeck, Lieutenant Gerard and Mr. Trench standing beside him. Midshipman Lee approached the captain and saluted.

"Anchor's hove short, sir," he said.

"Thank you, Mr. Lee," Bush replied. "Mr. Gerard, take her out, if you please."

"Aye, sir," Gerard saluted and picked up a speaking trumpet. "Stand by the capstan! Man the bars! Heave round!"

The hands at the capstan put their chests against the bars and pushed for all they were worth. Slowly, they began to make their way around.

Gerard raised the trumpet to his lips again. "Hands aloft to loose the headsails!"

Hands clawed their way up the shrouds. The headsails fell from the yards.

"Hands aloft to loose topsails!"

The anchor broke water, and HMS *Lydia* began to move toward the open sea.

"Thank you, Mr. Gerard," Bush said. He turned to the sailing master.

"Once clear of the harbor, set your course due east."

"Make my course due east. Aye, sir."

Captain Bush invited his officers to supper after they left Gibraltar.

They gathered in the captain's cabin at the appointed hour. Bush, Captain and host, Lieutenants Gerard, Brewer, and Starling, and Captain James of the Royal Marines. Mr. Trench, the sailing master, rounded out the group. No sooner had they all arrived than dinner was served. Each man found his place, and the stewards filled the glasses. Thomas Goodnight, the Captain's steward, came in carrying a huge tray filled with the largest roast of beef any of them had ever seen.

"Captain!" Gerard cried, "How big was the animal this came from? Mr. Brewer, you grew up on a farm. How large would you estimate this beast to have been?"

Brewer shook his head in uncertainty. "I'm sure I couldn't say, Mr. Gerard. Not a small one, to be sure."

"God bless him," Gerard said. "The man knows his cows."

The assembly roared with laughter, and the rest of the banquet was brought in. Platter followed bowl, kidney pie and peas, pudding and cauliflower in quick succession.

After they had feasted, and the stewards had removed the dishes and poured wine for anyone who wanted it, Captain Bush rose from his seat at the end of the table and cleared his throat loudly.

"Gentlemen," he said, "I'm sure you are wondering about our orders. I may now tell you that we are bound for the city of Cagliari to pick up a convoy which we shall then escort to Leghorn. From there, we are to escort a brig carrying the new British consul to Naples."

"Where's Cagliari?" Starling asked.

Gerard spoke up. "Southern tip of Sardinia."

"As of now, we are the only escort," Bush said, "although I am in hopes of getting a sloop or two to assist us. There are scheduled to be six merchantmen in the convoy. Mr. Gerard, please make sure we have extra lookouts aloft during every daylight hour."

"Aye, sir," Gerard said.

"I want sail and gunnery drills morning and afternoon," Bush continued as he resumed his seat. "Remember what Lord Exmouth said regarding the Barbary pirates. They are not, for example, noted for their gunnery. It seems their favorite tactic is to rush in and board. His lordship strongly advised us to stay away from them and pound their xebecs into matchsticks. Those boats of theirs are fast and maneuverable. Therefore, we must be even more so."

"Aye, sir," was heard from each of the assembled officers. Bush nodded his head and sat back in his chair, and small talk broke out around the table. He sat back and watched these men, his officers, some picked by him and some not. He was glad to have had the chance to see them in battle before they got to the Mediterranean. Now he knew he could rely on them. Training was vital, but a captain never knew just how his officers (and, by extension, his crew) would

69

behave until they had round shot and grape coming at them. His men had done well.

He looked to Gerard, who was engaged in an animated discussion with Brewer and Mr. Trench. Gerard had made himself indispensable to Bush. The Premier had kept HMS *Agamemnon* at peak efficiency during the year-long commission at St. Helena, where all they had to do was circle an island. Bush thought it was almost as boring as blockade duty had been outside Le Havre during the wars.

He thought about Mr. Brewer, who had performed so brilliantly while detached at St. Helena. Bush had taken a chance in recommending him for the post. He had come within a hair's breadth of sending Gerard; he knew Hornblower and would have served him well, but something told him Brewer was the man. The Lieutenant proved himself worthy of his captain's trust, including an episode where he stood nose-to-nose with the Corsican himself! Bush smiled and shook his head; how he wished he had been there to see that!

He shifted his attention to young Mr. Starling, sitting in his seat and sipping his wine, listening with half an ear to two or three different conversations but not really engaging in any. Bush frowned. He had inherited Starling when he took command of HMS *Agamemnon* prior to the St. Helena commission. His eyes narrowed. Starling had performed adequately during their last commission, but Bush sensed there was something deeper, something that was holding the youngster back. Bush had already noticed that he drank too much, but it had never been reported as interfering with his duties. He tried to remember the young man's background, second son of a country squire in Norfolk, sent to sea in order to make a name for himself, if the stories he had heard were to be believed. Bush resolved to speak to Gerard about him at a later date.

Bush stood and quiet descended upon the room. "Gentlemen," he said, "I thank you once again for your efforts thus far, and I look forward to the glories to come."

"Prize money!" Gerard said.

Bush grinned. "And plenty of it, let us hope, Mr. Gerard. Now, I bid you good night."

The assembly rose and bid their captain a collective good night. They made their way out of his cabin quietly, lowered heads indicating that one or two of the conversations were ongoing. He wondered how many of them would make it home again.

HMS *Lydia* made an uneventful voyage to their destination. The crew were constantly drilling, getting used to the hot Mediterranean sun. The sea was calm for the most part, and they entered the harbor at Cagliari a full day sooner than expected.

Captain Bush went ashore to pay his respects, and when he returned he had information about the convoy from the Port Authority.

"Mr. Gerard," he said, "hoist this signal. *'Captains of convoy M-23 report aboard.'*"

"Aye, sir," Gerard said. "Mr. Hanson! Signal to be sent!"

"Aye aye, sir!" Hanson had been close enough to hear the signal as Bush said it, and he went to work at once.

"Mr. Gerard," Bush said, "when the captains come on board, I want you in the meeting with us. We must impress on these men the men the importance of staying together and reporting any strange sail in the area."

"Agreed, sir. What will be our position?"

Bush thought for a moment. "Our orders do not say, and I have not decided. I am considering putting *Lydia* between the convoy and any shorelines to prevent any attacks dashing out from shore."

Gerard nodded. He hoped his captain could convince these merchant captains to cooperate with them, but he remembered his old days working on a slave ship. Nobody told him how to sail his ship. He hoped they didn't encounter too much of the same attitude now.

It took about two hours for all six captains to report aboard HMS *Lydia*. As soon as the last arrived, Gerard closed the door behind him, and Bush called the meeting to order.

"Gentlemen," he said loudly to get their attention, "if you will please take a seat, we can get started."

Gerard moved quickly to sit at his captain's right hand. The six captains found a place as well, and all looked to Bush, standing at the head of the table.

"My name is William Bush, and I am captain of His Majesty's frigate *Lydia*. I have been charged by Admiral Fremantle, commander-in-chief of the Mediterranean Fleet, with ensuring your safe passage to Leghorn. I will tell you right now, I will need your help to make that happen."

Gerard watched for any reaction by the six to the Captain's words, but he saw none—yet. He has read the information that the Port Authority had given Bush, including the short biographies on each of the captains assembled. Seated across from him was Captain Johnson of the *India*, a tall, thin man with thick blonde hair and beard. His skin looked toughened by years in the cold northern latitudes. Next to him was Captain Allison of the *Kent*. Allison was not nearly as tall, probably closer to Captain Bush in height, but he was solid muscle from head to toe. Gerard thought even the man's ear lobes must have muscles. He chuckled to himself over his little joke and turned his attention to the next man, Captain O'Malley of the *London*. Gerard frowned. O'Malley was an Irishman, which in

Gerard's book automatically made him a suspect in any imaginable crime; Gerard privately wondered if he could betray his ship to the pirates. He made a mental note to discuss the possibility with Captain Bush as soon as possible. On Gerard's right sat a big Scot named McDonald, captain of the *Glasgow*. He was a huge man with fiery red hair and huge sideburns who smoked a large clay pipe. Gerard liked him instantly. Beside him was Captain Jameson of the *Rose*, a Londoner with a Cockney accent and a pearl-handled dagger in his belt. The final man at the table was also the only Continental. Giuseppe Calipari was captain of the *Roma*, a Tuscan merchantman added to the convoy at the last minute. Gerard was suspicious of Calipari. The Italian looked nervous, almost hunted, his eyes darting back and forth between the others at the table and Captain Bush.

Bush sat down and continued, "The Port Authority confirmed that the *Lydia* will be the sole escort for the convoy. This makes the matter of early identification paramount. Every ship will need to post extra lookouts during daylight hours."

That caused a stir at the table. Captain Johnson spoke up for the group.

"So, now the Royal Navy is going to tell me how to run my ship?"

"If you want to arrive safely, yes," Bush said. "Another thing. Since HMS *Lydia* is the only escort at present, it will be necessary for the convoy to stay together, especially if the pirates should attack."

"You would have us become sitting ducks!" Captain Allison cried.

"*Lydia* cannot be everywhere," Bush said, trying to keep his cool. "If you scatter, you make yourself a target for boarding by the pirates. If you stay together as much as possible, then we have the chance to intervene. You know as well as I do that these villains attack in packs; if we have to chase you, then the rest of the convoy is wide open to boarding."

"You are to protect us!" Calipari shouted in fear.

"I cannot if you run." Bush sat back in his chair. "Let me be plain, C aptains. HMS *Lydia* will not leave the convoy to help anyone who scatters. You will be on your own."

The captains erupted. Gerard rubbed his chin to cover his smile. Evidently, nobody had ever told these merchant captains that before. Bush just sat at the head of the table, seemingly above it all, and waited for the storm to blow itself out. Gerard thought it was a performance worthy of Hornblower himself.

The din eventually died down. Bush looked around the table, careful to meet each man's eye, then he nodded.

"Now that we're all agreed, here is what I propose. The convoy will be organized in two groups, one forward, and the other aft, with enough space in between for *Lydia* to dash from one side of the convoy to the other at a moment's notice. When we pass within sight of an island, *Lydia* will be stationed inboard of the convoy. Sightings must be signaled immediately, and all signals must be repeated by everyone. *Lydia* must be able to pick it up from whatever ship is closest to her. Signals from *Lydia* to the convoy should be similarly repeated. Any questions?"

There were none, and the rest of the meeting went swiftly. Bush turned the meeting over to Gerard, who went over night signals and rendezvous in case of separation. It struck Bush that this was not so very different from when they escorted convoys during the wars. They were fighting a different enemy, to be sure; swifter, perhaps, and more unconventional than the French, but every bit as dangerous. *Oh well,* Bush grunted to himself, *at least this time we won't have to convince anyone to volunteer.*

The meeting broke up soon thereafter. Gerard was not surprised to see that most of the captains returned to their ships without the courtesy of shaking either his hand or Bush's. The only one who did was the big Scot, Captain McDonald.

"I trust, Captain, that should we sight that turncoat Murad Reis, you will hold him just long enough for me to put a bullet in his head."

Bush grinned. "I will certainly keep my eyes open, Captain. Tell me, what earns him your special attention?"

"Me dad sailed with the traitor on the *Betsy* back in '96. He never came home. When I got old enough, I shipped out to support me mum and sisters. The first time I sailed into the Med, I heard about Reis—so he calls hisself now—and what happened to the *Betsy*. Ever since that day, I've saved a bullet for him."

Bush's expression sobered. "I'm sorry for your loss, Captain. I hope that when I do catch him, you are somewhere in the neighborhood. I just might be tempted to turn my back."

The Scot nodded. "I'd be obliged, Captain."

When they were alone, Gerard grunted. "Why do I think this convoy is going to be like herding cats?"

The convoy left Cagliari on schedule with the morning tide. Brewer was at his post, his eyes roaming the harbor, taking in activity on the ships that should be sailing with them in the convoy. He looked back to the quarterdeck in time to see Captain Bush say something to Gerard. The First Lieutenant raised his hat and then picked up a speaking trumpet and began bellowing out the orders that would set HMS *Lydia* in motion. Brewer saw the yards braced around and felt the ship turn on her keel and begin to edge toward the harbor entrance.

The convoy was divided into two sections, with *India, Kent,* and *London* in the first group and *Glasgow, Rose,* and the Tuscan *Roma* bringing up the rear. Bush kept *Lydia* out in front of the convoy for the first four hours, then he brought the ship around, making a full circuit of the convoy before taking up a night station a quarter mile to windward of the convoy.

The next morning, Brewer was on deck talking to Mr. Trench when Lieutenant Gerard came on deck.

"Good morning, gentlemen," he said.

"Morning, sir," Brewer touched his hat.

"Have we lost anyone yet?" he asked, looking at the two ships that were visible to their north.

"Not yet," Brewer said with a note of disbelief in his voice. "We had all six at last count. We are due for another at the turn of the watch."

"Deck there!" the lookout cried. "Signal from the convoy! *Enemy in sight!*"

"Which group signaled?" Gerard called.

"It came from the lead group, sir!"

"I have the deck!" Gerard shouted. "Mr. Trench, call all hands to make sail. Alter course to the starboard group. Mr. Brewer, my respects to the Captain. Please inform him of the signal and that I have altered course to close on it as per his standing orders."

"Aye aye, sir." Brewer touched his hat and went below to inform his captain. The marine guard admitted him to find Goodnight, the captain's steward, helping him with his hanger and his coat.

"Report, Mr. Brewer," Bush said.

"Sir, Mr. Gerard send his respects and asks that I inform you that the forward group of the convoy is signaling *'Enemy in Sight'*. He has called all hands to make sail and has altered course toward the signal, in obedience to your standing orders."

"Very good, Mr. Brewer," Bush said. He adjusted his coat before grabbing his hat and heading for the door. "Follow me."

Bush appeared on deck with Brewer hard on his heels. Gerard met him on the quarterdeck and saluted. He handed the Captain a telescope.

"Report, Mr. Gerard," Bush said.

"Our course is NNE, toward the lead group, sir. They're the ones who raised the signal. We have not sighted the enemy ourselves yet. I have sent a follow up signal asking where the enemy is."

"Signal coming in!" Hanson called. *"Enemy three points off starboard bow!"*

"I have the deck!" Bush bellowed. "Mr. Trench, alter course two points to starboard! Lookout! What do you see?"

Brewer looked up to the maintop and saw the lookout studying the sea ahead of them and to starboard. Brewer nearly grabbed a glass and went up to help him when the man homed in on his objective.

"Sail ho!" the lookout called. "Three, no four points to starboard!"

Bush, Gerard, and Brewer all rushed to the starboard rail and searched the horizon. It wasn't but a few moments before Gerard pointed.

"There, sir!"

"I've got it," Bush said. "Steady as she goes, Mr. Trench! We'll try to head her off."

"Aye aye, sir; steady as she goes!"

"Mr. Gerard, beat to quarters."

"Aye, sir! Beat to quarters!" Gerard bellowed, and the sound of the *rat-a-tat-tat* from the Marine drummer boy's instrument sent the crew of HMS *Lydia* scurrying to their battle stations. Brewer reported below to his guns in time to see the last of the bulkheads being taken down. It always amazed him how quickly his home was transformed to a ship of war.

On deck, Captain Bush was studying the enemy ship carefully. He lowered his telescope and called, "Mr. Gerard, load the guns with shot but do not run them out!"

"Aye, sir!"

"Deck, there! The enemy is raising sail and moving away from us! Looks like she's headed for the other side of the convoy!"

"Mr. Hanson! Signal to convoy. *Maintain course and speed.*"

"Aye aye, sir!"

"Mr. Trench! Port your helm. Take us between the two groups."

"Aye, sir!"

Brewer did his best to remain calm in front of his men, but the anticipation was beginning to wear on him. With the gun ports closed, he was blind to what was happening. They all felt it when *Lydia* adjusted her course. He looked over to Gerard, who shrugged.

"Captain's probably heading for the gap to beat the pirate to the other side of the convoy."

Brewer nodded as he looked back to the men. Almost without exception, they were looking back at him.

"Steady, men," he said calmly. "Captain Bush will tell us when, and that will be the end of one Barbary pirate."

He was pleased to how his words affected his men. Many smiled at him with gap-toothed smiled and several more bobbed their heads in agreement. At that moment the order came down to run out the guns. Gerard and Brewer repeated the order and their men cheered as the lids were raised. Men pulled on the gun tackles for all they were worth to run the guns out and then stood back, ready to fire when given the order. Brewer had command of the larboard battery, and when he looked out the open port, he could just see the after group of the convoy flying past. Again he steadied his men; it would not be long now.

HMS *Lydia* burst from the north side of the convoy, and the lookout was quick to pick up on their quarry.

"There, sir!" the lookout said and pointed. "Three, no four points off the starboard bow!"

Bush rushed to the rail and put his telescope to his eye. He trained it along the bearing indicated by the lookout and was rewarded immediately. The pirate was farther north than *Lydia*, giving Bush the weather gage. She was coming around toward the convoy.

"Hard-a-starboard!" Bush shouted. "Stand by, larboard battery!"

Suddenly, the pirate reversed course and bore away until all the sail she could carry. Bush had just turned to speak to the sailing master when the lookout alertly called his attention to the pirate's change of course. Bush went to the rail and studied the situation. Should he pursue the pirate or remain with the convoy? He lowered the glass and stared after the pirate for a fraction of a second before nodding to himself, his face set like a flint.

"Hard-a-larboard, Mr. Trench!" he cried. "Let's get after them! Ready on the long nines! Midshipman of the watch! My compliments to Mr. Gerard; ask him to report to the quarterdeck!"

"Aye aye, Captain!"

Gerard was there in moments and touched his hat. "You sent for me, sir?"

"Yes, Mr. Gerard. The pirate has turned tail, and I have

left the convoy to pursue. I want you to take personal charge of the long nines. Let me know when we're in range, and we'll try one alongside him."

"Aye, sir," Gerard touched his hat again and went forward. Bush paced back and forth for several minutes before deciding he could not stand the wait, and he followed his premier forward. He arrived to find the two long nines, HMS *Lydia's* bow chasers, loaded and run out, and Lieutenant Gerard studying the pirate through a telescope. Bush said nothing as he stopped and put his glass to his eye. It was immediately obvious to him that the gap was closing quickly; *Lydia* was simply too fast for their enemy.

Bush lowered his telescope. "Report, Mr. Gerard."

Gerard lowered his glass and saluted his captain. "Sorry, sir; I didn't hear you approach. We are closing the gap rapidly, sir. It shouldn't be long now before we can try a ranging shot."

"Very good," Bush said. Both men went back to studying their enemy.

About five minutes later, Gerard lowered his glass. "I think I can hit them now, sir."

Bush nodded. "Agreed, but put the first one to the side. I want to make them surrender if we can."

"Aye, sir." Gerard knelt behind the starboard long nine to check the aim, then he stood and nodded. The gun captain set the gunlock and handed the lanyard to Gerard. The Premier waited until just after the high point of the uproll to fire the gun. It went off with a deafening roar, and moments later Bush saw the splash of the ball off the pirate's port quarter.

"Well done, Mr. Gerard!" he said. "Now we'll see if he's smart enough to surrender."

They did not have to wait long for an answer; within three minutes the pirate's sails came down and a white flag was run up. Bush lowered his telescope and smiled as the gun crews around him cheered.

"Come with me, Mr. Gerard," Bush said. The two men went aft to the quarterdeck.

"Heave to, Mr. Trench," Bush said. "Put them at pistol shot under the starboard battery. Mr. Gerard, I want you to take the launch and the cutter and board her. Have Captain James load the launch with marines, just to make sure you have no trouble over there. Secure the ship before they have the chance to destroy any papers they may be carrying. Take Mr. Brewer with you; he needs the experience. Send back any papers you find with him, then we'll see about a prize crew."

"Aye, sir. Mr. Hammersmith! Ready the launch and cutter! Pass the word for Captain James and Mr. Brewer!"

Lieutenant Brewer said nothing as he sat in the stern sheets of the cutter, his sword at his side and a pistol in his belt. They were trailing the launch, which was crowded with marines. Lieutenant Gerard and Captain James were visible in the stern, ready to be the first to board the pirate luggar. When they reached the pirate, the marines followed the officers up and over the side in a flash. The deck was secured by the time Brewer set foot on it.

"Orders, sir?" he asked Gerard.

"Get down to the captain's cabin. Secure any papers you can find. Grab *everything*. We'll take it back to the Captain and let Ali read them. Take two marines with you."

"Aye, sir." Brewer touched his hat and called for two marines to follow him.

He entered the cabin to find a man desperately trying to start a fire in a pile of papers on the table. Brewer pointed his pistol at the man and ordered him to stop, praying that he understood English. The man froze, and the marines swept past Brewer to secure the room.

"Take him up on deck," Brewer said to one of the marines. "Inform the first lieutenant."

Brewer and the remaining marine began to search the room. The marine pulled a box down from a shelf overlooking the captain's bed. Brewer opened it and examined the papers inside, but he could not read any of them. He placed the papers the pirate was trying to burn inside the box as well. A further search failed to turn up anything else, so Brewer returned to the deck and made his report.

"Very good, Mr. Brewer," Gerard said. "Take your box back to the Captain immediately. I shall remain here while we complete our search of the ship."

"Anything so far, sir?"

Gerard shook his head. "No, it seems to be a typical pirate. Everything sacrificed to the ability to carry more men. Only six guns, six-pounders by the look of it. We've taken thirty-seven prisoners, but I would estimate the ship could hold more than two hundred. If the rest of them went to prize crews, then we are missing an awful lot of ships." He sighed. "Well, perhaps that box of yours will give us some answers. Off with you, William; take the cutter."

"Aye, sir." Brewer touched his hat and was gone.

Back on board HMS *Lydia*, Brewer went immediately to the captain's cabin to make his report. Bush listened without interrupting to his second lieutenant. His eyes studied the box when Brewer told what was in it. When Brewer finished, Bush called for two glasses of wine.

"Pass the word for Ali, Mr. Brewer," he said.

The Arab arrived a minute later. He nodded a greeting to Brewer as he entered.

"You sent for me, Captain sir?"

"Yes, Ali. Mr. Brewer brought back this box from the

luggar. Mr. Brewer will explain it to you."

Brewer opened the box and lifted out the first group of papers. "We found a pirate trying to burn these when we entered the captain's cabin. The remainder were found in the box."

"I need you to translate them," Bush said. "You may use the table in the dining cabin."

"Aye aye, Captain sir."

The young man picked up the box and went to the outer room. Bush watched him go and then looked at his second.

"Mr. Brewer? Something on your mind?"

Brewer shrugged. "I just hope he's as good as Lord Exmouth believes."

Bush looked back toward the door and said nothing.

Within minutes Ali was back, holding a paper. "Captain sir, I think you should see this now. It is from the government of the Bey of Tripoli, and it gives the captain permission to attack and capture any English ship he encounters."

"A letter of marque, by God!" Bush exclaimed.

"But Captain sir," Ali persisted, "do you not see whose signature is affixed to the letter?"

"What does it say? Whose signature is it?"

"Captain sir, the signature reads, *Signed, Murad Reis, Grand Admiral of the Bey of Tripoli!*"

Bush stared at the signature at the bottom of the letter. Murad Reis!

"Can you tell where he is?" he asked.

"There is nothing in the letter to indicate that," Ali said. "I will look on the other papers. I thought you should see this at once."

"Quite right, quite right."

Bush considered for a moment, and then gave the paper

back to Ali. "Return to your work. Please copy each out in English. My clerk will help you. Mr. Brewer, please pass the word for Mr. Bell."

The clerk duly arrived and was instructed to copy out what Ali translated, and both men were sent to the clerk's office to complete their work. Bush considered for a moment before turning to Brewer.

"Have we identified the captain of the luggar yet?" he asked.

Brewer shook his head. "No, sir; at least, not when I left."

Bush considered a moment. "Return to the luggar. If the captain has been identified, bring him back. If not, bring the man who you found in his cabin. My compliments to Mr. Gerard, ask him to finish the inspection of the luggar and return to report. I will send a prize crew to take the ship to Malta."

"Aye aye, sir." Brewer picked up his hat and left.

He stepped up on the deck of the luggar and looked around to spy Lieutenant Gerard on the quarterdeck. He walked up and saluted, then spent the next several minutes making his report. He told the Premier of the letter of marque with Murad Reis' signature on it. Gerard raised his eyebrows in surprise and whistled.

"Have we identified the captain yet?" Brewer asked.

"No, he still refuses to come forward, and the crew will not give him up."

"In that case, the Captain wants to see the man I found in the captain's cabin. Where is he?"

Gerard turned and pointed to him, sitting by the lee rail by himself, under guard. "I thought it best to isolate him until we found out who the captain was, just in case."

"I congratulate you, sir," Brewer said. "The Captain wants me to bring him back with me."

"Are there any orders for me?" Gerard asked.

"Yes. Forgive me for not telling you at the outset, sir. The Captain sends his compliments and asks that you return to the ship when the search of the luggar is completed. He will send a prize crew to take the ship to Malta."

"Thank you, Mr. Brewer. Take your prisoner and two marines back to *Lydia*. My respects to the Captain, I shall return as soon as I confer with Captain James. I will leave Mr. Midshipman Kennedy in command of the luggar until the prize crew arrives."

"Aye, sir," Brewer touched his hat. "Thank you, sir."

Back on board *Lydia*, Brewer ordered the pirate held isolated until the captain sent for him and went to report to the Captain. He found Bush reading the first of the translations made by Ali and Bell.

"Come in, Mr. Brewer," he said as he set the letter down. "What have you to report? Have we found the captain yet?"

"No, sir, no-one wants to admit to commanding the luggar. I have brought the man I found in the captain's cabin back with me. Mr. Gerard had him kept in isolation, just in case, and I have ordered the same for him here until you can speak to him. Mr. Gerard sends his respects, Captain; he will return as soon as he return as soon as he confers with Captain James. He says he will leave Mr. Midshipman Kennedy in command of the luggar until you send the prize crew to take over."

Bush nodded. "Very good. I am reading the first pages translated and copied. This luggar, which appears to be named *Sword of Allah*, has taken thirteen English merchantmen of various sizes over the last twenty-seven days. Their prizes have all been sent back to Tripoli."

"Not any more, thanks to you, sir."

"Yes, well," Bush murmured, seemingly embarrassed by

the compliment. "Let us see what we can learn from your would-be arsonist. Pass the word for the prisoner, if you please."

The prisoner was brought to the Captain's cabin and put into a chair in the middle of Bush's day cabin, still clad in irons and a marine guard on either side of him. His face bore a hunted look as he surveyed his surroundings.

"I am Captain William Bush of His Majesty's frigate *Lydia*. Do you understand? Do you speak English?" The pirate just stared at him. Bush turned to Brewer and nodded once. Brewer stepped out of the cabin and returned a moment later with Ali. Bush repeated his words to Ali, who duly translated them into Arabic. Still the pirate sat, deaf and dumb.

Bush rose from his chair. "I have no time for imbeciles. Ali, inform this man that he will be hung as a pirate the day after we reach Malta. Sergeant, lock him up in the cable tier."

The marines lifted the pirate from his chair, and he exploded in loud and terrified gibberish. Bush looked to Ali.

"He says you cannot do this, Captain sir," Ali repeated calmly. "He says he is not a pirate; he has a letter of marque from his Bey."

"Well, well," Bush cooed as he sat, signaling for the marines to return him to his seat. "It seems our friend *can* speak. Ask him his name, Ali."

Ali spoke, but the pirate was again silent.

Bush's face grew dark, his tone menacing. "I shall not be merciful again."

Ali translated, and then a moment later said something else. The pirate looked at him and then looked to the deck in defeat. He mumbled something. Ali nodded and turned to Bush. "His name is Yasser Muhammed."

Bush focused on Muhammed. "Are you captain of the *Sword of Allah*?"

Ali translated. Again the prisoner mumbled. Ali said, "Yes."

Bush picked up the letter of marque. "This letter is signed by Murad Reis, Grand Admiral of the Bey's navy. Where is he?"

Ali translated the answer. "I do not know. The letter was delivered to my vessel by messenger just before we sailed."

"Was the ship *Meshuda* at Tripoli while you were in harbor?"

Ali posed the question. "The *Meshuda* sailed from Tripoli harbor two days before he did. He claims he does not know their destination."

Bush leaned forward, his elbow resting on his desk. "Was Murad Reis on board when she sailed?"

Ali seemed surprised at the answer but duly translated it. "The Grand Admiral is *always* on board the *Meshuda* when she sails."

Bush sat back in his chair and quietly considered what Muhammed had said. "Return the prisoner to the deck and hold him in isolation until we return him to his ship." To Muhammed: "You will be sent with your crew to Malta where an admiralty court will decide your fate."

Muhammed spoke to Ali as he was lifted to his feet. Ali translated, "Captain sir, he wishes to know if you will inform this Admiralty court of his letter of marque."

Bushed smiled, giving Muhammed a bad moment. "Inform him that copies of all papers taken from his ship will be forwarded for the court's consideration. You may also tell him that if he gives us any trouble, I will shoot him myself and throw his body to the fish. Those will be my orders to the prize crew as well."

Muhammed nodded dumbly and shuffled out with the two marine guards. Bush waited until they were gone and then looked to Ali.

"When I asked his name, you translated the question and then added something. What did you say?"

Ali stared as though trying to remember. "I told him not to be stupid."

Bush blinked and tried not to smile. Brewer stared at the Arab.

"Well," Bush said, "don't do it again, Ali. Your job is to translate, word for word. Understood?"

"My apologies, Captain sir. It will not happen again."

"Very good. You may return to your translating work. We need those papers translated and copied as soon as possible."

Ali was no sooner out the door than the marine sentry announced the arrival of Mr. Gerard.

"Ah, Gerard," Bush said. "Is everything ready on the luggar?"

"Aye, sir," Gerard said. "The crew is secured below decks. I spoke to Mr. Trench; he estimates a four-day journey to Malta. Have you decided on a prize master?"

Bush named a petty officer in Starling's division. "He's got a master's warrant. Select a prize crew to include six marines. We will pick them up again when we reach Malta. I shall write out orders before they transfer to the *Sword of Allah*."

Gerard grinned. "*Sword of Allah*, sir?"

Bush pointed to the papers he was reading. "That's the luggar's name. The man you sent over is the captain, name's Yasser Muhammed. He says that Murad Reis sailed on the *Meshuda* from Tripoli two days before he did."

"Interesting. I don't suppose he knows where they were bound?"

Bush shook his head. "Claims not to."

"Do you believe him?"

Bush took a deep breath and expelled it loudly. "Who

knows? He will return to the luggar with the prize crew and go to Malta for trial. Ali and my clerk, Bell, are translating and copying the papers Mr. Brewer found in the box, but so far there's not much of interest."

Gerard looked puzzled. "Bell reads Arabic?"

"No, Mr. Gerard," Bush said. "Mr. Bell's copies are for us."

"Ah," Gerard smiled.

"Signal Mr. Kennedy to get the cutter ready to get under way," Bush said as he rose. "She will accompany us while we rejoin the convoy. Prize crew will sail her to Malta as soon as Ali is finished translating the documents."

"Aye, sir."

The two ships sailed on the course Bush laid out for them, one point east of ENE, and the convoy was sighted within three hours. Mr. Trench was on deck with Brewer when the call came from the tops that the convoy was in sight. Brewer had just sent a midshipman to inform the captain when he turned to see a look of modest shock or perhaps awe on the sailing master's face.

"What is it, Mr. Trench?" he asked.

Trench glanced at him and looked back at the convoy, shaking his head. "No sightings, Mr. Brewer. Do ye realize that? *No sightings!* He did it all in his head, and he took us straight to the convoy." He smiled and shook his head in mock disbelief. "That's *seamanship*, Mr. Brewer. I doubt even the old man himself could have done better!"

It took Brewer a moment to realize the sailing master was referring to Lord Hornblower. He looked at the other man, who was still staring at the convoy, but his eyes shows no trace of any disrespect toward the admiral, only admiration for his captain's feat. Brewer smiled to himself and agreed.

The remainder of the voyage to Leghorn passed without incident. The incident with the luggar convinced the merchant captains to get serious about maintaining a strong lookout; HMS *Lydia* was kept busy investigating false sightings. The luggar was dispatched to Malta on the second day, the prize crew being commanded by a master's mate named Dawson. Brewer and Gerard stood at the fantail and watched it sink over the horizon.

CHAPTER FIVE

HMS *Lydia* was forced to spend two days in the harbor at Leghorn. It was a busy harbor, and that was the soonest that a water hoy could be spared for them. Bush fumed at the office of the Port Authority, but both the clerk and his supervisor simply smiled at the English captain and said that no water hoy was available any sooner. Mr. Smalley, the purser, along with the captain's steward and the gunroom steward, took advantage of the time and went ashore to procure as many fresh fruits and vegetables as they could. Mr. Goodnight wanted to get the captain a half-dozen chickens which he would then fatten up on a diet of weevils and crumbs from the empty bags of ship's biscuit before cooking. Coles, the gunroom steward, managed to find a fair-sized pig from which he hoped to get several chops and a couple hams.

Captain Bush and Lieutenant Gerard were invited by the new British consul to dinner on the brig. The two officers went and made the acquaintance of the envoy, whom Gerard described upon his return as "all talk and no substance," and to discuss their route and arrange signals with the brig's captain. Neither officer seemed impressed when they returned.

Other than the visit to the brig, Bush himself spent most

of their forced reprieve in his cabin, pouring over the copies made by Mr. Bell of the documents Ali translated. The neatly written pages—there were fifteen in all, besides the letter of marque—began to paint an interesting picture of Reis' ideas and intentions for using his ships. Bush set the papers on his desk and sat back to think for a moment, his eyes darting faster and faster around the room as his thoughts began to coalesce into a plan. Finally, he rose from his desk and opened his door.

"Pass the word for Mr. Gerard," he said.

He closed the door and returned to his seat, his mind still racing, turning his new plan over to examine it from every angle. He needed Gerard's input on this, just to make sure he wasn't grasping at straws. The Premier arrived within minutes. Bush poured them each a glass of Madeira, and they sat on the settee under the great stern windows of the frigate.

"I want you to read these papers from the luggar, Gerard," Bush said. "One is the letter of marque, of course, but there are fifteen others, and I think we can use them to our benefit."

"How so, sir?"

"It seems to me they reveal bits and pieces of some sort of grand strategy, sort of an overall plan of how Grand Admiral Reis plans to use his ships against us. Now, if we can add anything to it, say from other ships we may encounter, might they not be made to fit together as a puzzle, and may we not glean from it where he might be at a particular time? If luck is on our side, we just may be able to surprise the traitor and take him!"

Gerard was surprised to hear his captain talk this way; frankly it sounded much more like something Hornblower would say than Bush, but he had to admit it was an intriguing idea. He took a long, slow drink of his wine to give himself an extra moment or two to think, and when he was finished, he looked at his captain and nodded.

"It sound plausible, sir," he said. "When do we start?"

Bush rose and retrieved the copied pages. He set the letter of marque aside and kept the coded page for himself, handing Gerard the remaining fifteen.

"I have already read these," Bush said. "I want you to read them, then we'll talk."

The men worked in almost complete silence for the next three hours, interrupted only by Goodnight, who asked what the Captain would like for his dinner. Bush left it in the steward's capable hands, adding only that the First Lieutenant would be joining him.

They stopped only grudgingly to eat, realizing that their legs and backs needed to stretch and their stomachs were growling for food. Goodnight produced a very good tongue, the aroma of which was the final straw in convincing the men to set their work aside for a time. Carrots and pudding rounded out the simple fare. Bush sat back in his chair, puffing a cigar to life, while Gerard finished the last of his pudding.

"I wonder," Bush said from behind a cloud of blue smoke, "if we might need some help."

"What do you mean, sir?"

"Do you remember when the Admiral came out to *Agamemnon* after Bonaparte's abortive escape attempt? Do you remember his saying that Mr. Brewer had a hand in figuring out what was going on?"

Gerard sat back in his chair, his narrowed eyes betraying his attempts to remember, his success told by those eyes going wide.

"Yes, sir," he said. "I believe I do. Do you think Brewer may be able to help?"

Bush shrugged. "Who knows? He may have a suggestion

that has eluded us. Let's have him in, shall we? Pass the word for Mr. Brewer, if you please."

"With pleasure, sir." Gerard grinned and went to the door to pass the word. The two officers retreated to their seats under the stern windows to wait. It was not long before the marine sentry admitted the Second Lieutenant.

"You sent for me, sir?" Brewer asked.

"Yes, Mr. Brewer," Bush said. "I have a question for you: On St. Helena, was it you, or was it not you, who figured out how Bonaparte planned to escape the island?"

Brewer came close to recoiling physically at the Captain's question. It was literally the last thing he thought he would hear when he entered the cabin. His eyes hid behind narrowed lids and flashed from one officer to the other and back again while he tried to decide what light his answer would cast upon his mentor.

Unfortunately for him, his captain saw through his hesitation. "Mr. Brewer, I strongly urge honesty in whatever you are about to tell us. I am sure I speak for Mr. Gerard as well when I say that what you say will not leave this room."

Brewer sighed in surrender and lowered his eyes. "I... may have said something to his lordship that proved to be correct."

Bush and Gerard shared a knowing look, and Gerard nodded.

"Goodnight!" Bush called. The servant appeared in the pantry doorway. "Wine, if you please. Mr. Brewer, please sit down."

Goodnight returned with three glasses filled with wine and set them on the table before withdrawing. The three men each picked up a glass, and Brewer was a bit surprised when Bush raised his glass in a silent toast before indulging.

"Mr. Brewer," the Captain began, "Mr. Gerard and I have undertaken a project, and I would like to enlist your help.

Murad Reis is the Grand Admiral for the Bey of Tripoli. He is also a turncoat Scot who was born Peter Lisle before he deserted and went Turk, and he is wanted by the Admiralty. Ali translated the papers you took from the privateer, and Mr. Bell made me a copy of them before they were sent with the prize crew to Malta. Mr. Gerard agrees with me that they seem to present pieces, as it were, of Reis' plans for the plunder of Mediterranean shipping. If his plan was a puzzle, we believe we have one or two pieces. What we plan to do is to gather information from whatever sources we encounter to see if we can't complete the puzzle ourselves. Should we be able to accomplish that, we may be able to predict his movements to a great degree and capture him. We want you to help us analyze this and any new information."

"I see, sir," Brewer said.

"Understand, William," Bush said quietly, "this is a secret project of our own doing. I want it to remain so. No one is to know about this. Do you understand?"

"I do, sir."

Bush handed him the copied papers. "Good. Here are the copies. One is the letter of marque, and I want your ideas on the rest. Read them, and then we'll talk."

Brewer took a drink of his wine and then spent the next hour pouring over the pages handed him by the captain. When he finished, he stretched his back and drained his glass.

"Well?" Bush asked. "What do you think?"

Brewer shrugged. "If this is a puzzle, we are still missing many pieces."

Gerard smiled. "That much we already knew, William."

Brewer sighed. "The papers are vague references to places and times of the year, but I fear that many of them must have a significance in Muslim culture. It may give us a clue."

"Well, let me know if anything occurs to you. Mr. Gerard,

we sail on the afternoon tide tomorrow."

"Aye, sir."

Both officers rose and came to attention before exiting the cabin. Brewer glanced behind him as he closed the door to see Bush staring thoughtfully out the stern windows. He wondered idly what was going through the captain's mind, and why that coded page looked so familiar.

HMS *Lydia* departed on schedule, followed by the brig *Heracles* carrying the consul and his party. Their course was due south, with the Italian peninsula just over the horizon. Bush stationed *Lydia* one mile southeast of the brig, hoping to intercept any pirate ships. The brig had orders to run for the peninsula at the first sign of trouble.

The first two days of the run were filled with dull routine. The winds held, and the sea remained relatively calm with *Lydia* being careful to match the brig's four knot speed. Brewer kept his men busy while he himself thought about that coded page the captain had showed him. It was maddening, as though the answer of where he had seen it was just beyond his reach.

Two bells had just sounded in the afternoon watch on the third day when the tedium came to a sudden and permanent end.

"Deck there! Sail off the starboard bow!"

"Where away?" Brewer called.

The lookout pointed to the SSW. "Three points off the starboard bow, maybe four, sir!"

Brewer took a glass and went to the starboard rail to see. It took only a moment for him to zero in on the patch of white on the horizon, and only a few more to confirm that it was growing slowly. He lowered the glass.

"Mr. Bennet," he said to the midshipman of the watch, "my respects to the captain. Tell him we have sighted a strange sail to the southeast."

"Aye, sir," Bennet touched his hat was gone.

Brewer studied the approaching ship. It was still hull down, but the sail was still growing.

"What do you make of it, lookout?" he called.

He watched the lookout study it for a moment before the answer came. "Can't rightly tell yet, sir. Still too far away!"

Brewer figured as much. "Keep on it. Let us know as soon as you can!"

Brewer brought his eyes back to the deck in time to see Captain Bush arrive on deck. Bush looked around for a second, then marched straight over to him.

"Report, Mr. Brewer."

"Sir, we have sighted a strange sail off the starboard bow," he said, handing Bush his telescope and pointing. "Still hull down a moment ago; no identification yet, sir."

Brewer could tell by the way the glass steadied that the Captain had found his target. He watched it for more than a minute before lowering the glass.

"We'll keep this course for now, Mr. Brewer," Bush said. "Signal *Heracles* that we have sighted a strange sail to the southeast and that she is to keep this course for now."

"Aye, sir," Brewer said. "Pass the word for Mr. Thompson!"

Thompson, the midshipman in charge of signals, arrived, and Brewer relayed the captain's orders. The midshipman touched his hat and went aft to compose the signal.

"Signal acknowledged, sir!" Thompson called out minutes later.

"Very well," Bush said. He turned away from the railing and handed the glass back to Brewer. "Keep an eye on that ship, Mr. Brewer. I want to know as soon as she's identified."

"Aye, sir."

"Deck, there! Sail's changing course!"

Brewer handed Bush the glass again and turned to get another for himself. He joined his captain at the railing in time to see the small field of white elongate as though turning broadside to them and then narrow again.

"Appears to be moving away from us, sir!" the lookout bellowed.

Bush lowered the telescope and stared at the horizon for a moment before lowering his gaze. He turned and leaned against the rail, lost in thought. He looked to Brewer.

"What time is sundown?"

"Just after the turn of the second dog watch, sir. Maybe one bell of the first watch."

Bush nodded and handed the glass back to Brewer. "Notify me immediately of any further sightings. I'm going below."

"Aye aye, Captain."

As soon as the captain was below deck, Brewer turned and scanned the horizon again but found nothing. He looked to the lookout and caught his eye. The lookout shrugged and shook his head. The sail had dipped below the horizon.

At five bells, the lookout was heard from again.

"Deck there! Sail off the starboard beam!"

Brewer rushed to the rail and soon had the sail in sight.

"Mr. Bennet! My respects to the captain! Sail in sight off the starboard beam!"

The midshipman rushed off, and Brewer looked to the tops.

"Lookout! Is it the same ship as before?"

"Could be, sir! Sails look familiar!"

Suddenly the Captain was at his arm, and Brewer handed over his telescope.

"Sail sighted, sir. Lookout says it may be our friend from before."

Bush studied the horizon in silence. Brewer wished his captain would think aloud, so he could follow his thoughts. Bush lowered the glass.

"Steady as she goes, Mr. Brewer."

Brewer sighed. "Aye, sir. Do you think they might be sizing us up for something?"

Bush shrugged. "I have no idea. Pirates aren't known for their night attacks, according to the intelligence I've been given, so they must be seeing if we will react to their advances. As long as they sit on the horizon, we shall continue on our course."

"Aye, sir." Brewer looked out to the horizon, troubled by their shadow. He remembered that the Barbary pirates often attacked in packs, and he wondered at *Lydia's* chances against four or five pirates.

Bush handed the glass back to Brewer. "Same as before, Mr. Brewer. Call me if anything changes."

"Aye aye, sir."

Thirty minutes later, the lookout called down to the deck. "Sir! Looks like she's turning away again!"

Brewer swung his glass toward the horizon and saw the field of white elongate, just as it did before, and then fade over the horizon.

"Mr. Bennet, my respects to the captain. Please inform him that the sail's turned away again and has gone below the horizon."

"Aye, Mr. Brewer!"

Brewer watched the horizon for the next hour but saw nothing. He was beginning to think they were safe for the night when the lookout called down again.

"Deck there! Strange sail on the starboard quarter!"

Brewer went to the fantail and scanned the horizon.

"Same one, lookout?"

"Think so, sir!"

"Mr. Bennet, inform the Captain."

"Aye, sir."

Once again, Bush appeared at his lieutenant's side. Brewer handed him a glass and pointed out the sail now trailing them on the horizon. Bush studied the image and lowered the glass again. Brewer did not like the look on his captain's face.

"This fellow is toying with us!" Bush said under his breath. "Mr. Trench! Time until dark?"

The sailing master studied the sky for a moment. "I would put it at five hours at most, Captain."

"Time enough," Bush said. "All hands! Make sail! Mr. Trench, give me an intercept course for that sail! Mr. Brewer, signal to *Heracles! 'Stay on course. Am investigating strange sail sighting'.*"

"Aye, sir!"

"Stand by to go about! Man the braces!"

Lydia came alive as the hands hurriedly scaled the shrouds and the bow swung around to the northwest. The ship picked up speed as the cloud of canvas above her grew. Bush went to the bow to get a better view of their quarry, now fully aware of *Lydia's* change of course. The other ship was now turning away and crowding on sail of her own.

"Lookout!" he called. "Can you make her out?"

"Hard to say, sir—a brig, maybe!"

Bush lowered his telescope and handed it to a nearby midshipman before marching back to the quarterdeck. If they moved smartly, there may just be time to take their shadow before they could escape into the darkness.

Gerard was on the quarterdeck talking with Brewer when he returned. The Premier turned and touched his hat; Bush acknowledged the gesture quickly.

"I want every stitch she'll carry, Mr. Trench! I want to overtake them before dark."

Trench looked uncertainly at the mass of canvas above them before acknowledging the order and going to take the wheel himself. Bush cast an eye over the sails himself before joining his lieutenants.

"It appears we have a shadow," Gerard said.

"First appearance was to the sou'east, then to the east, and now she's nor'east," Bush said. "Trying to see if we're guarding anything inshore, I'd wager. I'm hoping we can either take her or at least scare her off before dark."

Gerard automatically cast an eye westward. It was a clear night, and Brewer saw he was estimating for himself the amount of daylight left. Gerard called for a telescope and studied the chase, now under full sail themselves, and tried to estimate the rate at which the gap was closing. Brewer noted that he was not smiling. He lowered the telescope and stared out into space; Brewer thought he was doing math in his head. He focused on their quarry one more time before turning and heading for the captain, handing Brewer the glass as he passed.

"Sir," Gerard said softly as he saluted Bush, "may I speak with you?"

Bush turned. "Yes, Mr. Gerard?"

Gerard took a step closer and spoke quietly. "Sir, it is my judgment that we will not overtake the enemy before dark. I recommend we turn back to ensure the safety of the consul and his party."

Bush looked at his first lieutenant in silence for a moment. "Walk with me, Mr. Gerard." The two men began to pace the quarterdeck together. "I thank you for your recommendation. It will be noted in the log. However, I believe we can overtake them in time. I do not intend to lose this chance to take or sink a pirate."

"As you say, sir," Gerard surrendered gracefully, but he was concerned. He had never thought Bush to be one to take chances or gamble the mission this way, but he could see the Captain's blood was up and further talk would do no good. He hoped his estimates were wrong, but he had the nagging feeling they were not.

Bush stopped and faced his Premier. "Thank you, Mr. Gerard. You have the deck. Do whatever you must to close the gap."

Gerard touched his hat. "Aye aye, sir." Gerard watched his captain go below, and then went over to Brewer. "I relieve you, sir."

Brewer saluted. "Thank you, sir." He looked around discreetly and then lowered his voice. "We're not going to make it, are we?"

Gerard did not look at him. "The Captain says we will."

"Aye aye, sir."

Gerard sighed and looked at Brewer. "To answer your question, William, it was my recommendation to the Captain that we abandon the chase and return to the consul's ship. No, I do not believe we will make it. The Captain listened to my counsel and decided to reject it. That is, of course, his prerogative. It also ends the matter."

"Aye, sir." Brewer had the sense to look chastised and stepped away from the first lieutenant. He looked back to see Gerard begin to pace slowly up and down the quarterdeck, retracing the path he walked with Captain Bush only minutes before. The look on his face was equal parts frustration, resignation, and concern, and gave Brewer the impression of a man who knew he was making a mistake.

Brewer took advantage of his relief to go below. He entered the gunroom to find the large table empty.

"Coles!" he called. The steward appeared almost at once.

"Yes, Mr. Brewer?"

"Some wine, if you please. Do we have any more of that cheese lying about?"

"Yes, sir. Shall I bring you a sampling?"

"Yes, thank you." The servant disappeared on his errand, and Brewer ducked into his cabin. He selected Gibbons' *Decline and Fall of the Roman Empire* from his shelf and returned to the table. He had promised Lord Hornblower during the voyage home from St. Helena that he would read the book and write him with his opinion of the work, but so far he had not been able to make much headway. He was determined to finish the book before they left the Mediterranean and returned to England; that way, he could either write his lordship or possibly stop over at Smallbridge a day or two to discuss it with him.

He no sooner took his seat than Coles reappeared with a tray containing a glass of wine and a plate with several wedges of cheese. He set them in front of Brewer and noticed the book.

"Enjoying the book, Mr. Brewer?"

"I hope to," Brewer answered with a smile. "Have you read it, Coles?"

The steward looked embarrassed. "Oh, no, Mr. Brewer. I never was one for reading, I'm afraid. It's just that I had an occasion or two to wait on Lord Hornblower on the way home from St. Helena, and I remember this one being a particular favorite of his."

"Well, that's where I got this one. Somehow, I promised Lord Hornblower I would read it and give him my opinion of the work. I'm not sure if he wants my opinion of Gibbons or of the Romans."

Coles shook his head and returned to his pantry. Brewer opened the book and absently reached for a wedge of cheese. It was many pages later that his attention was broken by his hand searching the empty plate for another wedge of cheese. He looked around to find the gunroom still deserted. His glass was empty; he had no idea if Coles had refilled it or how many times if he had. He took count of how many pages he had read before closing the book on what he considered a good day's work.

He replaced the book on his shelf and made his way back on deck. Lieutenant Gerard was pacing the quarterdeck, so Brewer made his way over to the wheel to speak to Mr. Trench.

"What's the situation?" he asked.

"We've closed the distance by half, but we only have about two hours' daylight left to us," the sailing master said. "The Captain's been up on deck three times in the last hour, each time his face looks darker than the time before. My guess is that we'll just have time to get the long nines a shot at him before we lose him to dark or a fog."

"I advise you to keep your guesses to yourself." It was Gerard, who had walked up behind them. "The Captain's in a foul mood, and he may not take kindly to it."

"Aye, sir," Trench said. He went back to his wheel.

Brewer grabbed a glass and went forward. He stood beside one of the bow chasers studied their chase. He had a reasonably good view of the hull, but he could not make out any name on the stern. He could just make out two forms that appeared at the fantail and wondered idly what they were talking about. He was just beginning to think the long nines might be able to reach when midshipman Lee, midshipman of the watch, approached him and saluted.

"Mr. Gerard's compliments, sir," he said, "and could you please ready the long nines for firing? Mr. Gerard asks that you let him know when you believe we are within range."

"Thank you, Mr. Lee," Brewer said, all business now. "My respects to Mr. Gerard. I will let him know. Please pass the word for Reilly."

"Aye, sir." The midshipman touched his hat was gone.

Within a few minutes, the gunner appeared. He was

about the same age as Brewer's father and possessed the same brownish, leathery, weather-beaten skin that marks a man who has spent much of his life exposed to the elements. He had shoulders like an ox, and his biceps nearly tore his sleeves. His hair was completely white, and he wore a bright blue kerchief about his neck. His movements were slow and deliberate, as would be expected of someone who spent his life working with explosives.

"You sent for me, Mr. Brewer?" he said. His voice was unexpectedly high and squeaky for a man of his size.

"Yes, Mr. Reilly. Mr. Gerard wants the long nines readied to fire at the enemy as soon as we can reach them. You are far and away the best man for the job."

"Aye aye, Mr. Brewer."

Brewer stepped back and watched as Reilly took command of both bow chasers. After having them loaded and run out, he personally sighted down each barrel, making the incremental corrections that would give the greatest probability of a hit at extreme range. Finally, he stood and stared at the chase. After several minutes of this, Brewer stepped up and asked him what he was doing.

"Waiting for the range, sir. Shouldn't be long, now."

Brewer stepped back and waited. Three minutes later, Reilly blinked twice and stared again for thirty seconds. Then he turned to Brewer.

"I think I can reach her now, sir."

"Mr. Lee!" Brewer called to the midshipman standing by. "My respects to Mr. Gerard. Tell him I think I can reach him now. Request permission to open fire."

"Aye, Mr. Brewer."

The midshipman hurried away, and Brewer turned back to the task at hand. He watched from behind Reilly, trying to understand the man's train of thought but not wanting to disturb him. He heard footsteps coming up behind him and assumed it was Lee returning with orders from Lieutenant Gerard. He turned and was surprised to see the Captain coming forward.

"Report, Mr. Brewer," Bush said. He put his telescope to his eye.

"Ready to open fire, sir."

Bush lowered his glass. "Oh? Think you can reach her?"

"Mr. Reilly does, sir."

Bush turned to the gunner, who was standing respectfully between his guns, awaiting the Captain's permission to fire.

"Very well," Bush said. "Mr. Reilly, you may open fire."

"Aye, sir!" Reilly said. "Alright, lads! Steady! Steady! Fire!"

The two long nines belched fire and smoke. Bush and Brewer put glass to eye in time to see twin water spouts erupt from the sea barely twenty yards behind the chase.

"Well done, Mr. Reilly," Bush said. "You may fire at will."

"Thank you, Captain! Reload lads! Here, slow down, mate! Sponge out that gun first!"

Bush looked to the sky, then down at the chase again. The light was fading rapidly. He motioned for Brewer to step away with him.

"Mr. Brewer," he said, "I'm afraid the light is giving out on us. Mr. Reilly is to continue firing as long as he can see the target. I'm hoping he'll get lucky and bring down their mizzen. Report to the quarterdeck when you are done here."

"Aye, sir," Brewer touched his hat. "Mr. Reilly, you may fire at will as long as you can see the enemy. Your target is their mizzen."

"Aye, sir."

The sun gave way to a moonless night. Reilly had to cease fire after only thirty minutes, during which he got off six shots with each gun. Brewer was impressed by the steady fire. Slow by broadside standards, the gunner fired one at a time, taking pains to get the best aim he could in the fading light. Brewer saw four hits to the ship, but unfortunately the mizzen stood defiant.

"You did the best you could, Mr. Reilly," Brewer said. "Secure your guns. I need to report to the captain."

Brewer made his way aft and found the captain in conversation with Mr. Gerard and Mr. Trench. Bush stepped away from his men and stood alone on the quarterdeck as the darkness descended around them.

"Mr. Trench," he called, "any chance of getting a burst of speed to try a quick broadside before she disappears?"

"None, Captain," the master said sadly. "She's carrying all she can carry. There's not room for a single stitch more."

Bush nodded but said nary a word for several moments.

"Mr. Gerard," he said finally, "Dowse the lights. Order more lookouts forward to see if we can catch her changing course."

"Aye, sir!" Gerard said. He picked up the speaking trumpet and gave the order before turning back to his captain.

"What do you think, sir?" he asked.

Bush looked at him and shrugged. "I think you were right. I shouldn't have left the consul's ship. Odds are they have already slipped away to port or starboard while I was debating what to do. We'll continue on this course for a bit, just to make sure, then we'll abandon the chase and head back to our charge."

Gerard was surprised at the resigned way in which his captain spoke. Hornblower would have been furious at their failure to damage the enemy somehow and slow him down. He knew his chief well enough to know that Bush was every bit as angry, both at himself and at the fates, and as he stepped beside the captain, he could see the set of his jaw and knew that he was right. He also saw the captain's eyes, and they said something was terribly wrong.

Bush turned to Gerard. "Turn us about. Set course to rendezvous with the consul's ship as soon as possible. I'm going below. Set extra lookouts. I want to know as soon as we sight her."

Gerard touched his hat. "Aye, sir."

He watched Bush go below. Brewer came up beside him.

"Is anything wrong?" he asked.

"I believe there is," Gerard answered. "Mr. Trench! Turn us about. Set course to intercept the consul's ship. Double the lookouts. Notify the captain as soon as the consul's ship is sighted. I believe it's Mr. Starling's watch. He has the deck. I shall be in the gunroom."

Gerard went below. Brewer followed him, choosing to get a couple hours sleep before he had to relieve Starling at the turn of the watch. Sleep was hard coming, Brewer's mind racing with scenarios that may occur due to their failure to catch the chase.

He relieved Mr. Starling at eight bells and posted the extra lookouts ordered by the captain to scan the horizon in search of *Heracles'* night signal. Nothing had been seen by the time Gerard relieved him at the turn of the next watch.

"I've got a bad feeling about this, William," Gerard said.

"Hopefully, we'll come upon them after dawn," Brewer said. "I'm going to get some sleep."

Brewer rose just before six bells and ate a hasty breakfast before going on deck. He found the Captain already there and in conversation with Lt. Gerard and the sailing master. They were gathered around a chart held by Gerard and Trench.

"They have to be in this area, sir," Trench was saying, drawing a small oval on the chart with his finger. "That's based on the best possible speed for the brig if the wind held all night."

Bush studied the chart. "And where were they when we left them?"

"About here, sir." The master's finger moved almost an inch north along the coast.

"And where do you estimate our position to be now?"

"About here, sir." The finger moved half an inch south and slightly east.

"Very well," Bush said. "Turn us northwest. We will hold that course for an hour or two. I want to close with the coast to make sure the brig wasn't driven to the shore. Then we'll race south to Naples, checking the coast as best we can."

Brewer looked past Bush to Gerard, who was standing behind him. The look on his face was one of having his worst fears come to pass.

They found nothing on their passage northwest, and the feeling on board began edging from bad to worse. Bush spent every daylight hour of their southern search on the quarterdeck, alternately pacing or standing at the lee rail, his hands behind his back, staring out to sea. His officers left him in peace; only Gerard intruded on the captain's solitude to make a report when necessary.

The search for the *Heracles* was slow, frustrating, and taxing on the nerves of everyone on board the *Lydia*. Extra lookouts were aloft from dawn till dusk, with more scanning the horizon from the shrouds. Every passing ship was questioned, and every harbor was visited to see if the missing ship had put in there. Tempers very nearly flared during a three-hour period in which the *Lydia* was becalmed. Lieutenant Gerard, Mr. Trench and the quartermaster were speaking in low tones regarding their situation. The captain was pacing on the opposite side of the quarterdeck and overheard a remark the sailing master made about the calm not helping them in their search. He ceased pacing and marched over to the group.

"I'll thank you to keep your opinions to yourself, Mr. Trench," the Captain said hotly. "Unless, of course, you happen to have some wind up your sleeve! Or perhaps you think you were better in command!"

The three men stared open-mouthed at their captain, quite unable to overcome their shock at his outburst. The quartermaster recovered first; he looked at the deck and made his way back to the wheel as unobtrusively as he could.

"Captain!" Gerard cried when he found his voice.

"What, Mr. Gerard?" Bush said. "Am I to be confused with the Almighty, that I can but say the word and the wind should appear? Well, sir? Or do you mean to tell me that had we followed *your* plan, we would not be in our present troubles?!?"

The sailing master recoiled at his captain's words. Gerard immediately came to attention, his eyes forward and unmoving and his jaws clamped shut. Mr. Trench opened his mouth again to defend the first lieutenant, but Gerard stopped him with a motion of his hand. He stood unmoving before his captain. Bush for his part stood poised for a fight, his eyes flying from one man to the other as his rage boiled over.

"Well?" he yelled.

That drew the attention of the attention of the quarterdeck and beyond. Gerard and Trench stood unmoving and silent, Gerard at attention and Trench ready to flee behind the wheel at the first sign of trouble.

Suddenly, the Captain blinked. He looked around and saw the stares of those aft of the mainmast, some curious and some frightened at this display of the wrath of Zeus upon mortals. He looked back at Gerard and drew a deep slow breath to help regain control. His eyes dropped to the deck and he exhaled. When he looked up again, the rage was gone from his eyes. He reached out and patted Gerard on the arm. To the sailing master, "As you were, Mr. Trench."

He stepped back. "Please come to my cabin, Mr. Gerard. Mr. Trench, you have the deck until he returns."

Without another word, Bush turned and went below, knowing that his number one was right behind him. The sentry opened the door to allow them to enter. Bush called for the steward and ordered two glasses of Madeira. He tossed his hat and coat on the table and led Gerard to the day cabin. When the glasses arrived, he handed one to Gerard.

"Mr. Gerard," he said, holding his glass up in salute, "I apologize for my words on deck. They were undeserved. Man to man, I ask for your forgiveness."

Gerard was stunned. He had served with Bush off and on for more than ten years, watched him learn from Hornblower all those years, and never had he heard anything like this from his Captain. He suddenly realized he was staring and blinked his eyes back into focus. He smiled and raised his glass as well.

"Right willingly, sir," he said. The two touched glasses and drank.

"I will admit, Mr. Gerard, that in hindsight you were quite right. That sail was obviously a lure to entice us away from the *Heracles*, and I allowed it to work to perfection." Bush sat before the stern windows and called for more wine. "I'm afraid I may have much to answer for, Mr. Gerard, if the consul has been taken captive or murdered."

"We'll find them sir," Gerard said. "*Heracles* is probably waiting for us in Naples."

Bush smiled ruefully. "I'm afraid that brigs do not fly, Mr. Gerard." The steward arrived to refill their glasses. "In any case, we shall soon know, one way or the other. We should pull into the harbor at Naples tomorrow, and we shall see if the good ship and consul are there. Then I must report to the British authorities." He drained his glass and stood. "Now, if you will excuse me, Mr. Gerard, I must write my report for the admiral."

"Aye aye, sir." Gerard set his glass down and came to attention before leaving the cabin. His head was still spinning, trying to process first the Captain's lashing out and then his apology. Both actions were unlike Bush, and Gerard could only put them down to the strain the Captain was under due to the missing consul. Gerard fervently hoped they would fine *Heracles* at Naples, but a nagging little voice in the back of his head told him that was not going to happen.

HMS *Lydia* slid into Naples' harbor at six bells of the forenoon watch. A pilot was sent to guide the frigate to her berth roughly in the center of the bay. Gerard had extra lookouts searching the large harbor for any signs of the *Heracles*. After the pilot left, he reported to his Captain.

"I'm sorry, sir," he said quietly. "There's no sign of the *Heracles* anywhere in the harbor."

Bush sighed. "Thank you, Mr. Gerard. I am going below to change. Please call away my gig. I must go ashore to see the British authorities."

In less than half an hour, Bush found himself seated in the stern sheets of his gig being rowed to the getty. According to the information given him at Gibraltar with his orders, the leading British diplomat in Naples was the Envoy Extraordinary Sir William à Court, Lord Heytesbury.

After alighting on the getty, Bush made his way to the British mission. A copy of his report was in his hand, to be given to the British Envoy, but Bush did not feel it exonerated him for failing to protect the incoming consul.

Bush saluted the sentry at the gate to the mission and walked quickly up the long drive to the mission door. Off to the left, on the other side of the landscaped lawn he saw a bunkhouse where the garrison resided. As he neared the door, he saw a roving patrol come around the corner of the house and wondered at the security.

The door was opened by a liveried servant who would have done honor to the finest manor house in England. Bush was asked to wait in a small library while the servant to his report to Lord Heytesbury. Bush thought it a room used for just this purpose, and he perused the bookshelves and admired the portrait of Lord Nelson that hung on the wall. He smiled to himself when he noticed that there was no clock in the room.

The servant returned and asked if Bush would kindly follow him. He was led up a grand staircase to a door at the top of the stairs. The servant knocked twice and then opened the door and announced him. Bush marched past the servant to find Lord Heytesbury standing in the middle of the room. A look of concern was on his face.

"Welcome, Captain," he said. "I presume you are going to explain to me where my consul has gone. I have skimmed your report, so I am familiar with the chain of events. I would like to hear it from you."

He led Bush to two chairs set on either side of a window overlooking a garden with a low table in between. As if on cue, a servant entered carrying a tray with two glasses on port. He set it on the table before bowing to the envoy and leaving the room. The envoy picked up his glass and sipped it. Bush picked his up as well, but he only allowed the merest taste of the nectar to touch his lips before setting it down and beginning his tale. Heytesbury listened in silence for the most part, interrupting only twice to ask for clarification.

When he finished, Bush sat back in his chair and waited. Heytesbury took a drink of his port and looked out the window, obviously digesting what his guest had told him.

Bush could tell from the way his eyes darted from here to there and back again that Heytesbury mind was working furiously, so he sat still and bided his time. Finally, the envoy sighed. He looked at his glass, drained it in a single draught, and set it on the table. When he sat back in his chair again, there was a look of resignation on his face.

"Thank you, Captain," he said. "I believe I see clearly now the chain of events. You are not the first captain to fall victim to that trick, and I am sure you will not be the last. The question now is, what happened to the *Heracles*? If the pirates got her, we should be getting a ransom demand for the consul and his wife at the very least, possibly for the return of the ship and crew as well. However, it is entirely possible that the pirates will sell the crew into slavery without a second thought. It's what they did before Exmouth taught them a lesson back in 1816, and I have heard rumors that they have resumed the practice."

There was a sudden and urgent knock at the door, which flew open to admit a young man in his mid-twenties carrying a sheet of paper.

"Hawkins?" Heytesbury said. "What is the meaning of this?"

"My apologies, my lord, but I thought you should see this at once." He handed Heytesbury the paper, and the Envoy scanned it hurriedly. He laid it on his lap for a moment and thought. He handed it to Bush.

"Well, now at least we know."

Bush read the letter. It was a ransom demand for the consul and his wife. It warned that failure to pay would result in the hostages being sold into slavery. The ransom of £5,000 was to be delivered to the Bey of Tunis by the end of next month.

Bush paused his reading, burning with shame that his error in judgment had led to this. His embarrassment turned rapidly to rage when he read the rest of the letter and saw the signature at the bottom—Murad Reis!

Bush stared at the signature before handing the letter back to Lord Heytesbury. His lordship handed it back to his aide.

"Hawkins, how did the letter arrive?" Heytesbury asked the aide.

"It was sent here in Heracles' launch, my lord. It was crewed by the second mate and four sailors."

"What? Let's have them in!" Heytesbury rose, and Bush followed suit.

"Yes, my lord." The aide left the room and returned with a man Bush recognized from his visits to the Heracles, although he could not recall the man's name.

"What is your name, sir?" Heytesbury asked.

"James Abernathy, my lord. I was second mate on the Heracles. Captain Bush! It's good to see you, Captain! We almost stopped at the Lydia when we entered the harbor, but we was told to come straight to his lordship, so that's what we did!"

"Please tell us what happened, Mr. Abernathy," Heytesbury said.

"Well, yer lordship, the Captain here signaled us that they were going to investigate a sighting to the nor' west. We was a bit concerned when it got dark and they weren't back yet, but we kept on the southern course as ordered. A couple hours after dark we saw a ship appearing out of the darkness. We thought it was *Lydia*, Captain, honest to God we did! The size was about right. We didn't realize until it was too late that she was coming in from the wrong direction—it was a point or two south of east. They closed to a half pistol shot before we knew it and ran out the broadside. A voice called over to us to surrender or they would fire. The cap'n hauled down the flag. Bloody pirates came over the rail and terrorized the passengers! Their admiral was the worst of the lot, my lord. He came aboard and asked who the captain was. When the cap'n spoke up, the blighter shot him down in cold blood! Took any fight out of the crew, let me tell you! Then their admiral called for me and gave me the letter."

"Just a moment," Heytesbury said. "He called you by name?"

"No, my lord, he called for the second mate. He ordered me to take the launch and four men and sail for Naples to deliver the letter."

"You've been on the southerly course the whole time?" Bush asked.

"Aye, Captain."

Bush stared. "We must have passed you during a night."

Abernathy shrugged. "Could be, sir; we didn't see you, that I can tell you."

Heytesbury stirred. "Yes, well, thank you, Mr. Abernathy. Please go with Mr. Hawkins. He will show you where you can write me a report on what you told us."

Hawkins left with Abernathy in tow. When the door closed behind them, Bush turned to Heytesbury. The man had his arms crossed on his chest with his chin resting in one hand. He was staring at the floor, lost in thought.

"What happens now, my lord?" Bush asked.

Heytesbury walked to his desk and sat down. "You and HMS *Lydia* are released to your next assignment, Captain."

"What about the consul?" Bush asked.

"My office will handle that from here," Heytesbury said. "We have a lot of experience dealing with the Bey in these matters."

Bush stood there, wondering what his own admiral was going to say when he heard the consul Bush was supposed to see safely to Naples had been kidnapped by Murad Reis! Heytesbury must have seen the look on his face, because he sat back in his chair.

"I shouldn't worry over much, Captain," he said. "As I said, you're not the first to fall for Reis' tricks, and you certainly won't be the last. I know Admiral Fremantle rather well; I think you can expect a severe tongue lashing for your error, but hardly more than that." Heytesbury picked up a pen and looked up at Bush. "However, I wouldn't fall for it again, were I you."

"No, my lord," Bush said.

CHAPTER SIX

Bush returned to the Lydia with his face set in a hard, unreadable mask to hide his feelings. He was embarrassed by the loss of the consul and hopeful that Lord Heytesbury was right is his estimate of the admiral's reaction. He acknowledged Lt. Gerard's salute.

"Are we ready for sea, Mr. Gerard?" he asked, surprising himself at the edge in his own voice.

"Aye, sir," came the reply. "The water lighters came out while you were ashore sir. The purser along with your steward are ashore. We can put to sea as soon as they get back."

"Very well," Bush said. "Inform me as soon as they return. Make all preparations for putting to sea."

"Aye aye, sir. May I ask our destination?"

Bush paused and turned back to his first lieutenant. "South to the Straights of Messina, and then on to Tripoli. I have to see a man about a ransom note."

HMS *Lydia* left Naples and the Kingdom of the Two Sicilies behind with little fanfare and turned south for the Straights. They traveled under all plain sail over the calm Mediterranean waters, the lookouts ever vigilant in their lookout for pirates. None were kind enough to show themselves, however; other than the coastal traffic, Lydia seemed to have the seas to herself.

Lieutenant Brewer came on deck to a clear, starlit night to take the middle watch. He made his way to the quarterdeck and found Lieutenant Starling in conversation with a quartermaster's mate at the wheel.

"I relieve you, sir," Brewer said.

Starling turned to him and saluted. "I stand relieved."

The two officers stepped away from the wheel as the new watch came on deck and relieved their fellows. Brewer did not notice that Starling had not gone below until he spoke.

"I hope the Captain's not going to get in too much trouble," he said.

"I wouldn't know about that," Brewer replied, trying his best not to get into a conversation. Much to his dismay, the third lieutenant did not appear to have anywhere else to be.

"Do you think the admiral will hold him responsible for the consul and his wife being kidnapped?"

"I really have no idea," Brewer said, watching the waves crest and slide past them.

Starling watched the activity on the deck for a few minutes, and Brewer hoped he would go below. His hopes were foiled when Starling looked at the deck in concentration.

"But don't you think-"

Brewer turned on him and cut him off unmercifully. "Mr. Starling! I have no idea what will happen to the Captain, if anything at all! What I do know is that this is one subject you would be better off keeping your thoughts to yourself!"

Starling made as though he would answer in kind, but he caught himself and instead came to attention.

"Aye, sir," he said, and he turned and marched below decks.

"Mr. Brewer."

Brewer turned to see Captain James walking up from behind.

"Captain."

James stopped and nodded after the departed Starling. "I'm dashed if I know how you put up with that young snipe."

Brewer shrugged. "He's young. He'll learn."

"I'd love to help teach him, if you'll let me have him for a week or so."

Brewer turned to see the playful look on the Marine's face and had to laugh himself.

"No, thank you," he said. "Although we may take you up on it one day."

"Well," James said as he continued on his way, "you know where to find me."

Brewer smiled as he watched the captain make his way forward, stopping to inspect a tackle or inspecting one of his men on their patrols, and he was glad to have him aboard. In a moment of honesty with himself, he was glad that someone else thought the same of Starling as he did.

Then he frowned. *Blast Starling!* he said to himself. *Why did he have to bring up the Captain?* Brewer had deliberately followed his own advice and not dwelt on the topic at all. Now, however, he suddenly could think of nothing else.

He looked out at the passing waves and shook his head. He hoped that Bush would not be held responsible for the disappearance of the consul and his wife. It would be terrible if Bush was forced to give up the *Lydia* due to an error in judgement. His brows furled as his considered. Any captain would have done what Bush did and gone after that ship. Who knows what information they may have obtained had they been able to catch and board her? Why, Murad Reis himself may have been on board!

Brewer frowned and looked down the deck. Like many of his fellow officers, he was distrustful of the judgments of admirals, most of whom were considered to only care for their own relatives or protégés. It was highly unlikely that a decent captain without connections could get a fair hearing from such men, let alone a correct and righteous answer to the charges.

He walked aft to the fantail and looked out over their wake. It's not fair, he thought, and immediately he chided himself for his foolishness. He learned when his father told him never to return that life was not fair; why should he expect it to be for Bush?

He walked forward to do his duty.

HMS *Lydia* slid into the harbor at Tripoli just after dawn. A pilot was sent who guided the frigate to a spot near the center of the harbor. Brewer stepped up on deck and immediately felt like a sheep tied down in the midst of a pack of wolves. He looked over at the Captain, standing alone at the starboard rail of the quarterdeck, hands behind his back and his coat opened despite the morning mist. He also saw Mr. Gerard and Mr. Starling speaking with Mr. Trench and the Quartermaster beside the wheel. He strolled casually over to the outskirts of this group.

"Keep the ship ready to move, Mr. Trench," Gerard was saying. "The anchor may be an issue, but we'll deal with that when the time comes. Hopefully, we won't have to fight our way out of this harbor." Brewer swallowed hard at that. Gerard went on: "The Captain wants marine guards walking the rails day and night. No boat approaches without being challenged."

Starling and Trench acknowledged the order. Brewer looked forward, his attention drawn by Captain James briefing the first squad to begin their patrol. Obviously,

Brewer thought, the Captain had reached some decisions while he was sleeping. Behind him, the meeting broke up, and he found himself alone with Lieutenant Gerard.

"Good morning, sir," Brewer said as he touched his hat.

"Good morning, Mr. Brewer," Gerard said. He stood there with his hands behind his back and looked at the big citadel at the harbor entrance. Brewer followed his gaze and studied the stone fortress. Between gun ports and battlements, he estimated close to two hundred guns could be brought to bear on the harbor and its entrance. If they had the capability to heat shot, then it would be a formidable obstacle indeed. Behind him, Gerard cleared his throat, and Brewer turned back to him.

"Mr. Brewer," the Premier said, "I was going to brief you when you awoke, but I believe you know the basic plans." Brewer flinched (only on the inside, he hoped) at the implied chastisement of his eavesdropping. He expected a dressing down, but Gerard continued. "If all goes well, the Captain's plan is to visit the Bey and return to the ship. We would then leave the harbor and take up our patrol position."

"Do you expect all to go well, sir?" Brewer asked.

Gerard smiled. "We shall see, Mr. Brewer. Call away the Captain's gig. Make sure the men are smartly turned out."

"Aye, sir." Brewer saluted and went forward to find the bosun. Brewer issued his orders regard the gig and its crew and returned to the quarterdeck. No sooner had he reported to Lieutenant Gerard than Captain Bush emerged from the companionway stair. He was dressed in his best uniform, complete with the hundred guinea sword presented to him for his actions in the Baltic in 1810 when he commanded HMS *Nonsuch* under Hornblower. Brewer always thought the sword was really for bringing Hornblower home alive before the fever could kill him.

Bush walked up to Gerard and himself, and the junior

officers saluted.

"The gig is ready, sir," Gerard said.

"Thank you," Bush said. "Mr. Gerard, if I am not back aboard by midnight, you are ordered to take HMS *Lydia* and leave Tripoli at once. Your immediate destination is Malta. If the admiral is not there, take the ship to Gibraltar for orders. Under no circumstances is anyone to leave the ship and go ashore." Bush looked his premier in the eyes. "Nobody, Mr. Gerard. Do you understand? I say that because it is entirely possible that you will receive a messenger with a note saying I am the Bey's prisoner. *Nobody* leaves the ship."

"Aye, sir," Gerard said.

Bush nodded and walked to the entry port. As the bosun piped him off the ship, Brewer wondered if he would return.

The same thought occurred to Captain Bush as he sat in the stern sheets of the gig, although he made sure it didn't show on his face. He sat silently as the coxswain kept the hands to a smart rhythm over the smooth seas. Bush had never been prouder of a crew as he was of these men when they pulled up to the wharf.

"Well done, coxswain," he said, just loud enough for his men to hear. "Return to the ship. I shall signal when I am ready for you. Ask Mr. Gerard to have a lookout keep an eye on this wharf."

"Aye, sir."

Bush made his way to the end of the wharf, where he was met by man elegantly dressed in silks, his turban fastened in front by a large ruby. He bowed to Bush.

"Pardon me, sir," he said in studied English. "Are you the captain of the British warship that has just anchored in our harbor?"

"I am," Bush said with a bow. "Captain William Bush, of His Majesty's frigate *Lydia*. I have come ashore to pay my respects to the Bey."

"Excellent," the envoy said with a smile. "I have been sent to meet you and conduct you to His Excellency. I am Elijah Ali, Chamberlain to His Excellency, Hassan Bey." He stepped aside to allow his footman to open the door to the carriage and gestured to Bush with a bow.

"If you please, Captain?"

Bush nodded his thanks and took his seat in the carriage. He had to admit that, despite the terrible condition of the roads, this was the best carriage he had ever ridden in. He inquired where the Bey got it.

"It was part of a ransom demand for some Christian slaves some years ago," Ali said very matter-of-factly. "His Excellency takes great pains to see that it is kept in good repair. An excellent ride, is it not?"

Bush muttered an agreement as he turned away and studied the scenery as they passed by. He thought the town dirty, the houses run down. Smallbridge looked like a paradise by comparison! Soon they left the town behind and proceeded inland, finally pulling into the drive of a beautiful palace, cornered by four tall minarets.

"What a beautiful house," Bush said.

"Thank you," Ali said as the carriage stopped at the door. "It was built for the Bey just two years ago."

Two years ago, Bush thought. *Right after Exmouth shelled them into submission. Smart of the Bey, moving himself inland and out of the range of British naval gunfire.*

Bush followed his host into the house and past the bowing servants. They walked upstairs and into what Bush took to be a very large library. In the far corner of the room sat two overstuffed leather chairs, similar to those he sat on during his briefing with Lord Exmouth. In front of the chairs stood a mountain of a man, fully six feet, six inches in height, with shoulders that would allow him to easily press a yardarm over his head. He stood perfectly erect with his chin held high, but not so high that he would appear to look down his nose at his guest. His beard was trimmed close, after the European fashion. His whole physical presence proclaimed power, but it was his eyes that interested Bush the most. He had picked up a trick or two from Hornblower over the years, and one of them was to watch the eyes. The Bey's eyes twinkled with enjoyment. Bush smiled to himself. These were not the eyes of a wise ruler or warrior. This man was purely and simply a bully.

"Excellency," Ali said. "May I present to you Captain William Bush, Captain of His Majesty's frigate *Lydia*. Captain, His Excellency, Hassan Bey."

Bush bowed. "I am honored, Excellency."

"Of course you are, Captain," the Bey said. Bush was surprised to hear him speak English, and the Bey picked up on it right away. "You are surprised that I can speak your language? My father made sure I was tutored by Englishmen when I was young. That way I could better deal with your countrymen when they appear in my waters. So. What can I do for you, Captain Bush?"

"This is purely a social call, Excellency," Bush said. "My ship and I are new to the Mediterranean, and I have come to pay my respects."

"Thank you," the Bey replied. "Would you care for a drink?" Bush nodded, and the Bey gestured to the Chamberlain, who left the room.

"Would you care to sit, Captain?" The Bey indicated the leather chairs, and the men sat.

"Wonderful, aren't they?" the Bey said as he rubbed the armrest admiringly. "I saw one on a visit to London when I was young, and when I became Bey, I ordered two for my library."

He paused as the Chamberlain returned with two glasses

filled with dark liquid. He handed one to each man before turning to his Bey for further instructions.

"Thank you, Ali," the Bey said. "That will be all. Leave us."

The Chamberlain bowed and retreated from the library, softly closing the door behind him.

The Bey raised his glass to Bush. "Your very good health, sir."

Bush returned the gesture, and both men sipped their drink. Bush was surprised again to find it to be a very good Port.

"I keep surprising you, Captain! A good game, is it not? Yes, it is true that our religion... discourages the use of alcohol, but I have found it an important tool when dealing with British emissaries."

Bush drained the small glass in a single draught. "Excellent." He set the glass on the table beside the chair. "May I ask you a question, Excellency?"

"Of course." The Bey set his glass down as well. He had a smile on his face.

Bush sat back in his chair, elbows on the armrests and his fingers steepled. "Where is Murad Reis?"

The name caught the Bey by surprise, but he recovered quickly. "I do not know. Why do you ask?"

"He took something that was in my care."

The Bey smiled again. "Really? And what would that be?"

"The new British consul for Naples and his wife, along with the brig they were sailing in."

The Bey's brows arched and his lips pursed in a mocking tsk-tsk gesture. "How careless of you to have lost them, Captain. Why come to me?"

Bush's eyes gleamed hard. "Because he is grand admiral of your fleet. And there is also the little matter of the ransom note."

"Oh? What ransom note?"

"The one that demanded £5,000 be paid to you by the end of next month for his safe return."

"Really?" the Bey did his best to look resigned. "I am not surprised. Between us, Captain, Reis tends to go rogue. He kidnaps dignitaries and leaves ransom notes like this one, instructing the ransom to be paid to me, but I never see it. Somehow, he intercepts the couriers and confiscates the ransom. But I suppose it is fitting, since I do not have the consul, his wife, or the brig in any case."

Bush leaned forward in his chair. "Excellency, I have information that he was here, in Tripoli, less than two months ago."

The Bey sat back and relaxed. "Yes, that is so."

"Where did he go?"

"He did not tell me his plans."

"What did he say to you?"

The Bey smiled. "That, sir, is none of your affair."

Bush smiled and rose, rudely signaling an end to the meeting. The Bey remained seated.

"Please pass a message along to the Grand Admiral when you see him next. Tell him I will meet up with him sooner or later to settle accounts with him."

The Bey smiled. "I will certainly pass along your good wishes to the Admiral."

"Then I will bid you good day and thank you for the most excellent glass of port."

"You are most welcome. Ali!" The Chamberlain opened the door. "Please conduct Captain Bush safely to his ship."

Bush bowed to the Bey and left the room without looking back.

Bush stepped up onto the *Lydia's* deck and saluted the quarterdeck and Lieutenant Gerard.

"That was quick, sir," Gerard said.

"Not pleasant company, I'm afraid, Mr. Gerard," Bush said. "Any luck in the harbor?"

"None, sir. Neither the *Heracles* or *Meshuda* are here."

"Well, no sense in hanging around where we're not wanted. Get the ship under way, if you please."

"Aye, sir!" Gerard picked up a speaking trumpet and began bellowing orders, calling hands to make sail and others to man the capstan. Bush stood on the quarterdeck, at the lea rail, his eyes on the citadel that guarded the harbor entrance.

HMS *Lydia* was soon sliding toward the open sea under reefed tops'ls and jib. Gerard stood beside his captain and followed his gaze.

"I say, Captain," he said softly, "that citadel is impressive. I almost expect El Supremo to present himself on the battlement."

Bush looked at him in stark amazement and burst into laughter.

Gerard looked to his captain. "Seriously, Captain, do you think they have the capability to heat shot?"

Bush pointed, and Gerard turned to see smoke rising from the fortress.

Gerard looked grim. "Did Lord Exmouth say anything about heated shot?"

"No," Bush replied. "It looks like they have been making improvements."

HMS *Lydia* sailed past the citadel and into the blue Mediterranean waters. She spent the next three days cruising off the port, stopping merchant ships and searching their cargo. Five ships were searched, but all five were let go after their searches came up empty.

That night, Captain Bush hosted many of his officers for dinner. After the plates had been cleared by the stewards and their glasses had been refilled, the Captain raised his glass and all heads turned his way.

"Mr. Vice," he said, "The King!"

Everyone turned to Mr. Hanson, the senior midshipman, who sat at the end of the table next to Captain James. As the junior officer present, the honor and privilege of toasting the King's health fell to him. He swallowed hard to calm the nerves caused by the scrutiny, then he picked up his glass and stood.

"Gentlemen!" he said, "the King!"

"The King!" the assembly echoed, and everyone drank.

Bush raised his voice to get their attention. "Well, gentlemen! I imagine you are as tired as I am of this useless sailing back and forth, stopping ships for no reason." A general murmur of agreement arose. "I propose to change that. Beginning at dawn tomorrow, we will start hunting our adversaries, rather than waiting for them to come to us. During my briefing with Lord Exmouth, one of the things he told me was that the African shore in this part of the world was positively peppered with coves and small bays where these pirates like to hide out. We are going to investigate every one we come across and capture or sink every one of those buggers we find."

A cheer arose around the table, and Bush sat back, satisfied. He let them carry on for a time; they felt the stigma of the loss of the *Heracles* as much as he did, and they deserved to look forward to the prize money. He knew that within an hour or so of the breakup of this meeting, word will filter down to the crew, and their morale should improve as well. Finally, he stood, and the clamor died.

"Gentlemen," he said in a voice that sounded tired but hopeful, "I thank you all for your fellowship tonight. I will tell you, it has cheered me considerably. And now, I will bid you a good night, and good hunting tomorrow."

As one man the company arose, and they began to make their way to the door. As they bid their Captain a good night, Bush noticed a light in their eyes that he had not seen for many a day. As his servant readied his bed, the Captain found he was looking forward to the morning.

Lieutenant Brewer had the morning watch, so he was on deck when the dawn broke. Like the rest of the crew, he was anxious to start the hunt. He listened all night as the men made plans for all the prize money they expected to win in the next few days. Brewer smiled; the same thoughts had been running through his own mind. He turned in time to see Lieutenant Gerard come on deck with Mr. Trench.

"Good morning, sir," he said, touching his hat to Gerard and nodding to Trench.

"Good morning, Mr. Brewer," Gerard said. "Is the crew ready?"

Brewer grinned. "They've been talking about nothing else, sir. Can't wait to get going, let me tell you."

Gerard was about to reply when Captain Bush appeared on deck. Both officers came to attention and saluted. The Captain acknowledged and looked around the deck.

"I don't think I've seen the crew so happy," he said.

"Well, sir," Gerard said, "it seems word of your announcement has made its way around the ship."

Now Bush grinned. "Has it indeed, Mr. Gerard? Well then, let's not keep them waiting, shall we? Mr. Trench!" he said loudly. "What is *Lydia's* current position?"

"Approximately forty miles west of Tripoli, Captain. Course due east."

"Very well," Bush said. "Let's get to it. Mr. Trench, change course to due south. Take us close enough to shore that the lookouts can see clearly with a telescope."

"Aye, sir!"

A cheer went up from the hands on the deck. Bush turned to them, grinning broadly. He had been right in his thinking last night; *they* needed this as much as he did.

HMS *Lydia* approached to within range of the coastline before resuming their easterly heading. Lookouts in the tops peered eagerly to the south, and as many idlers or those off watch who could lay their hands on a glass or had very good eyes stationed themselves in the shrouds all along the larboard side, hoping to be the first to bring prize money to them all. Brewer posted two hands to the starboard shrouds as lookouts so nobody could sneak up on the ship during the preoccupation with the coastal search. When he saw how disappointed they were, he mollified them by rotating them out every thirty minutes. Anyone caught looking south had to pull another shift. The system worked to perfection.

It was three hours later, while investigating the fourth cove of the morning that they struck gold. Brewer, despite being relieved at the end of his watch, was still on deck—in the mizzen shrouds, in fact—scanning the shoreline when a petty officer in the foretop raised the alarm. Brewer recognized the brogue as belonging to an Irishman named O'Donnell.

"Deck, there!" he cried. "I see ships at the end of the bay!"

"Off tacks and sheets!" Bush bellowed. "Prepare the mains'l haul!"

Bush walked forward and settled at the larboard rail amidships. "Pass the word for Ali! Lookout! Let's hear you!"

The lookout studied the scene for a moment before lowering his glass and reporting. "Looks like ten small ships holed up in there, sir!"

Ali arrived at Bush's side. The Captain handed him a glass, and Ali studied the scene.

"They are feluccas, Captain," he said as he handed back the glass. "Small craft, swift, they can be powered by either sails or oars. Pirates favor them for quick raids on vessels passing too close to the shore. Of course, they are also used by merchants for the coastal trade."

Bush grunted and closed his telescope. "Ali, come with me," he said as he headed aft to the quarterdeck and Lieutenant Gerard.

"Mr. Gerard, I want you to take the launch and investigate those ships. Take some marines with you, just in case."

"Aye, sir."

"Board the closest one and examine the cargo. Take Ali with you; he can translate if need be. Report to me, and I will decide what to do with them." Bush looked down the bay again. "They look too small to take as prizes. We'd waste too many hands for too little prize money."

Gerard sighed and shook his head. "I'm afraid I agree with you, sir." He saluted and went off to give the orders for the launch and the marines.

"Mr. Brewer," Bush said as he watched his premier go, "run out the larboard battery, so they know we mean business."

"Aye, sir." A quick dash to the gun deck and a word to Mr. Starling, then he returned to the quarterdeck.

Brewer stood on the quarterdeck and watched as the launch pulled down toward the feluccas. He wondered if they would be worth it in the end.

The same thought crossed Lieutenant Gerard's mind, sitting in the stern sheets of the launch as they approached the assembled boats. He half-expected a show of resistance when they reached the first boat, but the marines in the front of the launch showed themselves ready to fight, and they made it aboard without incident.

Gerard stepped onto the deck with Ali and was met by the

sergeant of marines.

"Deck's secure, sir. I've sent two sailors and two marines below deck to search the cargo."

"Thank you, Sergeant," Gerard said. He turned to Ali. "Call for the captain."

Ali did, and a thin, elderly man with a grey beard and no turban stepped forward and said something. Ali turned to Gerard.

"He wants to know what you want."

Gerard grew perturbed. "Is he the captain, and what is his name?"

Ali translated and listened to the reply. "He is the captain. His name is Bekah."

"Cargo and destination?"

Ali inquired, then said, "Wheat for Tripoli."

"And the other ships?"

"The same."

Gerard looked at him hard. "He serves the Bey?"

Ali asked. "No, he says he is from Tunis."

A petty officer returned to the deck and reported to Gerard. "Cargo is wheat, sir. We couldn't find anything else below."

Gerard grunted, and said to Ali, "Tell him Tripoli is under blockade by the Royal Navy. I will return to my ship to ask my captain what shall be done with their ships."

Ali informed Bekah, and the Arab looked at Gerard with undisguised hatred in his eyes. Gerard and Ali descended back to the launch, followed by the sailors and marines. The marines kept alert for trouble as they made their way back to *Lydia*.

Gerard ordered the launch's crew to remain where they were for the time being while he reported to the Captain. He found Bush more or less where he had left him on the quarterdeck.

"Tunisians, sir, with wheat bound for Tripoli," Gerard said.

Bush thought for a moment. "Any armaments?"

"None, sir."

Bush thought again, weighing the benefit of taking the small ships to Malta or burning them. Finally, he shook his head. "If we take them all, we may not have enough men left to man our own ship. Burn them, and we'll look for bigger game. Have Mr. Starling take the cutter. Order their crews ashore, then burn the ships and cargos. Mr. Brewer! Take command of the larboard battery from Mr. Starling, and have him report to me."

"Aye, sir," Brewer said. He went below, disappointed not to be going in the cutter himself.

Starling came on deck and reported to Bush. "You sent for me, sir?"

"Yes, Mr. Starling," Bush said. "We are going to burn those ships in the bay. You will take the cutter and accompany Mr. Gerard. We will give the crews a chance to abandon their ships, and then you and Mr. Gerard will burn them. See to the loading of combustibles in the launch and cutter, if you please."

"Aye aye, sir," Starling touched his hat and was gone.

In less than thirty minutes, Gerard and Starling were on their way back to the feluccas. Bush stood on the *Lydia's* quarterdeck, watching their every move through his telescope.

"Mr. Brewer!" he called. "Stand ready to fire!"

"Aye, sir!" Brewer moved to aft two guns and spoke to their captains. "Make sure you're trained on the two ships to larboard, in case the Captain gives us the order to open fire. Do not fire on the ship Mr. Gerard boards unless I specifically tell you to."

"Aye aye, Mr. Brewer," the captains said.

Bush watched as Gerard climbed aboard the same ship he boarded before, followed by Ali. He saw a commotion stir on deck, which told him that Ali had relayed his plans for their ships and cargo. He saw the word quickly pass from ship to ship, and he began to worry about his men if there were an uprising among the crews of all ten ships. His fear passed when he saw the crews of most of the ships climbing over the sides of their vessels and swimming for shore. His good mood was spoiled moments later by the voices of two seamen watching the ships from the mizzen shrouds.

"Captain!" they cried almost simultaneously. "We got a couple runners!"

Bush looked up at them and then followed the line they pointed. His glass came to his eye to show two feluccas on the larboard side raising sail and extending oars. They were beginning to move with the first few strokes of the oars.

"No, you don't, my friend," Bush muttered to himself. He went to the quarterdeck rail.

"Mr. Brewer!" he cried. "Two runners to larboard! Put a warning shot either through their sails or into their oars. Try not to sink them, if you please!"

Brewer smiled and saluted. "If you insist, sir!" He turned to his two gun captains. "We guessed right, lads! You heard the Captain. Peterson!" he said to the captain of the gun on the left, "Take the lead ship. Can you hit his oars?"

Peterson looked through the gun port for a moment before pulling his head back and shaking it in the negative.

"Not without putting a hole in his side, sir."

Brewer considered for a moment before turning to the captain of the gun on the right.

"What about you, Fitz?"

Shannon Fitzmorris-O'Sullivan was a great, muscular mountain of an Irishman with fiery red hair and a full beard of it to boot. It was said that some years ago, a man in a pub had kidded him about his first name being better suited for a lass of questionable virtue. O'Sullivan responded by ejecting the unfortunate patron from the establishment—through a plate glass window—and into the street beyond. For some possibly unrelated reason, he was known fore and aft simply as Fitz, and Brewer imagined it was considerably safer for all that it remain that way.

The Irishman pulled his big head back inside the port and patted his gun tenderly. "If you let me shift her a point or two, Mr. Brewer, I think I can take out the last half-dozen or so of his oars."

"Excellent!" Brewer said. "Do it. Peterson, put a nice hole in his sails. And if you happen to take out his mast in the process, I shall be happy to apologize to the Captain for your enthusiasm and skill."

Both gun crews cheered and got to work. Peterson went first, aiming carefully, and when Brewer gave the order to fire, he put a noticeable tear in the felucca's sail. Brewer laughed at his disappointment. It was Fitz's turn now. He muscled his gun's bearing one point, then another after rechecking, and when he was order to fire, several of the felucca's rear oars disappeared from sight. He wasn't sure, but Brewer thought he saw a hand or two flip through the air when his oar was destroyed by Fitz's ball.

They were rewarded by both runners lowering their sails and pulling in their oars. The entire battery cheered!

"Well done, Mr. Brewer!" Bush shouted from the quarterdeck. "Mr. Hanson! Take a boat and secure both ships. Captain James will help you with manning. Do not burn them, not for now, at least."

"Aye aye, Captain."

Brewer again felt a sting of regret that he was not given the assignment, but he knew from experience that the

Captain was loathe to leave only one officer aboard ship. He looked through the gun port and saw smoke begin to rise from the group of eight remaining feluccas and nodded in satisfaction.

"Beggin' yer pardon, Mr. Brewer," Fitz said, "but I wouldn't be so quick to be happy. We may have a problem."

"What's that, Fitz?"

"Well, sir, if I saw it right, Mr. Starling made a bad mistake. He should have gone to the rearmost ship and set fire to it first, then set fire to the remaining ships as he backed out of the pack. But he didn't sir; he set fire to each as he passed 'em. Now he had to escape past all those burning hulks!"

"Good Lord!" Brewer bolted for the stairs and made his way quickly to the quarterdeck and the Captain. He came to a halt and touched his hat.

"I beg your pardon, sir, but there may be a problem with Mr. Starling."

"I am already aware of it, Mr. Brewer," the Captain said irritably. "Unfortunately, all we can do at the moment is wait and pray they emerge from the smoke. I have just had to recall Mr. Gerard to stop him from going in to attempt a rescue."

Brewer turned to see the launch with Gerard aboard making her way slowly back to HMS *Lydia*. Behind them, the feluccas were beginning to burn beautifully. All hands lined the larboard rail, searching desperately for any sign of the cutter and Lieutenant Starling.

"There, sir!" cried a hand halfway up the mainmast shrouds. "On the starboard side of the fire!"

Bush and Brewer turned their telescopes just in time to see the cutter emerge from the smoke between the starboard-most feluccas and pull for all they were worth to get away from the fire and smoke. The entire rail erupted in cheers. Bush closed his telescope and sighed in relief.

"I'm going below, Mr. Brewer," he said. "Please ask Mr. Gerard and Mr. Starling to join me in my cabin when they come aboard. Also, I would like you to detail prize crews for the two remaining feluccas. Bring them to my cabin when you have them."

"Aye aye, sir," Brewer said as he touched his hat. Brewer got to work on his prize crews, pausing only to direct his two fellow officers to the Captain's cabin as instructed. He followed them fifteen minutes later with the list of two prize crews, each headed by a good petty officer with six hands to work the ship.

As he approached the Captain's cabin, he noticed that the marine guard was standing much farther away from the door than usual. As he neared the man, the guard indicated that Brewer should stop here, and Brewer soon discovered the reason. Even at that distance and through the closed door, he heard the faint sounds of Captain Bush shouting at his third lieutenant over nearly losing his boat and crew.

"He should be done in a minute, sir," the guard said.

Brewer nodded. "I believe I'll wait here with you, if you don't mind."

It wasn't a long wait. Within moments Bush was silent and the door flew open. Lieutenant Starling rushed past Brewer and the guard so fast that Brewer nearly missed the tears in his eyes.

"You may go in now, sir," the guard said simply.

Brewer made his way to the door and cautiously peered inside. Captain Bush was sitting behind his desk with his head in his hand, looking for all the world as though he had just finished trying to herd cats. Beside the door, Mr. Gerard was standing as silently as possible.

Bush looked up when he heard Brewer approach. "Yes, Mr. Brewer? What is it?"

"I have the lists of the two prize crews you asked for, Captain."

"What? Oh, yes; give them to me."

Brewer handed the lists to him, and Bush read them. Brewer noticed that his manner seemed to grow calmer as he did so.

"Johnson and Sims to command?" he mused to himself as he read. "Six hands each? Sounds right for that size. These look good to me. Well done, Mr. Brewer. Mr. Gerard, will you see that these prize crews are posted to the two remaining feluccas? I will have orders for them shortly. They are to sail to Malta and await our arrival there."

"Aye, sir," Gerard said, and he and Brewer made their exit. Brewer looked at his friend, but Gerard only shook his head. "Don't ask."

The prize crews were detailed, and the Captain came on deck to give them instructions and hand them their written orders. Brewer was among those who cheered as they left the ship.

Lydia remained in the area for another five days, but failed to find anything else hiding along the coast. The entire crew felt satisfied when the Captain gave the order to set their course for Malta.

CHAPTER SEVEN

HMS *Lydia* sailed into the harbor at Malta, preventing the setting of the sun by less than an hour. Captain Bush stood on the quarterdeck, surveying the harbor as he heard the anchor splash into the waters. He immediately noted the imposing bulk of HMS *Victory* and ordered Mr. Starling to take his reports to the admiral. He wondered idly how long it would be before the admiral called him to account for the incident with the consul. Bush shrugged and continued his survey of the assembled ships, noting two French frigates, one American sloop-of-war, a Spanish frigate, and two Venetian tartanes.

Lieutenant Gerard appeared by his side. "Quite a collection, wouldn't you say, sir?"

Bush shrugged and handed Gerard his glass as he pointed to the French frigates. "Do those frigates seem new to you?"

Gerard studied them briefly before lowering his telescope. "I suppose they do look rather fresh, if that's what you mean, sir. I hardly think they're carrying any advances; if they were, would the French send them here?"

Bush studied the frigates through the fading light. "You may be right." He handed Gerard his glass. "I'm going below. Call me if I am needed."

"Aye, sir," Gerard said. Touching his hat with one hand

and holding the telescope in the other, he felt a little ridiculous without knowing why. He wondered if Bush was beginning to worry about his upcoming testimony before Admiral Fremantle. He shook his head ruefully and wished there was something he could do to help.

As fate would have it, Bush would not have long to wait. Within an hour, there was a knock at the Captain's door. Bush looked up to see the sentry admit Lieutenant Gerard.

"Begging your pardon, sir," the Premier said. "Signal from flag. You are wanted aboard *Victory*."

"Very well, Mr. Gerard," the Captain said with more calm than Gerard gave him credit for. "Call away the gig. I shall be on deck within ten minutes."

Gerard left, and Goodnight entered the cabin and helped Bush into his best coat. The Captain picked up his hat from his desk and went up on deck. Gerard met him at the entry port and saluted.

"She's all yours, Mr. Gerard," Bush said without thinking.

"I hope not, sir!" Gerard replied. Bush looked at him but saw only concern and realized what he had said. He smiled and patted his First Lieutenant on the arm.

"Carry on, Mr. Gerard."

Bush was met at *Victory's* entry port by Captain Leeds, the admiral's Flag Captain.

"Good to see you again, Captain," Leeds said.

Bush saluted, and the two shook hands.

"The admiral is waiting, Captain," Leeds said. "If you'll follow me, please?"

Walking through the great ship reminded Bush of Trafalgar, and in his mind he heard the roaring of the cannon and the screams of the wounded who were decimated by the deadly combination of enemy fire and the hail of splinters that followed. He also thought of Nelson, cut down at the height of the battle but surviving just long enough to hear of the victory. At that moment, it angered Bush that someone like Fremantle sat in Nelson's chair.

They arrived at the Great Cabin, and the marine sentry let them in. It was much the same as on his previous visit. Bush stood beside Leeds and waited for the admiral to finish his reading.

Fremantle finally set the papers in his hand on the desk and looked up at Bush with a scowl. "Captain Bush, I have just finished rereading your report on the loss of the *Heracles*. I would not have expected a captain of your experience and background to fall for such an obvious trick. Your third lieutenant could have done better!"

"I'm sorry, sir," Bush said. "It won't happen again."

"I should bloody well hope so!" the Admiral exploded and pounded his desk with his fist. "Bad enough this renegade Scotsman plunders our shipping at will without our frigate captains as though they were puppets and he was pulling their strings!" He stared at Bush with rage spewing from his eyes before suddenly blinking and sitting back in his chair, as though the wind had been dumped from his sails.

"Captain," he said in a low, menacing voice, "if something like this happens again, I will send you back to London in irons for court martial. Do you understand me?"

"Yes, sir."

Fremantle glared at Bush for a minute or so longer before turning to look out the stern windows and shaking his head in disgust. When he turned back, he appeared to have put the episode behind him. He signaled to a far corner of the room.

"Come here, Lieutenant," he called, and an officer Bush hadn't known was there rose from his seat in the corner and came to stand beside the admiral's desk. He was a young man, probably no older than Mr. Brewer, his height and weight similar to those of Bush himself. His hair was the color of sand and neatly combed, his eyes were grey and carried himself with a self-confidence bordering on fearlessness.

"Captain Bush," Fremantle said, "allow me to introduce Lieutenant Calloway. He is to be the subject of your next assignment."

"Sir?"

Fremantle stood. "Just a moment, Captain. Can I have the room, please?" he called to the room at large. The others in the room, led by the Flag Lieutenant, made their way out, leaving only the Admiral, Bush, Leeds, and Calloway remaining.

"Gentlemen, please, be seated," the Admiral said. "Let me explain myself, Captain Bush. At this moment, there is a ketch, HMS *Intrepid*, is being converted into a fireship. She is being packed with five tons of black powder in one hundred barrels and one hundred fifty fused shells to inflict maximum damage in the surrounding ships. Lieutenant Calloway and a crew of ten will sail her into Tripoli harbor and set her afire. Your job is to escort her to her destination and then rescue the crew."

Bush stared at the Admiral and then at Calloway. His recent visit to Tripoli's harbor gave him doubts as to the plan's chances for success. The harbor was thickly patrolled by gunboats which, while not being much of a threat to a frigate like *Lydia*, could give a ketch like *Intrepid* a very bad time. Then there was the citadel overlooking the harbor entrance, which had obviously been repaired and strengthened since Exmouth pounded it into submission nearly three years ago now.

"You have doubts, Captain?" Fremantle asked.

"Well, sir," Bush said slowly, "I have just come from there. I saw many gunboats patrolling the harbor entrance day and night. They are big enough to give a ketch a very bad time. Entering the harbor in the dark of night will offer some protection against the citadel, but once the fireship is lit, fifty guns or more will open up on it."

The Admiral bristled at Bush's review. "Yes, yes, we have taken all that into consideration, *Captain*."

"We have taken additional precautions, Captain Bush," Calloway said. "First, *Intrepid* is to all outward appearances a Barbary ship out of Algiers. Second, we have among my crew two Arabs with us."

"Why two?" Bush asked.

Calloway smiled. "One Arabic speaker may not fool a guard boat if it challenges us, but with a second, they may be able to carry it off between them."

Bush considered for a moment before nodding his approval. Fremantle snorted.

"I am so glad you approve. As I said, your job is to make sure *Intrepid* gets there in one piece. On the night of the attack, *Lydia* may approach the harbor entrance after *Intrepid* has entered the harbor. *Intrepid* has a small boat hidden on deck for the crew to use to escape after the ship has been set afire. The ship is equipped with a delayed fuse that will give Calloway and his men approximately ten minutes to get away. The boat has a signal rocket that can be fired to help you locate them in the dark." Fremantle leaned forward with his elbow resting on his desk. "Captain Bush, there is one thing I wish to make unmistakably clear: Under no circumstances is HMS *Lydia* to enter Tripoli harbor. I repeat, *under no circumstances,* Captain. Do you understand?"

Bush's eyes narrowed at his hands being tied behind his back like this. He opened his mouth to speak, but instead closed it and stared at the Admiral. Fremantle's face openly showed that he did not like the order either, but it was evidentially a necessary part of his orders. He looked to Leeds and saw that the Captain was sitting quietly, hands folded in his lap and his face expressionless, and Bush realized that part of the Flag Captain's purpose in the room was to act as a witness to Bush's acknowledgement of his orders.

"Sir..." Bush began.

Fremantle cut him off. "Under *no circumstances,* Captain."

Bush looked to Calloway, but the Lieutenant's face was peaceful and confident, as though he knew all the risks and accepted them; somehow Bush doubted that was entirely true. He turned back to the Admiral and nodded.

"I understand, sir."

Fremantle sat back and relaxed, and the tension that had blanketed the room eased as well. "I am not unsympathetic, Captain," he said, "and your concern does you credit. You must believe me that the restriction is a vital one."

"Aye aye, sir," Bush said.

"The *Intrepid* is scheduled to be ready the day after tomorrow," Leeds said. "Your orders will be for you to sail as soon as possible afterward. Two days to Tripoli should place you off the harbor on the sixteenth. Moonless nights are the sixteenth and seventeenth this month. You should be back by the twentieth."

"Aye aye, sir," Bush said. Fremantle rose, and the others followed suit. The meeting was over, and on the way out Bush spoke to Calloway.

"Lieutenant," he said, "I want to invite you to dine with us on *Lydia.*"

"Of course. Thank you, Captain."

"Tomorrow, say? Turn of the first dog watch?"

"I look forward to it, sir."

Bush nodded and said his goodbyes. His return trip to

HMS *Lydia* was not as calming as he had hoped.

The next day, the water hoys were rowed up next to HMS *Lydia* to fill the casks the cooper and his mates had brought up on deck. Lieutenant Brewer stood calmly beside the rail and watched the operation as he basked in the warm Mediterranean sunlight. He mind was still on the Captain's briefing of the night before and the seeming hopelessness of the mission. Still, Lieutenant Calloway accepted the mission, so he must think there was a reasonable chance he would survive.

Brewer was so lost in his thoughts that he didn't hear Mr. Gerard approach until he spoke.

"Good morning, William."

Brewer was startled and turned to his friend. "Sorry, Mr. Gerard, I didn't hear you approach. Good morning."

Gerard stood beside him, hands clasped behind his back as he rocked gently back and forth from his toes to his heels. "Thinking about what the Captain said last night?"

Brewer grunted. "Am I that obvious? How did you know?"

Gerard smiled. "Because I've been thinking about it, too."

Brewer stared at the hoys. "And what do you think?"

Gerard leaned on the rail. "I think I'm glad they didn't offer it to me."

"So, you think those men have no chance?"

"You saw the harbor, William. Do you think an unknown ketch will be able to get in there unchallenged in the middle of the night, let alone be allowed to approach ships at anchor?" Gerard shook his head. "Not likely."

Now Brewer turned to face the first lieutenant and lowered his voice. "Then why go?"

"Well," Gerard answered just as quietly, "I wasn't there, of course, but I imagine Lieutenant Calloway considered it his duty to go."

Brewer stared at his companion. His eyes, first wide at Gerard's pronouncement, narrowed as he considered what he had heard and all that it implied. He opened his mouth to speak, but closed it again and turned to stare at the water hoys again. He knew that Gerard was right. Everything that Hornblower, Bush, and even Bonaparte had taught him came back to him mind in overwhelming fashion, and he was ashamed at his own thoughts of avoiding the trip, were it offered to him.

"Don't worry, William," Gerard said privately as they watched the cooper at work. "Every officer has thoughts like that, of avoiding duty that seems distasteful or even suicidal." Brewer frowned at his friend's seeming ability to read his mind. Gerard, for his part, ignored his friend's reaction and simply went on. "Duty is something that is learned, William; it is not inbred, not matter what one may think from watching certain other officers." Brewer wondered what that meant but dared not ask. "You and I, William, we have been blessed with some very good teachers, so I wouldn't worry, were I you. When it comes time, you will know your duty when you see it, and you will do what's right."

The Premier left him there to consider his words and watch the cooper. Brewer did not watch him go, but he fervently prayed that Gerard was right.

HMS *Lydia* and HMS *Intrepid* left Malta harbor under cover of darkness. The reasons for this were twofold: first, that the Bey's agents might not notice them leave, and second, *Intrepid* would only be able to manage 3-5 knots on the journey; Bush and Calloway were trying to time their departure so that they would not have to waste time heaved to in the open ocean over the horizon from their destination.

The trip was the longest two days Brewer had ever known. The slow speed combined with gloomy prospects for the survival of *Intrepid's* crew took the joy out of otherwise beautiful days and cool nights. He stood his watch with no smile on his face, and he avoided looking at the *Intrepid* following behind them whenever possible. He did his duty and kept the lookouts alert. He wished there was something else he could do, something that would change the odds.

In the afternoon sunshine of the second day, Captain Bush came on deck.

"I have the deck!" he announced to the quarterdeck at large. "Mr. Trench, heave to. Mr. Rivkins, signal to *Intrepid: 'Heave to. Captain come on board. We will send a boat.'*"

"Aye sir!" came from both men.

Brewer stood over by the wheel—he was officer of the watch at the moment—and kept a respectful distance from the Captain. *Lydia* came to an almost complete stop as the wind spilled from her sails; *Intrepid* did the same, gliding past her escort by thirty yards or so.

"Mr. Brewer," Bush said, "order the gig over the side to go retrieve Lieutenant Calloway."

"Aye, sir," Brewer said. "Mr. Hammersmith! Lower the gig to row to *Intrepid* and retrieve their captain!" He stood back and watched the bosun in action. The man was something akin to a conductor leading a symphony, and the proof was the sight of the gig seemingly within moments rowing across the seas toward *Intrepid*.

"Mr. Brewer," Bush said, "please escort Mr. Galloway to my cabin when he arrives."

"Aye, sir."

Brewer watched his captain descend the companionway stairs and knew by the set of his shoulders that Bush was worried. Brewer set his face as a flint, determined not to allow his thoughts to show as he turned and watched the gig make its way over the choppy seas toward the *Intrepid*. He wondered what Bush would say to Calloway once he arrived but quickly decided that he had better ways to spend his time. He picked up a speaking trumpet and told the lookouts to stay alert. Not that they needed to be told; Brewer knew he was doing it just to have something to do so he didn't have to do nothing and wait.

He looked out over the rail again and saw the gig on its way back, Lieutenant Calloway sitting straight in the stern sheets. Brewer stared at the man and could not for the life of him decide whether Calloway was the bravest man he'd ever met or simply resigned to being ordered on a one-way mission.

Brewer shook himself from his thoughts and went to the entry port to greet the Lieutenant. The two shook hands when Calloway stepped up on deck.

"The Captain asked that I bring you to his quarters the moment you arrived," Brewer said. "If you will follow me?"

"Of course. Lead the way, sir."

The two officers made their way to the great cabin. Brewer knocked once and opened the door. He was surprised to see Gerard standing beside the Captain's desk.

"Lieutenant Calloway, sir," he said, and he stood aside so the Lieutenant could enter. Calloway strode in purposefully, his hat under his arm, stopping before Bush's desk.

"Reporting as ordered, sir," he said.

"Welcome, Lieutenant," Bush said formally. "You may remain, Mr. Brewer. Please close the door."

Brewer did as he was bade, then he stood by the door and watched what would happen. Calloway took the seat in front of Bush's desk. The Captain remained seated, while Mr. Gerard had moved to stand behind his captain's shoulder. The tension in the room was thick enough to carve with a knife. Bush cleared his throat and spoke first.

"Mr. Calloway, is *Intrepid* ready?"

"Yes, sir," the Lieutenant said simply. "Everything is in order. We have closely watched the powder and charges, and all is in readiness to proceed."

"Very good, Lieutenant," Bush seemed to hesitate for a moment before continuing. "Goodnight! Bring that bottle of Port—the one I have been saving for a special occasion. Tonight we part company. The night signal to be used for parting is detailed in your orders. Oh, thank you, Goodnight." The servant set a tray on the Captain's desk that held the bottle of Port and four glasses. He bowed and withdrew silently. Bush continued, "Mr. Gerard, if you would do the honors?" He waited until they each had a glass in hand before raising his and saying, "Lieutenant, I wish you well on your mission. May it bring you glory and victory for England."

"Here! Here!" echoed Gerard and Brewer.

"Thank you, gentlemen," Calloway said. He drained his glass in a single draught. "I look forward to drinking with you again tomorrow."

Bush dismissed Calloway back to his ship, mostly to avoid any awkward silence. He truly wished the young man well, but he had a bad feeling that it wouldn't be enough.

Approximately ten hours later, eight bells tolled, signaling the end of the first watch. Before the echoes of their chimes faded in the wind, Captain Bush came on deck long enough to observe the *Intrepid's* night signal dip noticeably and then resume its normal station. He turned to Mr. Gerard, who was the officer of the deck, and nodded once. High above him, *Lydia's* night signal aped the motion of her consort's. Seconds later, *Intrepid's* night signal was extinguished, and she disappeared into the night.

BREWER AND THE BARBARY PIRATES

Lieutenant Calloway took the wheel himself for the final run into Tripoli. He'd been at his post ever since they parted from HMS *Lydia*. Not that he had anywhere else to go; the entire space below deck was crammed with powder or explosive shells. Now, he and his men were minutes from entering the harbor. The lookout reported seeing the lights of the harbor entrance nearly an hour ago, and now they were clearly visible from the deck.

The tension was so thick, they could cut it with a knife. Every man was at his station around the deck, ready to call for the two Arabic speakers to answer any challenges. All, that is, save two: Calloway had two men below decks. One sitting safely concealed in each hatch with orders to set the fuses the moment they came under attack. It was part of his fallback plan—if they failed to achieve surprise and subsequently came under attack, his two secret weapons would light off their fuses while he himself turned *Intrepid* toward the nearest big concentration of shipping and lashed the wheel to lock her on course. He hoped that, no matter what else happened, he and his men could still do some damage to the Barbary fleets.

They slid into the harbor without being challenged. Calloway made the decision to light the regular ship's lights in the hope they would blend in and not draw undo attention. He was pleased to see his plan worked to get them in the harbor, but as soon as he altered course toward a group of ships they were approached by two boats. A challenge came across the waves.

Calloway held his breath as he heard one of his Arabs reply to the challenge. The man answered back, and per the missions orders the second Arabic speaker was brought in to bolster the arguments of the first. Calloway could not understand a word of what was going back and forth, but he could tell that the tones were taking a jovial turn, and he began to breathe again. Just when he thought they may get out of this, a third gunboat came up from behind them, unseen, and challenged them. The seaman at the rail panicked and cried out in English. That was enough for the gunboat; they fired at the *Intrepid*. Two minutes later, the citadel opened fire as well.

It was the fire from the fort that first alerted Captain Bush and the crew of the *Lydia* that something was wrong. Mr. Starling was the first to hear the repercussion of the guns.

"Captain! Gunfire, sir!"

Bush, Gerard, and Brewer rushed to join Starling near the larboard bow and strained their ears to listen. Within moments, the next breath of wind brought the sounds of another round of fire.

"Mr. Gerard," Bush said, "call the hands to make sail. Mr. Brewer, tell the sailing master I want a course to Tripoli harbor."

Both officers saluted smartly and departed on their appointed errands.

Brewer interrupted Mr. Trench speaking with his quartermaster.

"Pardon the interruption, Mr. Trench," he said, "but the Captain wants a course for Tripoli harbor."

Trench nodded. "We're ready, Lieutenant. Been figuring that course since we heard tell of gunfire."

Brewer turned when he felt the ship's speed pick up. He saw Captain Bush returning to the quarterdeck.

"Ready, Captain," Trench reported.

"Get on with it, man!" Bush snarled. Trench touched his hat and turned to give the orders to put the ship on its new heading.

Brewer was amazed at their speed. The ship was on her

best point of sailing, and the last casting of the log gave a speed of eleven knots. Suddenly the horizon was set on fire, and the sound that reached them was that of a great explosion.

Bush stared in horror at the horizon. "Something's gone wrong," he said at last. He turned to Trench. "Give her every stitch she'll carry. Take us in. Load both batteries, but don't run out the guns yet."

Gerard stepped up. "Captain, may I speak to you?"

Bush looked irritated at the interruption, but his training held. He led Gerard to a private spot across the quarterdeck.

"Yes?" he said testily.

"Captain," Gerard said in a low voice, "you can't go in there."

Bush said nothing, but Gerard felt as though his captain's eyes were running him through with sabers. Nevertheless, he stood his ground silently. After several seconds, Bush blinked and looked out over the dark sea.

"I know," he said.

"And so did Calloway," Gerard added softly.

Bush's eyes snapped to his Premier, and for a moment Gerard thought he had gone too far. Then the eyes dropped for a moment before searching the sea again. Bush nodded and said, "Thank you, Gerard. Reduce sail and have Mr. Trench lay us off the harbor entrance. Do not enter the harbor."

"Aye, sir," Gerard said. He touched his hat and departed on his journey. In moments Bush felt the ship slow down, and he walked to bow to better see what was happening. The sky was still on fire, and occasionally there was an additional flash that gave him hope that additional magazines were exploding. The closer they got, the clearer the sound of continuing gunfire reached their ears.

When at last they reached the harbor entrance, what they

saw was horrifying. Several ships were on fire, but Bush could not make out the *Intrepid* from the rest. The pirates were doing what they could to contain the damage, either by attempting to tow those on fire away or else by firing into them to sink them before they could infect their neighbor. The citadel was also firing at the ships on fire. Gasps were heard across the deck when they saw several burning forms jump off the ships and into the harbor.

"Merciful God in Heaven!" Starling breathed.

"Deck there!"

Bush and Gerard looked up. The younger men could not take their eyes from the harbor.

"We're under fire, sir!" the lookout cried, pointing to the citadel.

Bush could now see the muzzle flashes pointing toward them and realized that the same flames that lit the harbor must have also betrayed the presence of the *Lydia* to gunners who were thirsting for revenge. Bush tried to ignore the fire while they desperately searched the harbor for any sign of Calloway and his men in their getaway boat, but by the third salvo shells were beginning to drop around the frigate, and Bush knew he had to look to his ship.

"Mr. Trench," he said loudly, "take us to ten miles off the harbor entrance."

The Sailing Master hesitated only for an instant before acknowledging his captain's order and turning the *Lydia* due north. To Brewer, standing beside the mizzen mast, it was clear that Mr. Trench did not agree with abandoning the crew of the *Intrepid*.

Brewer went to stand beside the Captain and First Lieutenant as they watched the carnage that was Tripoli Harbor recede to the horizon. The Captain watched through his glass for a time, then he closed it and handed it go Gerard.

"I am going below," he said to his Premier. "Call me when we reach the ten-mile limit."

Brewer turned to say something to Gerard, but he didn't when he saw the worried look on the First Lieutenant's face.

"Double the lookouts, Mr. Brewer," he said. "I have the deck."

"Aye, sir," Brewer touched his hat and moved off to post the lookouts. For the time being, he thought it best to follow Gerard's example and keep his thoughts to himself.

HMS *Lydia* took two hours to reach the ten-mile point; the sun was making its ascendency. Even at ten miles from the port, Brewer could still see a faint column of smoke rising from the previous night's action. Captain Bush came on deck as soon as he felt the ship swing to the east to begin her patrol for the missing comrades. Gerard and Brewer saluted.

Bush led them to the chart beside the wheel. "Mr. Trench, a moment if I may. Now, gentlemen, here is what I plan to do. I want *Lydia* to patrol on a line of about fifteen miles from this point. Keep our speed around seven to eight knots as much as possible, Mr. Gerard. Approximately every two hours, we should be turning around and retracing out steps. Call me at once if we sight anything heading into Tripoli. Lookouts need to keep their eyes open for the signal rocket. Mr. Gerard, please note my instructions in the standing orders. We shall remain here until I am satisfied that there is no reason to remain any longer."

"Aye, sir," the three officers said.

"Also," Bush said, "I will give £100 of my share of our prize money to the man who sights any of the *Intrepid's* crew." He leaned in close to Gerard. "I don't think you need to put that in the standing orders."

"No, sir," Gerard grinned.

"Very well, gentlemen," Bush said, "let's get to it."

HMS *Lydia* began her lonely vigil. Word of the Captain's

bounty got out quickly, and nearly every hand in the ship found a spot in the shrouds or along the rails, hoping to be the one who rescues Lieutenant Calloway and his crew and pockets the hundred quid. Hour rolled into hour with no sightings. The forenoon watch came and went, and the afternoon watch was coming to a close when Captain Bush appeared on deck. Gerard and Brewer touched their hats as their captain approached.

"Still on deck, gentlemen?" Bush asked. "Where is Mr. Starling?"

Gerard pointed to a spot halfway up the main shrouds where Mr. Starling was diligently searching the horizon with a glass.

"Ah," Bush said, "I see. Is there anything to report, Gerard?"

"No, sir," came the answer. "Nothing."

Bush sighed and nodded. He moved to the lee side of the quarterdeck and began to pace, his chin firmly planted on his breast and his hands behind his back. Brewer knew he was debating calling off the search, and he didn't envy his commander the responsibility for the decision.

About thirty minutes into the captain's pacing, *Lydia* reached the western tip of her search pattern.

"Prepare to go about, Mr. Trench," Gerard ordered routinely.

"Belay that," Bush said. He ceased his pacing and rejoined his officers. He looked at Gerard with a huge sadness in his eyes. "I don't believe we have reason to remain any longer. Make your course for Malta."

Gerard looked to the deck for a moment before looking in his captain's eye.

"Aye, sir," was all he said. Bush nodded and went below.

"Mr. Trench, make your course for Malta." The First Lieutenant's words sounded like a death sentence, but

Brewer knew that any sentence had already been carried out. The ship settled on her course under all plain sail. Gerard stood off by himself at the fantail for well over an hour before he stirred.

"Mr. Brewer," he called, "you have the deck. I shall be with the captain."

Brewer barely had time to acknowledge the order before Gerard disappeared below deck. He went quickly to the captain's cabin, hardly pausing to allow the marine guard to announce him.

He found Bush writing his report, and from the amount of paper on the desk with lines crossed out and writing in the margins, he guessed it was nowhere near his first draft.

"Yes?" Bush said testily.

"I was wondering if there was anything I could do for you, sir," Gerard said.

"Yes," Bush said. "Bring me Lieutenant Calloway and his men."

Gerard said nothing at this manifestation of his captain's frustration, choosing to purse his lips in silence and look at the deck. Bush set his pen down on the desk and rubbed his face with both hands.

"I'm sorry," he said. "That was cruel of me."

"I understand, sir."

"To answer your question, No, there is nothing you can do. I'm trying to write my report, but it doesn't seem to be coming together very well. Please, sit down."

"May I ask what you're going to say?"

"I believe the explosion we heard was probably the *Intrepid* exploding after being hit multiple times by shot from the citadel. Subsequent damage to shipping in the harbor was not nearly what we had hoped. I am listing the lieutenant and his crew as missing, presumed dead."

Gerard folded his hands in his lap and studied them

intently. "I see, sir."

Bush picked up his pen again. "Please see to it that I'm not disturbed until I finish this."

"Aye aye, sir." Gerard rose as his chief's pen resumed its scratching across the paper. He closed the door softly behind him and instructed the marine guard that the captain was not to be disturbed and that all visitors should be sent to him until further notice. The guard assured Gerard that he would do so.

The Premier went on deck. Lieutenant Brewer touched his hat at Gerard's approach.

"The Captain is not to be disturbed," he said plainly. "He is composing his report on the action at Tripoli. Call me if anything needs attention. You have the deck."

"Aye aye, sir. May I ask how he listed the *Intrepid's* crew?"

Gerard hesitated a moment before dropping his head and lowering his voice.

"Missing, presumed dead."

Brewer nodded, and Gerard went below. Brewer spent the next several days of the voyage to Malta dwelling on the meaning and reality of sacrifice.

Two months later, a note arrived at the British consul's office at Malta from the Bey of Tripoli. He wrote that seven bodies were found floating in the harbor or washed up on shore in the days following the raid. All were torn and burned beyond recognition, but some pieces of British uniforms were still recognizable. He ended by saying he was merciful enough to allow Christian slaves to bury the bodies and recite a Christian burial ritual over them.

CHAPTER EIGHT

HMS *Lydia* slid into the harbor at Malta worn down in every way. The loss of the *Intrepid* still weighed heavily on them. No sooner had they dropped anchor than a boat came out from shore to collect the captain's reports and pass on a note that the Port Admiral would see the captain in three days' time. The ship was granted three days of glorious rest at Malta while they were resupplied. Captain Bush granted shore leave for the entire crew, one watch at a time. Mr. Starling took the starboard watch ashore, and when they returned, Mr. Brewer took the larboard. Mr. Gerard said he had no need of time ashore and much preferred to remain aboard to supervise the resupply effort. Bush was very proud of the behavior of his crew. Out of both watches, a single tar failed to return to the ship. An investigation found him at the naval hospital ashore; he had fallen and broke his right leg while on his way back to the ship.

HMS *Victory* was not in the harbor when *Lydia* arrived, and as she had not arrived by the end of the three days, Bush paid his visit to the Port Admiral, Admiral Wallingsford. The Admiral received Bush graciously.

"Ah, yes, Captain Bush," Wallingsford said as he rose to shake hands. "Glad to finally make your acquaintance at last. Forgive me for postponing this meeting, but I make it a habit to read a captain's reports before I see him. I have read your report on Calloway and the *Intrepid*. Bad luck, that. In such circumstances, I have found it best just to move on." He picked up a packet from his desk and handed it to Bush. "Your orders, Captain. Admiral Fremantle left them for you when HMS *Victory* departed three days before you arrived. We're sending you back out on the hunt again. You are to show the flag at all three major Barbary ports before putting in at Gibraltar in four to five months' time. Orders say for you to start at Tripoli and work your way west. Sink, burn, or take as a prize every pirate ship or privateer you encounter."

Bush accepted the packet and rose to attention, knowing the meeting was at an end. The Admiral resumed his writing and did not look up again, so Bush quietly made his way from the office. The orderly in the hall returned his hat and showed him to the door. Outside, he paused to look back at the house and wondered how it is that some people make it all the way to flag rank.

He arrived back aboard the *Lydia* and went straight to his cabin. Goodnight was there and helped him with his coat and hat before bringing his captain a glass of wine and leaving him alone. Bush sat down at his desk and sipped his wine before opening his orders and perusing them lightly the first time through. They appeared to be exactly what Admiral Wallingsford said they were. He was being sent out to hunt enemy ships. They were to leave as soon as *Lydia* was provisioned. He called for the sentry to pass the word for Mr. Gerard, then he refilled his glass and reread his orders more closely. He took note of the prohibition of entering any Barbary port, including in the course of a pursuit of the enemy. He frowned at that, even though he understood the order and the reasons behind it.

A knock at the door heralded the arrival of Mr. Gerard.

"You sent for me, sir?" he asked.

"Yes," Bush said, handing the orders to his Premier. "Our orders. We're going hunting for the next 4-5 months before putting in at Gibraltar."

Gerard grinned broadly as he sat and read their orders. "Too bad we're not still at war with Napoleon. The navy isn't buying prizes like she used to."

Bush shrugged. "True, too true. That's why I've decided to sink a lot more then we will capture."

"Sir?"

"I'm not willing to risk the life of one man on this ship in a boarding action for nothing. Unless I am sure that the navy will purchase her, I intend to stand off and sink most of the pirates we encounter."

"I understand, sir."

"Good," Bush sat back in his chair. "How's the provisioning going?"

"We are ready for sea in all respects but one, sir: Water. I scheduled the water hoys to come out this afternoon and top off the open casks. We can on the evening tide, if you like."

Bush thought about that for the moment. There were advantages to leaving at night, but unlike their last mission, there was no need for secrecy or timing their arrival off Tripoli. Bush shook his head.

"That won't be necessary, Mr. Gerard. We'll sail on the morning tide."

Gerard grinned, glad for one more night in port. "Aye aye, sir!"

HMS *Lydia* left the port at Malta behind to sail into a beautiful Mediterranean Sea that she found to be strangely empty. Bush set a wide, zigzag course toward Tripoli in order to increase their search area, but it only yielded two sightings, both of which immediately disappeared below the horizon.

They finally arrived off Tripoli and began their hunt in earnest. Many from the off duty watch lined the shrouds, watching for contacts and hoping to lay claim to some prize money. Lieutenant Brewer had the first watch on that first night of the hunt. It was a cool evening. He smiled when he saw half the hands abandon the shrouds after darkness fell; a good number of them gathered forward and sang for a while. Brewer looked around the deck and was generally pleased with what he saw. His watch—and the entire crew—were ready for action.

Six bells had just wrung when the call came.

"Deck there!" cried the lookout in the mizzen tops. "I think I see a ship's light dead astern!"

Brewer grabbed a telescope and went to the fantail. He put the glass to his eye, but he could make out nothing.

"Lookout!" he called. "What do you see? Is the light still there?"

"Comes and goes, sir! Must be just on the horizon!"

Brewer lowered his glass and thought for a moment, then he turned to the wheel.

"Quartermaster! Bring us about! Call hands to make sale! Mr. Bennet! My respects to the Captain, tell him we have sighted a light on the horizon, and I am altering course to intercept as per his standing orders!"

"Aye aye, Mr. Brewer!" The midshipman saluted and disappeared.

HMS *Lydia* came around and picked up speed as the additional canvas caught the air and held it. Brewer was just about to go forward when he saw Captain Bush appear on deck.

"Report, Mr. Brewer," Bush said.

"We've come about, sir; our heading is now east on an intercept course."

Bush nodded as he accepted a glass and raised it to his

eye.

"Deck there!" the lookout cried. "The light's gone out!"

"What do you mean?" Brewer asked.

"I was looking right at it, and all of a sudden it was gone! Like someone blew out a candle, sir!"

Brewer looked to his captain, who was staring into the darkness ahead of them.

"Have they seen us, sir?"

Bush raised the glass to his eye for a few moments before lowering it in frustration.

"Beat to quarters, Mr. Brewer."

Brewer picked up a speaking trumpet. "Beat to quarters!"

Within moments the marine drummer boy was beating out the incessant *rat-a-tat-tat* on his drum that sent the crew scurrying to their individual battle stations. Brewer waited until both Mr. Trench and Lieutenant Gerard reported to the quarterdeck to report to the larboard battery.

"Mr. Brewer!" the Captain said as he went to leave, "don't load or run out until ordered."

"Aye, sir!" Brewer touched his hat and went below.

When he got there, his well-trained crews were ready to load and run out their guns, and they looked to him expectantly.

"Belay, boys!" he called. "Captain's orders! Don't load or run out 'til we get the word!"

A murmur arose at the strange order, but Brewer squelched it in a hurry.

"Silence!" he called. "Stand by your guns!"

Gerard made his way below deck now, and Brewer stepped up to meet him.

"Any word?" he asked.

Gerard shook his head. "Nothing," he said. "Just stand by. The Captain's about to alter course to the north, then dowse our lights and swing back to the southeast. I think he's trying to trick them into relighting their lamps so we can get a fix on their position."

Brewer's eyes grew wide at that. "We don't know where they are?"

Gerard shook his head. "No. There's been no sightings since the lookout reported the light going out. Did you see it?"

Brewer paused as he felt the ship swing to port and steady up on the northerly course.

"No," he said. "I presumed it was below the horizon from the deck. I questioned the lookout, and he said it was there one second and gone the next, like it kept dropping below the horizon."

Gerard thought for a moment, rubbing his chin as though it would help somehow. "So," he said quietly, "nobody's actually seen this mysterious light, *except* the lookout. Who was in the tops?"

Brewer thought for a moment, then closed his eyes in an 'oh, no' sort of gesture.

"Ferguson," he said quietly.

Gerard nodded his understanding, and perhaps his sympathy. "I thought as much. Not the most reliable of witnesses." Ferguson had a reputation of sorts for misidentifying targets and, according to some, seeing things that weren't there. Brewer had no idea how he could have allowed him to man the tops alone, but he was sure the Captain would want an explanation.

"If you'll excuse me," Gerard said with a note of sympathy in his voice, "I shall go inform the Captain."

Brewer nodded and touched his hat as his friend left. He felt sick and miserable at having made such an obvious mistake. Everybody knew about Ferguson; the trouble was that the man simply *loved* to be in the tops, and he took every opportunity to get up there. Somehow, he got up there without Brewer noticing when they came on watch, and Brewer didn't realize his mistake when Ferguson made his sighting.

Ten minutes later the word came down to stand easy, and the ship went back to a normal routine. Three minutes after that, Brewer hung his head as he heard the word being passed for him to report to the captain's cabin. Reluctantly, he made his way aft, only to be greeted outside the cabin door by a marine sentry wearing the pitiful expression Brewer had ever seen. The sentry opened the door and announced the lieutenant before stepping back. Brewer walked past him, ignoring the sentry's pity.

Captain Bush was sitting behind his desk, catching up his log. Brewer stood at attention until his captain took notice of him.

"Stand easy, Mr. Brewer," the Captain said without looking up from his writing. Brewer noticed that he had not been invited to sit down.

He stood easy, his eyes fixed on a spot on the bulkhead directly over the captain's head. It took nearly ten minutes for Bush to finish his writing and put down his pen. The look on his captain's face when it rose from the page made his heart sink.

"Mr. Brewer," Bush began, in a tone that could only be described as ominous, "words fail me to describe my disappointment at the events of this evening. Frankly, sir, I expected better from an officer of your caliber."

"I'm sorry, sir," Brewer said, trying to hold his voice steady by only partly succeeding. "It won't happen again."

"Oh, I can assure you of that, sir!" Bush exclaimed. He stood and came around his desk to stand before his second lieutenant. "You were lucky, Lieutenant. Sending the ship off on a wild goose chase based on the word of a hand who is known to be unreliable is nothing short of scandalous. Assign Ferguson to a gun crew in your division, Mr. Brewer. You will be directly responsible for him from now on. You may tell him from me that if he ever goes *near* the tops on duty again, or ever tries to make a report like that again, I will have him flogged! Do you understand me, sir?"

"Aye aye, sir!" Brewer replied, snapping to attention, his voice rising in the heat of the moment.

Bush looked him hard in the eyes before turning and going back to his seat. Brewer remained as he was, honestly afraid of even twitching.

"You are dismissed," the Captain said quietly. Brewer noted that he hadn't even raised his eyes from his desk to dismiss him. He silently turned and left the cabin.

Once past the sentry, Brewer made his way back on deck. He stopped before mounting the companionway stairs, leaning against the railing and taking several deep breaths to calm his nerves. He ascended to the deck and saw Mr. Gerard on the quarterdeck speaking to Starling. He approached and touched his hat to Gerard.

"Gentlemen," he said.

"Mr. Brewer," Gerard said. "It's good to see you survived." Brewer wondered what he meant, but Gerard to turned Lieutenant Starling. "You have the deck. Walk with me, Mr. Brewer."

The walked forward along the lee rail. Gerard had his hands clasps casually behind his back; Brewer thought it best to imitate the Premier's calm until he found out what was going on.

"I'm glad he left a little skin on you," Gerard said quietly. "I was afraid he would skin you like a fox."

Brewer closed his eyes in shame and then looked out toward the sea. "I feel like I've... I don't even know what to call it. It's worse than disappointing him, almost a personal betrayal of his trust."

Gerard gave a sympathetic smile and nodded. "I know what you mean. I got my chewing out from Hornblower." Brewer saw Gerard shake his head at the memory. "Don't worry about it, William. I can tell you two things: One, the Captain will never mention the incident again. He considers the matter closed; if he were going to punish you, he would have done it then and there. And two, if you ever do it again, you will not walk out of his office a free man. In fact, you will be lucky to retain your rank."

Gerard stopped and faced him.

"Tomorrow morning, you begin rebuilding his trust. You may have to prove yourself all over to him; if that's what it takes, so be it. You do what you have to do, and you do it willingly and to the best of your ability. He will notice."

Brewer looked out over the waves again, his face unreadable. He was angry with himself for allowing this all to happen. He shook his head. No matter; he would do what he had to in order to prove himself to the captain and regain his trust. He turned back to Gerard.

"Thank you," he said. "I shall do my best not to let you down. By the way, the Captain has made me responsible for Ferguson for the remainder of the voyage. He is to be reassigned to a gun crew in my division."

Gerard smiled broadly at that. "I wondered if he would do that. No problem, Mr. Brewer. I shall adjust the watch bill and reassigned Ferguson. Now I suggest we both get some sleep. Hopefully, tomorrow will give us all a chance to prove ourselves."

Lieutenant Brewer came on deck the next morning in time to assume the forenoon watch. He relieved Gerard as the sound of eight bells was carried away on the brisk sea breeze. Gerard smiled and quietly wished him luck before going below. Brewer noticed the Captain pacing along the lee rail but didn't bother him. Instead, he went to the wheel and greeted Mr. Trench, verifying their position, course, and speed, as well as when the next change of course was scheduled. Satisfied, he looked over the deck to make sure that all was as it should be. He was almost done when he heard it.

"Deck there!" cried the lookout. A quick look reassured Brewer it was not Ferguson. "Sail three, no, *four*, points off the larboard bow!"

Brewer reached for a glass and went to the rail to see for himself. A quick glance over his shoulder told him the Captain was doing the same. He raised the telescope to his eye and quickly saw the patch of white on the horizon, obviously outward bound from Tripoli.

"Let me hear you, lookout!" he cried.

"Looks like a barque, sir! Don't think she's seen us yet."

Brewer lowered his glass and considered for a moment. He nodded to himself, and then turned to the Captain.

"Orders, sir?"

Bush lowered his glass and looked briefly at Brewer before raising the telescope to his eye again. Thirty seconds later, he lowered the glass and snapped it shut.

"Call the hands, Mr. Brewer," he said. "Make all sail. Let's close the gap and see what we have here."

"Aye, sir," Brewer said. He grabbed a speaking trumpet and raised it to his lips. "All hands! Make sail! Make sail! Mr. Trench, steady as you go!"

The hatches erupted, spewing men like a volcano did lava and sending them skyward. Within minutes, HMS *Lydia* leapt forward to close on their quarry.

"Mr. Rivkins!" Brewer said to the midshipman standing at the rail. "Take your glass and join Jones in the foretops. Keep your eyes on the enemy; I want to know the moment he sees us and alters course."

"Aye, sir!"

Brewer resisted the temptation to look to the Captain for approval. Bush had not taken the deck, therefore he was still in command until relieved.

"Mr. Trench," he said, "I am going forward for a better look."

He made his way forward along the larboard rail, but the view when he arrived was no better than what he had on the quarterdeck. The patch of white that was the strange barque was definitely growing little by little, but the hull was still below the horizon. Brewer wondered if they had been spotted, and the enemy was turning away or perhaps trying to retreat into Tripoli.

"What about it, lookout?" he cried.

"She's changing, sir! Stand by!"

Brewer could see the shape of the white patch changing, indicating a change in course.

"Definitely a barque, sir!" Rivkins called down. "She's turning away from us and crowding on sail!"

Brewer headed aft to report to the captain. He found him speaking to the Sailing Master.

"Lookout reports the chase is definitely a barque, sir. She is turning away from us and crowding on sail. Not sure of her new course yet."

"Thank you, Mr. Brewer," Bush said. "Alter course four points to larboard."

Brewer looked to Trench, who was standing right there, and nodded.

"Aye aye, sir," Trench said.

Lydia settled on to her new course, which took her almost directly at the barque. The gap was closing fast, so the enemy's hull was clearly visible on the horizon. Brewer counted ten gun ports along the barque's side as she came around. He also saw her run up her colors.

"She's flying a Venetian flag, Captain!" he called.

"Thank you, Mr. Brewer," Bush said. "I have the deck. Clear for action, Mr. Brewer."

"Aye, sir!" Brewer said. "All hands! Clear for action! Clear for action!"

Brewer waited for Gerard to arrive on quarterdeck, and then he went to check on his battery below deck. He was pleased to find all in readiness when he arrived.

"What's the word, sir?" a gun captain asked.

"We're closing on a barque we intercepted coming out of Tripoli. He's running."

The man chuckled. "For all the good it'll do him."

Brewer went back on deck. He joined the Captain and First Lieutenant.

"Mr. Gerard," Bush said, "how much longer would you say before they're within range of a long nine?"

Gerard jumped up on the mizzen shrouds to get a clearer view and was back in moments.

"I'd say we're very nearly there now, sir. Might take a bit of luck at this range, but it's possible."

Bush thought for a moment. "Go forward. Get the starboard nine ready. Let me know when you think you can lay one off her larboard quarter."

"Aye, sir," Gerard said.

"Mr. Brewer," Bush said calmly, "beat to quarters, if you please."

"Aye, sir! Beat to quarters! All hands! Beat to quarters!"

The drummer boy took up his rhythm and was quickly joined by the scurrying of bare feet on the decks as hands reported at speed to their stations. It was a sight Brewer never tired of seeing.

"Mr. Brewer," Bush said, "load the starboard battery, but

do not run it out until ordered."

"Aye, sir!" Brewer saluted and reported to his guns.

"Starboard battery! Load but do not run out! Larboard battery, stand by!" he called when he arrived. His men were well-drilled in their duties and set about their tasks with almost mechanical precision. Within minutes every gun captain in the battery signaled his readiness.

Back on deck, a messenger brought word to Bush that Gerard was now confident of the range, and Bush sent back his permission. He watched as Gerard and the gun captain carefully adjusted the aim and the elevation of the long-nine before backing away from the piece. A moment later, the gun went off, and Bush looked up in time to see a wonderful splash in the water about twenty yards off the barque's port quarter. He raised his glass to see the enemy's reaction. He saw an officer at the barque's fantail, glass in hand, studying the approaching *Lydia* intently. He turned and walked forward, and the barque went over to the starboard tack and away from her pursuer.

"Oh, no you don't," Bush muttered to himself. He walked forward to the waist and looked down. "Mr. Brewer! Run out the starboard battery! Load the larboard battery, but do not run out yet!"

"Aye aye, sir!" Brewer turned to the starboard battery crews. "Run out, you men! Heave! Larboard battery! Load, but do not run out! Hurry, lads! Heave, I tell you, heave!"

Bush turned to a midshipman. "Run forward to the First Lieutenant. Tell him I said to fire at will."

"Aye, sir!" The lad saluted and was gone.

Bush turned to the Sailing Master. "Two points to starboard, Mr. Trench. They've offered us their stern, and I intend to take full advantage of it."

"Stand by, Mr. Brewer!" Bush called. "We're going to rake

her stern!"

"Aye, sir!"

Forward, Gerard was able to get off two shots before the increasing angle took the barque out of range. At least one of the shots was a definite hit. Gerard came aft and reported to the captain.

"Well done, Mr. Gerard," Bush said. "Report to your guns, stand by for the order to fire. As soon as you fire, I am going to come about and try to rake their stern again. As soon as the turn is completed, run out the larboard battery and fire as the guns bear."

"Aye, sir."

Gerard went below, and Bush looked to the enemy, trying to time the best moment to open fire. They were coming up on her fast now, and Bush was about to give the order when the barque suddenly turned hard to port and threw back the main topsail, bringing them to an almost immediate stop. To Bush's horror, he saw their larboard gun ports fly open and their battery run out and fire.

He ran back to the waist to give the order for Gerard and Brewer to fire, but he knew it was too late. Canister fire belched from the enemy's guns and ripped across *Lydia's* deck, making havoc of woodwork and human flesh as the British frigate shot past her. Bush was knocked to the deck by the concussion, but he got back to his feet quickly. Fortunately, either Gerard or Brewer realized what was happening and gave the order to fire. About four of *Lydia's* guns were able to reply before the barque was past them.

"Hard to starboard!" Bush ordered. He spun to look aft, and, just as he feared, the barque was turning to port to try to cut across his stern. He turned back to the waist.

"Gerard! Fire as your guns bear!"

The remaining guns of the starboard battery fired. Bush's maneuver may have saved his stern, but it exposed them to the barque's broadside. Ten twelve-pounders were out and threw fire and ball at the British. Bush's carronades on the quarterdeck belched canister, and Bush saw that it had swept the enemy's deck very effectively.

"Hard to port!" Bush ordered. "Stand by the larboard battery!"

Brewer stood behind the larboard battery now, waiting for the order to fire. Behind him, Gerard was rallying his men. The barque's broadside had disabled one gun and killed most of the crew of another, but Brewer could not worry about that now.

"Steady, men!" he called. "Stand ready!"

He looked up and down the line, meeting the eyes of every gun captain and nodding. He also saw Ferguson, wide eyed and scared but standing to his post as a member of number three gun crew. Brewer smiled and nodded to him, and the man took heart.

The ship continued to come around. As she steadied up, Brewer ran from gun to gun to make sure all was in readiness for the order. He turned and looked up to the quarterdeck; what was the captain waiting for? Finally, after a seeming eternity, the Captain appeared at the waist and looked down.

"Fire!"

"Fire, men!" Brewer called. "Fire!"

The broadside was a tad ragged, with one or two guns going off, followed by the remainder of the battery. The noise was horrific. Brewer ran up and down the line.

"Reload, blast you! Sponge out and reload! Smartly now!"

His crews were doing their utmost to reload and run their guns out again when a broadside from the barque hit the larboard side of the frigate forward of the mainmast. Brewer happened to be aft when the broadside hit, but two guns were put out of action and three men killed. One man in the starboard battery went into hysterics after being covered with brains of the captain of the larboard battery's number two gun. His own gun captain silenced him by dropping him with a right cross to the chin and then ordering two powder monkeys to drag the unconscious man out of the way.

Brewer moved forward to get the men back into the fight.

"You two men! Take the wounded below to the surgeon! You men, there! Get over here and see about getting these guns back into action! Not you two! You tend your own gun! Are you ready to fire? Then stand by for the captain's orders! Ferguson! Take Duncan below and get back here!"

"Aye, Mr. Brewer!"

Brewer turned around to see if he could help on the starboard side, but Gerard had things well in hand; in fact, one of his disabled guns was already back in action. He looked up toward the quarterdeck, but nobody was there to tell them what was going on or what to do. Brewer shook his head, angry with himself for letting his mind wander. Now, back to his guns...

Trench had brought *Lydia* out of her turn slightly behind the barque, and so the broadside loosed by Brewer was only partially effective. The barque took advantage to turn in toward *Lydia* and loose the broadside that hit the forward part of the gun deck. Now Bush decided to turn his enemy's own trick on him.

"Mr. Trench!" he called. "In a moment, I am going to call to back the main topsail. I want to slow us down, but only for a moment to allow the barque to leap ahead. As soon as he does, I want the topsail put right and the wheel put over hard to port. If all goes right, that should put us across his stern with our starboard battery ready and waiting to rip him open."

Trench did some calculations in his head as he looked

first at the main topsail and then at the approaching barque. It was fifteen seconds before he looked back at his captain and nodded.

"We can do it, sir," he said, "provided we can surprise them."

"Stand by," Bush told him. He ran to the waist and called down, "Starboard battery ready?"

"Ready, sir!" Gerard replied.

"Stand by!" Bush turned to Trench. "Now!"

The Sailing Master began bellowing orders, and the main topsail was backed. HMS *Lydia* slowed almost immediately, allowing the barque to pass. The sail was quickly set to rights, and the wheel was put hard over to port. A sudden gust of wind cleared the smoke and allowed Bush to see the astonished look on the enemy captain's face as he realized what the British were doing. *Lydia* picked up speed rapidly as they approached the barque's unprotected stern. Bush walked to the waist.

"Now, Gerard! Fire as your guns bear!"

It took a moment for Gerard to judge the moment was right before the starboard battery began to spew flame and solid shot. The guns went off two or three at a time, a testimony to Gerard's careful aim and timing. Before the smoke hid the barque from view, Bush had the pleasure of watching shot after shot make a shambles of the barque's stern and send showers of splinters down the hull of the ship on their murderous courses.

Now he delivered the *coup-de-gras*. He had held the 32-pounder carronades on the quarterdeck in reserve; now he would unleash their fury on the barque's quarterdeck. He turned to the midshipman in charge of the battery and nodded, and the six carronades erupted as one. In a way, it was a mercy that the smoke obscured the enemy ship for a few moments; Bush decided he would not have wished the sight of that sort of mutilation on anyone. Sure enough, when the smoke cleared, the only one visible on the barque's quarterdeck was a lad who was hastening to lower their colors in surrender. Bush immediately called for a cease fire and passed the word for Mr. Gerard.

The First Lieutenant came up on deck and surveyed the damage their broadsides had inflicted on the barque. Her upper deck was a wreck, the carnage being visible to all as the smoke cleared and HMS *Lydia* closed the range to lower a boat. The hull itself wasn't in much better shape.

"Dear God, sir," was all Gerard could say.

"Yes," Bush answered. Gerard looked at his captain and saw at once that Bush was not pleased by any means, his mouth compressed into a thin line at what duty had forced him to do.

"Mr. Gerard," he said quietly, "take Mr. Brewer and the launch and board that wreck. See what intelligence you can gather before she goes down. Take a surgeon's mate as well."

Gerard touched his hat and called for the bosun to lower the boat. He found Brewer still on the gun deck, tending to his guns.

"Mr. Brewer," he said formally, "you and I have been ordered to board the Venetian and learn what we can before she goes down."

A gun captain pulled his head back inside a gun port and said, "Looks like she's starting to settle already, sir."

Gerard looked at Brewer with a fateful grin on his face and motioned for him to follow.

The ride over to the Venetian was strange to Brewer's mind. Other than the occasional glance from the deck, or a head momentarily appearing in one of the many holes in the hull, their approach was almost totally ignored by those left alive on board. Previously, the enemy crew had glared with hatred at their approach, or at least made their distain known somehow or other, but these Venetians were a breed unto themselves.

They reached the ship, and Gerard sent six marines up the ladder to the deck first. As soon as their sergeant gave the okay, Gerard and Brewer followed along with the remainder of the boat's crew. Brewer tried not to get sick as he surveyed the deck and took in the massive slaughter their guns had wreaked. Judging from the number of bodies and pieces of bodies strewn about, he was sure the hail of canister from the quarterdeck carronades was what broke the back of their resistance.

Gerard was with the marine sergeant.

"Anyone speak English here?" Gerard asked.

The sergeant indicated a boy, younger than an English midshipman. "This lad does, sir."

Gerard looked down at the boy, who had a small trail of blood seeping down the side of his face. "Where is your captain?"

The boy turned and pointed to a place toward the back of the quarterdeck where several bodies had fallen. "De capitan is dere."

Gerard took the boy by the arm and headed that way. "Show me."

The boy led him there but would only point from a distance to one of the bodies. Gerard left him to go to the indicated man. He turned the man over and found a pulse in his neck. He turned and called for the surgeon's mate.

Brewer came over with the mate and stood back out of the way along with Gerard while the man ministered to the Venetian captain.

"He don't look too bad, sir," the mate—whose name was Varny—said. He's got a crease on his head, probably from a canister round." He started unpacking the bandages he brought and applying them to the wounded man's head.

Gerard turned back to his guide. "What is your name?"

The boy looked at him with a blank look on his face, and Gerard repeated his question.

"Benito," he said, staring again at the surgeon's mate at work.

Gerard took him by the arm and turned him away. "Benito, are there any more bandages on board? Bandages?" He pointed to the work done by the mate.

The boy nodded and ran off. Gerard looked back to the mate briefly before turning to Brewer.

"Take a marine with you and find the captain's cabin, if there's anything left of it. Hopefully, you can find something as big as you did the last time."

Brewer nodded and touched his hat. He grabbed a marine private and went below decks and turned aft. The two men had to tread carefully due to the destruction wrought when they raked the Venetian's stern. Brewer noticed there were few bodies among the debris, for which he was profoundly thankful.

The captain's cabin—such as it was—was wrecked in the battle. Pieces of what furniture was in the room were now strewn about nearly as far forward as midships. Brewer shook his head at it all.

"Well, start poking around," Brewer said. "Hopefully, something survived all this that we can take back to the Captain."

"Aye, sir," the private said as he began poking amongst the debris.

Brewer turned over what was left of a desk, but found nothing worthy of his efforts. The private searched the wreck of an armoire before picking through the mess across the stern. Brewer watched the man long enough to satisfy himself as to the marine's competence and then turned forward. There was probably more debris from the cabin around the mainmast than there was aft. He began to sift through it slowly, using his saber to move things or turn them over for his inspection. Papers were strewn everywhere, and Brewer passed the word for two men to come below and gather up everything that was legible.

Brewer moved a little farther forward, and he got to a point where he had to step around a body on the deck. He took special notice of it, because it was pretty much intact, which was unusual after what he had seen on deck. The head was mostly gone; Brewer presumed it was blown off by a direct hit, as the head was not lying near the body. A few feet in front of the body was a packet tied with a scarlet ribbon lying as though it were dropped when the corpse was hit. Brewer picked it up and turned it over, examining it before he untied the ribbon. Most of the pages were written in Arabic, but one was not. It was written in English. It was a Letter of Marque, and when Brewer saw the signature at the bottom, he took it up on deck immediately and showed Lieutenant Gerard.

"Reis again," Gerard said when he saw the letter. "It seems you've done it again, William. The boat is just about to leave, taking prisoners and wounded back to *Lydia*. I want you to go with them and take these papers to the captain. The Venetian's captain is going along, and I know Captain Bush will want to see these before he interrogates him."

"Aye aye, sir."

Brewer boarded the *Lydia* and headed straight for the captain's cabin.

"Begging your pardon, sir," he said after the sentry opened the door, "but Mr. Gerard felt you would want to see these at once."

Bush took the papers Brewer had found during his search of the Venetian, quickly discarding those in Arabic before reading the one in English.

"Pass the word for Ali," he muttered as he read it through again. Brewer went to the door to pass the word and returned to find the Captain reading the letter yet again, his eyes wide in astonishment.

"Pass the word for the doctor, Mr. Brewer," Bush said. Brewer did as he was instructed, pausing to allow Ali to enter.

"Here, Ali," Bush handed him the papers in Arabic. "I want you to translate these, please."

There was a knock on the door, and the sentry announced the doctor. Brewer actually recoiled as Dr. Wallace walked past him; the stench of alcohol on the man was very strong. Brewer noted that the Captain did not seem to notice.

"Doctor," he said, "is the captain of the Venetian conscious yet?"

"Aye, sir," the doctor wheezed, his breath projecting a cloud of foul alcohol before him. "He woke about about fifteen minutes ago. He went to sleep almost immediately. Not unusual at all, considering his head injury."

"Can he move?"

The doctor thought for a moment. "I'd advise not, sir; not right now, anyway. The morning would be better."

"Very well," Bush said.

At that moment, Lieutenant Gerard entered the cabin.

"Forgive the intrusion, sir," he said, "but I thought it best to report as soon as I returned."

Bush sat back in his chair.

"Well, sir," Gerard began, "I'm afraid there was very little paper left that was legible in the Venetian. We brought back about ten or fifteen pages; they all appeared to be in Arabic, so I left them with Ali for translation." Bush nodded his approval, and Gerard continued. "We brought back about a dozen crewmen. Mixed lot, Moors, Europeans, Africans,

Turks. Our carronades did their work far too well this day, sir. I estimate the crew to be over 200 when the day began."

Bush shook his head at the butcher's bill, hating the waste but knowing he did what he had to do. "What of the ship? Is she worth a prize crew taking her to Malta?"

Gerard shook his head in an 'I-don't-know' sort of gesture. "We found a couple leaks below the waterline, sir, but they weren't of our doing. Other than that, she looks seaworthy enough, but I don't know if the navy would buy her."

Bush looked out the stern window at the Venetian and found he had to agree with Gerard's assessment. He stood and walked back to the windows, hands behind his back.

"Very well, Mr. Gerard," he turned and said. "Let's get everything off her we want, then burn her."

"Aye, sir," Gerard said. "May I suggest sending Mr. Starling with a bosun's mate and a dozen hands to arrange the combustion?"

Bush smiled. "Make it so, Mr. Gerard."

Mr. Starling's crew made short work of their assignment, winning the applause of their shipmates by bringing back several cases of Italian wine and sausages. Thirty minutes after they returned to HMS *Lydia*, the Venetian was in flames from stem to stern. Ten minutes later, her magazine exploded, and she disappeared beneath the waves.

The following morning found Gerard and Brewer in the captain's cabin. Bush sat behind his desk, the letter of marque from the Venetian sitting before him.

"This makes two we've found with his signature," Gerard said. "Why does he sign them? Why not the Bey?"

"Perhaps it gives the Bey a way to deny involvement," Brewer said. "He gets to blame it on Reis."

Bush shrugged. "We'll ask Reis when we catch him."

Gerard smiled. "Perhaps our friend in sickbay can tell us where he is."

"Capital idea, Gerard," Bush said. "Let's have him in. Mr. Brewer, pass the word for two marines to fetch him."

Brewer did so, and as the men waited, Ali came in and made a preliminary report.

"Captain," he said, "these are intelligence reports on movements of British shipping." He held one up. "This one says four ships are scheduled to leave Malta on the seventeenth." He held up another. "And this one says that ships will find good hunting ground off the Neapolitan coast for the next three months."

"Well done, Ali," Bush said. "Get with Mr. Bell; I want a translation ready to go with the originals to the admiral along with a copy to stay with me. How goes it with the papers Mr. Gerard brought back?"

"They appear to be more of the same, Captain, sir."

"Very good. The same goes for them, then."

"Aye, sir." The Arab departed on his errand just as the Venetian's captain appeared with two huge marine guards to encourage his good behavior and cooperation. Bush motioned for them to bring him in and seat him before the captain's desk. He was a small man, stocky in build like a teamster, broad in the shoulders with muscular arms. Deep set dark eyes dart about the room before settling on the man seated behind the desk.

"I am Captain William Bush of His Majesty's frigate *Lydia*," Bush said. "What is your name?"

The man looked about like a trapped animal, eyes hooded, until one of his marine guards nudged him with the butt of his musket.

"Me name is Sean Blakely."

"An Irishman."

Blakely's chin rose. "And proud of it, too."

"An Irishman," Bush leaned forward, his voice menacing, "with a letter of marque signed by Murad Reis."

Blakely shrugged. "What of it?"

"A letter of marque signed by a turncoat," Bush sneered. "You must be just as much traitor as Reis! Corporal, get him out of my sight!"

The corporal standing behind the prisoner took him by both shoulders and lifted him bodily from the seat.

"Ay! 'Ere, now, Captain!" the prisoner barked. "You got it wrong!"

Bush nodded to the marine, who dropped the Irishman back into his chair.

"I may raid British ships—under a letter of marque, mind you; I ain't no pirate—but I do it for a United Ireland! I ain't no blankethead, and I'm not about to turn away from my Catholic roots, neither! Reis may be a traitor to his country, his church, and his shipmates, but not me!" He shook his head in disgust. "What do you expect from a bloody Scotsman, anyway?"

Brewer turned away to hide the smile that crept across his face. He swallowed it as fast as he could before turning back to the Captain's interrogation of the prisoner.

"Now, Mr. Blakely-"

"Captain Blakely!" the Irishman interrupted.

Bush ignored him. "Where is Murad Reis?"

Blakely shrugged. "How should I know?"

"He gave you this letter of marque, didn't he?"

Blakely shook his head. "Delivered by messenger two hours before we sailed, along with our retainer in silver coin."

Bush looked to Gerard. "Did Mr. Starling recover that?"

Gerard flashed one of his patented fabulous smiles. "Indeed he did, sir."

It took an effort, but nobody laughed out loud at the

crestfallen looked on the Irishman's face.

Bush thought for a moment before an idea struck him.

"Was the *Meshuda* in port when you sailed?"

Mr. Trench was having a pleasant conversation with Mr. Starling and the quartermaster at the wheel discussing the various treasures that Starling's men had liberated from the Venetian before she was sent to the bottom, when Lieutenant Brewer burst from the companionway stairs and made his way quickly to the sailing master.

"Captain's orders!" he said. "Bring us about! Set your course for Tripoli harbor! All hands to make sail!"

Trench and the quartermaster immediately consulted the chart while Starling reached for a nearby speaking trumpet.

"All hands!" he called. "All hands! Make sail!"

The wheel was put hard over to port, and HMS *Lydia* steadied up on a course of southeast. She was picking up speed when the Captain and Lieutenant Gerard appeared on deck. Brewer went to report.

"Course southeast, sir," he said as he touched his hat.

Bush looked up at the expanse of canvas over his head. "Speed?"

"We're preparing to cast the log now, sir."

Bush glanced over to where Mr. Hanson, the senior midshipman, and Mr. Bennet were preparing to cast the log, and he noticed young Mr. Lee, the most junior midshipman and barely twelve years old, watching them with great interest.

"Mr. Lee," Bush said, "have you ever cast the log?"

"No, sir."

"Mr. Hanson, allow Mr. Lee to take Mr. Bennet's place, if you please. Let us take the opportunity to teach the lad some new skills."

"Aye, sir! Come along, Jon."

The boy bounded after Hanson, and soon Brewer saw them standing at the fantail as Hanson explained how the log worked and pointed out the knots in the cord.

"Since this is your first time, you get to work the timer." Hanson saw the boy's disappointment at not getting to heave the log into the sea. "Listen to me, Jon; your task is vital. You turn the glass over when I tell you to, and then you yell out to me as soon as the last grain of sand has drained into the bottom. I stop the cord at that moment, then you and I count the knots as we reel the log back in. The number of knots is our speed, which you will then report to the Captain."

"I'm ready!" Lee said as he took his place at the glass.

Hanson heaved the triangular log over the stern. "Now, Jon!"

Lee turned the sand-glass over and watched diligently as the sand drained into the bottom. The instant he saw the last grain fall, he gave the signal.

"Nip!"

Hanson caught the cord, and Lee came to help reel in the log and count the knots. As soon as they were done, Lee reported to the Captain.

The junior midshipman saluted with a pride that was almost comical.

"Ten knots, Captain!"

Mr. Trench spoke up. "With all due respect, Captain, may I ask why we're heading back for Tripoli?"

Bush looked at Gerard and nodded. Gerard flashed one of his patented smiles and said, "The Captain neatly boxed the Venetian's captain into admitting that *Meshuda* was in Tripoli when he sailed."

"We are on the way to take a look into Tripoli harbor," Bush said. "If *Meshuda* is there, we will blockade the harbor until she sails. We can send the next prize we take to Malta to let the admiral know what we're doing."

Mr. Trench spoke up. "And if she's gone?"

Bush looked up at the capacious clouds of canvas overhead. "Then we head for Tunis. Now, if you will excuse me, gentlemen, I will retire below. Call me when we reach Tripoli."

They watched him disappear below, and then Gerard and Brewer turned and stared at the Sailing Master. At first, he tried to ignore them, but he soon withered under their piercing glare. Finally, he turned back to them and sighed.

"Sorry."

At four bells of the afternoon watch the following day, Captain Bush was summoned to the deck.

"Yes, Mr. Gerard?" he said.

"We are about to begin our pass across the mouth of Tripoli harbor, sir," the Premier said. "In order to get the best view of the entire harbor, it will be necessary to pass within range of the guns of the citadel."

"Very good," Bush said. "Call all hands to make sail. Post extra lookouts. We are only going to get one chance at this; let's make it count."

"Aye, sir!"

Orders were bellowed and hands posted. Once more the sky over HMS *Lydia* became obscured by the mountain of canvas. The ship picked up speed, and the pass in search of *Meshuda* began. Every telescope on the ship was in use, pointing to larboard and the harbor. Bush stood in the center of the quarterdeck, his hands behind his back. He was taking a gamble, and now he had to let it play out. As *Lydia* had approached harbor last night, Bush had opted to bypass the harbor in order to make his run from east to west during the afternoon sunlight. The alternative would have been to double back on his course for an east to west run during daylight. This would have exposed them to attack by any ships that managed to get out of the harbor in an attempt to intercept them after they turned west again.

The trouble with the east to west run is that the great citadel is at the western end of the harbor mouth—plenty of time to see the British frigate coming and get off several salvoes during the pass. As it turned out, that is exactly what happened. *Lydia* had barely begun their run when the first shots rang out from the huge fort. They fell well short, but it showed Bush that they were in for a dangerous pass.

"Mr. Gerard, warn the lookouts to keep a sharp eye out! Mr. Trench, prepare to alter course."

"Aye, sir."

Brewer stood by anxiously as their ship approached the extreme limit of the citadel's range. About thirty yards from it, the Captain stirred.

"Two points to port, Mr. Trench."

The Sailing Master acknowledged the order, and as he turned to the wheel Brewer could see him swallow his angst and personally direct the movement of his mates at the wheel.

The volleys of the citadel's guns began to cause geysers to erupt on either side of *Lydia*. Brewer looked to the Captain and found his standing in the same pose on the same spot, immoveable, only his eyes darting from place to place, missing nothing. The sight reminded Brewer of Bonaparte and how he might have looked during a battle.

"One point to starboard, Mr. Trench," Bush said.

Gerard stepped up. "Mr. Brewer, take a position forward on the rail. Keep the looks alert; warn them of the Captain's evasive maneuvers."

"Aye, sir."

Brewer took his telescope and found a place for himself on the larboard rail just forward of the mainmast. He turned his eye toward the approaching harbor entrance, but he couldn't help but worry about the gauntlet *Lydia* was forced to run. He scolded himself, told himself to worry about his own job and quickly looked around to make sure the men were alert. Every eye, telescope or no, was fixed on the harbor they were passing.

"Take note of everything you see, lads!" Brewer cried. "We are looking for *Meshuda*, but the Captain will be interested in any new information he can get!"

He put his glass to his eye and searched the harbor diligently, trying his best to ignore the splashes of the near-misses. Once he and those around him were sprayed when the captain had altered course to starboard and a shell landed not ten feet from them, right where *Lydia* would have been, had the captain not acted. As they approached the citadel and the end of their run, two of the rounds crashed into the upper works and rigging, one of them taking with foretop mast with it and killing two men. Brewer turned and looked back to the quarterdeck, but Captain Bush was still there, rooted in that same spot.

Finally the wheel was put over hard to starboard, and the ordeal was over. Brewer silently breathed a sigh of relief and questioned everyone in his area, but none had seen anything in the harbor that was close to *Meshuda's* size. He went to report to Gerard, who nodded and said his section said the same.

Gerard carried the report aft to the captain.

"Report, Mr. Gerard," Bush said.

The First Lieutenant saluted. "I'm sorry sir, but no sightings of *Meshuda* or anything else that big in the harbor. If she was there, she's sailed."

Bush pursed his lips and said nothing for a moment. "Damage report?"

"We're looking at it now, sir. The foretop mast received a solid hit. It's gone. It appears the hit blew two men over the side and killed them. I'll have a full report on your desk by eight bells."

Bush nodded. His eyes dropped to the deck for a second. "I'm going below. You have the deck."

"Aye, sir," Gerard touched his hat, and Bush went below. Gerard knew what his master was feeling; both of them had learned it from Hornblower. Two men lost for nothing. Not that the mission was a waste; they had to find out if *Meshuda* was there or not. But to come up empty and still lose two men—that was like pouring salt in an open wound. Gerard did not envy his captain the night to come.

CHAPTER NINE

Mr. Franklin, the carpenter, and Mr. Hammersmith were able to make repairs to the ship without having to divert to Malta. HMS *Lydia* was cruising westward just off the coast of Libya heading for Tunis.

The night air was cool, a fact that never ceased to amaze Brewer. He leaned against the lee rail and sighed. The middle watch was his favorite—the cool breeze and the moonlight in the middle of the night gave a welcome respite from the cares and worries of his duties. He looked up and watched the sail overhead billow softly and he envied the quartermaster's mate an easy watch at the wheel.

He saw Mr. Midshipman Rivkins come aft. He was the senior midshipman on Brewer's watch, but Brewer realized that he had never taken any opportunity to speak to the lad and learn anything about him. The lad paused to say something to the mate at the wheel before going on to stand by the fantail, staring at *Lydia's* wake.

Brewer studied the midshipman. He thought Rivkins to be about fifteen years old. The boy was of medium height and looked to be well on the way to developing a muscular physique. Even the way he carried himself made Brewer wonder whether he had family connections that could help him with promotions that are hard to come by in the peacetime Royal Navy. He rose and walked quietly aft and stood beside the midshipman.

"Pleasant night, Mr. Rivkins," he said.

The midshipman touched his hat in salute. "Aye, sir."

Brewer was hoping the lad would be more inclined to talk, but he tried again. "Are you getting along all right?"

He did not take his eyes from the sea. "Well enough, sir."

"Is there anything I can do for you?"

He shook his head. "I don't think so, sir."

Brewer sighed. "How old are you, Mr. Rivkins?"

"I'm seventeen, sir."

"And why did you join the Navy and go to sea?"

"It was expected of me, sir," he said with just a hint of bitterness in his voice. "I had no choice."

Brewer looked down at the boy. "Excuse me?"

"It was expected of me," he said again. "My mother's side of the family has been going to sea for generations. Her uncle was Lord Nelson. After Trafalgar, my father decided that I would uphold the family tradition and take up my uncle's mantle. So, when I turned twelve, my father wrote to the Admiralty in London and secured me a midshipman's berth on *Agamemnon*. I was transferred to the *Lydia* during the refit, and here I am."

"I see," Brewer said. Inwardly, his mind was racing. *Nelson? Good Lord!* Suddenly near panic set in when he had no idea what to say to the midshipman. Brewer chastised himself for his hesitation and decided to charge ahead.

"Yes, well," he said, "I take it from your tone that you are not pleased?"

Rivkins smiled as he shrugged, but it was a smile born of an ancient wound being reopened.

"I suppose you could say that, sir," he said.

Brewer chuckled and shook his head.

That got Rivkins' attention. "What's so funny, sir?"

"Nothing, Mr. Rivkins," Brewer said. "I apologize if I have offended you. It's just that, here you are, with a family tree that includes the greatest sea hero England has ever produced, having to be forced to go to sea to uphold the family tradition, while I have been disowned for defying my father and going to sea." He shook his head. "There's something wrong with the world."

"You were disowned?"

"Yes. My father wanted me to stay and work our family farm as he had done with his father. On the night I left to join my first ship, my father said that if I stepped through that door, then I would never be allowed to reenter." He paused, as the memory struck a raw nerve. "I went, and I have never been back to this day."

Rivkins stared at him. "You can't go home?"

"No."

"You've not heard from him? In all these years?"

Brewer looked out over the waves and sighed. "No. I wrote him once, about a year after I left home, but he never wrote back. I write my mother, and my sisters and brother. That's how I know my father received my letter; my mother said he got it." Brewer shrugged, hoping the hurt didn't show. "I don't even know if he read it."

Out of the corner of his eye, Brewer noticed that the midshipman was staring at him with shock written all over his face. He hoped he had not just made a mistake in admitting so much to the lad. Rivkins' breeding regained control quickly, and he stared out over the waves again.

"I'm sorry, sir; I didn't know," he said. "I thought, when the Captain chose you to go ashore at St. Helena to work with the Governor that you had some kind of family backing or the Captain was doing your father a favor."

"No, nothing of the kind."

"I see. You must have wanted to go to sea very badly, defying you father the way you did."

"More than anything. It called to me."

Rivkins nodded. "That's how my mother said it was with her uncle, Lord Nelson. She stayed with his family during the summer. They played together when they were children."

Brewer looked at him. "It was like that for him, but not for you, eh?"

"No, sir," he said. "I wanted to go to university and study law or engineering. But when I was twelve, my father called me into his study and told me that it was my duty to enter the Royal Navy and uphold the family tradition. He told me the family name and honor was on my shoulders." He shook his head in frustration. "I never knew Nelson. I was three year old when he died." Brewer thought for a moment that the lad would bread down and cry, but once again the breeding reasserted control and his back straightened. "Honestly, sir, my only fear is that I may not have the chance to bring glory and honor to the family name before we return to England. I can't go home until I do."

Brewer stood beside the boy and studied the stars. What could he say? If there was a polar opposite to his own situation on the *Lydia*, it was Rivkins. He knew nothing of the forces that drove the lad to the King's service and held him there until he could emulate his famous uncle to some degree. Still, he felt he couldn't leave things as they were.

"Well," he said, "I confess I'm not sure what to say. Let me tell you one thing, though. Since you have been in my division, Rivkins, I have found you to be an excellent midshipman. You work hard, the men respect you, and I believe you have the makings of a fine officer. What I'm trying to say is, don't rule out the fact that your father may have done you a favor. I think you would make a good officer if you continue to apply yourself." Brewer turned to the lad.

"Let me give you some advice that a friend once gave me. He said that opportunity comes but once in everyone's life, and you must be ready to seize it by the throat like a wolf and wrestle it to the ground and make it your own. That, he said, was how to make yourself the master of your own destiny." Brewer turned back to the sea. "Be careful you don't miss an opportunity."

Rivkins was silent for several minutes. All he did was look out over *Lydia's* wake, and Brewer began to wonder if he had gone too far. Suddenly, the midshipman leaned over and asked a question in a subdued voice.

"Your friend, the one who gave you the advice, was it by chance Bonaparte?"

"Yes, as a matter of fact, it was."

Rivkins nodded thoughtfully. "Sounds like him. Thank you, Mr. Brewer."

He touched his hat and walked forward.

HMS *Lydia* moved west to the waters off Tunis, looking for fresh hunting grounds. The weather was abominable when they arrived, so Bush kept the ship out to sea. The high seas played havoc throwing items around the deck. Brewer, who suffered through the worst of the squall during his watch, was grateful the guns stayed where they were.

They ran south out of the squall, and Bush took *Lydia* in close to shore to search for prizes. They followed the coastline south until it turned west, and then headed north again toward Tunis. On the third day of searching, they hit pay dirt.

"Deck there!" cried the lookout. "There's a ship at the back of the cove!"

"Back the main tops'l!" Gerard ordered. He picked up a glass and saw a long ship rather low in the water, angled so that they could see down most of one side. "Mr. Bennett! My respects to the Captain; please inform him that we have sighted a ship hidden at the back of a cove."

Bush came up on deck and joined Gerard at the rail.

"Thank you, Mr. Bennett," Bush said as the midshipman handed him a glass. He trained it on the unknown ship they had trapped. "What do we have, Mr. Gerard?"

"Looks like we've caught a pirate xebec, Captain, probably towed backward down the cove for a quick exit. I sent Dewey to the tops for a good look, and he counted ten or eleven gun ports."

"Begging your pardon, Captain, sir." It was Ali, who had come up on deck. "I believe it is a *polacca*, rather than a xebec. See the square sails on the main and mizzenmasts? I believe it is a sort of cross between a xebec and a brig. Very maneuverable. Very dangerous to our side."

"Not for long," Bush said. "Mr. Gerard, can we reach her?"

The first lieutenant studied the situation. "Maybe with the long nines, sir."

"Call the hands to wear ship. Let's bring the long nines to bear. Mr. Brewer, see to the guns."

The hands went aloft, and HMS *Lydia* came around slowly, making a three-quarter circle round to starboard that left the ship poised to enter the cove and bringing the long ranged bow chasers to bear on the *polacca*. Bush ordered the Sailing Master to heave to at that point, and he and Mr. Gerard went forward.

Lieutenant Brewer and Mr. Reilly the gunner were already there, working on the guns. Both men saluted as the captain and first lieutenant approached.

"Yes, Mr. Brewer?" Bush said.

"Both guns ready, sir," Brewer said. "Mr. Reilly and I have set both guns to maximum elevation. We think we can just reach that ship."

Mr. Reilly agreed. "With any luck, Captain, the plunging fire will come down through her deck and hole her hull."

Mr. Brewer held out one of the lanyards to the Captain. "Sir? Would you care to do the honors?"

"Thank you, Mr. Brewer." The Captain took the lanyard and squatted down behind the gun to check its aim. Satisfied, he stepped back and to the side and gave the lanyard a mighty pull. The long nine erupted and spewed flame and smoke out of its muzzle. They struggled to see the fall of the shot through the smoke.

"I think it went long, sir," Gerard said.

"I agree," Bush said. "Mr. Reilly? Opinions?"

The gunner scratched his chin for a moment as he thought. "I'd rather lessen the powder than decrease the elevation, sir. Plunging fire is our best hope to sink her where she lies."

Bush stared at the *polacca* as he considered the options. He nodded and said, "Agreed."

Reilly and Brewer worked on the second bow chaser. Gerard turned and said, "Pass the word for Mr. Dewey." The quartermaster's mate had the best eyes in the ship. When he arrived, Gerard handed him a glass. "Up to the foretops with you, Mr. Dewey. I want you to see the fall of our shot on that ship out there."

"Aye, sir!" He saluted and jumped for the shrouds to make his way aloft.

Bush turned from watching the exchange to find Brewer handing him another lanyard. The Captain stood back and pulled. Ignoring the smoke and flames, the officers turned and looked up to Dewey in the tops.

"The range is good, Captain!" the lookout called down. "It landed about twenty feet to starboard, but the range was right on!"

Bush handed the lanyard back to his second lieutenant.

"It seems your aim is off, Mr. Brewer. Correct for both guns and fire at will."

"Aye, sir!"

Bush and Gerard moved aside to allow Brewer, Reilly, and their hands to get to work.

"Lookout!" he called. "What's going on out there?"

"A lot of scurrying about, sir!" The lookout smiled down at them. "It appears that they don't have any guns they can bring to bear!"

Bush smiled and turned as the first salvo went off behind him. Brewer had opted to fire both guns at once. The three officers turned their heads skyward and waited.

Dewey almost jumped out of the tops as he pointed toward their quarry. "We got her, sir! We got her! One hit for sure; maybe two, I'm not sure!"

Bush turned to Brewer and Reilly. "Well done, gentlemen! Let's keep it going."

"Aye, sir!"

Two minutes later the guns erupted again. Dewey reported two clean hits this time, one of which took down the main yard on its way down.

Two more salvoes were lobbed down the cove when Dewey called down to the deck.

"Deck there! Looks like they're abandoning ship!"

"Cease fire, Mr. Brewer," Bush said. "Let the smoke clear, so we can see what's going on."

By the time the smoke cleared, they could see one boat in the water, full of men and clear of the ship and pulling for shore as well as another that was lowered and filling with men. Several swimmers were also on their way to shore. Within minutes, Dewey reported that there was no sign of movement on the ship.

To Gerard's surprise, Bush returned to the quarterdeck and began to pace. Gerard followed and went to stand by Mr.

Trench. The Sailing Master shot him an inquisitive look, but Gerard could only shake his head. After several minutes, Bush stopped pacing and raised his telescope to study the *polacca* again. Gerard decided to risk his captain's displeasure and walked up to him.

"Begging your pardon, sir," he said. "Shall I take a boat and board her?"

"I had considered that, Mr. Gerard," Bush said. He lowered the telescope and looked at the first lieutenant. "But I'm not sure I want to expose you or anyone else in my crew as sitting ducks rowing down that cove."

Gerard looked down the cove with shock on his face. He saw immediately what his captain was talking about—the cove was long and narrow, with heavy foliage on both sides, narrow enough that anyone rowing down it would be easy prey for snipers on either shore. He turned away from the captain to hide his embarrassment at not having seen it himself. He was saved from further recriminations by a call from above.

"Deck there! Boats are moving out from the shore! Looks like they're trying to reboard her!"

Bush and Gerard made their way forward quickly to see for themselves. One boat had reached the *polacca* and another was right behind it. The Captain lowered his glass.

"Mr. Brewer, open fire."

"Aye, sir."

Ninety seconds later, both long nines erupted. Ninety-five seconds after that, they fired again. Each salvo was reported as hits by the watchful Dewey in the foretop. It was right after this that Bush heard the sound of a gun going off.

"Deck there!" Dewey cried. "They've fired a signal gun, sir! Looks like they're surrendering!"

Bush strained to see through the slowly dissipating smoke. Finally, he was able to make out someone standing beside the bowsprit waving a white flag. He also noticed their colors were being lowered.

"Well, well," Bush said under his breath.

"Do you think they've had enough this time, sir?" Gerard asked.

"If they haven't, Mr. Gerard, I promise they won't get another chance." Bush studied the *polacca* again while he tried to decide what to do. He turned to Gerard.

"Gerard, I want you to take a boat and—"

He was interrupted when the *polacca* suddenly exploded. No one who witnessed it could claim to have seen anything as devastating; the main and mizzen masts were each blown 150 feet into the air, their yards, shrouds, and stays still attached and flapping as they rose into the air and fell back to earth, landing almost exactly where they were launched from and devastating what was left of the ship. Bodies were blown through the air as well, their screams brief but haunting nonetheless.

Bush turned away from the devastation, and the rest of them lowered their eyes.

"Mr. Gerard," the Captain said, "please get the ship under way. Set course for Tunis."

"Gladly, sir."

HMS *Lydia* prowled the waters of Tunis for a fortnight but took only two prizes, both English merchantmen taken by the pirates. *Lydia's* boarders set the ships' crews free and sent them to Malta.

Something was different. It was obvious to all who were on the deck that day, but none of them would speak of it. The overwhelming power of the blast that took the *polacca*, the bodies that followed the masts skyward, nobody seemed to be able to forget. Sailors were a superstitious lot by nature; it was almost as if they felt under a curse now.

Captain Bush decided not to linger in Tunisian waters; He turned *Lydia* west to hunt off Algiers.

The voyage to Algiers was long and tedious, as there seemed to be thousands of coves and inlets along portions of the coast, all of which had to be investigated, and all of which turned out to be empty. Brewer watched as the tedium of searching empty cove after empty inlet worked on the crew. They grew irritable and frustrated, causing tempers to flare and angry words to be exchanged. Brewer himself had to step in between two of the hands in his division to prevent blows from being struck.

"Any more of this foolishness," he yelled at them in front of the rest of their mess, "and I'll flog you myself! *Now get out of my sight!*"

The hands were so taken aback by the uncharacteristic outburst that the entire mess disappeared forward in a hurry. Brewer stood there for a moment, alone and somewhat embarrassed. He turned and made his way as quickly as dignity would allow to the ward room. He was disagreeably surprised to find Gerard sitting at the table, reading and nursing a tankard of beer. He hesitated for only a second before entering.

"Hello, William," Gerard said. "Have something to drink? Coles! A beer for Mr. Brewer! Sit down, sir, sit down. Was that you I heard forward a moment ago?"

"Yes, I suppose it was," Brewer nodded his thanks to Coles for the beer. "I intervened to prevent a fight at a mess in my division, and my temper got the better of me."

"Certainly sounded like it. Something wrong?"

Brewer shrugged. "Nothing new. Ever since Tunis, the crew has... *felt different*, is the only way I can put it. And then with this endless checking of coves and inlets and always coming up empty, well, the frustration is almost more than the men can bear. I guess it got to me as well." He took a healthy draught from his tankard. "I almost wish we would run into *Meshuda* and have it out with them."

Gerard smiled and raised his eyebrows mockingly. "My, my, but you are a bloodthirsty devil, Mr. Brewer! Be careful, my dear sir, be careful!" He shook his head playfully and made a *tsk-tsk* noise. Finally, he sat back in his seat and sighed. "Don't worry, William, we've all been there. You can't let yourself get in that sort of position. In short, Lieutenant, we are not allowed to lose our tempers. It makes it too easy to lose control of your men. Remember that. Trust me, you don't want to have the Captain remind you."

"Aye, sir," Brewer said. He finished off the tankard and put it on the table. "Thank you, Gerard. I will remember what you've said." He rose. "If you'll excuse me, I'll try to get some sleep before I have to go on watch. Could you ask Coles to wake me at seven bells?"

"Of course. Sleep well, William."

Two days later, Lieutenant Brewer came up on deck at eight bells of the morning watch to relieve Mr. Gerard. It was a dreary and somewhat overcast morning, and Brewer was tempted to send below for his cloak but decided against it. He reported to the first lieutenant for his briefing.

"Good morning, Mr. Brewer," Gerard said. "As you can see, the weather went sour on us during the night. Right now, our course is due north; we are scheduled to turn back due west at three bells to continue the search. However," Gerard paused to rub his chin, "the way the weather has reduced our visibility, I wouldn't put it past the Captain to try something... unusual."

"Like what, sir?" Brewer asked.

Gerard shrugged. "I have no idea, Mr. Brewer. You have the deck. I shall be in my cabin, trying to sleep."

"Aye aye, sir," Brewer touched his hat. He spoke briefly with the sailing master and the bosun before reviewing the standing orders. Nothing had changed since his last watch, so he picked up a telescope and walked to the lee rail to scan the horizon.

A voice spoke up from behind. "It looks almost close enough to touch, wouldn't you say?"

He turned to see Captain Bush standing behind him.

"Oh! Good morning, Captain. I'm sorry, but I didn't hear you approach."

Bush took the telescope from his second and scanned the horizon. "I can see that in all the time you've been commissioned, Mr. Brewer, you've not been taught to have someone on your watch alert you when the captain comes on deck."

Brewer bowed with his head. "Thank you, Captain."

Bush handed him back the telescope and smiled. "Not at all. Come with me." He led Brewer to the wheel where Mr. Trench was standing with the quartermaster and two of his mates.

"Mr. Trench," Bush said, "I want to find a fogbank we can hide in."

"A fogbank, sir?"

"Yes. I want to lie in wait for a prize to come by, and then emerge and take them by surprise."

"Very good, sir. I shall notify you at once when we find one."

"Thank you." Bush acknowledged their salutes. "Come, Mr. Brewer. Walk with me."

"An honor, Captain."

The two men returned to the lee side of the quarterdeck, where Brewer fell into step with his captain as he began to pace up and down the deck.

"I don't want to give a pirate the chance to see us first in this bad weather and avoid us, or, worse yet, use the advantage to send his prizes around on a circuitous route into Algiers while he keeps us busy. If we can hide in a fogbank, or perhaps a squall, then he will walk right into our trap. We can burst from our hiding place and be on him before he can evade or even defend himself."

"I see, sir," Brewer replied. "But isn't there a danger that our concealment could work against us?"

"Aye," said Bush, "we'll have to maintain good lookouts and keep absolute quiet on deck. Sometimes, you can hear them before you can see them."

Bush paused his pacing when he saw young Tucker, the youngest of the quartermaster's mates, standing patiently, waiting to be noticed.

"Yes, Mr. Tucker?" Bush said.

"Pardon the interruption, Captain," the lad said, "but Mr. Trench sends his respects and wishes me to inform you that he believes he has found what you were looking for."

"Has he indeed? Well, let us see if such is indeed the case."

Bush led Brewer and Tucker across the quarterdeck. "Well, Mr. Trench?"

Trench handed him a telescope and pointed to larboard. "Three points forward of the larboard beam, sir, looks to be a wonderful wall of fog. Being that we are at the far eastern end of our patrol area, I respectfully suggest that we sail into it and see where we come out. Based on where the other end is, you can decide if you want to hide in it or not."

Bush raised the glass to his eye and studied the fogbank as he considered the sailing master's plan. After several minutes, he lowered the telescope and nodded.

"Let's do it. Quartermaster, hard to larboard. Put us into that fogbank. Mr. Brewer, clear for action. I want the guns loaded but not run out. Pass the word for Mr. Gerard."

HMS *Lydia* underwent the conversion from sailing ship to machine of war as within minutes walls were taken down and everything was made ready for battle. The Captain, now joined by the First Lieutenant, stood and watched it all with pride.

Brewer reported back to his captain. "Ship cleared for action, sir."

"Very good, Mr. Brewer. Mr. Gerard, when we enter the fog, I want no noise on deck. No lights. Hands to line the rails to keep lookout. Pass the word."

"Aye, sir." Gerard saluted and went forward along the larboard rail, motioning for Brewer to take the starboard side. Both men passed the captain's instructions as quickly and quietly as they could as the ship entered the fog. Brewer sent Rivkins below to make sure the gun captains knew to keep their men quiet. On his way aft again, Brewer had to remind several hands to keep quiet.

Sailing through a fogbank is one of the most disorienting experiences Brewer ever endured. All sense of direction is lost as the fog simply envelops the ship. At times, it's hard to know if you are moving at all. It was all very disconcerting.

"Are you all right, Mr. Brewer?" Gerard asked quietly.

"I suppose so, sir," Brewer whispered back. "It's just so *strange*. I don't like it."

"Not many do, especially when you consider that, at any moment, an enemy might appear at half pistol shot or more and open fire before you can react."

Brewer shivered slightly at the thought, although he hoped Gerard didn't notice.

"One of the strangest things," Gerard went on, "about sailing through a fogbank is that you never know when you'll reach the end of it. I heard a story once that, during the wars with Napoleon, a British warship came out of a fogbank at night right in the middle of a French fleet! Fortunately, she was able to get away before dawn."

Brewer shook his head in disbelief. To find yourself suddenly in the midst of so many French warships? Good God!

Captain Bush joined them. "Well, Mr. Brewer, what do you think of the fog?"

Brewer shrugged. "Well, sir, but for the smell—or the lack thereof—one might just think he's in London."

Gerard and Trench laughed. Mr. Midshipman Lee came up and saluted Bush.

"Mr. Starling's respects, sir, but he thinks we're fixing to leave the fogbank."

"Thank you, Mr. Lee," Bush said. "My compliments to Mr. Starling. Please keep me informed."

The midshipman touched his hat and was gone. Within minutes, the fog was clearing and HMS *Lydia* slid out of her hiding place. Within seconds the call came.

"Deck there! Two sail bearing nor'west!"

Brewer followed Bush and Gerard to the starboard rail. The Captain raised his telescope to his eye for all of fifteen seconds before turning to the wheel.

"Hard to port!" he ordered. "Mr. Trench, put us back in the fogbank!"

The Sailing Master leapt to the wheel and helped the quartermaster's mates put it over.

"Mr. Gerard," Bush said, "I am going forward. When we enter the fog again, I want you to put us about again, and then stop the ship while she's still in the fog. I am hoping those two ships didn't see us, and we will be able to spring upon them as they approach."

The Captain departed forward, and Brewer moved to stand with Gerard as they reentered the fog.

"What's the plan?" he asked.

"Did you see those ships?"

Brewer shook his head.

"A xebec and an English merchantman."

Brewer stared wide-eyed at his senior. He blinked and thought furiously, trying to follow his captain's plan.

"The Captain intends to cut out the merchantman?"

Gerard looked over at him in surprise. "My dear Brewer, the Captain wants them *both*."

Brewer smiled, nodding to himself. Of course he would want both. *I have to quit thinking so small!* he thought.

Gerard walked over to the wheel and gave the orders that brought the ship about again and heaved to inside the fogbank. He was still talking with Mr. Trench when the captain returned aft and called Gerard, Brewer, and Trench to his side.

"I have given Mr. Starling his instructions," he said. "We cannot see out of the fogbank. Bad luck, but it means we shall have to estimate when our prey shall arrive. Mr. Gerard, how long would you estimate it will be before they reach our position?"

Gerard rubbed his chin for a moment. "I would guess about an hour, sir, maybe a little more."

"That was my estimation as well. Mr. Starling is at the bowsprit, listening for all he is worth in the hopes that he can catch a noise to let us know when they approach. Failing that, we shall have to trust to time and pray that they have not increased their speed or altered their course."

He looked around to make sure everyone understood.

"At this moment, we have both batteries loaded but not run out. Mr. Brewer, your crews must be ready to run out at a moment's notice. We may not have a lot of time to react when we jump from our hiding place."

"Aye, sir."

"My plan is to disable the xebec in passing and go for the merchantman. That merchantman is everything to me, gentlemen; I will not be responsible for a single Englishman becoming a slave if we can prevent it. If necessary, we shall let the xebec escape in order to take the prize. Understood?"

A chorus of "Aye, sir" and nodded heads followed Bush's statement. All were in agreement; not a single Englishman—or European, for that matter—would be enslaved on their watch.

"Gentlemen," Bush said, "thank you. Your determination in this matter is a great comfort to me. Dismissed."

The gathering scattered, and Brewer made his way forward. He found Lieutenant Starling just where the Captain said he would be, at the bowsprit, listening.

Brewer touched the third lieutenant on the shoulder so as not to startle him.

"Anything, Jonah?"

Starling shook his head. "Nothing. It's so frustrating to think that they could sneak right past and we would hear nothing!"

"Don't worry," Brewer reassured him. "The Captain knows. Honestly, he doesn't expect you to hear anything. You are here on the off chance that they may set off a bell, or you may hear some work on deck to give us some warning. The Captain and Mr. Gerard estimated it would take those two ships about an hour to reach our position; that is what they are going by."

Starling considered. "An hour? Yes, that sounds about right."

Brewer spread his hands in a "there-you-have-it" gesture.

"Keep your ears open, just in case," he warned.

"Aye, sir."

Brewer returned to the quarterdeck and passed what he would later call the longest hour of his life. Between the eeriness caused by the fog and the need to stay as still and quiet as possible (so as not to give themselves away), Brewer was convinced that he would soon be seeing imaginary fairies and pixies coming at him out of the fog. He was saved when he turned and saw the Captain pull a watch from his pocket and compare the time with Mr. Gerard. Both officers nodded, and Brewer knew the wait was over.

The Captain said a few words in Gerard's ear, and Gerard went to speak to the Quartermaster at the wheel before heading forward. He went right past Brewer without saying a word, so Brewer stayed where he was and waited for orders.

Gerard passed the word of the Captain's orders forward quietly. Topmen made their way aloft to make sail and get *Lydia* moving out of the fog. Brewer realized immediately that Gerard was sending the crew to quarters for the battle, but without the incessant beating of the drums that usually alerted the hands and drove them to their posts.

"Mr. Brewer."

Brewer turned and found himself looking at Captain Bush. "I'm sorry, sir; I didn't hear you approach."

"Report to your guns. Have your men at the ready, and I will send you the word on which battery to run out."

"Aye, sir."

Brewer made his way below. As he reached the gun deck he felt the deck move beneath his feet, and his pulse quickened.

"Gun captains, check your guns!" he called to his men. "Make sure everything is ready! The Captain will let us know which battery to run out! Get ready!"

Brewer walked up and down the deck, his eyes everywhere, speaking to gun crews on both sides to encourage them and get them ready for the coming battle. At one point, he turned and looked up over his shoulder through the waist and saw the sky clearing, and part of him wished he was on the quarterdeck with the Captain.

HMS *Lydia* emerged from the fogbank ready to fight, but it was not to be. Captain Bush saw immediately that for whatever reason, their quarry was past them by a mile or more, the xebec on the near side and the merchantman just beyond. Bush silently cursed whatever fates had caused him to misjudge his exit.

"Mr. Gerard! Call the hands to make all sail! Quartermaster, hard to port! Give me a course to pass with pistol shot of the xebec's stern on the way to the merchantman."

He stood back to watch his crew. Gerard had a speaking trumpet and was bellowing orders to the hands; within minutes he would feel the acceleration in his legs. The Sailing Master and Quartermaster watched those two ships, and Bush knew his mind was racing, figuring in the enemy's speed, *Lydia's* speed, and the angles necessary to give the proper intercept. Too far to port and the xebec would be in a position to intercept them while the merchantman escaped. Too far to starboard and they may not be able to disable to xebec sufficiently, allowing them to counterattack as *Lydia* went for the merchantman. Bush did not envy the man his job at the moment; there was a great deal of pressure on the Sailing Master just now. Of course, Bush was running the computations in his own head as well.

He frowned for a moment. It was times like these that Bush wished he possessed a brain like Hornblower's. How many times had he seen his friend run similar computations in his head with no mistakes, every result coming true, and all of it seemingly without effort. Bush shook his head; his brain just wasn't wired that way. Once, Hornblower had tried to help his friend with the spherical trigonometry used in navigation, but all Bush got out of it was a headache.

He smiled at the memory. Bush was an old sailor who'd been in enough battles over the years and chased down enough of England's enemies to allow him to develop a "feel" for what to do. It's one of the things that made him one of England's best fighting captains.

Mr. Trench came over to him and saluted. "Three points west of south is the course you want, Captain. That should put us close to half-pistol shot to rake the xebec on our way to the merchantman."

"Thank you, Mr. Trench," Bush said. The Sailing Master's course agreed with his own. "Steer that course, if you please. Mr. Gerard, kindly go forward to the long nines. Let me know when you think we're in range."

"Aye, sir."

"Mr. Kennedy," Bush said to the midshipman of the watch, "my compliments to Mr. Brewer, and would he please join me on the quarterdeck?"

"Aye, sir."

Brewer presented himself and saluted.

"You sent for me, sir?"

"Yes, Mr. Brewer," Bush answered. "If you will turn and look forward, you will see our situation. I plan on passing behind the xebec and raking her across the stern before making a run for the merchantman. Of course, that plan may be altered based on when the xebec might do. If the ships split, we will do our best to get around the xebec and go for the merchantman. Should the merchantman run, I will have Mr. Gerard put a ball off her bow with a long nine. If that does not convince them to heave to, I will order you to load with chain shot or bar to fire into her rigging."

"I understand, sir."

"Good lad. Now, back to your guns, and stand ready!"

"Aye, sir!" Brewer saluted and was gone.

Bush looked toward the wheel. "Mr. Trench, I'm going forward."

He made his way to the bowsprit to find Gerard and

Starling looking through telescopes at the fleeing enemy. He went to stand next to Starling, quietly and without ceremony, and raised his glass to his eye, startling his junior officers into hurried salutes.

"Report, Mr. Gerard," Bush said gruffly.

"I think we're almost in range, sir," Gerard answered. "Do you want us to elevate the guns, as we did for the *palacca*?"

Bush lowered his telescope and thought for a moment. He noticed Mr. Reilly on the lee rail.

"Mr. Reilly? Your opinion?"

"It's almost impossible to get a plunging hit on a moving target, Captain," the Gunner said.

Bush nodded. "My thinking exactly. Mr. Starling, are the long nines loaded? Run them out, then." The guns' crews sprang into action and muscled the weapons into firing position. The captains looked to Bush.

"Ready? Fire!" the Captain roared.

The twin cannon erupted, belching fire and smoke and obscuring the fall of shot to those on deck. The officers looked to the foretop.

"Shot fell about twenty yards short, sir!" the lookout cried.

"Another twenty minutes, sir?" Gerard asked.

"Perhaps," Bush said. He turned and looked at the mountain of canvas over his head and then looked back to the chase ahead of them. He was just about to head back for the quarterdeck when Gerard prevented him.

"Sir! Those two ships are altering course!"

Bush rushed to the rail and raised his glass. "Where away?"

"They've gone south, sir!" Gerard said.

"Heading for the coast?" Starling ventured.

"So it would seem, Mr. Starling," Bush said. He studied he ships for a moment. "I think we're still overtaking them.

Mr. Gerard, fire on the xebec as soon as we're in range. I'm returning to the quarterdeck. Keep me informed."

Bush went aft and resumed his pacing. His chin on his chest as he walked back and forth, he couldn't help but wonder how many passengers and crew were on that merchantman, men—not to mention the possibility of women and children—doomed to a life of slavery if he did not recapture that ship. Approximately twenty minutes into his pacing, he heard the bow chasers fire, followed by additional volleys at two-minute intervals. Strangely, it was the cessation of their fire that caused the Captain to pause his pacing and turn forward, and that was when he noticed Midshipman Lee standing there patiently waiting.

"Yes, Mr. Lee?"

The Midshipman saluted. "Mr. Gerard sends his respects, sir, and would you please come forward?"

"Lead the way, Mr. Lee."

Bush followed the midshipman forward. When he arrived, the crowd of watchers parted almost like magic to allow their captain access to the rail. The scene that presented itself for his inspection was hardly what he expected.

The xebec was damaged. The mizzenmast was toppled, and she had fallen off to port. It looked like she was trying to turn to port and present her broadside to *Lydia*, but evidently her steering was damaged as well, because she was having great difficulty in making the turn. Bush now noticed that the xebec was also listing slightly to port. Beyond the xebec, it looked like the merchantman was running for all she was worth toward the coast, which Bush guessed was now only five miles or less away.

"Report, Mr. Gerard," he said.

"Those last two salvoes did the trick, sir," the first lieutenant said. "We took out his mizzenmast and holed her port aft. Apparently, when the mizzen went over, it damaged their steering."

"Good shooting, gentlemen," Bush lowered the glass and thought for a moment. He turned to his Premier. "Mr. Gerard, go aft and tell Mr. Trench I intend to pass the xebec to starboard and that he is to head straight for the merchantman once we are past her."

"Aye, sir," Gerard saluted and headed aft.

"Mr. Lee," Bush said to the midshipman, "go below. My compliments to Mr. Brewer. He is to run out the larboard battery and prepare to fire on my order."

"Aye aye, sir!" the lad knuckled his forehead and disappeared.

Bush studied the ships before him for a few minutes more. The xebec was definitely in a bad way; he could see them trying to lower boats from her deck. He noted the *Lydia's* change of course to starboard to safely pass the xebec, and he headed for the quarterdeck. Gerard greeted him on his arrival.

"On course as ordered, sir," he said.

"Thank you, Mr. Gerard," the Captain replied. He wandered to the rail at the waist and looked down to see Mr. Brewer awaiting orders.

"Larboard battery run out and ready, sir!" he called.

"Thank you, Mr. Brewer," he said. "Stand by."

"Aye, sir!"

Bush watched as *Lydia* approached and began to slide past the xebec. He smiled, glad he was not close enough to hear what the Arabs who were shaking their fists at him were yelling. He looked down.

"Mr. Brewer, fire as your guns bear."

"Aye, sir!" Brewer ran to the forward guns. "Steady, boys, wait until your guns bear. Gun captains, fire as you bear!"

On the quarterdeck, Bush and Gerard heard *Lydia's*

larboard battery of 12-pounders went off in twos and threes and walked to the larboard rail. The smoke was dense, so Gerard called to the lookout in the mizzen top.

"She's wrecked, Captain!" the lookout called down a moment later. "Mr. Brewer's finished her proper!" A cheer went up from the hands on deck.

Lydia sped past the xebec and resumed her southerly course in pursuit of the fleeing merchantman. Bush and Gerard went to the fantail for a look at the xebec, and it was quickly evident that the lookout was not exaggerating. Even from this angle, the British officers could see that the xebec's stern was wrecked, and it looked like the damage extended far forward.

"Apparently, they are not very well constructed," Gerard commented.

"So it appears," Bush agreed. "All the more reason to follow Lord Exmouth's advice to stand off and pound them at long range."

Lydia rapidly closed the range on their remaining quarry. Gerard was again sent forward to try his skill on the long nines, although this time with a stern warning from Bush not to hit the merchantman.

Fifteen minutes later, the Captain heard the bow chasers fire, followed a minute later by cheers. He went forward to see the merchantman's flag being lowered. The ship turned to port and the main topsail sheets were loosed, allowing the wind to spill from the sails and bringing the ship almost to a stop.

Bush lowered his telescope. "Pass the word for Mr. Brewer."

The Second Lieutenant appeared and saluted.

"Mr. Brewer," Bush said, "I want you to take a boat and board the merchantman. Standard crew and marines should do."

"Aye, sir!" Brewer saluted. "Thank you, sir!"

Gerard watched him head aft to speak to the bosun about lowering the boat and gathering the boarding crew.

"What do you think he'll find, sir?" he asked Bush.

Bush studied the merchantman for a moment before lowering his glass. "Nothing."

Gerard looked confused. "Nothing, sir?"

"Just that," Bush answered and raised his glass again.

Brewer and his men were soon in the water and pulling toward the merchantman, whose name was soon visible across her stern—*Sandal Rose*. Brewer sat in the stern sheets as the coxswain called to the ship and received no reply. They hooked on to the ship and scrambled up to the deck as quickly as they could. The deck was completely deserted. Noise in the water drew them to the opposite rail, where they saw the entire pirate prize crew swimming for dear life for the shore, which Brewer estimated was less than two miles away.

The sergeant of marines came up to him and saluted. "Permission to fire, Lieutenant?"

Brewer's head snapped his direction. "Fire?"

"On the pirates, sir!"

Brewer was appalled. "In the back? While they're running away?"

The sergeant shrugged. "They're pirates, sir."

"Not while I'm in command, sergeant," Brewer turned away from the man, disgusted with him. "Send a detail below, sergeant. Find the crew and set them free. Have the captain report to me."

"Aye aye, Lieutenant." The sergeant saluted.

Brewer looked around the deck. Nothing looked damaged, and there was no sign of any kind of a fight. Apparently, the merchant's crew had surrendered rather than be boarded.

"Mr. Pearl," Brewer called to a passing petty officer, "take two men and search the officers' quarters below. You're looking for anything the pirates may have left behind."

"Aye, Mr. Brewer."

"Mr. Brewer!"

Brewer turned to see a marine private escorted one of the merchant crew to him.

"This here's the captain, Lieutenant," he said.

"William Jorgenson, sir," the man said, shaking Brewer's hand. "We're very grateful for the rescue."

"Not at all, Captain," Brewer replied. "It was our pleasure, believe me. Are all your people alive and well?"

"I believe so, Lieutenant. They didn't hurt us, just locked us up below and helped themselves to our cargo."

"Which was?"

"Wine and cheese from Naples, bound for Gibraltar."

Brewer grunted. "I'm surprised any of them could still swim."

CHAPTER TEN

It was a beautiful day, and the midday sun was beating down on the crew of HMS *Lydia* as they slid into the harbor at Gibraltar. The harbor was packed with merchant shipping from a dozen different nations as well as warship of every stripe from the smallest sloop to the first rate HMS *Victory*.

Captain Bush and his officers stood on the quarterdeck taking in both the sunshine and the scenery. The prize attraction was a Russian frigate anchored on the far side of the harbor. Brewer and Starling had never seen a Russian warship before, let alone a frigate, and both men studied her closely.

"I don't know," Starling mused. "There's something... wrong about her, somehow. She just seems..."

"Dirty," Brewer said, a telescope to his eye. "Even the officers on the quarterdeck look slovenly."

"They were like that when we were at Riga in 1812 as well," Bush chimed in. "The only ships I saw the entire time that were clean and polished were those associated with the Russian court."

"Boat approaching from *Victory*, sir!" the lookout shouted.

Gerard looked to his captain and smiled. "The admiral wants your reports, I wager."

Bush shrugged. "Some things never change. I shall be in my cabin."

"Aye, sir." The officers saluted their captain and turned their attention back to the Russian.

"What would you say, Mr. Brewer?" Gerard asked. "Twelve pounders? Or eighteen?"

"Oh, twelve, I should say, sir," Brewer replied. "The gun ports look a shade small for eighteens."

The flag lieutenant came aboard for the captain's reports and left immediately. Gerard shared a look with Brewer as the flag lieutenant went back over the side. Brewer shrugged, and Gerard smiled. Apparently, the man did not feel like talking.

It was late in the afternoon when HMS *Victory* hoisted the expected signal with *Lydia's* number ordering the captain to report on board.

"It's about time," Gerard muttered. He handed his glass to a quartermaster's mate. "Acknowledge the signal. I'll inform the captain."

He made his way below and was announced by the sentry. He was surprised to find the captain sitting beneath the stern windows, sipping on a glass of wine.

"Ah, Mr. Gerard," Bush said, "will you join me?"

"No, thank you, sir. Signal from the flagship, sir; you're wanted on board."

"Of course," Bush drained his glass and stood. "How's the provisioning going?"

"We need two days at least, sir," Gerard answered. "The yard claims to be short of provisions at the moment, and I had to schedule the water hoys for the day after tomorrow."

"I'll see what I can do with the admiral," Bush said as he put on his best coat and buckled on his sword. "Well, let's not keep the good gentleman waiting, shall we?"

Bush was shown in to Admiral Freemantle's great cabin, and as usual he found the admiral behind his desk reading reports. Bush wondered if this was a favorite pose of the admiral's to receive guests. As on his previous visits, Bush waited until the admiral deigned to take notice of him. He bit his tongue, but for the life of him, it wasn't something he could ever picture Lord Exmouth doing.

"Ah, there you are, Captain Bush," Freemantle said as he set his papers aside. "I finished reading your reports this morning. Quite an adventure you had, I assure you! The way that *polacca* exploded and sent her masts skyward! I've never seen the like, I can tell you that!" He motioned for someone to join them. The man who joined them was a small man with dark hair and eyes. From his dress, Bush guessed him to be a foreign office operative. He bowed gracefully, and Bush nodded in return.

Admiral Freemantle made the introductions. "Captain Bush, this is Tobias Lear, special envoy for American President James Monroe. Mr. Lear, may I present Captain William Bush of His Majesty's Frigate *Lydia*."

The two men shook hands.

"Your mission, Captain, is to ferry Mr. Lear to Naples as a goodwill gesture to our American cousins. After that, report to Malta for further orders."

The admiral picked up his quill and began to write. Bush was surprised at both the rudeness of the dismissal as well as the strange mission he had been given. The Royal Navy does not usually lend itself out as a taxi service.

Bush did not realize he was still standing before the admiral's desk until the flag lieutenant touched his elbow.

"Captain," he whispered, "if you would please follow me?"

Bush cast one last look at the admiral before turning and following the flag lieutenant from the cabin.

He was fuming by the time they arrived on deck.

"Lieutenant," he said rather sharply, "where is Captain Leeds?"

The flag lieutenant had the good sense to look somewhat embarrassed.

"I'm afraid Captain Leeds is ashore at present, sir."

Bush held his tongue, knowing that taking his anger out on the lieutenant would accomplish nothing. Instead, he turned his back and marched directly to the entry port, followed by Lear and the flag lieutenant.

"Be sure that Mr. Lear's dunnage is sent to HMS *Lydia* at once," Bush said to the lieutenant.

"I'll see to it immediately, sir," the lieutenant said as he saluted. "Good luck."

The ride back to HMS *Lydia* was silent, as Bush did not trust himself to speak. He felt sorry for Lear and determined to apologize to him tomorrow or the day after. Never had Bush been so ill-treated in public by a superior officer. It was all he could do not to lose his own comportment over the matter. He did his best to take a deep breath, let it out slowly, and set his face like a flint.

They stepped on deck and were greeted by Gerard and Brewer.

"Mr. Gerard, Mr. Brewer," Bush said hurriedly, "this is Mr. Lear, Special Envoy from American President Monroe. We shall be transporting him to Naples. Mr. Lear, may I present Mr. Gerard, my first lieutenant, and Mr. Brewer, the second lieutenant. Mr. Gerard, please see Mr. Lear settled into one of the cabins in the gunroom. I shall be in my cabin. I hope you gentlemen will join me for supper." Without further ado, he turned his back and descended below deck.

The lieutenants looked at each other in bewilderment and then to their guest for an explanation. None was forthcoming.

"Well, Mr. ... Lear, was it?" Gerard said. "Right. Come along and we'll get you settled in the gunroom. Mr. Brewer, will you lead the way?"

Lear nodded his thanks and followed the second lieutenant below.

"Coles!" Brewer called as they entered. The steward appeared. "This is Mr. Lear. He'll be sailing with us as far as Naples. Can you set him up in the end cabin? His dunnage will be delivered before we sail."

"Aye aye, Mr. Brewer."

"Mr. Lear," Gerard said as he came in, "Coles here is the gunroom steward. If you need anything, just ask him."

Lear smiled and bowed to the steward. "Thanks much, Mr. Coles. I'm obliged to you."

Coles blushed. "Oh, none of that, now, Mr. Lear. It's just Coles."

Gerard sat at the table and asked Coles to bring three glasses of wine.

"Now, Mr. Lear," he said quietly. "What can you tell me about what happened on *Victory*?"

"To be honest, gentlemen," Lear said as he accepted a glass of wine and thanked Coles, "I'm not sure it's my place. I don't know your captain well enough to know whether or not I would offend him by telling what I saw, so I think I must unfortunately decline. I hope you won't hold it against me."

"No, of course not," Gerard said absent-mindedly, thoroughly confused over what could have upset the captain so greatly. They were simply going to have to wait for the Captain to tell them, if he ever would.

"Mr. Lear," Brewer said, "what will you be doing in Naples, if I may ask?"

"Please, call me Tobias," Lear said. "My job is to scout out new trade routes for American goods in the Mediterranean. You know, find new markets and the like."

Brewer was confused. "Is that a good idea at the moment? What with the Barbary pirates stirring up trouble again, I mean?"

"I'm not worried. You British tars will whip them again in no time. Now, if you have no objection, I'd like to rest up before our dinner engagement with the captain."

The three men knocked on the captain's door at the appointed hour and were admitted by the Goodnight, the captain's steward. Bush was in the dayroom, seated beneath the frigate's stern windows, drinking a glass of wine.

"Come in, gentlemen," he called, waving his glass. "Join me. Goodnight! Glasses!"

The faithful steward entered with a tray containing three glasses of wine and gave them to the newly arrived guests. Bush rose and raised his glass.

"A toast," he said. "To the Royal Navy.

The three newcomers raised their glasses and echoed, "The Royal Navy."

Gerard caught Brewer's eye, but he could see the second lieutenant had as little idea about what the toast meant as he did.

Bush resumed his seat. "Sit, gentlemen, please. We have a few minutes before Goodnight serves us. Tell me, Mr. Lear, what is your job in Naples?"

Lear sat beside the Captain. "My president has charged me with opening new trade routes in the Mediterranean for American goods, Captain."

Bush chuckled. "More business for the pirates, Mr. Lear?"

"I'm not worried," Lear said. "You British will teach them some manners."

"I beg your pardon," Brewer said, "but we quit protecting out for American shipping over forty years ago."

The American brashly waved the objection aside.

"England knows what's good its national interest, and that is the growth of American trade. The more America trades with other nations, the more money it has to purchase British goods."

"So we should just forget the wars?" Gerard asked.

"The wars are in the past," Lear said. "I say leave them there."

"Those who fought those wars may not think so," Bush chimed in. "Did you fight in the wars, Mr. Lear?"

"No, I didn't. I was too young for the Revolution, and by 1812 I was in the State Department."

"May I ask what you did while you were growing up?" Bush asked.

"I was a personal secretary for fourteen years."

"Whose, if I may ask?"

A glint appeared in Lear's eye. "George Washington."

Bush reacted to that. "Washington? Do you mean the General who commanded the American army during your revolution?"

"The same. He was also the first President of our republic."

Brewer leaned forward. "When did you work for him?"

Lear sipped his wine. "From 1786 until his death in 1799."

"Incredible!" Gerard said.

"So you were there while he was president?" Bush asked.

"Yes, sir, although I handled mostly his private correspondence, not that associated with his office."

Goodnight appeared in the doorway. "Dinner is served, sir."

"Thank you, Goodnight." Bush rose, followed by the others, and they made their way to the table.

"Actually, this is not my first time in the Mediterranean," Lear said. "President Jefferson sent me here in 1807 as the

American General Counsel to the North African coast."

"Really?" Bush said. "Then you know the name Murad Reis?"

They found their seats at the table, and Lear answered.

"Oh, yes. I am very familiar with that renegade. We tried to capture him, but he always eluded us."

"We would love to get our hands on him as well," Gerard said.

Lear grunted. "Good luck to you. Many before you have tried and failed. You know, there's a reason he's the Grand Admiral of the Bey of Tripoli's fleet, such as it is. He's good at what he does, unfortunately for our side."

The meal was served and the conversation lagged as the men turned their attention to filling their empty bellies. In honor of their American guest, Bush allowed Goodnight to prepare the last of the chops he had purchased the last time they had called at Gibraltar, along with stewed potatoes and a medley of cauliflower and peas. Bush had been assured that this was a very 'American' meal, and Lear dug into it with gusto.

After the dishes were cleared away, Bush distributed cigars and Goodnight refilled the wine glasses. The men moved back into the dayroom.

"Tell me, Mr. Lear," Bush asked, "if you were the British admiral, how would you go about capturing Murad Reis?"

Lear considered for a moment, blowing a ring of cigar smoke heavenward. "I would lay a trap for him, Captain. It must be well conceived and laid out perfectly, each point followed exactly. I would take two months spreading rumors and false information regarding uprisings in the east, perhaps Cyprus or one of the Greek islands."

Gerard laughed. "That information may not be false."

Lear smiled. "At the end of the two months, make it plain that the situation is so dire that the fleet must respond to the emergency. Send them east. At the same time, a convoy should be scheduled to start from Naples west to Gibraltar. Due to the redeployment of the fleet, the convoy will only be guarded by two or three small ships, schooners or luggers, perhaps. Reis will find out about the escort—his intelligence network is too good for him to miss something like that—and then we hope he takes the bait."

"Hope?" Brewer asked.

Lear shrugged. "There is no way to know for sure. Anyway, immediately after the convoy sails, the fastest ships in the fleet immediately leave their positions and sail west at top speed to try to catch the pirates as they pray on the convoy. A second group could be sent to intercept anything trying to enter Tripoli harbor."

Bush considered the plan as he stared into a cloud of smoke. "Sounds interesting, Mr. Lear. I wish we could try it out. Well, maybe one day."

"A question, Mr. Lear, if I may," Brewer said. Lear waved his cigar by way of permission, so Brewer asked, "I am interested in the time of your Revolution. Would you say Washington was the dominant man of the period?"

"Without doubt, Lieutenant. Oh, I know there are those of my countrymen who would bring up Franklin or John Adams, but trust me, without Washington, the whole thing would have dissolved into anarchy."

"You'll forgive me, I'm sure," Bush said as he rose, "but part of me wishes it would have. It would have saved British arms much embarrassment."

The assembly laughed as they rose.

"Thank you all for an enjoyable evening," Bush said. "I must now bid you good night."

The officers came to attention and bade their captain good night before leading Lear out of the cabin. Gerard halted them when they arrived at the companionway steps.

"I have to step up on deck to make sure we are ready to sail in the morning," he said. "Mr. Brewer, will you see our friend Tobias to the gunroom and safely to his bed?"

Brewer grinned. "Aye, sir."

Gerard flashed his patented smile and hurried up the steps. Brewer turned to Lear.

"Sir, if you'll follow me?"

The two made their way to the gunroom. As they entered, Brewer turned.

"What can you tell me about him?" he asked. "Washington, I mean. What meant the most to you?"

Lear sat in a chair and shook his head in sadness. "That would have to be his death."

Brewer sat on the table. "You were there?"

"Indeed I was, though I wish to heaven I hadn't been." He looked down, and Brewer thought he saw a tear escape from Tobias' eye. He sniffed and said, "Do you know, I held his hand as he died? I heard his last words."

Brewer leaned in. "What were they?"

Lear looked up and took a deep, ragged breath. "He said, *'Tis well."* and died." He grinned at the look on Brewer's face and rose. "Now, *Lef*tenant, if it's okay with you, I shall bid you good night."

"Good night, Tobias."

Three nights later, HMS *Lydia* was well on her way to her destination, and Captain Bush, feeling uncharacteristically generous, hosted a second dinner party, this time inviting Lear and his officers. Goodnight outdid himself, serving a veritable feast of boiled beef, roast mutton smothered in onions, French beans, potatoes, beaten butter, and tarts, with apple pie for dessert. The officers of the *Lydia* had never seen such fare, and all did their best to do it justice. The room erupted in laughter when Gerard playfully challenged Brewer to a duel for the last piece of apple pie, and Starling suggested potatoes at twenty paces.

Afterward, they adjourned to the dayroom for Madeira and cigars. Lear had the seat of honor, beside the Captain, and after puffing his cigar to life, he turned to his host.

"I pray I do not offend you, Captain, but now that we are safely at sea, I can reveal to you my primary mission in these waters. President Monroe has charged me with investigating reports that Americans are again being taken by these pirates and sold into slavery."

Gerard grunted. "I think we can safely assure you the reports are true."

Lear turned to him. "How so, Lieutenant?"

"Have American ships gone missing?" Gerard asked. Lear nodded, and Gerard responded with a there-you-have-it gesture. "They don't kill what they can sell."

Lear pondered Gerard's point. Bush leaned forward.

"Pardon me if I seem forward, Mr. Lear," he said, "but I have a question. Your President Monroe, is he from the northern United States or the southern?"

"Southern, Captain. He is from Virginia."

"As you are yourself?"

"No, sir, I was born in New Hampshire; it is in the northern part of the country known as New England."

"I see," Bush said as he sat back again and blew another cloud of rich blue smoke toward the deck above. "I'm not sure I understand why your president, or indeed your people, are so upset about something you yourself practice."

Lear stared hard at Bush for a moment before lowering his gaze. "Yes, well..."

"Do you yourself own any slaves, Mr. Lear?" Brewer asked.

"No, Mr. Brewer, I do not."

"May I ask," Bush said, "what is your opinion of slavery,

Mr. Lear. You need not worry about offending us in any way; it may interest you to know that Mr. Gerard here once worked on a slaver."

Lear gave Gerard an appraising eye before nodding and looking back to Bush. "Well, Captain, as an emissary of my President, I must tell you that our constitution says that slavery is legal within the borders of the United States."

Nobody said a word as he paused for a drink of wine.

"However, if you are asking my *personal* opinion, I will say, privately to you gentlemen, that I find slavery to be an abomination, a black mark on my country."

"Washington owned slaves, did he not?" Bush asked. "And he never freed them?"

"He did own slaves," Lear confirmed, "but in his will he freed them all upon the death of his wife Martha."

"I see," Bush said. "To your knowledge, did any other of your nation's founders do something similar?"

Lear looked into his glass. "Not to my knowledge, no."

"Interesting," Bush said as Goodnight appeared to refill their glasses.

The conversation drifted to other topics, and the party eventually wound down. Bush said good night to his guests, who made their way back to the gun room. Brewer went to his room for a few minutes, but decided that he would rather write a letter at the table. He walked out again with his pen, ink, and paper.

"Coles?" he called. The servant appeared. "Is there any coffee about?"

"I'll brew some right away, Mr. Brewer!"

Brewer thanked him and sat down to write his sister about their latest adventures. He was not three lines into his letter when Tobias Lear came out of his cabin.

"Oh, I'm sorry to disturb you, William," he said. "I thought I heard someone say the word *coffee*."

"You certainly did, Tobias. Have a seat; Coles is brewing some now."

"Thank you. Writing home?"

"Yes, a letter to my sister. She worries about me. It's hard to describe our adventures out here without giving her more cause to worry."

Lear chuckled. "It's funny you should say that; I remember the General saying something very much along those lines while we were filing his correspondence from the war."

Brewer set down his pen. "The General? You mean Washington? Tell me, what kind of man was he? What kind of leader?"

At this point Coles came in bearing a tray with two steaming cups of coffee, which he set on the table. Brewer looked up and smiled.

"Coles, you *are* a magician!"

"No, young sir, but I was blessed with good hearing."

Lear watched as the servant retreated from the gun room, tray in hand. When he was gone, he looked to Brewer and said in a low voice, "Now *that's* a good thing to keep in mind."

Brewer merely nodded before returning to his topic. "But what about Washington? What can you tell me?"

Lear muttered a curse under his breath upon discovering that the cup was as hot as the liquid within. He tried again, using the handle this time, bringing the cup to his lips and blowing on the rim before taking a tentative sip. The taste was every bit as good as the aroma predicted. He set it down carefully.

"If you're asking about his wartime experiences, William, you must remember that the war ended, for all intents and purposes, in 1783, and I did not begin to work with him until 1786. Still, there were times when he was in a mood to reminisce, and he was as full of stories as any man."

Brewer considered for a moment. "What kind of a man was he?"

Lear smiled. "I would say he was a very *singular* man, if you know what I mean? There was no pretense, no putting on of airs, no acting a certain way in front of certain people. He was what he was, and that was all he was. He had certain convictions he lived by, but that did not mean that he would not do what was necessary in extreme emergencies. He helped everyone he could, and when he couldn't, he said so."

Lear paused to take a drink of his coffee. "As you could imagine, a man as famous as the General has people coming to Mount Vernon almost daily to visit him, either to meet the great man for themselves or ask his advice or aid on a particular venture."

Brewer interrupted. "Excuse me—Mount Vernon?"

"That's the name of his estate. It's located near the present day capital of Washington City." Brewer nodded his understanding and sat back, cup in hand, to allow his friend to continue.

Lear drained his cup and set it down. "You asked what kind of a leader he was. I wasn't there during the war, as I said, but I was present during his presidency. He was decisive, but not monarchial. He listened to all the advice he could gather before making his decision. Perhaps his greatest achievement was his decision to lay down power after only two terms in office. Can you believe it? He could have been President as long as he wanted—the people would have elected him forever after what he did during the war—and he walked away from it after only two terms. And do you know what? It cost him his life."

Brewer was confused. "What do you mean?"

Lear sighed. "The General caught something while riding out in a snowstorm, and two days later, he was dead. If he had stood for just one more term as President, maybe he would not have been out on that horse! He would have been in the President's Mansion, safe and warm, and maybe he would still be here..."

Lear, on the verge of breaking down, stopped and dropped his head. Brewer heard a couple of ragged breaths before he looked up again. "I'm sorry. I guess the thought still overwhelms me at times."

"Perfectly understandable, I assure you," Brewer said. "More coffee? Coles! More coffee!"

The steward refilled their cups. "If I may ask," Brewer said, "what was it that killed the General?"

Lear thought as he drank. "Let me see... I believe the doctors said it was the croup that actually killed him."

Brewer shuddered. "I remember we had a young child, a girl, I think, die of croup." He looked away. "Painful way to die."

Neither man spoke for several minutes. Then Brewer stirred.

"Washington's been dead, what? Not twenty years yet, right?"

"That's right. He died in December, 1799."

"Has anyone written a biography of him yet?"

Lear thought for a moment. "Not that I know of; not a good one, anyway. A couple of hucksters have put out some tripe that's not much better than fiction. Wait a minute.... Let me see... It seems I have heard of a new biography coming that is rumored to be fairly reputable, but the author's name escapes me."

"I shall watch for it."

"Good," Lear said. He downed the last of his coffee and stood. "And now, William, I will bid you good night."

"Good night, Tobias." Brewer watched him walk to his cabin and wondered what it must have been like to work with a man like Washington for all those years.

HMS *Lydia* made port at Naples two days later, arriving at five bells of the afternoon watch. Captain Bush came on deck briefly to bid their passenger farewell. The very next morning, Bush had *Lydia* warped out of the harbor in order to set sail for Malta.

Two days later, Bush guided his frigate into the harbor at Malta just as the sun was rising high to dominate the clear blue sky. In the outer harbor, he noticed what looked like a convoy gathering. He also saw two sloops anchored nearby and fervently hoped that the convoy would be their problem rather than his.

A pilot took *Lydia* to where she could drop her anchor. Bush began to pace the quarterdeck, and Gerard and Brewer each took a glass and examined the sloops.

"Sixteen guns," Brewer said.

"Eight pounders, I'd wager," Gerard added.

"Agreed," Brewer said. "So, what do you think?"

Gerard lowered his glass. "The same as you: that we'll be escorting that convoy out of here, probably bound for Gibraltar."

At that moment, Mr. Lee, the signals midshipman, approached the Captain during his pacing and duly waited to be noticed.

"Yes, Mr. Lee?" Bush said.

"Signal from the shore, sir; our number: *'Captain to report ashore.'*"

Bush turned to see for himself—mainly to verify the number—and saw that the lad was correct.

"Very well, Mr. Lee. Acknowledge the signal, if you please. Mr. Brewer, call away the gig. Mr. Gerard, please come below with me."

Gerard followed his captain below deck, leaving all the

activity behind. The two went into the captain's cabin, and Bush began to change into his best uniform.

"What are the odds?" he asked.

"Odds, sir?" Gerard replied.

Bush stopped dressing and stared at him.

"Oh, you mean the odds that we're about to be saddled with another convoy? I would say better than fifty percent. Our best hope is that those two sloops are part of the bargain. There were at least ten merchant ships sitting over there!"

"I know," Bush said as Goodnight fastened his hanger around his waste and adjusted his coat. "Best to be prepared, I suppose. Goodnight, make sure you go ashore today or tomorrow morning. Be ready to give a dinner party for eight tomorrow night."

"Aye, sir," Goodnight said as he pulled a piece of lint from his captain's shoulder.

Bush nodded his thanks and looked to Gerard. "Let's hope you're right about those sloops."

"Captain Bush, sir," the aide said as he announced the captain of HMS *Lydia*. Bush strode in and came to attention before the port admiral's desk.

"Captain Bush," the admiral said, waving Bush into a seat, "good to see you again. I trust all has been well with you and your crew?"

"Both ship and crew are well, sir," Bush said.

Wallingford stopped his writing and looked at Bush over the top of his pince-nez. "That may be the understatement of the year, my dear sir! To date, HMS *Lydia* has brought in more prizes than any other ship in the fleet! Well done, Captain, well done indeed! Please tell your crew I said so."

Bush smiled from ear to ear. "Thank you, sir."

The admiral handed Bush a packet of sealed orders from

the side of his desk.

"Your orders, Captain. Convoy escort. You probably saw it as you entered the harbor. Thirteen merchantmen bound for Gibraltar. I am giving you two sloops to help you, HMS *Titan* and HMS *Pilgrim*. Their captains already have their orders. The last ship in the convoy should be ready to sail by noon tomorrow. Sail as soon as your ship is provisioned."

"Aye, sir," Bush said. He waited a moment, and then rose when Wallingford began writing again. He came to attention and left the room.

Back on *Lydia*, Bush went straight to his cabin, pausing only to motion for Gerard to follow him. Once the door closed behind them, he tossed his packet onto his desk and turned to face his Premier.

"You should be burnt at the stake for witchcraft," he said as he removed his hanger and coat.

Gerard smiled. "So, the convoy's ours, sir?"

Bush grunted. "Thirteen ships, scheduled to be ready to sail after noon tomorrow. We do get the two sloops to help, though."

"Destination?"

"Gibraltar," Bush answered as he sat at his desk and began to open the packet with his orders in it. "Coffee, Gerard? Goodnight!"

It was Bell, the captain's clerk, who appeared.

"Goodnight's gone ashore, sir. What can I get for you?"

"Coffee for two."

Bush opened his orders and read them through carefully. They contained no special instructions. He passed them to Gerard and sat back in his chair.

"Nothing special here, sir," Gerard commented as he flipped through the tight, handwritten pages. "Looks fairly standard. Will you speak to the captains?"

Bush nodded. "Send Mr. Starling with invitations. I want the two sloops tonight for dinner at the turn of the first dog watch, and all captains tomorrow at two bells of the forenoon watch."

Gerard rose. "Aye, sir. I will ask your clerk to write the invitations for the commanders of the two sloops. Signals should due for tomorrow."

"Agreed."

"Thank you, sir," Gerard came to attention and left the cabin.

Bush watched the door close behind his first lieutenant. He had sailed with Gerard for more than ten years now—or most of it, anyway—and he saw now what Hornblower did when he took him under his wing. Once his ego had been brought to heel by Hornblower, Gerard first developed and then blossomed into one of the best officers Bush had ever seen. Cool and rock-steady in action, he was also unintimidated by personal status. Bush smiled as he recalled the discussion Gerard had with Bonaparte regarding naval versus army artillery when the latter toured *Lydia* with the governor. Gerard quickly overcame his apprehension and at one point was actually lecturing the ex-Emperor regarding naval gunnery tactics. Bush chuckled at the memory of Gerard having to stop himself to allow Hornblower to interpret. Later, Hornblower told Bush how impressed Bonaparte was by Gerard and his tactical abilities. To Bush's utter surprise, when he informed Gerard of the compliment, the first lieutenant did not laugh or even smile—he simply looked at the deck in humility and nodded.

HMS *Lydia* led her charges out of the harbor at Malta on schedule. Bush's two meetings, first with the sloop commanders and then with the captains of the merchantmen, went about as well as he hoped. A couple of the captains objected to being forced into the convoy, but they withdrew their objections quickly once Bush gave them permission to leave if they wanted—along with a promise not to come to their aid when the pirates attacked.

He led them to a point ten miles north of Malta where the convoy formed up and headed west for Gibraltar. The convoy sailed in two columns, with *Pilgrim* to the north, *Titan* to the south, and *Lydia* roaming the waters in between, ready to race to any point where an enemy was sighted. The convoy never managed more than five to seven knots over the course of the voyage. Bush's overriding orders to both groups were to stay together above all else; he would leave no stragglers behind for the pirates to plunder.

One week later, HMS *Lydia* saw her charges safely enter Gibraltar. Bush was surprised to have only four sightings of pirate or unidentified craft on the horizon, each of which disappeared over the horizon as soon as *Lydia* showed up to investigate. Twice Bush had to recall an over-enthusiastic sloop commander from pursuing a tempting target.

No sooner had they dropped anchor than Mr. Lee approached Lt. Gerard and saluted.

"Signal from flag, sir," he said. "Our number. *'Captain to come on board.'*"

"What? Already?" Brewer said.

Gerard sighed. "Acknowledge the signal and inform the captain, Mr. Lee." He turned to Brewer and said, "I've got a bad feeling about this."

CHAPTER ELEVEN

"Captain Bush, sir," the flag lieutenant said before he stepped back to allow Bush to enter the cabin.

"Come in, Captain, come in," Freemantle called. Bush found them in the great Day Cabin, the Admiral and his Flag Captain seated beneath the stern windows and drinking wine. To Bush's surprise, both men stood when he entered the room, and the Admiral stepped forward to shake his hand.

"Good to see you again, Captain," he said. "Does the flag lieutenant have your reports? Good, good. Congratulations on bringing your convoy in. That timber is needed in England, let me tell you. Will you join us in a glass of wine? Haskins! Some wine for Captain Bush. Thank you. Your arrival here is very propitious, Captain. Please sit down."

Bush accepted his glass from the steward and took his seat to the admiral's left.

"Captain," Leeds said, "what is the condition of your ship? Is there any battle or weather damage needing repair?"

"Nothing, sir," Bush replied.

"Good," Freemantle said in a low tone. "What I am about to tell you, Captain, you cannot share with anyone until after you have sailed. Rumors have been circulating since shortly after you left about a captured French warship at Tripoli. We received confirmation only this morning that the French frigate *Liberté* of forty-four guns did indeed run aground outside Tripoli harbor while chasing a pirate xebec. The French commander surrendered rather than fight, presumably when he realized there was no hope of freeing his ship before every ship in the Bey's fleet arrived. The pirates refloated her, and she is now in the harbor sitting under the guns of the citadel."

The admiral paused to drink his wine, and Bush thought about what he had been told. It was quite impossible for the British to allow the Bey to retain possession of such a ship; if the French could do nothing about it, then it fell to the Royal Navy to act. But what? How? Bush remembered the last time their last attempt to enter the harbor and how it cost Lieutenant Calloway and his crew their lives. And that was without the Arabs on the alert with such a big prize to guard.

Freemantle set his glass on the table and turned to Bush. "Your mission, Captain, is to cut out the *Liberté* or burn her. I have two items to help you do it. Sentry!" The guard came in. "Ask Mr. Catalano to join us. We have a captured pirate xebec for you to use to sneak into the harbor. Catalano will pilot her in for you. Take it from me, Captain, there is no one better suited for the job than he is. He is an Italian who speaks flawless Arabic, right down to the accent. He has worked for us before, infiltrating pirate strongholds. He hates the pirates like nobody you've ever seen—something to do with a personal vendetta, I'm told—just so you are aware."

At that point, the sentry opened the cabin door to admit a person Bush could only assume was Catalano. He was of a short, stocky build, the muscles in his shoulders and arms evident even through his thick fisherman's tunic. His unruly hair was black as coal, his eyes nearly as dark and close set on his face. He wore a thick moustache, although the rest of his face was only covered by a day or two's growth of beard.

His legs resembled logs of the strongest oak, his muscles like springs ready to leap on an enemy.

Freemantle rose. "Signor Catalano, allow me to present Captain Bush of His Majesty's frigate *Lydia*. Captain Bush, this is Signor Salvadore Catalano, the man who will pilot the xebec into Tripoli harbor for you."

"Signor," Bush said, holding out his hand.

"Capitano," Catalano replied, nodding once and taking Bush's hand in a firm grip.

"As I was saying, Captain," Freemantle said, "Catalano will take your strike force into the harbor an hour after dark, eight days from now."

"Excuse me, sir," Bush said, "but what is to make this intrusion more successful than Lieutenant Calloway's?"

Freemantle's eyes grew cold and hard, and for a moment Bush thought he had gone too far, but the admiral blinked. His gaze went to Leeds, his flag captain, then back to Bush again, and he cleared his throat loudly to regain his composure.

"There's a very good reason," Freemantle said. "The Arabs will be eating."

Bush blinked. "Excuse me, sir?"

Freemantle turned to the Flag Captain. "Captain Leeds?"

Leeds leaned forward and set his glass down. "You see, Captain, right now the Arabs are celebrating their holy month called Ramadan, which involved fasting during daylight hours. After dark, they are allowed to break their fasting, usually with a large meal. That is what they will be doing when the xebec enters the harbor."

"Any questions, Captain?" Freemantle asked. Bush had none. Freemantle looked back to his flag captain. "You may explain the plan of battle, Captain Leeds." To Bush: "Should you decide to burn her."

Bush sat back and listened for the next hour as Leeds laid

out an extremely detailed plan for the destruction of the *Liberté*. He had to admit, it sounded plausible if they could achieve surprise and board the frigate before any alarm was raised. He wondered what Catalano would say about the plan once they were back on board *Lydia*.

"Your men can use the fire and subsequent explosion of the *Liberté* to cover their escape." Captain Leeds finished his delivery and looked to the admiral.

"Questions, Captain?" he asked.

Bush thought for a moment. "None, sir."

Freemantle rose. "Then you sail on the morning tide. Catalano will join *Lydia* immediately. His dunnage will be sent over by the turn of the next watch. Good luck to you, and God speed."

He put his hand out, and after a moment's hesitation, Bush shook it, followed by Leeds'. He came to attention and left the cabin. He was met outside by the flag lieutenant. He handed Bush a packet.

"Your orders, sir. Stores for the demolition will be ferried to *Lydia* within the hour. If you'll both follow me to the entry port?"

Bush and his guest stepped on to the *Lydia's* deck to salutes from his officers.

"Mr. Bush," he said, "this is Signor Catalano. Please see that he is squared away in the gun room. His dunnage will be coming aboard soon. As soon as that is done, please join me in my cabin."

Gerard saluted again. "Aye, sir."

Bush turned and went below decks without another word. Gerard looked after him for a moment before turning to Brewer.

"Lieutenant Brewer, please see that our guest is settled in to a cabin in the gun room."

"Aye, Mr. Gerard," he said. "If you'll follow me, sir?"

Brewer led the way below to the gun room.

"Coles!" he called. The servant appeared. "This is Mr. Catalano. He will be sailing with us. I'm putting him in the end cabin starboard. Please stow his dunnage there when it arrives. Sir," he said to Catalano, "this is Coles, the gun room steward. If you need anything, just ask him."

The steward acknowledged the order and greeted the newcomer before disappearing again. Brewer got Catalano settled in his room before returning to the deck. He stood along the starboard rail, hands behind his back, thinking, until a voice beside him broke in.

"So, sir, who's the new guy?"

He turned and saw Starling standing beside him.

Brewer looked back over the harbor. "You know as much as I do, I'm afraid."

Starling grunted in disbelief. "What, you mean he didn't say a word?"

Brewer shook his head. "Not a one."

"Too bad," Starling sighed. "I was hoping for some answers."

Brewer looked down at him. "What do you mean?"

"Turn around, sir."

Brewer turned to look across the deck and saw a xebec being towed toward *Lydia*.

Gerard entered the great cabin to find Bush examining their orders. The captain motioned for him to be seated while he finished reading. When he was done, Bush folded up the papers and locked them away in his desk before leaning back in his chair and looking out the stern windows. Gerard folded his hands in his lap and patiently waited for his captain to speak.

"Gerard," Bush said finally, "I want you to detail a prize

crew under a petty officer to man a xebec. It will be sailing with us on the morning tide."

Gerard's eyebrows flew up, and it was all he could do not to blurt out questions. He mastered himself as quickly as he could. "Aye, sir."

Bush turned back toward the window. "Thank you, Mr. Gerard. I shall see you in the morning."

"Aye, sir." Gerard rose and came to attention before leaving the captain's cabin. He pulled the door closed gently behind him and wondered what the future held.

The morning was overcast when Captain Bush came on deck. He looked around and saw that all was in readiness to depart. Gerard, Brewer, and Trench stood together by the wheel, giving him the option of pacing the deck in solitude. Tempting as it was, he decided to forego it in order to get underway as soon as possible. He walked over to the group.

"Good morning, gentlemen," he said.

"Good morning, sir," Gerard answered for the group.

"Are we ready to get underway, Mr. Gerard?"

"Aye, sir. Anchor's hove short."

"Good. Mr. Lee! Signal to flag: *Ready to proceed.* Mr. Brewer, how's our guest doing?"

"He hasn't come out of his cabin since he arrived, sir."

Bush considered it and shrugged.

"Reply, sir! *God speed.*"

"Mr. Gerard, get the ship under way, if you please. Mr. Lee! Signal to xebec! *Proceed to sea.*"

Bush watched as Peters translated the signal in his head and issued the orders to his crew. They sprang into action, and he waved to acknowledge.

"Acknowledged, sir."

"Yes, Mr. Lee, so I see."

Gerard bellowed his orders, and HMS *Lydia* was soon gliding toward the open sea with her consort in attendance. Once clear of the harbor, Bush turned to his sailing master.

"Turn us west, Mr. Trench," he said. "Match whatever speed the xebec makes under all plain sail. Mr. Lee! Signal to xebec. *Course due west. Proceed under all plain sail.*"

He went to the fantail and arrived in time to see Peters' crew working the lateen sails on the xebec. It was very different from a square-rigged sail, like those on the xebec's foremast or on *Lydia*. It would be interesting to put a xebec through her paces to see if she maneuvered better than a frigate. *Oh well, maybe one day...*

The day wore on with nothing out of the ordinary happening, which means it dragged on forever for Gerard, Brewer, and anyone else who was aching to know why the xebec was trailing them and why Catalano was secluded in his cabin in the gun room. Gerard even went so far as to order extra gun and sail drills, just to keep himself occupied. Brewer wisely decided to spend his hours off-watch in the gunroom, writing a letter to Lord Hornblower.

Once *Lydia* was well clear of the harbor and set on her course, Bush returned to his cabin. As he entered, he asked the sentry to pass the word for Sig. Catalano. He closed the door softly behind him and went to sit behind his desk. He unlocked the drawer and took out their orders. He set them on the desk and waited for his guest.

Catalano was admitted by the sentry and bowed to his captain.

"Welcome, Signor," Bush said, indicating that Catalano should sit opposite from him. "I wanted to talk to you privately regarding our mission. As I understand it, we have the option to either retrieve the *Liberté* or burn her. Which do you favor?"

Catalano shifted in his chair. "Burn her, *Capitano*. To take her out of the harbor will require more men, which means we cannot move fast enough in boarding her to make it out of the harbor alive."

Bush considered this for a moment. It was what he thought the Italian would say, but still... "Do you not consider a ship of that size worth trying to save?"

"No, *Capitano*," his guest shook his big head. "No ship is worth that many lives. If we try to save her, in my opinion, we condemn the entire boarding party to death. The time it would take to get the ship moving, even assuming they have taken no extraordinary measures, would be more than enough for the pirates to man the guns of the citadel and pummel the ship with heated shot. The ship would be lucky to make it out of the harbor before she sank or blew up."

Bush leaned forward and placed one hand of the packet containing their orders. "If I agree with you, and we do decide to burn her, are you content with the plans for doing so as laid out in our orders?"

"Si, *Capitano*. I helped develop it. It is designed to create maximum damage over a wide area. Speed is the key! If we are quick, we shall live."

Bush nodded his head. "I agree. Very well, Signor; we shall burn the *Liberté*."

He was surprised when Catalano rose.

"If you will excuse me, *Capitano*," he said, "I shall return to my cabin and meditate."

Bush rose. "Of course, Signor." He escorted his guest to the door and opened it. When the Italian had gone, he turned to the sentry.

"Pass the word for Mr. Gerard."

"Aye, sir."

Within minutes, the sentry announced the first

lieutenant. He found his captain staring out the stern windows, hands behind his back.

"You sent for me, sir?"

Bush turned and sat down. "Yes, Mr. Gerard. Tomorrow night, I would like to ask you to join me for supper, along with Mr. Catalano, Mr. Brewer and Mr. Starling, Mr. Trench, and Captain James. Make it at the turn of the first dog watch."

"Aye, sir."

At the appointed time, Gerard collected everyone invited to dine with the captain, and they made their way to his cabin. They were admitted by the sentry and found the captain seated beneath the great stern windows.

"Welcome, gentlemen," Bush said as he rose. He shook hands with each man, making his way to Catalano last.

"Signor," he said. "I hope you are settled in?"

"Yes," he said, "thank you, *Capitano*."

"Gentlemen!" Bush called to get their attention. "I'm afraid we may have a long night ahead of us, so please make your way to the table. Sig. Catalano, please sit here, at my left."

"Thank you, *Capitano*."

Goodnight's feast was up to its usual standards, Bush noting the quiet at the table and taking it for the compliment that it was. The only one who did not dig in with relish was Catalano; he ate, but not with the gusto of the *Lydia* men. Bush wondered if he was wishing it was lasagna instead. When the last plate was clean, the stewards cleared the table, and Goodnight passed out brandy and cigars.

Bush waited until all the cigars were lit before he stood, calling the meeting to order.

"I brought you here so I could brief you on our mission. The French frigate *Liberté* ran aground chasing a pirate xebec into Tripoli harbor. The pirates captured her, refloated her, and imprisoned her crew. *Liberté* is a 44-gun, 18-pounder frigate. We cannot allow the pirates to keep her. The French are either unable or unwilling to do anything about the situation, so it falls to us."

The Captain paused to gauge the reactions. The corner of his mouth turned up in a slight smile when he saw they ran the gambit from pure shock and amazement to the what-else-would-you-expect-from-the-French look on Captain James. He looked down at the table in order to get hold of himself.

"Signor Catalano will pilot the xebec into Tripoli harbor to the *Liberté*. He will be accompanied by Mr. Gerard, Mr. Brewer, and a team of forty men. They will transfer to the xebec along with the combustibles needed for the attack the day before we make the approach to Tripoli. They will be divided into four teams for the attack. Team One will set fire to the berth deck and the forward stores. Team Two will take care of the wardroom and steerage. Team Three will the cockpit and stores, and Team Four will handle the magazines. Each team will have a fast-burning three inch candle with the wick soaked in turpentine to make them flammable. This should allow just enough time for you to make your way back to the xebec and make your escape, but you must be fast. Combustibles will also be taken to assist in the burning."

He paused again. He could tell they were remembering the last time they sent a ship into Tripoli harbor.

"Now let me tell you what you do not know," he continued, "which is the reason that this incursion will succeed. Do any of you know what the Muslim month of Ramadan is?" No one did. "Ramadan is a month in which Muslims are required to fast during daylight hours. The fast is broken nightly by an elaborate meal after the sun goes down. That is what the Arabs will be doing when the xebec enters the harbor. It should delay their reaction just long enough for our teams to do their work and get out again.

"The xebec will slide as unobtrusively as possible into the harbor as soon as it's dark. Timing the entrance will be the trickiest part of the mission. We must allow the Arabs time to do their prayers and be well into their meal before any alarm is raised. HMS *Lydia* will remain below the horizon until well after dark. Then she will approach the harbor to draw the fire of the citadel and provide cover for your escape. Any questions?"

Lieutenant Starling raised a tentative hand. "Who will lead the four teams, sir?"

Bush counted them off on his fingers. "Mr. Brewer will lead team one, Master's mate Peppers will lead team two, Mr. Hanson will lead team three, and Mr. Gerard gets the magazines with team four." He looked to Gerard, who smiled and nodded. "You, Mr. Starling, will remain on board as acting first lieutenant."

"Aye, sir." Brewer thought the disappointment in his voice sounded rather insincere.

"As for the makeup of the teams, Mr. Gerard and I will make those assignments. Any other questions?"

"Will you be taking volunteers, sir?" Mr. Trench asked.

"Only to a point," the Captain answered. "I still need the right men aboard to sail *Lydia* and fire the guns." Several of the men chuckled at that. "However, I will consider some on an individual basis. Anything else?"

There were none.

"Very well," Bush said. "I remind you all that this is not to be discussed with the crew. I thank you for the evening, gentlemen, and bid you goodnight. Mr. Gerard, if you will be so kind as to remain, we can begin to comb the muster book and flesh out our teams."

On his way out, Brewer pulled Gerard aside.

"If you can sir, I should like Midshipman Rivkins to accompany me," he said.

Gerard nodded. "I'll see what I can do."

For the next two days, HMS *Lydia* sailed under a cloud. Not only the overcast in the sky, but there was a second cloud that settled over the men, for they had not yet been told their mission, and that did not settle well with many of them. Sailors were by and large a superstitious lot, and they did not like being kept in the dark.

That came to an end on the third day as the first bell of the afternoon watch rang out. Captain Bush came on deck, accompanied by the First Lieutenant. The men took notice, as this was the first time the two had appeared on deck since they secluded themselves in the captain's cabin following the dinner party a couple days back.

"Mr. Gerard," Bush said, "kindly call all hands aft."

"Aye, sir," Gerard replied. He picked up a speaking trumpet. "All hands! All hands! All hands lay aft!"

"Lads!" Bush addressed them when they had gathers before the quarterdeck, "it's time I told you where we're going and what our mission is. Listen closely." Over the next half-hour, he told them of the plight of the *Liberté* and how the French could do nothing to regain their ship. He said their mission was to set her on fire to deny her to the pirates, and introduced Sig. Catalano as the man who would pilot the xebec into Tripoli harbor. He told them of Ramadan and how the Arabs would be feasting when they moved on the captured frigate, which would give them the edge in making their escape after putting the French ship to the torch. Finally, he pulled a list from his pocket and read the names of the forty men who would accompany the xebec. He put the list away and leaned on the railing. "I know there's not a faint heart amongst you, and those who were not chosen are bound to be bitterly disappointed!" There was a murmur of laughter at that. "Never fear, I'm sure your turns will come! Now, I want those men whom I called to come aft. The rest of you are dismissed!"

The forty moved aft and sat down on the deck. Bush handed out the team assignments and introduced the team leaders, then he let them split off to discuss their individual assignments. Brewer took his team to the mizzenmast, where he sat down with his back to it. His team sat around him.

"First things first," he said. "Midshipman Rivkins is my Number 2. If I go down, take your orders from him. Understood?"

Ten heads nodded.

"Right. Now listen. Our objective is to set fire to the berth deck and the forward stores. As soon as we board the frigate, we'll rendezvous at the foremast and proceed below. Four men will be carrying our combustibles, and the rest will have swords and pistols drawn. Their job will be to protect those who's got the combustibles. That'll be Johnson, Petey, Smoke, and myself. Mr. Rivkins will be in charge of our protection. I haven't seen it yet, but I'm told that the stuff we're taking will make that ship go up like putting a match to paper, so we have to be fast about it. That means we stay together as much as possible, and you do what you're told without question. Understood? Good. As I see it now, when we get below, Johnson, you and Petey will head for the forward stores. Smoke, you and I will work on the berth deck. We have three inch candles that we'll light to give us time to get away before the combustibles ignite, but watch out—the wicks in those candles have been soaked in turpentine to make it burn through the candle fast. So don't waste any time! Set it up well, then light that candle and get back to the deck at fast as you can! Any questions?"

"Yes, sir; what's this about the party the pirates will be having?"

"It's not a party, it's a religious celebration. Sort of like when we go through Advent before Christmas back home. Anyway, they're not allowed to eat during the day, so they make a big prayer and then have a huge meal after the sun goes down. That's just when we'll be heading for the frigate. That's all the edge we should need."

Brewer watched their eyes as they digested what he'd said. He smiled when he saw the grins on their faces and their heads begin to bob up and down.

"We'll transfer to the xebec the day before the attack," he went on, "and then head for the harbor. Signor Catalano is already aboard the xebec, teaching the crew aboard how to do things in the Arab way. He also took over Arab clothing for them. The plan is that by dressing like pirates and setting the sails like they do, it might help make them—*and us*—a little more invisible, if you know what I mean."

They smiled openly at that. Even Rivkins looked like he might live through this after all. Brewer stood up.

"Right. Remember, don't waste your time gabbing about the job with the rest of the crew. They've got their jobs to do, and you've got yours. Let's leave it at that. You can tell them all about it after we get back. Dismissed!"

Ten knuckles went to their foreheads before wandering away. Brewer turned to see Rivkins standing beside him.

"Something you need, Mr. Rivkins?" he asked.

"I was just wondering, sir, whether you asked for me on this mission."

Brewer looked up at the sails overhead. "And why is that important to you?"

"I suppose it isn't, sir. I was just wondering, is all."

Brewer looked at the midshipman. "Your job is to watch my back, Mr. Rivkins. I've only got one set of eyes, you see, so I have to keep them on the job at hand. I'm trusting the rest to you, sir." He smiled at the younger man. "Bring me back alive, Mr. Rivkins."

The midshipman came to attention. "I'll do my best, sir." He saluted and went aft.

Brewer watched him go and wondered if that would be good enough.

Three days later, Brewer and his team gathered again, this time at the entry port as they made their move to the xebec. Captain Bush was there, along with Lieutenant Starling, to see his men off and wish them good fortune. He shook hands with Gerard and Brewer before they saluted him, just as he had with the first two team leaders when they transferred.

"Don't waste any time," Bush urged them. "Get in there, put that beast to the torch and then get out of there. *Lydia* will be waiting for you outside the harbor."

"Aye, sir," Gerard said.

Brewer stood on the xebec's quarterdeck and watched as *Lydia* was swallowed up by the darkness. He turned to see Gerard speaking to Signor Catalano, who was manning the wheel and seemed to be trying his best to ignore Gerard. Brewer smiled and shook his head; he knew that Catalano thought he was to be in command of the xebec and that he did not take it too kindly when Bush said that Gerard was in command. Space did not allow them to bring along any of *Lydia's* marines, but Brewer determined to be there if it looked like Mr. Gerard needs someone to back him up.

It was crowded below decks, so Brewer elected to find a quiet corner on deck to close his eyes. He dreamed about playing with a candle in his grandfather's barn when he was just five or six years old. The lit candle had toppled over in the hayloft and the barn had burned to the ground. Brewer saved himself a whipping (probably more than one) by saving his grandfather's cows and horses from the fire. He awoke with a start, flames still dancing before his eyes as he leapt to his feet. He blinked his eyes free and leaned against the railing. He was disagreeably surprised to find his shirt soaked with sweat despite the cool night's breeze. He sat back against the lateen mast and rested his head against the cool wood, praying his foolish childhood memories did not interfere with his ability to perform his duty.

The day's passage was miserable for all who were to take part in the enterprise. Gerard agreed with Catalano's "request" (to Brewer it sounded more like a demand) that the strike teams stay below deck. Brewer had to admit the Italian's reasoning was sound; they were in British uniforms (a precaution against be executed as a spy, should they be captured), a dead giveaway should another pirate ship see them on deck. The teams spent the time going over their individual assignments and rechecking their equipment.

At one point late in the afternoon, Catalano came below decks and sought out Gerard.

"We approach the harbor too fast," he explained. "We need to reverse course for one hour, possibly two, depending on the wind." Gerard considered his proposal. Catalano said, "If we enter the harbor too soon, all will be lost."

Gerard nodded, bowing to the wisdom of the Italian's words. Catalano nodded and disappeared up on deck and the xebec put about.

Brewer looked at him, but Gerard merely shrugged. "What could I say? The blighter was right!"

Both men laughed and went back to checking their equipment.

The xebec slid into the harbor in the wake of two cargo ships. Catalano quickly spotted the *Liberté* and made course for her. Gerard, Brewer, and their teams stayed as quiet and still as they possibly could; Brewer wondered if it helped that Gerard had let it be known six hours before that he would flog any man who made a sound or went up on deck before he did.

Catalano guided the xebec slowly and expertly toward the big frigate, which surprisingly seemed to be under little or no guard. As they approached their target, a challenge came from the frigate's deck. Brewer could hear Catalano speaking with whoever issued it. Suddenly a cry of "Kafir! Kafir!" (which Brewer knew to mean "Infidel! Infidel!") told him the jig was up.

Gerard knew it as well and bounded out of the xebec's hold ahead of his men. The xebec's crew had grappled near the forward chains. The first lieutenant caught Brewer by the arm.

"You take your team in through the open gun ports!" he said in Brewer's ear. "Meet us back on deck when your job is done!"

Brewer acknowledged the order and handed his box of combustibles to a hand. The frigate's gun ports were all open with none of the guns run out. They were quite accessible when he stood on the xebec's rail and leaped. Once inside, a rope was tossed to him, which he used to pull the xebec closer before securing it to a nearby gun barrel. He reached out the gun port and took back his box, then he moved inward to allow his men to enter. The gun deck was dark, but Perkins found a couple lanterns which were quickly lit.

"Johnson," Brewer said, "you and Petey head for the forward stores. Take your time and get it right, just like we practiced. Off with you, now!" He watched them head out, followed by their protection. "Now, Smoke, let's do for the berth deck. Lead the way, Mr. Rivkins."

Gerard and the other three teams vaulted over the railing onto the frigate's deck and quickly attacked the thirty or so pirates they found. The fight was swift and brutal. A dozen or so pirates escaped over the side, swimming toward shore to spread the alarm. Gerard looked around to make sure the only pirates left were the dead ones.

"Right!" he said. "Peppers, Hanson, off with you, now! Be quick about it!" He watched them disappear below before turning to his own team. "Now it's our turn, lads." He led them below. They found a lantern and used it as they made their way to their destination.

"Let's get a powder keg open. Lay me out a line of powder from here back to those kegs." Gerard looked around. "Where's that fool candle? Thank you, Masters. The rest of you, spread those combustibles out like we talked about. Yes! Just like that! Are we ready? Start up, then, you men. I'll be right behind you."

Carefully, he lit the candle. He stayed just long enough to make sure it would not go out. The delay proved very nearly fatal.

Gerard made it up on deck to find Brewer counting off the men.

"All present, William?" he asked.

"Aye, sir. We can leave any time."

Gerard nodded. "After you, Mr. Brewer."

Columns of smoke were already rising as the British fled to the xebec. As the smaller ship raised sails to move away, flames shooting out the open gun ports very nearly caught the xebec's sails on fire! Two of the hands saved the day by dousing that bit of sail with water. The xebec began to move away as fire engulfed the big frigate. Mr. Hanson smiled.

"Found quite a bit of rum, sir," he said to Gerard. "I took the liberty of having some of the men smash several full bottles around the deck to help it burn."

"Good idea." Gerard turned to see the flames spreading. Gunfire was beginning to erupt from the citadel, but none landed close yet. Gerard thought it strange that no fire was coming from any of the ships nearby; perhaps their crews had all gone ashore for the nightly feast.

Catalano steered a straight course for the harbor entrance. Gerard watched the citadel as more and more cannon were brought into readiness to fire on the xebec. They were getting the range as well. The next couple shots bracketed the small ship. Gerard looked again at the massive fort, only this time he saw cannon balls impacting its walls and disabling several of its guns. He turned to scan the darkness outside the harbor, and there he saw HMS *Lydia* illuminated by her own broadsides.

Suddenly he was thrown to the deck as the *Liberté* exploded. The xebec was tossed over the waves by the force of the blast, but under Catalano's expert hand she righted herself quickly. Brewer ran to join Gerard at the fantail to watch what was left of the *Liberté* burn. Pieces of the ship continued to rain down on the harbor; Gerard estimated that over a dozen pirate vessels moored near the frigate were destroyed by the blast.

The xebec joined up with *Lydia* and both ships moved north away from Tripoli. Three hours later, Bush signaled for both ships to heave to, and he welcomed his victorious warriors aboard. Every man shook the Captain's hand and received his personal congratulations for a job well done. When he was finished, Bush looked around.

"Where's Sig. Catalano?" he asked.

Suddenly, Catalano bounded from below decks on the xebec and scrambled on to *Lydia's* deck.

"*Capitano,*" he said, "you may want to move your ship."

Bush didn't understand until he noticed over Catalano's

shoulder a glow building on the xebec. He quickly turned to Mr. Trench and ordered the *Lydia* to move off. The xebec was engulfed in flames by the time they reached pistol shot.

Catalano nodded in satisfaction. "Too bad we cannot send her back into the harbor now."

Bush watched the ship burn as the Italian turned his back and went below decks.

CHAPTER TWELVE

The journey back to Gibraltar was as close to a pleasure cruise as HMS *Lydia* had had since she entered the Mediterranean. After dropping Signor Catalano off at Malta, they proceeded under normal sail on their westward trek. It wasn't that Captain Bush went out of his way to make it an easy voyage, it just worked out that way. The entire crew was bursting with pride at the burning of the *Liberté*, and even more so as it was accomplished at the cost of only one British tar wounded and none killed! The wound was received when the unfortunate sailor was thrown against the xebec's mainmast by the frigate's explosion.

Bush himself sat in his cabin, writing his report and wondering how long this good feeling would last. The crew even went about their drills with smiles on their faces, and the tunes and dancing that seemed to spring up spontaneously nearly every night were like he had never heard. And the Captain had to admit that he himself was not unaffected by the good feelings permeating the ship. He hosted a dinner party the night after they abandoned the burning xebec to honor the team leaders and Signor Catalano, and he also authorized an extra ration of rum for the other thirty-six team members (plus the xebec's crew) who risked their lives. Three days later, the Captain was the guest of honor in the gun room, where Coles unexpectedly showed that he was nearly as good a cook as Goodnight.

And yet, it was not all "smooth sailing" as the saying goes. Bush set down his pen as he remembered debriefing Gerard and Brewer after their return to the ship.

"You should have seen them, sir," Gerard had said. "We boarded her, and those so-called pirates fell before British steel like they were standing still! About a dozen or so got smart; they threw down their swords, dove overboard and swam for shore!"

"I see," Bush said. He looked at Brewer, who didn't seem to share the first lieutenant's enthusiasm. "And you, Mr. Brewer?"

"I was not there, sir," Brewer answered. "At Mr. Gerard's instruction, my team entered the frigate through some open gun ports."

Bush nodded and turned back to Gerard. "The operation was well done all around, Mr. Gerard. I shall be pleased to note your leadership in my report to the admiral. There is one matter I feel I must bring to your attention, however; I would not be so quick to dismiss the fighting qualities of the Barbary Pirates as a whole based solely on those whom you chased from the frigate's deck. They have proven their mettle against both British and American steel, as you put it, many times over, and you overlook this fact at your peril, sir."

Gerard had the good sense to curb his enthusiasm and look properly admonished.

"Aye, sir."

HMS *Lydia* glided into the harbor at Gibraltar for what Bush estimated would be a minimum of three days of rest, refitting, and resupply—always assuming there wasn't another emergency for the admiral to throw their way. As usual, Freemantle had the guard boat fetch Bush's reports almost as soon as they had dropped anchor. The mail the boat brought out only reinforced the good feeling that still held the crew in its grasp. Bush himself enjoyed two letters from his sister before turning in early.

At four bells in the forenoon watch, the expected signal from HMS *Victory* was seen: *'Captain come on board.'* Bush was on deck when it came, speaking with Gerard, Brewer, and Mr. Trench.

"Acknowledge the signal, Mr. Lee," he said. "Mr. Gerard, Mr. Brewer, would you accompany me to the flagship? I want to present you both to the Admiral."

"Thank you, sir!" Gerard said. Both lieutenants hurried below to put on their best uniforms.

On board the flagship, Bush presented the two lieutenants to the flag captain, who met them at the entry port and escorted them to the Great Cabin for their meeting with the admiral. As they entered, Gerard and Brewer stood by the door while Bush made his report. When he finished, the admiral was all smiles.

"Very well done indeed, Captain!" he said. "This will be a feather in your cap, I can assure you of that!"

"Sir," Bush said, "may I present two of my officers who led the mission? This is Lieutenant Gerard, my first lieutenant and commander of the strike force, and Lieutenant Brewer, who led one of the teams."

Freemantle came around his desk and shook Gerard's hand. "Mr. Gerard, your name shall figure prominently in my report of this mission to the Admiralty, sir! Once word of your exploit gets out, none will dare doubt the ability of British arms in the Mediterranean! Well done!"

"Thank you, sir!" Gerard said.

Freemantle patted him on the arm and moved on to Mr. Brewer.

And his whole countenance changed.

"Mr. Brewer," he said, "I confess to having heard your name before, young man. Congratulations on this marvelous feat of arms, by the way, although I'm not at all sure that it would make your friend very happy."

Brewer was confused. "Friend, sir?"

Freemantle stopped in front of Brewer and looked up at him, his face growing more hostile by the minute.

"Bonaparte, of course," he said in a low, menacing voice.

"Sir—" Bush stepped forward, but he was cut of when Freemantle exploded.

"Don't 'sir' me, Captain! Is this, or is this not, the man who was Hornblower's secretary and personal aide during his disastrous tenure as Governor of St. Helena? And was he, or was he not, complicit in Hornblower's *treasonous* friendship with England's greatest enemy? Of course he was! Did he not help make that Corsican Usurper's life one of ease and comfort, when he should have been left to rot on that God-forsaken spit of land on bread and water? Of course he did! *This* is a man you think England should honor?"

This was too much for Bush. He leapt to his lieutenant's defense.

"Admiral, I protest! No matter what you think of Lord Hornblower's term as governor of St. Helena, you have no right to take it out on Lieutenant Brewer! He has performed his duties flawlessly since we have arrived in the Mediterranean! He risked his life to burn that damned French frigate!"

Freemantle looked from Bush to Brewer and back again.

"Are you certain it wasn't burned *in spite of him?*"

"Admiral!" Bush roared.

"And don't think *you* have escaped my notice in all this, Captain!" Freemantle cried as he turned on Bush. "You, who sailed for so many years with that traitor Hornblower! The only reason I agreed to allow you to keep your command was that you only commanded the squadron patrolling around the island, so you could not have been directly involved in their treason. But do not think you are immune to the beach, sir! Lord Exmouth may have given you your command, but it can be taken away. So I advise you to watch your step, sir!"

Brewer and Gerard stood there at attention, Brewer's face plainly showing the betrayal he felt.

Bush also came to attention. "Admiral, in the presence of Captain Leeds, I formally protest your actions here today. Lieutenant Brewer in no way has acted in a manner which could be called insubordinate, let alone treasonous, and—"

"*Silence!*" Freemantle screeched. "You *dare* speak that way to me? You shall pay for that, sir, you may depend upon it! Captain Leeds, get these *gentlemen* out of my cabin and off my ship! At once!"

"Aye aye, sir," Leeds said as he made his way directly to the door and opened it, ushering the three shocked *Lydia* officers out of the room. All eyes watched them as Leeds escorted them to the entry port.

The three officers saluted the flag captain, and when he returned the salute, Bush read the approval in his eyes that he could not voice.

The crew of HMS *Lydia* wondered what had happened on the flagship to make their Captain and two lieutenants return with such angry visages. Bush and Gerard paused on deck, but Brewer did not stop. He went straight to the companionway and disappeared below deck. Gerard looked to his captain and was pleased to see worry on Bush's face.

Brewer did not stop until his cabin door slammed closed behind him. He fell on his bed and buried his face in his pillow, willing himself not to weep in shame. He had no idea how long he lay there, but he didn't move until he heard a knock at his door.

"Yes?" he called, with more courtesy than he felt like giving.

"It's Mr. Lee, sir. Captain wants to see you in his cabin."

"I'll come."

"Aye, sir."

Brewer rose and paused to gather himself. He laid his coat out nicely on his bed and went to see what the captain wanted.

He was admitted by the sentry, who announced his arrival. He found the Captain looking out the stern windows at HMS *Victory*. He turned at the sentry's voice.

"Ah, William, come in," he said. "Goodnight! Madeira for two. Sit down, William."

Bush sat and indicated Brewer should sit beside him. Brewer wondered if sitting with their backs to *Victory* and the admiral was symbolic or not. Goodnight returned bearing a tray with two glasses. After he departed, Bush turned to his second lieutenant.

"William, I'm sorry for what you went through on the flagship. You did not deserve it. I hope you realize that it was political in nature, not military."

"Political, sir?"

"Yes. Freemantle belongs to the same clique as Lowe and the rest of his murdering cohorts. They and their friends in Parliament thought the work that you and Lord Hornblower did on St. Helena was nothing so much as treason to the state. That was the reason we were all recalled from the island so precipitously. Fortunately, Hornblower's brothers-in-law, the Duke and his brother, squashed any formal punishment of any kind.

"Frankly, William, I am astounded at the Admiral's rebuke. Had I known he was of that stripe, I would never have asked you to accompany me to the flagship." He shook his head in disbelief. "I haven't seen that kind of behavior in a senior officer since I joined Lord Hornblower aboard the old *Renown* and ran into Captain Sawyer, and he was a certifiable lunatic!"

The two sat in silence for a time, sipping their drinks and allowing the conversation to wander. Finally, Bush finished his drink and rose. Brewer hastily followed suit.

"Well," Bush said, "I would advise you to determine how you will answer such accusations in the future, Lieutenant."

"Sir?"

"I'm sure Freemantle isn't the only one who has heard your name in connection with St. Helena. You will run into men of his stripe for the next several years, both in and out of the service, I daresay, who will want to take you—and indirectly thereby take Lord Hornblower, although they'd never dare say it to his face—to task for what they imagine you did for Bonaparte. My advice to you is to let them think what they want. They formed their opinion without any attempt to verify the truth, so your giving it to them now will likely do little to alter that opinion. In any case, all will be forgotten when we put to sea."

"Put to sea, sir?"

"Yes. While you were in your cabin, the admiral sent new orders for us. We sail as soon as we are ready for sea. We patrol off Algiers this time. Fresh hunting grounds for us, and hopefully many new prizes!"

Brewer smiled. "I hope so, sir."

CHAPTER THIRTEEN

Lieutenant Brewer decided the captain was wrong about one thing: all was not forgotten when they put to sea. Again and again, Brewer heard the admiral's vitriol as it replayed in his head. Even though he knew the truth, knew what the admiral had said was wrong, the accusations ground him down, slowly but surely.

It was during one such bout that Brewer got his first taste of relief. He was standing at the fantail awaiting the turn of the second dog watch when he would take the deck from Mr. Peters, and he was in the throws of another episode when he became aware of the presence of Mr. Starling beside him. His guard immediately went up; his hands clasped behind his back, his jaw clamped shut, and he deliberately looked the other way, hoping the younger man would take the hint and go away. Sadly, it was not to be.

"Good evening," Starling said. "I hope I'm not intruding, but I wanted you to know that I have heard some stories about what happened when you and the captain and Lieutenant Gerard went over to the flagship."

Brewer's head spun to the third lieutenant, but Starling was looking out over their wake, his attitude almost as guarded as Brewer's. Brewer very nearly began to interrogate him, demanding to know how and where and above all from whom he had heard these stories, but the captain's warning to let them be rang in his ears. He clamped his jaw shut again and forced his eyes back to the sea.

Starling continued. "Just the sort of thing that almost makes one wish that one could challenge an admiral to a duel, don't you think?"

Brewer said nothing, but inwardly thought it wasn't such a bad idea.

Starling shrugged. "It was just an idea. Strange how people form opinions without getting to know what they're talking about, isn't it?"

Brewer spared a glance at his companion, but the third lieutenant was still staring at their wake. Brewer did the same.

Starling turned and said, "I just want you to know that, in my opinion, anyone who thinks you are a traitor is absolutely mad. Crazy as the proverbial loon. And I'll gladly share that opinion with anyone who asks. Good night, sir."

He walked away without waiting for a response. Brewer thought about it for a few moments, then turned in time to see Starling disappear down the companionway. Eight bells tolled, and he moved from the rail to take the deck for his watch. For the first time in days, he was smiling.

HMS *Lydia* took up her patrol outside the port of Algiers. The first week, she stopped and searched eleven merchantmen in total, finding no captives or war-making material to confiscate, so they were allowed to proceed on their way.

It was a warm Mediterranean morning when the monotony finally broke. Lieutenant Brewer had the morning watch that day, and HMS *Lydia* was running under all plain sail on the western leg of her patrol pattern. Brewer was conferring with the quartermaster's mate at the wheel. The sun was barely over the horizon when the call came from above.

"*Sail ho!*"

"Where away?" Brewer cried.

"Off the starboard beam! Hull down on the horizon, sir!"

Brewer and the quartermaster went to the railing and raised telescopes to their eyes. It took Brewer only a few seconds to locate the small patch of white sitting on the horizon. It was growing, bit by bit, but there was no lateral shift; whatever it was, it was coming right at them. The captain's standing orders were very clear. Brewer lowered his glass and turned to the quartermaster's mate.

"Hard to starboard," Brewer said. "Straight at them, Mr. Evans."

"Aye, sir," the mate replied. "Straight at them."

"Mr. Rivkins, my compliments to the captain. Tell him we've sighted a sail on the horizon, and I've altered course to intercept."

"Aye, sir." The midshipman touched his hat and was gone.

Brewer turned to the mate. "I'm going forward."

He went to the bowsprit and turned his glass on their growing quarry. He could detect a slight shift to starboard now; whoever she was, she was definitely heading for Algiers.

"Report, Mr. Brewer."

He turned to see the captain standing beside him with a glass to his eye.

"We sighted a sail on the horizon, sir. In accordance with your standing orders, I altered course to intercept immediately and informed you."

"Yes," Bush said. "What do you make of it?"

"Course indicates she's definitely heading for Algiers, sir.

She's nearly hull up on the horizon now. I'd say she was most likely a sloop, or perhaps a brigantine."

"I'd go with the brig, Mr. Brewer," the captain said. "Return to the quarterdeck. Order Mr. Trench to alter our course three points to starboard. Beat to quarters; load the guns, but do not run them out yet."

"Aye, sir," Brewer saluted and headed aft. "Beat to quarters! Beat to quarters!" The drum of the marine drummer beat out the alert as men sprang to their action stations. Brewer himself went below to see to his guns.

Brewer felt the ship shift slightly in response to Bush's alteration to their course. *Lydia* was now moving to cut off the chase. He looked back at the captain, wondering why he had not ordered the hands to make all sail yet, but when he looked back at the chase he saw it may very well cause them to overrun it.

"Sir!" he heard Gerard call. "She's putting on sail!"

The captain was immediately beside him to see for himself.

"Mr. Trench! Another three points to starboard. Mr. Gerard! Ready the long nines. On my signal, use one to put a shot across her bow. If she doesn't heave to, we'll use the other to do some damage."

"Aye, sir!" Gerard touched his hat and went forward.

Bush watched the gap carefully as it closed. He didn't want to let this ship get past him, nor did he want to be forced into threatening her with a broadside. He would signal Gerard to fire as soon as they were within range. *Surely they saw our colors*, he thought. *That means they're running for a reason.* He put the glass back to his eye, wondering as he always did at times like this what was going through his counterpart's mind and whether or not he would fight.

Mr. Lee came to him and saluted.

"Mr. Gerard's respects, sir. He's ready to open fire."

"Very good, Mr. Lee. You can tell Mr. Gerard he may fire when ready."

Bush had thought to watch from the quarterdeck, but his curiosity got the better of him and he went forward. He arrived just to fine both the long nines run out and Gerard just pulling the lanyard tight.

"Oh, hello sir," he said as he touched his hat. "I was just about to put one across her bow. Would you care to do the honors?"

Bush held up his hand. "I wouldn't dream of it. The honor is yours."

"Thank you, sir." Gerard sighted down the gun barrel one last time before standing to the side. He pulled the lanyard tight again, then gave it a good tug.

The long nine erupted, throwing flame and smoke before it. Seconds later, a geyser of water appeared thirty yards off the chase's bow.

"Well done, Mr. Gerard," Bush said proudly. "Now let's see if we shall need the other one."

It didn't take long. The brigantine lowered its colors and hove to very quickly.

"Excellent," Bush said. He turned to Gerard. "You have the deck, Mr. Gerard. Heave to, and pass the word for Mr. Brewer."

"Aye, sir." Gerard touched his hat and headed aft, bellowing orders along the way.

Bush took one long look at the brigantine before following his premier aft. Brewer appeared on the quarterdeck as soon as he arrived.

"Mr. Brewer, I want you to take the gig and board the brigantine. Standard crew, sailors and marines."

"Aye, sir." Brewer saluted and went to find the bosun.

Bush and Gerard watched the gig as it rode up and down

over the waves on its way to the prize. As they approached the other ship, Bush turned to Gerard.

"Mr. Gerard, I want *Lydia* turned a little past broadside to the brigantine. Have the larboard guns loaded and run out. Load them with chain and aim for their rigging."

"Aye, sir."

Bush put his glass to his eye and watched what was transpiring on the prize's deck. He didn't anticipate any trouble, but he always liked to have an option in his hip pocket.

Lieutenant Brewer stepped up on the deck of the brigantine and headed for the quarterdeck. His crew of tars and marines kept a wary eye on those on the deck.

Brewer stopped before a group of men at the wheel. "My name is Lieutenant Brewer, of His Majesty's frigate *Lydia*. Who is your captain?"

A short man stepped away from the group. His skin was darkened by the sun and leathery, and he had a perpetual squint to give as much shade to his eyes as possible. He had a turban on, and his beard was full and fiery red with streaks of grey throughout.

"I am the captain, Lieutenant. What can we do for you?"

"We will search your ship, Captain. If we find Christians being held captive, or if you are transporting materials of war into Algiers, we will take your ship as a prize of war."

"No," the captain said, "I don't think you will, Lieutenant. Raise sails! Cut his boat loose! Make for Algiers!"

The brigantine's crew jumped for the sails while the British boarders gathered around Brewer.

"You fool!" Brewer cried. "As soon as Captain Bush sees what you're doing, he will open fire on you!"

The captain laughed. "With you on board? I think not!"

Brewer stood there for a moment, not knowing what to

do. Suddenly something in him snapped. When he thought about it later, he wasn't sure if it was the captain's laughter or the memory of something Bonaparte once said to him. Whatever the cause, the effect on Brewer was undeniable. He got angry and drew his sword.

"I order you to heave to," he commanded.

The brigantine's captain stepped forward and drew his sword.

"No."

Brewer raised his sword high. "*Lydias!*" he shouted. "Take this vessel!"

He charged the enemy captain.

"Sir?" Mr. Rivkins said. "The brig is making sail."

"What?" Bush rushed to the midshipman's side to see for himself. He turned to Gerard.

"Mr. Gerard, I want you to go below and put a broadside into that ship's rigging. Reload immediately with the same and give them a second. If that doesn't stop them, we'll have to close and board her."

"Aye, sir."

Bush put his glass to his eye to watch what was happening on the brigantine, but he couldn't make out much more than the fact that Brewer had attacked. He lowered the glass for a moment, his lips pressed into a firm line. *Well, if worst comes to worst, at least I'll have that to write to his family and Lord Hornblower.*

The broadside went off, and Bush automatically began to count in his head, timing the reload. He had just said 'sixty-eight' in his head when the second broadside went off. He made a mental note to congratulate Gerard and Brewer on the readiness of their gun crews. Bush turned back to the brigantine and waited for the smoke to clear.

Brewer was in the fight of his life against the Barbary captain. Thus far, his opponent had parried every thrust or slice he had attempted, and Brewer came within an inch of his life a couple of times fending off his attacks. *Lydia's* two broadsides did significant damage to the brigantine's upper works, and—even better—distracted its captain. Brewer gave ground and side-stepped several times, looking for an opening in his enemy's defenses but finding none. Brewer found himself with his back against the wheel when he ducked a slashing attack that buried his enemy's saber in the wooden wheel. Brewer quickly stepped to the side and struck at his opponent's forearm, feeling the blade bite until it hit bone. The enemy captain cried out in pain and fell to his knees when Brewer pulled his sword free. He quickly stepped up and put his sword point to his enemy's neck.

"Surrender," he said coldly.

The captain looked at him for a moment before dropping his gaze to his wounded arm and nodding.

"I... yield," he said.

Brewer stepped back and raised his sword. "He has yielded!" he called out as loud as he could. "The ship is ours!"

The last couple individual battles ceased at his pronouncement and the cheers of the British boarders. Brewer looked around and saw *Lydia* approaching.

"Leslie," he said to one of his boarders, "get some men together and get those sails down. Captain, do you have a doctor on board? No? Then we must get *Lydia's* here at once. Harrison, you and Blake look to the wounded, ours first. Where is the Sergeant of Marines? Sergeant of Marines!"

The sergeant marched up to Brewer and came to attention before saluting. Brewer noted that both of his pistols were missing and his bayonet and musket barrel were covered in blood. So was the man's uniform, in fact.

"Are you hurt, sergeant?" Brewer asked.

"Nothing worth mentioning, sir. Bruised, mainly."

"Good. I want you to take two men and search the stores below deck. Send another two to the captain's cabin to look for any papers."

"Aye aye, suh!"

"Mister Brewer!"

Brewer turned to see Captain Bush hailing him. He went to the railing and cupped his hands around his mouth.

"Sir!"

"Report!" Bush cried. "What happened?"

"The captain tried to take the boarding party hostage, sir! But we attacked and took his ship!"

Brewer saw Bush lower the speaking trumpet he was using and turn to Gerard standing next to him. He saw a smile creep over his captain's face as the two officers exchanged words, and he wished he was close enough to hear what they were saying.

"Sir?" he called.

Bush and Gerard looked to him.

"Sir, we need the doctor over here!"

Bush raised the speaking trumpet to his lips. "How many of your men are injured?"

"Two of the boarding party, sir, but many of the brig's crew, including their captain."

Bush and Gerard spoke again, then Bush turned back to Brewer.

"Mr. Gerard is bringing a relief over, including the doctor. As soon as their captain is able to travel, bring him to my cabin. Well done to all, Mr. Brewer!"

"Thank you, sir!"

Brewer watched Gerard depart on his assignment, and the captain stepped over to speak to the quartermaster. Despite his heart still beating in his chest like a racehorse, he sighed and turned back to his prize.

Yes, *his* prize. He was in command of the boarding party, and he made the decision to fight. He looked over the deck and wondered what the Corsican would say. Probably something like, *Poor M. Brewer, he takes one little ship and acts as if he single-handedly charged the guns at Lodi, eh?* or *M. Brewer seems to have confused one little ship with storming the Pratzen or dictating peace terms in Vienna!*

Brewer chuckled and remembered their last talk, when Bonaparte urged him to play the wolf and seize opportunity by the throat and to be ready to follow his star. Brewer could hear the Frenchman's voice in the back of his mind: *Well done, mon ami, but do not lower your guard. You must follow your star to the heights of glory, but it is a fickle thing. Look what it did to me...*

"Lieutenant?"

Brewer blinked his eyes clear and saw it was the brigantine's captain who was calling him.

"Don't worry, sir," he said as he stepped over, "our doctor is on his way."

"I am not worried," the other said. "Your man bound it well; perhaps I may yet keep the hand, who knows? No, I wanted to present you with my sword. It is yours by right of conquest."

He pointed to the spot on the deck where the sword lay. Brewer picked it up and was astonished at the workmanship. The blade was of a quality he had never seen in his life, and the hilt had some very intricate workmanship—obviously the work of a master craftsman.

"Very well, Captain," Brewer said, "I shall accept—on behalf of my captain."

Lieutenant Gerard arrived and took command of the brigantine. The doctor made his rounds of the wounded, starting with their captain. Brewer watched as the doctor applied a new bandage to the captain's injured arm.

"So?" he asked. "Will he lose the arm, Doc?"

Peter Wallace, *Lydia's* doctor, was better known aboard ship for his ability to win at cards and consume huge amounts of alcohol than he is for his doctoring skills. His face betrayed all the marks of a heavy drinker—his bulbous red nose, to start with—and he was rarely without the smell of drink on his breath. He was unkempt in his dress, like many of his profession; Brewer was thankful that he had not faced the need of the doctor's services.

Wallace scratched his chin. "I don't think so, Mr. Brewer. It's all a matter of infection now. Avoid that, and you're safe as houses. But if infection sets in, I may have to take the arm to save his life."

"Can he travel to *Lydia*, Doctor?" Brewer asked. "The Captain wants to see him as soon as he is fit enough."

Wallace thought for a moment and shook his head. "I'd rather not, Mr. Brewer, until I know what's going to happen with that arm."

"Mr. Brewer," Gerard said, "I suggest that you return to the ship and report to the captain. I shall send their captain along as soon as he is able."

"Aye, sir," Brewer said. He touched his hat and picked up his prize. Gerard whistled when he saw it.

"Say, she's a beauty! Where'd you get that, William?"

"From him," Brewer answered, nodding toward the brigantine's captain, still sitting on the deck and nursing his arm. "He gave it to me when he surrendered his ship."

"A beauty!" Gerard repeated. "That's the sort of thing you send home to be stored in a London bank, *Mr.* Brewer!"

Brewer gave the first lieutenant a grand salute with the blade, just as he'd seen done on parade grounds, and boarded the next boat for HMS *Lydia*.

He reported to Captain Bush in his cabin. When he finished his report, he handed Bush the sword. The Captain took it and cast an admiring eye over it.

"The other ship's captain surrendered it to me when I took his ship, sir," Brewer said. "I accepted it on your behalf."

Bush's eyes snapped to his second lieutenant. "On *my* behalf? Oh, no, William—she belongs to you, and don't you let any man tell you otherwise. You *earned* her on the field of battle, so to speak. I believe even the Corsican would approve." Bush handed him back the sword. "Besides, it will give you something to write Lord Hornblower about."

Brewer grinned. "Aye, sir, that it will."

"Good," Bush said. "Now, then, to business. We are going back on patrol as soon as the brigantine is ready. I am keeping the ship with us until I can speak with her captain to see if he has any useful intelligence for us. Did the good doctor say when he might be up to traveling?"

"No, sir."

Bush shook his head. "As I thought. Ah, well, there's no hurrying it, I suppose. Mr. Gerard has orders to stay aboard the brigantine for now, so you will fill in as acting first lieutenant until he returns."

"Aye, sir." Brewer swallowed nervously.

"You'll do fine, William," Bush said as he handed the sword back to him. "I have every confidence in you."

"Thank you, sir."

Bush smiled as he sat down behind his desk. "I want you to go up on deck and relieve Mr. Starling. Send him below for some sleep and ask him to relieve you again at the turn of the next watch. Put us back on our regular patrol for now, as soon as Mr. Gerard signals the brigantine is ready to sail. Call me if you sight anything; I shall come and decide if we shall alter course to intercept."

"Aye, sir." Sensing the interview was over, Brewer came to attention before picking up his hat and sword and turning to go.

"Mr. Brewer?"

Brewer paused at the door and turned to his captain.

"Put that last in the standing orders, will you?"

"Aye, sir."

Brewer went up on deck, relieved Starling and sent him to bed with orders to be back at the turn of the watch. As soon as Starling was gone, Brewer wrote the captain's new orders in the standing order book. He walked around the quarterdeck, his left hand unconsciously patting the Barbary sword now dangling from his hip and a smile on his face. Nobody asked him about either.

Two hours later, Gerard signaled that the brigantine was ready to move, so Brewer ordered HMS *Lydia* back on patrol eastward. The brigantine fell into place, three miles north of Brewer's frigate.

After two days on patrol, word came to Bush from the brigantine that its captain was finally deemed well enough by the doctor to make the journey to *Lydia* and be interrogated by Captain Bush. He was escorted over by two marine guards. When he stepped up on *Lydia's* deck to be met by Lieutenant Gerard, he looked around at the deck and upper works with an appraising eye, as if he was making plans for making *Lydia* his own. Gerard angrily hurried the prisoner below deck.

When they entered the captain's cabin, they found Bush seated behind his desk. Gerard was surprised when his captain did not rise to greet them. Instead, he remained seated and watched as the guards brought his prisoner in and sat him in the chair opposite. Gerard closed the cabin door and stood in front of it.

"You are the captain of the brigantine?" Bush asked. "What is your name?"

The captain sat there, looking at Bush and saying nothing.

Bush looked past his captive to Gerard. "He does speak English, does he not?"

"Yes, sir," Gerard replied. "He spoke it with Mr. Brewer. No problems."

Bush looked at the captain. "I will ask you again. What is your name?"

The captain looked at his hands, bound in chains in his lap, and sighed.

"It is so hard to speak civilly when one is uncomfortable," he said.

Gerard saw Bush's left eyebrow rise—never a good sign.

"I grow tired of your games, sir," Bush said. "Either tell me your name, or I shall have you taken to the cable tier, to be held until we arrive at Gibraltar where you will be hanged as a pirate."

Gerard was shocked when the prisoner laughed.

"Captain," he said when the laughter passed, "you have no idea how many times I have heard that in my lifetime, and yet here I am."

Bush leaned forward, one forearm on the desk. "One last chance. Your name?"

The captain looked at his hands again and sighed. "Pasha. My name is Pasha."

Bush sat back. "Now then, Mr. Pasha—"

"I beg your pardon, Captain," Pasha interrupted, "but would it be possible for me to go to the head before we begin?"

Bush granted the request, but he warned the guards to keep a wary eye on the prisoner. After Pasha shuffled out of the cabin, Bush looked at Gerard in exasperation.

"Well," he said, "the fellow has nerve. I'll give him that!"

Gerard could only agree.

"Goodnight!" Bush called. "Coffee for two!"

Goodnight brought in the two cups on a tray and set them on the desk. He turned just in time to come face-to-face with Pasha when he returned. Goodnight turned white as a sheet at the sight of Pasha entering the cabin. He dropped the tray.

"You!"

Pasha stopped at the outburst and backed up against the guards behind him. Bush and Gerard stepped in between the two, looking from one to the other in confusion.

"Goodnight?" Bush said. "What's going on?"

The servant looked nearly hysterical as he tried to focus on his captain. "What's going on? Sir! Do you not realize who you have here?"

Gerard stepped up. "Who, Goodnight? Who do we have here?"

Goodnight's eyes flew in disbelief from one to the other before focusing on Gerard.

"Who? Lieutenant, *that's Murad Reis!*"

CHAPTER FOURTEEN

Bush and Gerard stared at the man they knew as Pasha in wide-eyed disbelief. He made no attempt to deny the accusation.

"It is true then?" Bush said. "You are Murad Reis?"

'Pasha' looked at them with a silent defiance.

Bush turned to Goodnight. "How do you know this?"

Goodnight looked at Bush. "You never forget the man who killed your parents, sir."

He collapsed into the chair.

Bush turned to the guards. "Take him back to the cable tier. Keep him under strict guard. Nobody talks to him."

After they were gone, Bush and Gerard helped Goodnight to the couch under the stern windows.

"Gerard, some wine."

Gerard brought the wine, and Bush helped Goodnight take a couple gulps. The servant coughed and seemed to come around.

"Goodnight?" Bush shook him by the shoulders. "Goodnight, are you all right?"

Goodnight took a couple deep breaths and sat up straight on the couch. He took another drink of wine and squeezed his eyes shut for a moment before blinking them clear. He flushed and seemed embarrassed.

"My apologies, Captain," he said.

"Nonsense, sir," Bush said. "Tell me how you know that man is Murad Reis."

Goodnight drew a deep breath and shuddered, as though calling up a terrible memory.

"Twenty years ago, my parents and I took passage on a packet bound for Malta. Our ship was taken by Reis and his pirates. My father was one of those who fought back; he was cut down by three pirates. I saw him fall. Reis gave my mother to the three who killed my father. They dragged her below decks... to have their way with her with her, I suppose. They eventually came up without her, and I never saw her again. I believe I heard her screams, though, coming up from below. Anyway, they came up, smiles on their faces, and Reis *congratulated* them! I swear, sir, I wanted to kill them all, but I was only ten years old! I could do nothing! Nothing!" He broke down and lowered his head into his hands, weeping openly.

Bush had no idea what to do. In the end, he patted Goodnight on the shoulder and left him alone for a while, motioning for Gerard to follow him.

They turned at the desk. Goodnight had not moved, his head still in his hands, sobbing.

"What do you think, sir?" Gerard whispered.

"I don't know," Bush whispered back. "I believe Goodnight's grief and rage are genuine. The question is whether his memory is reliable after twenty years."

"He doesn't seem to have any question, sir."

"No, none at all," Bush crossed his arms on his chest and rested his chin in one hand as he thought. "Well, let's hope the prisoner settles it for us by admitting it."

Goodnight coughed and blew his nose. Bush and Gerard joined him.

"Feeling better?" Bush asked. "Goodnight, I'm sorry for the pain I have caused you."

"You couldn't have known, sir."

Bush sighed. "Goodnight, I have to ask—are you *sure?*"

The servant looked up at his captain, tears filling his eyes again. "Yes sir. I *know*. That man is bloody Murad Reis!"

Bush patted him on the shoulder. "Thank you, Goodnight. Run along, now; back to your mess."

"I can do my work, sir."

Bush shook his head. "No. I'll be bringing the prisoner back soon, and I don't want you anywhere near here when I do. Run along, now."

Goodnight rose and shuffled toward the door.

Bush called after him. "Oh, and Goodnight? Stay away from the cable tier."

"Aye, sir."

The servant shuffled out of the cabin, the sentry closing the door behind him.

"So, what's the plan now, sir?" Gerard asked.

"We bring the prisoner back in and hope he admits to being Murad Reis. Pass the word for the prisoner, if you please."

Gerard did so, and Bush resumed his place behind the desk.

The prisoner was brought in and returned to his seat. He wore the same mask of silent defiance he had when he left.

"You are Murad Reis," Bush said. "It matters not if you do not admit it. I know of five people presently in Gibraltar who have seen Reis with their own eyes. When we get there, you will stand before them, and then we shall know."

The man known as Pasha looked down at his hands, still chained in his lap, and a smile broke out on his face. After a moment, he chuckled to himself and raised his head haughtily.

"It is as you say, Captain," he said. "I am Murad Reis."

"A pleasure to make your acquaintance, sir," Bush said. "The hangman awaits you in England."

"On what charge?"

"Piracy and treason for a start."

"What piracy?" Reis cried. "I was an officer in the navy of the Bey of Tripoli, serving my liege lord the same as you do your king, Captain. We fought at all times under either a declaration of war or a letter of marque, both of which making the seizure of British merchant shipping perfectly legal. And treason, did you say? Just because I chose to go with the Muslims who captured my ship rather than be cut down? I have always considered religion a coat to be worn when needed and changed when it suits you."

"I doubt that philosophy will help you," Bush said. "It certainly will not excuse all the men your murdered over the years, or the women and children you have tortured and abused by letting your men have their way with them. There will certainly be payment demanded for that."

Reis shrugged. "War is an evil business, Captain; one is forced to choose sides. Unfortunately, someone has to lose."

Bush saw Gerard twitch behind Reis and knew all he had to do was leave the room for a moment and it would all be over for Murad Reis.

"Well, sir, now it appears that you are on the losing side," Bush said. "We are at present on course for Gibraltar, from which you will be sent until heavy guard to London and, hopefully, an appointment with the executioner in the Tower."

"That would not be wise, Captain," Reis said.

"Why not?"

Reis sat back and smiled. "To my knowledge, the Bey in Tripoli has between 150 and 300 Europeans held captive. Of course, that number does not include those held by the Deys of Tunis and Algiers. I can promise you one thing, Captain: the minute the Bey hears or even suspects that I am no longer alive, he will begin killing his captives. I can well imagine that his brothers the Deys will also do the same when they hear."

Bush's face immediately became like flint. Gerard could see it in his eyes—judgment had been passed. The Captain stood.

"That was precisely the wrong thing to say to me. Guard, take him back to the cable tier and hold him in isolation. You, sir, have warrants out for your execution on charges of treason. You are a traitor and a murderer. Get him out of my sight!"

The guards hauled Reis to his feet and quickly muscled him out of the captain's cabin.

Gerard closed the door behind them.

"Do you think he was serious?" he asked. "Are we going to regret this?"

"My only regret," snarled Bush, "is that I cannot put a pistol to his head and pull the trigger myself."

HMS *Lydia* and her prize arrived at the harbor at Gibraltar just after noon on an overcast day that threatened rain. As they approached the entrance to the harbor, Lieutenant Starling raised an alarm.

"Sir?" he said to the Captain, who was speaking with Mr. Gerard at the fantail, "something's up in the harbor."

"And what would that be, Mr. Starling?" Bush asked as he picked up a telescope.

"I have no idea, sir. *Victory's* in harbor, but she seems to be draped in black. At least, that's the way it looks to me."

"Black?" Bush was at the railing, observing the goings-on in the harbor. Gerard was beside him.

"Have you ever seen anything like that before?" Starling

asked.

Gerard lowered his glass and shook his head. "Not me."

"I have," Bush said. "After Trafalgar."

"What happened, sir?" Starling asked.

"HMS *Victory* was towed back here after the battle. In fact, if I remember right, she was moored very close to where she is now. By the time I pulled in with *Tremeraire*, the scene was almost the same as you are seeing now. The flagship was done up in mourning for Nelson, and his body was being transferred to the ship that took him to the funeral in London."

Gerard turned back to the flagship. "So, if she's made up like that again..."

Bush nodded. "Freemantle."

Just then, the pilot came aboard and confirmed that the admiral had passed away three weeks ago. His replacement arrived only days ago, and now the ship that brought him was taking Freemantle's body back to England for burial.

The pilot guided HMS *Lydia* to her berth and departed. Bush, his officers and men lined the railings and climbed the shrouds to watch as the giant crane lifted the flag-draped coffin from *Victory* to the Indiaman moored next to her. It was an impressive sight, to be sure, moving slowly and almost majestically from one ship to the other. They could vaguely hear a band playing somewhere, the melody barely reaching them on the winds.

Soon after the ceremony was over, the usual boat came around to collect the captain's logs and reports and take them to the flagship. Brewer stood next to Gerard and Mr. Trench and watched it pull away.

"I wonder who the new commander is?" Brewer asked.

"I suspect we'll find out soon enough," Gerard said. "I imagine the captain will be called to report aboard today or tomorrow."

Three hours later, a long boat loaded with marines pulled toward *Lydia*. When they arrived, the captain of marines presented Lieutenant Gerard with an order signed by the new commander-in-chief, Vice Admiral Sir Graham Moore, to turn over Murad Reis. Gerard excused himself and took the order to the captain.

"So, it's Moore, is it?" Bush mused aloud. "Do you remember him, Gerard?"

"The name is familiar, sir."

"I should hope so, Mr. Gerard! He was in command of four frigates that captured a Spanish treasure fleet in 1804! You can imagine the prize money he got from that! In 1808, the Portuguese royal family escaped to Brazil on his ship only hours ahead of the French armies entering Lisbon." Bush tapped the desk with the order while he thought. "Well, well."

"Sir," Gerard said, "What do we do about the order?"

Bush frowned and read it again, and he realized he had no choice but to turn the traitor over to the marines. He had harbored the slight hope that he and *Lydia* would be assigned to take Reis back to England. He shook his head ruefully and handed the order back to Gerard.

"Give them what they want, Mr. Gerard."

"Aye, sir." Gerard picked up his hat. "Will you be coming on deck, sir?"

Bush grunted. "To say goodbye to *that?* I don't think so. If I can't hang him, it's best he be gone."

Gerard smiled. "Aye, sir."

As he left the captain's cabin, Gerard called for the master at arms to bring Reis up on deck. There, he turned him over to the captain of marines. As he was leaving, Reis looked to Brewer.

"Take good care of the sword, lad."

Brewer did not answer, and Reis was taken over the side.

The next morning, a boat pulled out from the flagship and headed straight for HMS *Lydia*. All the tars working the oars were dressed to the nines, and the officer who sat in the stern sheets had a uniform of such quality that Brewer could only dream about it as he watched it approach. He stood beside Gerard as they received him.

The newcomer saluted smartly. "I am Lieutenant Moody, flag lieutenant to Admiral Graham. I have a letter from the admiral to your captain."

Gerard returned his salute. "I am Lieutenant Gerard, the first lieutenant. May I present Lieutenant Brewer, our second lieutenant? Now, if you'll follow me, I take you to the captain."

He led the flag lieutenant to the captain's cabin and was admitted by the sentry.

Bush rose from behind his desk. "Yes, Mr. Gerard? What's all this?"

"Sir, may I present Lieutenant Moody, flag lieutenant to Admiral Graham? Lieutenant, this is Captain William Bush."

Moody snapped to attention. "An honor to meet you, sir. Your deeds in the Mediterranean are fast becoming legendary."

"Thank you, Mr. Moody. Please, sit down," Bush said as he resumed his seat. Gerard assumed his usual position just inside the cabin door. "Now, what can I do for you?"

Moody reached inside his coat and produced a letter, which he handed to Bush.

"Admiral Graham has charged me with delivering this into your hands, sir."

"Thank you." Bush broke the seal and unfolded the letter. He read the one-page missive twice before refolding it and setting it on his desk.

"Lieutenant, you may tell the admiral that we shall be

honored to accept."

Moody rose and came to attention. "Thank you, Captain. With your permission, I shall return to the flagship."

Bush rose. "Granted, Mr. Moody. Mr. Gerard, please see our guest to his boat."

"Aye, sir. This way, Lieutenant?"

After they were gone, Bush went to the door and spoke to the sentry.

"Pass the word for Mr. Brewer."

"Aye, sir!"

A knock at the door three minutes later announced Brewer's arrival. He found Bush seated on the couch beneath the stern windows.

"You sent for me, sir?"

"Yes, Mr. Brewer. We have just had a visit from the new flag lieutenant, a Lieutenant Moody. He brought an invitation for myself and my second lieutenant to dine with him this evening aboard the flagship."

"Me, sir?"

"Yes, Mr. Brewer. Apparently, the admiral wishes to congratulate the captor of Murad Reis personally." Bush smiled and handed him the letter to read. "I presume you can have your best uniform ready in time to leave the ship at the turn of the first dog watch? Don't worry, William; I daresay you will get more decent treatment on this trip."

"Aye, sir."

Bush and Brewer stepped through the entry port of HMS *Victory* and were greeting by Captain Leeds, the flag captain.

Leeds shook Bush's hand. "A pleasure to see you again, Captain."

"And I you," Bush said. "May I present my second officer, Lieutenant Brewer?"

"A pleasure to see you again, Lieutenant," Leeds said as Brewer saluted. The flag captain looked at Bush. "Is he the one?"

Bush smiled. "Aye, sir."

Leeds turned back to Brewer. "A pleasure indeed. If you gentlemen will follow me, our new commander in chief awaits."

"May I offer my condolences on your recent loss?" Bush said.

"Thank you," Leeds answers discreetly, "but let us say things are looking up."

Bush looked at Brewer, each wondering what the flag captain's words could mean.

They were admitted to the great cabin, where they found the new fleet commander sitting beneath the stern windows. He rose as Leeds brought in his guests.

"Sir," Leeds said, "may I present Captain William Bush of His Majesty's frigate *Lydia*, and his second officer, Lieutenant William Brewer. Gentlemen, may I present Vice Admiral Graham Moore, K.B., recently appointed commander-in-chief, Mediterranean Fleet."

The officers came to attention, and Moore nodded his acknowledgement. He stepped up to Bush and offered his hand. Moore was of medium height, and inch or so shorter than Bush himself and a good head shorter than Brewer. His hair was sandy blonde with the streaks of grey one would expect to see in the head of someone with Moore's reputation for action. His eyes were dark and piercing, and he carried himself with a quiet confidence and self-assurance that was totally self-contained and autonomous. This man didn't need anyone's approval—he made all his own decisions.

"A pleasure to meet you, Captain," Moore said. "I read your reports last night before I retired and could hardly put them down. You seem to have had more than your share of excitement since joining the fleet—and certainly more than your share of prize money!"

"Thank you, sir," Bush said with a slight bow.

Moore moved down and looked up to Brewer. A quick nod from the flag captain confirmed his suspicions.

"May I shake your hand, Lieutenant? We've been chasing Murad Reis for nearly twenty years before you caught him. Believe me, you shall receive full credit in my report to the Admiralty that shall accompany Reis to London. Is that the sword you took from him? That's quite a souvenir of war, let me tell you. Well done, Lieutenant, very well done."

Brewer blushed. "Thank you, sir."

A steward arrived at that moment carrying a silver tray with four glasses of wine. After he had departed, Moore raised his glass.

"A toast," he said. "To the departed Admiral Freemantle. He served his king and country for his entire life, and Europe is a safer place for his having served. Admiral Freemantle!"

The other three echoed his toast, and they all drank to the admiral's memory.

When the glasses were empty, the steward reappeared with four more glasses on his tray. When each man had exchanged his glass and the steward departed, Moore said, "Please, gentlemen, be seated."

The admiral sat on the couch beneath the stern window, Bush and Brewer on either side of him, while Captain Leeds sat in a plush chair to the side. Moore turned to Brewer.

"Excuse me, Lieutenant," he said, "but was it you who acted as Lord Hornblower's secretary during his tenure as governor of St. Helena?"

"Aye, sir, I had that honor."

Moore nodded. "I thought as much. I understand the two of you did some good work out there. Pity it's all being torn down by the current administration."

"As you say, sir."

"And you, Captain, weren't you there as well."

"Yes, sir. I commanded the squadron guarding the island."

"Ever meet Boney?"

"Twice, sir. The first time was at a dinner party at the governor's house. The second time was when the governor brought him along during an inspection of my flagship."

"A bit odd, don't you think? Bringing a prisoner aboard a British ship of the line?"

"Bonaparte was an artillery expert above all, Admiral. I believe the governor sought to expose him to the power and accuracy of British naval artillery. He wanted to leave him with no doubt that we would not allow him to leave the island alive."

"Ah," Moore said with an exaggerated nod, "now I understand. A message Boney could not possibly misunderstand."

"Just so, sir," Bush agreed.

Moore set down his drink and sat back in the couch. "You may relax, gentlemen. I am aware of Admiral Freemantle's opinion of both Mr. Brewer and Lord Hornblower regarding their time on St. Helena, and I can assure you I do not share his opinion." He smiled as he saw both officers relax a little. "I am also aware of the admiral's words the last time you were here. On behalf of myself, Captain Leeds, and the Royal Navy, I want to apologize to you, Captain Bush, and especially to you, Lieutenant Brewer, for what my predecessor said. In my opinion, it was neither warranted nor deserved."

"Thank you, sir," Bush said, answering for them both.

The admiral's servant appeared. "I beg your pardon, sir, but dinner is served."

"Ah," Moore said as he rose, "I believe you gentlemen are

in for a real treat."

Moore took his place at the head of the table with Leeds on his right hand and Bush on his left, and Brewer sitting next to Bush. The procession began with platter after platter of roast goose, tarts, beaten butter, potatoes, French beans, fruit fritters, bacon, carrots, cauliflower, roast mutton, and apple pie carried in by the stewards. Moore was obviously a man who liked to dine well, which surprised Brewer because of how thin and fit the admiral appeared. Still, each man did his best to do the fare justice, and Brewer for his part came away from the table sated as he had not been since they left Smallbridge.

The admiral sat back in his chair as the stewards cleared the plates and passed out cigars and poured coffee for each man. He puffed his cigar to life and blew a cloud of smoke toward the deck above.

"And now, Captain," he said, "let us get down to business. At dawn tomorrow, I am putting *Lydia* into drydock for a seven day refit." The admiral paused to send another cloud of smoke heavenward. "We are sending you back to Algiers. We are receiving intelligence reports that the Dey is gathering a large fleet of xebecs and gunboats to try to interfere with our trade routes between Gibraltar and Malta and Naples. We believe he has dispersed some of the fleet along the coastline on either side of the port itself. We are also sending with you ten gunboats, each with an 18-pound carronade in the bow, and sailors and marines to man them, of course. You will have to tow them to the target. You will have to supply and officer or petty officer to command each boat, but that shouldn't be too much of a problem. I shall leave the operational planning entirely in your hands, Captain. Do you have any questions?"

Bush considered for a moment. "I fear my force is too small to do as much damage as I would like to the pirates' forces. The first attack I make, no matter where it is, word is going to spread like lightning of my presence, and all the other ships will put to sea and scatter. Is there another frigate available, or a sloop of war at least, that we can use to build another strike force around? That way, we can hit twice at the same time and then combine forces to take on the port itself."

Leeds shook his head. "The rest of the fleet is out on convoy escort as well as watching Tunis and Tripoli. I'm afraid *Lydia* and the gunboats are all that can be spared at the moment."

"And there's no chance of postponing the attack, either," Moore added. "The orders from the Admiralty in London make that quite clear. Their Lordships want the Dey's fleet sunk before it can set sail in search of our convoys."

Bush sat silent in thought for a moment before looking to Brewer.

"Any questions, Mr. Brewer? Thoughts?"

Brewer shook his head. "No, Captain."

"Very well, Admiral," Bush said. "*Lydia* will sail as soon as the refit is done and she draws extra provisions for the gunboat crews."

"Good." Moore rose, and the other three quickly followed suit. He stepped toward Bush and held out his hand, which Bush shook warmly. "Good luck. I'm sure we'll talk again before you sail."

"Thank you, sir," Bush said. He and Brewer came to attention and followed Leeds out of the cabin.

"Well?" Leeds asked Bush.

"Quite a difference, that's for sure."

Leeds nodded. "Now you see why I say things are looking up."

The officers saluted at the entry port.

"If I don't see you," Leeds said, "good luck."

BREWER AND THE BARBARY PIRATES

The week that followed was one of the busiest in Brewer's young life. Gerard tasked him with working out the sleeping and eating arrangements for the extra 300 souls who would be making the trip with them and doing the fighting in the gunboats when they got there. There was also the matter of their arms, ammunition, and powder to be dealt with. It took him four days to get all the bugs worked out, but when the men boarded the ship after the refit was completed, he was ready for them. It was a secret source of pride for him that only two problems arose when they boarded the ship, and he was able to solve those with relative ease.

CHAPTER FIFTEEN

HMS *Lydia* sailed on the morning tide, her ten gunboats in tow. Gerard had never seen such crowded conditions in a frigate. Besides *Lydia's* normal compliment of 198 men, they had an additional 300 aboard for the gunboats! He stood there on the quarterdeck and shook his head in disbelief. Forward, he saw Mr. Brewer come on deck, no doubt rechecking the sleeping arrangements for their guests. When he gave Brewer the assignment for scheduling the feeding and sleeping arrangements for their passengers, he fully expected the lad to come back to him, asking for help. In fact, the opposite happened: Brewer got the schedule done and even tested it before men came aboard! Gerard made a mental note to write a write a report for the captain, praising Mr. Brewer's accomplishment.

Mr. Starling came up to him and saluted. "I relieve you, sir."

Gerard stared at him. Was his watch over already? He head the ship's bell ring eight times. He saluted.

"I stand relieved."

He started to go below, but Starling called after him.

"Excuse me, sir, but on my up I was stopped by the captain's sentry. The captain wants to see you in his cabin, sir, along with Mr. Brewer."

"Thank you, Mr. Starling. We shall go at once."

Gerard walked forward to where Brewer was talking with some of the marines who would man the gunboats.

"Excuse me," Gerard interrupted. "Mr. Brewer, the captain wants to see us both in his cabin."

"Oh? Yes, of course."

Inside the Captain's cabin, they found Bush studying a chart of the Algerian coastline. "Good evening, gentlemen," he said. "I called you here to discuss our plan of attack. Admiral Moore left me with complete tactical autonomy, so we must decide just how we are to wreak havoc and wreck the Dey's plans. Gather around the map, if you please. Now, the first place we are going to check is this little port of Oran. It was a rich trading center at one time. The Spanish took it back from the Ottomans in the early 1700s, but nowadays it wasn't profitable enough for them, so they sold it back to the Turks in 1792. It's just possible that the Dey is using the harbor to hide some of his navy. Probably thinking we wouldn't look for much trouble that far west of Algiers, and, truth be told, there are probably quite a few merchant captains who would think exactly that." He tapped the port on the map several times with him finger. "So, we'll just pay them a visit and have a look for ourselves.

"Now, then, I have decided that you two gentlemen will each command a division of five gunboats. Mr. Gerard, I want a list of ten men we can appoint to command the individual gunboats. You and Mr. Brewer will direct your divisions independently of each other. Our goal here is to inflict maximum damage, and that is just what I intend to do."

Gerard leaned in and studied the map closely. "That's pretty close to Gibraltar, sir. We should be there by tomorrow night."

Bush agreed. "We'll take in sail during the night so that we arrive just before dawn. I think a dawn raid is an excellent way to greet these pirates, don't you think?"

Gerard flashed that fabulous smile. "I do indeed, sir."

"As for your conduct with your divisions," Bush continued, "as I have already said, I want the maximum amount of destruction we can achieve. You gentlemen will have to judge how that can be accomplished for yourselves. We must destroy their ability to come after our convoys once and for all. I have the upmost confidence in your judgment, both of you, which is why I am not going to try to dictate your targets, other then the general guidelines I have laid down."

"Thank you, sir," Gerard said. Brewer nodded his agreement.

"There is one more thing," Bush said. "I have managed to procure a supply of special grape shot known as 'boarding dose' that contains 432 balls per canister. They are to be used prior to boarding. I was only able to obtain three of them. Use them wisely."

"Aye, sir!" Gerard said.

Dawn broke two days later and found Bush, Gerard, and Brewer on the deck waiting for the report from the lookout regarding what he saw in the harbor at Oran. The crews and supplies were already in the gunboats, ready to go; only the gunboats belonging to Gerard and Brewer were still tied to the ship.

"Deck there!" the lookout called. "The harbor's packed, sir! I estimate between twenty and thirty gunboats and luggars! No xebecs sighted yet, sir!"

"Twenty to thirty," Bush murmured to himself. He paced for a moment before turning back to his officers.

"Man your boats!" he said. "Take them out!"

"Aye, sir!" Both officers saluted and went to the rails and over the side to their boats.

Bush and Mr. Trench went to the railing and watched them approach the harbor entrance, just below the horizon from *Lydia's* deck.

"Alright, Mr. Trench," Bush said. "Now for Phase Two. I want *Lydia* to take up bombardment position right behind the gunboats to support them."

"Aye, sir," Mr. Trench said. He moved off to make preparations for carrying out the captain's orders.

Bush put a glass to his eye. He saw the gunboats enter the harbor and head for the Barbary gunboats. He saw the smoke from their first volley of grape, fired at extreme range into the pirates' first rank. Two minutes later, he saw another followed three minutes later by a third. Bush knew from conversations the night before that the extra time was due to elevating the carronade in order to hit the gunboats in the rear of the formation. Bush knew gunboats would not offer much protection from British fire, so hopefully the grape would dramatically tip the balance of the engagement in their favor.

Standing in the bow of his gunboat, Lieutenant Brewer was thinking the same thing. From when he could see, the damage from the canister was extensive.

"Stand by, muskets!" he roared. He waited until the range was down to nearly twenty yards. "Fire!"

Three volleys rang out from the marine sharpshooters. In the growing daylight, Brewer saw many pirates fall. "Johnson! Signal the division to turn to port! Giles!" he said to the man at the tiller. "Head straight for that group on the port bow!"

He saw Johnson raise the blue flag as Giles was putting the gunboat over to port. The other four boats followed his as it nosed over toward Brewer's intended destination.

"Is the gun ready? Fire!" he cried. Canister and muskets spewed death toward their new targets. "Stand by to board!"

Johnson lifted the red banner to signal the order to board, but only one boat was in range to comply, the other three had become slowed in the turn and were some minutes behind now.

Brewer led twenty men from his boat over the rails and into the Barbary ship. Their grape was extremely effective; Brewer estimated only about ten of the ship's crew were still on their feet to resist, and at least two of them were already wounded by the grape or supporting musket fire. Brewer drew his sword and struck down two of those that remained in quick succession; by the time he turned around, his men had finished the job. He saw the boarding party from his second boat was fighting for the vessel next to his. Caught up in the moment, raised his sword high.

"Come on, men! Follow me!"

He leapt over the railing into yet a third Barbary gunboat. Ten men had followed him before he heard a cry behind him. He turned quickly to see that the boats had drifted apart so that no more of his men could join him. He turned back to see that his ten were faced with around forty fresh pirates. Only then did it dawn on Brewer that he had allowed no time to send a grape volley into the rear ranks of the pirate gunboats. *Oops,* he thought ruefully. *Have to remember that for next time!* In the meantime, he did the only thing he could think of—he raised his sword.

"Charge!"

His ten men drove into the Barbary crew. Brewer struck two down before turning just in time to parry a blow aimed at his leg. He quickly pulled a pistol from his belt and shot the pirate before clubbing yet another in the head with it. He ran his blade up and under the pirate's ribs before he could recover, and the man fell where he stood.

The deck was fast becoming an issue, covered as it was with blood. Brewer was just about to find a better place to stand when he saw the crowd of pirates before him part like the Red Sea before Moses. Advancing on Brewer was a mountain of a man. Brewer estimated him to be 6'8" and around 300 pounds, all of it solid muscle. Oddly, the thought *This is what Goliath looked like!* flashed though Brewer's mind. This was evidently the captain of the boat.

"Surrender!" Brewer cried.

Goliath laughed. Then he roared, and charged at Brewer with his scimitar high.

Brewer moved to dodge the attack and promptly slipped on the bloody deck. His stumble threw off Goliath's attack, and the Barbary giant running into him as if they were playing a football game or wrestling. In any case, the blow knocked Brewer to the deck and caused him to slide several feet on the bloody surface. He spun to raise his sword to block the killing blow he expected to receive, but his life was saved by a British marine who jumped in and occupied Goliath's attention. As Brewer shook his head clear and scrambled to his feet, his savior was rapidly losing his fight with the giant. He later counted eleven slash and stab wounds on the marine's head, chest, and arms. Just as Brewer rose, Goliath raised his scimitar for a crushing blow to the marine's head. Brewer grabbed a pike off the deck and buried it in the giant's chest. The man just had time to scowl at Brewer before he fell dead at their feet. Somehow, the marine was still on his feet.

"Thanks," Brewer said.

"My pleasure, sir."

Brewer bent down and picked up the giant's scimitar and handed it to the marine.

"You're going to want to keep that. You earned it."

The man grinned. "Thank you, sir."

"Sit down," Brewer told him. "Be safe. You've done your part. Get back to the doctor as soon as you can."

"Aye, sir."

Brewer made his way to the other end of the Barbary gunboat. He could see the last three boats of his division were shelling the other five Barbary gunboats of this grouping before they could get away. He also saw that scores of Barbary pirates were in the water, abandoning their gunboats and swimming toward shore. He nodded to himself; not a bad morning's work at that. He headed back toward his own gunboat to organize a way to sink all these damaged gunboats.

Gerard was also satisfied with their initial grape barrage on the Barbary gunboats. When the range closed to about twenty yards, he raised his sword.

"Marines! Fire! Fire at will!"

His sharpshooters loosed two volleys before settling down to pick out individual targets. Gerard smiled and wished them well.

A tar grabbed his arm and pointed to starboard. "Sir! Look! Five of the buggers is tryin' to escape!"

Gerard saw the man was right. "Hoskins! Yellow flag!" This was the signal for the division to turn to starboard. "Yost! Steady up straight at that group trying to get away! Cut them off!"

"Aye, sir!"

Gerard's division made the turn in better order than Brewer's did, and soon they were traveling line abrest.

"Open fire!" Gerard shouted.

His carronade erupted grape and flame, and his other boats followed suit. The smoke prevented him from judging the success of his maneuver. Hoskins came up and shouted in his ear.

"Word from the next boat, sir! We've driven them aground, sir! All five!"

"Marvelous!" Gerard said. "Blue flag, Mr. Hoskins! Let's get back after the others!"

"But, sir! What about these?"

Gerard smiled. "I think we can rely on the captain to deal with them."

"Oh, aye, sir!"

"Sir!"

Bush turned at the call from Mr. Lee in the mizzen shrouds.

"Mr. Gerard is chasing five of the rotters off to starboard. Looks like they've run aground, sir!"

Bush went to the starboard rail to see for himself. "Right you are, Mr. Lee! And there's Mr. Gerard moving off, kind enough to get out of our way," he called. He went to the waist. "Mr. Starling! Run out the starboard battery. You have five sitting ducks beached coming up. Fire when your guns bear, and make every shot count!"

"Aye, sir!"

Bush moved back to the rail, hoping Starling would take that as a sign of the captain's confidence in him. Within three minutes, the first guns of the starboard battery went off. It continued with guns firing singly or in pairs throughout the broadside. Bush had the great satisfaction of watching shot after shot strike home. Debris was thrown skyward from each of the five boats until they were all pounded into matchsticks. Bush walked back to the waist.

"Well done, Mr. Starling!" he called below. "Reload and stand by!"

Gerard swung his division back around and straight into

the side of the main body of the Barbary gunboats. He kept his guns blazing, cutting down pirates as they tried to flee. Suddenly, he remembered a conversation he had with Hornblower when *Lydia* was on her way back from the Pacific Ocean all those years ago. Hornblower was telling him about an ancient weapon that the Greeks had but was lost to us today. What was it called? Oh, yes—*Greek fire!* Hornblower told him that witnesses described it as a blanket of liquid flame fired from a cannon of some sort! *That* kind of weapon would be perfect for destroying all these gunboats at a stroke.

Gerard set course for a group of seven gunboats and signaled his division to surround the pirates and board. They pounded the Barbary ships with grape as they approached, and it occurred to him that they might do better with 6-pounders rather then carronades, as the solid shot might have a better chance of holing and sinking the pirate gunboats.

His plan worked to perfection. Three of the Barbary craft collided, and their crews abandoned their sinking ships. He personally led the boarding party for one gunboat, but finding it abandoned by its crew and settling in the water, led took his men over the rail to another craft and captured it. He surveyed the scene and saw that his division had captured or sunk every one of the pirate ships.

He made his way carefully back to his own gunboat. Hoskins touched his arm again to get his attention.

"Sir!" he shouted in the first lieutenant's ear, "Signal from *Lydia*: *Recall.*"

"What?" Gerard spun and saw at once that it was true. "Why? Oh, it doesn't matter. Hoist the blue flag. Make course for the ship."

Bush watched the slaughter from the safety of his ship,

but he was far from satisfied. His men were killing Barbary pirates left and right, but so far few of the gunboats themselves had been sunk. The carronades were not capable of inflicting enough damage on the boats themselves to sink them. He snapped his glass closed and handed it to the quartermaster's mate while he walked to the other side of the quarterdeck to pace and think. Killing the pirates was not enough, he knew; they could always find more men. But without the *ships*, they could not attack the convoys no matter how many men they had. No, they had to find a way to destroy the ships themselves. Apparently, that was a job for *Lydia*.

He stopped pacing. "Mr. Lee, recall our gunboats immediately."

He watched as the gunboats made their escape from Oran, each towing several prizes behind them. He turned and walked to the waist.

"Mr. Starling!"

The third lieutenant stepped into view. "Sir?"

"We are about to enter the harbor," Bush said. "Have all guns loaded and run out. Your targets are the gunboats still floating in the harbor. On your order, all guns may fire at will, as they bear. Instruct your gun captains to make every shot count; we cannot afford to waste neither shot nor powder when we still have Algiers to deal with."

"Aye aye, sir!"

Mr. Lee approached him and saluted. "Gunboats returning, sir."

"Thank you, Mr. Lee." Bush grabbed a speaking trumpet and walked to the larboard rail. He looked down to see Mr. Gerard's boat about to hook on.

"Mr. Gerard," he called down to the boat, "you should come aboard now. Have your division proceed outside the harbor to wait for *Lydia* there. Tell them to be ready, in case we need to be towed out of the harbor."

The confusion showed on the first lieutenant's face, but he was too good an officer to allow it to affect him. He turned and gave some brief orders to his boat captain before springing to the ladder and making his way on deck. When he arrived, Bush handed him the speaking trumpet and returned to the quarterdeck, and Gerard repeated the captain's instructions to Brewer when he arrived.

The two officers found their captain speaking to the sailing master by the wheel.

"I'm just not sure we can get back out again, Captain," Trench said.

"The gunboats are standing by, in case we need towed out of the harbor, Mr. Trench," Bush reassured him. He turned to see Gerard and Brewer approaching.

"Gentlemen, congratulations on a job well done," he said to them. "I look forward to hearing your reports when this day is over. In the meantime, I find that I am dissatisfied with the actual damage done to the Barbary gunboats themselves. Now, now, Mr. Gerard, there is no need to protest or explain yourself. In watching the action, I realized that the pirates' boats are not built as flimsily as we thought, and the 18-pound carronade simply cannot sink one even within a half-pistol shot. Therefore, I have decided to take *Lydia* inside the harbor and sink those boats. Mr. Brewer, report to your guns. I must tell you, Mr. Brewer, that Lieutenant Starling did well in directing the guns during the day. I have given him orders already to the effect that on his orders, the guns may fire at will as they bear. I also cautioned him not to waste ammunition."

"Aye, sir." Brewer saluted and was gone.

"Now, Mr. Gerard, let's make some kindling."

Brewer stepped below deck and walked forward between

the batteries. Starling came up and saluted.

"Sir," he said, "the captain has ordered all guns loaded and run out. Gun captains are ready to fire at your order, and then they are to fire at will as they bear."

"Very well, Mr. Starling," Brewer said, "although I believe the captain said they were to fire at *your* orders. I wouldn't dream of countermanding that order. Besides," Brewer grinned at him, "I understand you did well this afternoon, so you earned it."

Starling grinned. "Thank you, sir."

Both men walked down the batteries as they felt the ship make her way into the harbor, checking with each gun captain to make sure they understood their instructions. Soon there came a cry down from the quarterdeck to stand by, after which the ship turned hard to port, presenting the starboard battery to the targets. Brewer watched Starling hold himself in check from giving the order to fire too soon; instead he waited until the ship had completed her turn and every gun had a target.

"Fire!" he roared.

The broadside was ragged, as might be expected when the captains were picking their own targets. Brewer and Starling watched as the guns went off singly or by twos or threes, then urged the crews to reload and fire as quickly as they could.

The view was obstructed to the men on the gun deck, but Bush and Gerard had climbed part way up the shrouds in order to avoid the smoke, and they saw the shot strike home. Time and again they saw the bows of the gunboats collapse when struck by the 12-pound shot or splinters fly high into the sky. The second broadside brought more of the same, with ships cleaving in two and going down within minutes.

"Mr. Gerard," Bush said, "order a cease fire while we go about."

"Aye, sir." Gerard jumped down and stepped over to the

waist. "Cease fire! We're going about! Fire as your guns bear!"

"Aye, sir!" Starling answered.

Bush jumped to the deck. "Mr. Trench! Take us about! Let's give the larboard battery a turn!"

"Aye, sir!" Trench grabbed a speaking trumpet and began bellowing orders, hands jumping to their tasks to turn the frigate around.

Gerard joined his captain on the quarterdeck. "What do you think, sir?"

Bush looked around. "I think if we don't run aground, we should be all right. Two broadsides and then we put to sea again."

They two again took their place in the shrouds, and were rewarded with more of the same, with shot sending splinters heavenward as it crashed through both sides of gunboat and then went into the one beyond. After the second broadside, Gerard ordered a cease fire and told Mr. Starling to secure the guns.

The captain jumped down to the deck and moved aft.

"Mr. Trench," he said, "hard to starboard. Take us out to sea to meet the gunboats."

"Aye, sir."

Bush pulled out his watch. The entire action had taken less then two hours, and they were leaving behind wreckage that would take the Dey a long time to replace.

CHAPTER SIXTEEN

They found the gunboats just over the horizon from the harbor's entrance.

"Heave to, Mr. Trench," he said. "Let's get the crews aboard and tend to the wounded."

Bush stood on the quarterdeck, feet spread and hands behind his back, and watched as his warriors came back aboard to rest. From what he could see, casualties were lighter than expected, but then there was the occasional man who was carried up on deck, bandaged and bloody, who reminded the captain how hard fought the battle was.

After the men were aboard and the gunboats rigged for towing, Bush turned the *Lydia* east and set course for Algiers. After making sure all was well, he turned to Gerard.

"You have the deck, Mr. Gerard," he said, "I am going to check in with the surgeon."

Bush made his was below. The sickbay was his least favorite place to visit on the ship, and yet he knew it to be the more important after a battle. The wounded needed to know that he cared.

He walked in and immediately found little room for maneuver. Mr. Wallace and his mates were busy sewing up slash wounds. It was all he could do not to cringe at the cries made when those wounds were probed for debris.

He was surprised to see Mr. Brewer in the sickbay, standing beside one of the marines who was badly wounded.

"Mr. Brewer?" he said. "Why are you here? Were you wounded?"

"Hello, sir," Brewer replied. "No, I wasn't wounded. I was checking on the man who saved my life. Sir, my I present Corporal Grouper? When I slipped and fell on a bloody deck, Grouper stepped in and fought a huge pirate. He received his wounds—how many did you say, Simmons?"

The surgeon's mate answered without looking up from his sewing. "Eleven."

"Eleven wounds, sir, holding off this pirate until I could get back on my feet and finish him off. I would have been dead, sir, were it not for him."

"Twas nothing, sir," the corporal grimaced. "Just doing my duty."

"Yes, well, I thank you anyway, Corporal," Bush said. "Your name will be featured in my report to the Admiralty."

The marine nodded his thanks as he bit his lip in an effort not to cry out.

Bush turned away and went to find Wallace.

"What's the butcher's bill?" he asked.

The surgeon wiped his hands on a rag and looked around. "Believe it or not, sir, we didn't lose a single man dead. We do have twenty-seven wounded, Mr. Brewer's marine being the most serious. No, I'd say we were lucky this time."

"Yes, well, thank you, doctor," Bush said. He turned and made his way out of the sickbay, pausing to speak to two or three men along the way. He stopped with his hand of the companionway step and decided to head to his cabin instead. When he arrived, he instructed the sentry to pass the word for Mr. Gerard.

The first lieutenant arrived and was admitted by the sentry. Bush set down his pen and motioned for his premier to sit down.

"I'd like to hear your preliminary report, Mr. Gerard."

"Aye, sir," Gerard replied. He spoke for over half an hour, detailing the actions of his division during the battle in Oran's harbor. For his part, the captain listened closely without interrupting until his first officer was finished.

"Pass the word for Mr. Brewer, if you please," Bush said.

"Aye, sir." Gerard went to the door and relayed the order to the sentry. When he returned, he found the captain sitting back in his chair with his eyes closed. His hands were clasped in front of his face, forefingers steepled and touching his nose. Gerard resumed his seat and waited for the arrival of Mr. Brewer.

When Brewer arrived, Bush opened his eyes just long enough to request his report. Brewer looked to Gerard, who motioned for him to proceed. Brewer's report was a little longer than Gerard's, but it differed little in general outline. When Brewer finished, Bush murmured his thanks to both of them, then he rose and began to pace the length of the day cabin. Gerard looked at Brewer and shrugged, and the two officers settled down to wait for their captain to finish his pacing.

When he finally ceased, Bush resumed his seat and picked up his pen.

"Thank you, gentlemen, for your reports," he said. "You've given me a great deal to think about before we reach Algiers. Mr. Gerard, I want you to arrange a meeting tomorrow at four bells of the forenoon watch. I want the three of us, the individual gunboat captains, and Captain James to attend."

"Aye, sir," Gerard said. "Might I suggest holding it in the gun room, sir? It's bigger and can accommodate the group better."

"Agreed," Bush said. He rose and shook each man's hand.

"I will expect your written reports then. And congratulations to both of you. Your work today was extraordinary. I shall see you are given full credit in my report to the Admiralty. Now I must bid you goodnight."

The officers came to attention and left the cabin.

After they had gone, Bush sat down and set his pen off to the side. During his pacing, he had come to realize that he was thoroughly disgusted with the day's achievements, but his disgust was not with the men in the gunboats but with himself. The destruction at Oran could have been total and complete had he only realized that it was not the men that had to be destroyed by the boats in order to safeguard the convoys. Had he realized that, he could have arranged with Admiral Moore to have the gunboats rearmed with 6- or 8-pounders firing solid shot. A couple hits with either of those would have been sufficient to sink a Barbary gunboat.

He rose and went to his cabin door to pass the word for Goodnight. When the servant arrived, he requested as pot of strong coffee. He sat down again and tried to resume his report to London, but he set his pen down again after only a few lines. In less than forty-eight hours he would be sending his men out again, this time into the harbor at Algiers itself. He unlocked his desk and pulled out the packet containing his orders and background papers. From that he extracted the map of the coast surrounding Algiers. There were any number of small harbors he could hit, but that would alert the Dey to his mission and the main force at Algiers would undoubtedly by dispersed immediately. He stared at the map and sighed. No, it had to be Algiers itself, and it had to be the day after tomorrow. He could neither afford nor justify giving the Dey the chance to either disperse his fleet or use it against British convoys.

He arose again and resumed his pacing. He was still faced with the same problem—how to ensure the destruction of the

Barbary gunboats. Obviously, he would not be able to take *Lydia* into the harbor to sink them at leisure. The map identified three strong forts guarding the entrance to the harbor. *Lydia* would have to keep them busy in order for the gunboats to get inside unmolested. So, if *Lydia* could not shell them, the obvious answer was to burn them, but how could he do that? All he had were his gunboats, and—

He pulled up. Wait, that was not *all* he had. He also had the gunboats brought out from Oran. How many did Gerard and Brewer say they brought out total? Eight? Twelve? It was then that an idea burst upon his mind like a star shell. Fireships! He could make those extra gunboats into fireships and turn them loose on the shipping at Algiers. Bush smiled. Yes, that would do nicely.

Bush walked into the gun room as the ship's bell struck the fourth time and walked straight to his place on Gerard's right hand. As the meeting was held in the gunroom and not in the captain's cabin, Gerard had precedence. Bush saw that everyone else was here. As soon as he sat down, Gerard rose and opened the meeting, turning the floor over to the captain.

Bush rose. "First, let me thank you all for the destruction wrought on the Barbary ships at Oran. Very well done. However, I was not satisfied, and the fault was mine, not yours. I should have realized that our main objective was to sink the pirate ships, not so much to kill their men. I mean, they can always get more men, but sink their ships and the convoys are safe. Had I thought of it, I could have asked Admiral Moore to rearm our gunboats with 6- or 8-pounders, which could have done some damage to their boats. Since then, I have been wracking my brain to find a weapon we can use, and I have found one. We shall use captured gunboats as fireships. How many did you bring out?"

Gerard looked to Brewer. "Seven?"

Brewer nodded, and Gerard looked back to Bush.

"We shall pack them with as much combustible material as possible. Mr. Gerard, ask the gunner to come up with a quick lighting process that cannot fail."

"Aye, sir."

"Those boats are small, and once they light up it won't take long for them to burn to the waterline. Make sure you don't light them off until you are practically in contact with the Barbary ships in the harbor. I hope this will give us a way to make sure that the Dey's fleet is useless to him by the time we leave.

"Remember, *Lydia* will not be there to come to your aid. I fully expect that our attention will be completely taken by the three forts that guard the harbor entrance. You will be on your own. Get in there, do your worst, and then get back out. Head past Lydia out to sea. We shall make sure none of the Dey's ships try to follow you."

Bush paused and looked around the room. He looked at the faces of the gunboat captains and found to a man a look of confidence on their faces. Gerard and Bush looked as though they were trying to figure out how to accomplish their mission; Bush smiled at that, knowing that when the time came, they would do their best, which was all he could ask of them.

"Any questions?" Bush asked.

There were none, and Bush dismissed the meeting. Afterward, Gerard and Brewer joined him in his cabin.

"Timing the incursion into the harbor is going to be difficult," Bush said as Goodnight handed them each a glass of port. If *Lydia* opens fire on the forts too early, it will alert the boats in the harbor that something is heading their way. On the other hand, any delay in opening fire may give the forts a chance to open fire on the gunboats before they can reach their targets."

"Hopefully, they won't see us for a while," Brewer said.

"Not likely," Gerard said. "We have to use the sails to go in; it would take too long to go in using the oars. We have to hit them before they can get a defense organized."

"Sir," Brewer said, "might I suggest that two or three of the gunboats be detailed to remain close enough to *Lydia* to tow her out, should she become dismasted?"

"Good idea, Mr. Brewer," Bush agreed. "You and Mr. Gerard detail whom you think necessary, but inform all your commanders to be ready, just in case."

"Aye, sir."

The dawn brought the British fortune by way of a heavy mist south of them in the direction of Algiers. Gerard and Brewer urged their men to load quickly so as to take advantage of the fog, and they bid the frigate goodbye a full thirty minutes early.

The captain and sailing master stood by the rail and watched their men fade into the semidarkness.

"I've got a bad feeling about this," Bush said.

"So do I, Captain," Trench agreed. "How are we going to follow them and engage the forts in this fog without giving them away?"

Bush turned to his sailing master and handed him his glass. "Very carefully, Mr. Trench."

Brewer was not entirely comfortable with the fog, either. Yes, it was hiding them, but he could hardly see the boats to his immediate left and right, and the fog might dissipate at any moment. He turned and looked behind him, trying to penetrate the mist to see the three of his boats that towed the fireships assigned to his division. He hoped those igniter packs the gunner came up with did their job. If they failed, he had managed to grab a length of quick match to use as a backup.

As they neared the harbor entrance, Brewer noticed patrol boats crossing their course to the south. If they saw the approaching British, or worse yet, if they collided with one of the oncoming gunboats, it would ruin the element of surprise. He was just about to alter course when they heard the sound of *Lydia's* 12-pounder guns going off. The captain must has opened fire against one of the forts. Brewer hurriedly signaled his boats to push on ahead. He looked around nervously; the fog was beginning to clear.

Gerard paid no attention to the fog. He saw, as Brewer did, the Barbary patrol boats cut across their path, and it was all he could do not to open fire on them. The reports of *Lydia's* guns engaging the forts were an unwelcome surprise, but he pushed ahead and concentrated on looking for the Barbary fleet. He was just about to curse the fog when his division ran out of it just as if they had passed through a curtain. The dim morning light revealed the harbor to be full of ships, few of which were larger than a schooner. He looked behind him to ensure the precious fireships were still with him, and he saw all four. Relieved, he turned forward to pick out his first target of the morning. He saw about ten gunboats gathered close in around a schooner. He changed course toward them.

Gerard orders his boat to fire one of the 'boarding doses' into the schooner; the force of 432 balls hitting something as lightly made as the schooner took the mast and left the hull settling in the water. Gerard didn't even bother to board her, so sure was he that she was done for. They grappled with a gunboat beside her, and Gerard led his men over the rail. No sooner did his boots land on the deck than he noticed a pirate across the deck pointing a pistol at him. He saw the pistol go off and felt it as the ball barely missed him and plowed into the railing next to his forearm.

A huge Mameluke appeared in front of him and lunged at Gerard with a pike. Gerard swung his saber to try to block the blow, but his blade broke when it impacted with the steel head of the pike. He did succeed in deflecting the pike; it ended up inflicting a flesh wound in his left shoulder. Gerard managed to knock the pike away as the big Mameluke tackled him. The two men wrestled on the deck, and Gerard ended up on top. He looked up just in time to see a pirate raise his scimitar high, intending to bring it down across his neck and back. His life was saved when a seaman named Daniel Frazier, already wounded in both arms, threw his body into the blade's path, sacrificing his own life for his lieutenant's. The Mameluke took advantage of Gerard's distraction to flip him over, holding him down by placing one huge hand in the middle of the Britisher's chest. Then, in one smooth motion, he reached into his waistband, pulled out a curved dagger, and made a thrust at Gerard's head. Gerard barely managed to hit his enemy's arm on its way down, causing the dagger to strike the deck with a thud, missing his head by two inches. The next thing Gerard knew, he heard a pistol being fired, and he felt the Mameluke fall to the deck beside him. He allowed himself to collapse against the deck for a moment to regain his breath, then he saw a hand in front of his face.

"Say, Lieutenant," the marine said, "what say we finish this, eh?"

Brewer, too, was surprised to burst from the fog and mist into the open air, and despite the dim morning light, he is able to estimate that between forty-five and fifty vessels crowd the harbor. Off to his right, he sees a brigantine at the head of some fifteen or more gunboats and changes course toward them.

He and the boat next to him hit the brigantine with the last two 'boarding dose' canisters, firing a total of over 850 balls across its deck and upper works. He led the boarding party over the rails and found dozens of pirates dead or dying on the brigantine's deck. He estimated less than fifty stepped forward to resist their action.

Brewer's men leapt into the fray. Brewer himself shot one pirate as he ran a second through. He freed the blade in time to parry a thrust. He pinned the pirate's sword to the deck while he pulled a dagger from his belt and ran it through the man's neck. He turned to find the next opponent and was surprised to find the deck empty. The pirates had abandoned the ship and fled over the rail to try to reach shore.

Brewer paused and looked around. Their canisters had done considerable damage to the ship's upper works; lines hung loosely and several small lengths of spars littered the deck.

"Spokes!" he called. "Take two or three men and go below. Let's burn this ship, and hopefully it'll take all these around her when she goes!"

The tar showed a huge gap-toothed grin. He saluted and dashed off on his errand.

"Turner!" Brewer called. "Get some of this debris over the side. I want to encourage the fire to travel from ship to ship."

"Aye, sir!"

The work was completed in ten minutes, by which time Brewer smelled smoke rising from below decks. Spokes and his men reappeared, and Brewer pushed them back to their gunboat. They pushed away from the brigantine and turned back toward the middle of the harbor. Brewer looked back to see flames licking out the open gun ports at the gunboats next to the flaming ship. Minutes later, the brigantine exploded as the flames reached her magazine. At least five gunboats were destroyed in the blast, and all the rest were on fire from falling debris.

And the best part was, he was just getting started...

The harbor at Algiers is protected by three forts, one to the west and the other two on a spit of land curving around to the east of the entrance. It was these that occupied Captain Bush and the crew of the *Lydia*. His plan was two-fold. First, he would bombard each of the forts in turn in order to keep their attention outward and not on the gunboats, and second, he would sink any craft that attempted a breakout from the harbor. After the gunboats disappeared into the mist, Bush called the sailing master to his cabin and spent the better part of an hour going over the charts regarding Algiers. They went back on deck and took *Lydia* off to the west before turning to approach the western fort.

"Mr. Starling!" he called from the waist, "fire as your guns bear!"

"Aye, sir!"

Bush walked back to the starboard rail and watched the fort through his telescope. It looked peaceful and quiet; that would change when Starling announced their presence. Bush only hoped that that would happen before they spotted *Lydia*.

His wish was granted when he heard the word "fire" drift up from below deck, followed immediately by a ragged broadside being launched at the fort. He hurriedly put the glass back to his eye and was rewarded by seeing several balls impact the fort and one or two hitting a gun port and disabling the gun. Habit built during years of command had him timing the reload, and he was pleased when a second broadside was fired seventy-five seconds after the first.

"Mr. Trench!" he called. "Bring us about!"

"Aye, sir!"

Bush went to the waist. "Mr. Starling! Well done, starboard battery! Now ready the larboard battery for two broadsides!"

"Aye, sir!"

Bush turned and watched the hands execute the sailing master's commands to bring the ship about and reverse her course. He moved to the larboard rail and again raised the glass to his eye. He saw the first shots from the fort being fired; he lowered the glass in time to see them land a good fifty yards short of the ship. Bush smiled; that meant that in all likelihood *Lydia* would fire her two broadsides and be away before the fort could get the range.

The larboard battery threw its flame and shot at the fort, and again Bush witnessed several of the balls strike the walls of the fort. The second broadside followed eighty-three seconds later.

"Mr. Trench, hard to starboard! Take us out to sea!" Bush cried.

"Aye, sir!"

Bush began pacing the quarterdeck while his ship appeared to make its escape. That was part of the plan—they hoped to fool the pirates into thinking that the frigate made its two passes at the fort and then fled for the safety of the sea. As soon as the fort dropped below the horizon, Bush implemented the next part of the plan.

"Mr. Trench," he said as he stopped pacing, "that's enough northerly. Make your course SSW. Mr. Lee, take your place with the lookout at the foretop and run messages for him. Tell him I need to know when he sees the harbor and the eastern forts."

"Aye, sir!" the midshipman saluted and ran forward.

Bush was counting on two things for this second phase of

his attack. One, that the pirates believed he had fled and were not watching for his return, and two, that the western fort had bad communications with its eastern brothers. There was nothing else for him to do but to stand, alone in the center of the quarterdeck, hands behind his back, and wait for events to play out. It wasn't very long before Mr. Lee returned.

"Sir, the lookout says land is visible, but he can't make out the harbor entrance or the eastern forts yet."

"Thank you, Mr. Lee," Bush said calmly. "Tell the lookout I need to know when he is sure."

"Aye, sir!"

Three rounds of pacing brought the return of Mr. Lee.

"Sir!" the lad panted, "the lookout reports he can make out the forts now!"

"Thank you, Mr. Lee! Mr. Trench, I'm going forward."

Bush made his way to the bow and put the glass to his eye. The forts were barely visible from the deck now. They were coming in at more steeply an angle than he wanted; their course would take them into the harbor.

"Mr. Thompson," he said to the midshipman, "my compliments to Mr. Trench. He is to stand by to alter course to the east."

"Aye, sir!" The midshipman went aft.

Bush studied their scene through his glass for a minute or so more, trying to get the timing down for his turn and the attack on the forts. Finally, satisfied, he headed aft.

"Stand by the starboard battery, Mr. Starling!" he shouted as he passed the waist.

"Aye sir!"

"Mr. Trench," Bush said as he stepped on the quarterdeck, "standby to change course."

"Aye, sir," the sailing master said. "On your command."

"Now, Mr. Trench."

The sailing master gestured, and HMS *Lydia* swung around until her bow pointed east and her broadsides were perfectly positioned to deliver more destruction to the Barbary forts.

Bush walked over to the waist.

"You may fire as your guns bear, Mr. Starling," he called calmly.

"Aye, sir," the young lieutenant answered. Bush smiled at the calm response. He was impressed with the third lieutenant's performance on this mission, and he determined to see that his name was prominently mentioned in his report to the Admiralty.

Within three minutes, Bush heard *Lydia's* 12-pounders going off singly or in pairs, the gun captains obviously being much more selective in their targets. Watching their impact on the fort, Bush guessed that Starling had told his captains to shoot for the gun ports. *Good thinking,* thought Bush as he observed the results. *Another point for you, Mr. Starling.*

The second broadside trickled out the same as the first, only the results were the best yet; Bush estimated seven or eight of the fort's guns were put out of action by that broadside alone. He walked to the waist.

"Mr. Starling!"

The Lieutenant appeared. "Sir?"

"Well done to the starboard battery!" Bush called down. "We are going to stay on this course and give the last fort two broadsides before we make our turn. Do you understand?"

"Aye, sir! Two broadsides with the starboard battery, then we make the turn."

"Very good. You may fire on the last fort when your guns bear."

"Aye aye, sir!"

Bush went back to the railing feeling confident and pleased with his ship's performance thus far. What he failed to notice was the third fort observed his attack on its neighbor and had calculated the British frigate's range. When Bush neglected to change course prior to his attack, his ship was a sitting duck.

The Barbary fort beat Mr. Starling to the punch and opened fire first. Their first two shots told, one going through the mains'l, and they other impacting the side of the frigate just aft of the mainmast.

Bush barely managed to remain on his feet. He looked over the side at the hole left by the fort's shot and estimated that his ship had been hit by a 24-pounder. Starling was answering now, but it was obvious to Bush that he had to take action.

"Mr. Trench! Alter our course four point to starboard!"

"Aye, sir!"

Lydia moved in closer to the fort, Bush hoping that the incoming shot might pass over them, but he felt two more hits strike the hull forward.

"Mr. Trench! Six points to port!"

"Aye, sir!"

He went to the waist. "Mr. Starling! Fire as you bear!"

"Aye, sir!"

Bush moved back to the rail, glass to his eye, trying to peer through the smoke to see how his shots were telling on the last fort. He estimated four of the enemy's guns had been put out of action. When Starling's broadside went off, he counted only eight guns. Lydia received another hit, this one on the starboard quarter, before the second broadside went out. Bush counted only seven guns.

He turned to the sailing master. "Take us away straight down the coast. On my command, steer NNE away from the land. Understand?"

"Aye, sir."

"I'm going below. You have the deck until I return."

"Aye, sir."

Bush made his way quickly to the gun deck. The scene that greeted him was not as bad as he feared it was, but it was still bad enough.

He counted six guns out of action, three, possibly four, of which could be put back into action within two or three hours. He counted maybe three or four dead on the deck; it was hard to tell as at least one had been pounded to pulp by an incoming round.

"Mr. Starling?" he called.

"Sir?" the Lieutenant answered. He was dirty and bloody across his coat and on leg, but he moved well enough that Bush judged the blood was not his own.

"What's the damage so far?" Bush asked.

"You can see we have six guns out of action," Starling replied. "We will work on getting as many as we can back into action before we have to man the larboard battery. Hopefully, we can get one or two up and ready by then. We lost ten men thus far, five or six of whom are with the surgeon."

"Understood," Bush said. "They are figuring out how to get our range. That means when we attack again, you are going to have to be more careful. Try to wait until we steady up parallel to the land to get off as many as you can. We will only have a minute or so before we have to change course again. Have your captains ready to fire in twos or threes; hopefully, that will eliminate those who try to fire as we make our next turn."

"Aye, sir."

Bush put his hand on the younger man's arm.

"You're doing very well, Mr. Starling," he said. "Keep it up, but be ready for anything."

"Aye, sir."

Bush went back on deck and looked at the sailing master.

"Now, Mr. Trench."

"Aye, sir."

Wounded though she was, *Lydia* came around to her new course as sweetly as she would on a parade at Spithead. Bush took a moment to look her over, a feeling of pride swelling in his breast.

"Mr. Lee! Find Mr. Franklin. Present him with my compliments, and ask him for a damage report, if you please."

"Aye, sir!"

Bush stopped for a moment to gather his breath. He began to pace again. He dared not stay away from Algiers for any period of time; the gunboats depended on his being there if he was needed. He pulled out his watch and found the action against the three forts had taken nearly an hour. He would follow this course away from the port for about fifteen minutes before making his turn and charging back again to turn a fresh battery against the forts. Hopefully, by the time they engaged the western fort, the gunboats will be on their way out of the harbor.

He stopped pacing and went over to join Mr. Trench and the quartermaster.

"Gentlemen," he said, "here is what I plan to do. As you can see from our last engagement, the enemy is getting far too good as getting our range. This is my plan. Mr. Trench, I want you to run an evasive course past the eastern forts. By that I mean for you to run parallel with the coast for ten to fifteen seconds only. After that, veer off to port or starboard, randomly and at your discretion, long enough to change our range to the fort, then run parallel to the land for another ten to fifteen seconds to give Mr. Starling a chance to fire. Do you understand?"

The sailing master considered for a moment before looking to the quartermaster and then back to the captain. He nodded. "Aye, sir."

"Good. I hope that will give Lydia some protection while still allowing us to inflict maximum damage on the forts. Now, remember, Mr. Trench: make your alterations as random as you can in both direction and distance. Don't wait for my command. Once we have been parallel for a maximum of fifteen seconds, turn!"

"Aye, sir!"

"We have about fifteen minutes before we go about and head back for the eastern forts. I'm going below for a few minutes."

As he made his way below, his fears were realized. The hit Lydia took on her starboard quarter was close enough to damage his privy. He turned in time to see Goodnight stepping from the pantry.

"I beg your pardon, sir," the servant said, "but the surgeon excused me for ten minutes to get a breath of fresh air. I came here instead to see if I could clean anything up."

Bush nodded. "Do you happen to have any port?"

Goodnight smiled. "I do indeed, sir."

Bush went and sat down under the stern window for a moment to rest his head and hopefully clear his thoughts. He closed his eyes for a moment and was surprised when Goodnight had to clear his throat to awaken him.

"Here you are, sir" the servant said, handing him the port. Bush sat up and took a drink, a tad embarrassed that he had fallen asleep. Goodnight said nothing about it, as befitting the faithful servant he was.

Bush finished his drink and rose. He set the empty glass on his desk.

"Goodnight?"

The servant appeared in the doorway. "Sir?"

"When this is all over and we take the Lydia back to England, they will probably pay her off, which means we shall be out of a job, unless you want to catch on with another ship. Is that what you want, Goodnight?"

The servant shrugged. "I haven't given it much thought, actually."

"I've pretty much decided to retire when Lydia is paid off, and I intend to purchase a small estate with my prize money. I wondered if you'd like to come with me."

"In what capacity, sir?"

"Whatever capacity you wish," Bush said. "You can choose. You can be cook, or you can be the manservant. My sister will be living there, so we know who will be running the house." Both men grinned at the inside joke. "You've taken good care of me, both at St. Helena and now here in the Mediterranean, and I'd hoped you would not mind doing it after we retire."

"That's a very kind offer, sir, to be sure," Goodnight said. "I will surely give it serious consideration before we make Plymouth again."

Bush nodded and left the cabin. He went back on deck and pulled out his watch. There were three minutes left of the fifteen he allotted for their run NNE. *Close enough,* he thought.

He turned to the sailing master.

"Alright, Mr. Trench," he said, "let's reverse our course and see if Mr. Gerard and Mr. Brewer are ready to go home."

Lieutenant Gerard was beginning to think it was time to head for home. His division had sunk or set on fire more than twenty gunboats as well as a schooner and two luggers. He had one fireship left, and he was approaching what he believed to be the last group of gunboats in the harbor. This battle had not been as easy as that at Oran; his men had paid the price in blood for every ship they sank. The best he could do for them was to make sure that no-one alive was left behind. He turned from his post at the bow of his boat to look at the ten wounded men lying in the stern; he guessed that two of them would not see the dawn. He turned back again and sighed. One more attack, and then he would make for the harbor mouth and the open sea.

He could see now the group he was heading for was six gunboats anchored behind an eight-gun schooner. He had three gunboats of his division still with him, and he signaled for them to take the Barbary gunboats while he went after the schooner.

Fortunately, the schooner did not have ports cut for any bow chasers, so his approach toward the bow was safe. His boat fired canister into the schooner, and Gerard saw many of the deck crew fall. He turned to his crew.

"Alright, men, one more and we make for home. Are you ready?"

They grappled with the schooner, and Gerard led the boarding party over the rails.

"Surrender!" he shouted, pointing his sword at the pirate behind the wheel.

The man came out from behind the wheel with his arms at his side.

"Very well, infidel," he said. "We surrender."

Gerard was caught off guard by the unexpected response just long enough for the Barbary captain to pull a pistol from his belt and fire.

His life was saved by the sailor next to him, who shouted a warning and tried to push Gerard out of the way. His shove caused the bullet to impact his upper right chest rather than the middle of his forehead. Gerard collapsed to the deck as three of his party pulled a pistol and shot down his treacherous assailant. The remainder of his party attacked the remaining pirates with such ferocity that none were allowed to escape. Gerard's assailant, though dead, had his head and hands cut off, as a message to the Pirates.

The tar who saved the first lieutenant immediately knelt beside him, first to shield him from further attack and also to administer first aid.

"Get the cap'n!" he shouted, referring to the gunboat commander.

"What happened?" the cap'n asked.

"Bloody pirate surrendered and then shot him," the tar replied. "We got to get him back to the ship."

"Right," the cap'n said. "You two, get Mr. Gerard back into the boat. Careful, now! You two, burn this piece of junk. Right! Everyone back into the boat, and let's push off."

They carried Gerard to the back of the boat and laid him down gently, his savior all the while keeping pressure on his wound. The grapple line was cut and they pushed off the burning schooner and made a course for the harbor entrance, leaving the other boats in the division to catch up with them.

Bush's plan for an evasive path past the eastern forts worked fairly well. *Lydia* took only three hits in passing both forts while Mr. Starling was able to get a total of five broadsides fired, albeit two or three guns at a time. They were just passing the second fort, and Bush was pleased with the results.

"Captain!"

It was the lookout in the mizzen tops who shouted.

"What see you?" Bush replied.

"Five ships trying to break out of the harbor, sir!"

"You're sure they're not ours?"

"Aye, sir! They're pirates all right!"

Bush went forward along the rail and put the glass to his eye. It did not take long for him to find them, and when he did, he agreed with the lookout. He went to the waist.

"Stand by, Mr. Starling! There are five pirates trying to escape! I am heading to cut them off. Wait for my orders to fire the larboard battery!"

"Aye, sir!"

"Mr. Trench, alter our course four points to larboard. I want to cut those ships off."

Trench looked at the ships and then back at his captain. He saw that the change of course would take them into the harbor itself, but he decided against pointing it out at that moment.

"Aye, sir," he said.

Lydia responded. The frigate entered the harbor mouth to cut off the escaping ships. The pirates in the forts on either side of the harbor mouth could not believe their luck. As soon as the frigate was between them, both opened fire with devastating effect.

Bush was surprised to be taking such heavy fire from both sides. He held his course long enough for Starling to destroy the five gunboats trying to escape. He turned to Mr. Trench to give the orders to take them back out, and the next two shots fired from the eastern fort struck solidly on *Lydia's* stern and quarterdeck.

In an instant, Bush saw Mr. Trench and a quartermaster's mate vanish in front of him in a cloud of blood and body parts as the ball ran them through. Bush felt something impact his own body, and he fell to the deck. He felt around his body desperately until he found two large splinters sticking out of the left side of his chest. He tried to pull then out, but he was too weak. His vision was blurred by blood running into his left eye; apparently one splinter creased his head as well. He was about to call for help when he discovered all he could do was to lay his head back as the darkness overtook him.

"Captain!" Mr. Lee screamed at seeing Bush fall. "Captain!"

He ran to the companion stair and jumped down to the gun deck.

"Mr. Starling!" he called. "The Captain's been hit!"

Starling bounded up the stairs and found several men assisting the captain. He had no idea what to do, but he realized he was the only officer on the ship.

"I have the deck!" he said. "You men, take the Captain below."

"Sir!" It was the quartermaster, covered in the blood of his mate. "We've got to get the ship out of here!"

"I know!" Starling said. He looked around and spotted Thomas, the signals midshipman.

"Recall our boats," he said.

CHAPTER SEVENTEEN

Brewer stepped out of a Barbary pinnace back into his gunboat while his men set fire to their latest prize.

"Right," he said. "What's next?"

"Sir!"

It was the boat's captain.

"Yes?"

"Recall order from the ship, sir!"

"What?" Brewer risked standing tall in the boat to see for himself. Sure enough, there was *Lydia* flying the recall... Wait! What was she doing in the harbor? She was getting pounded by the forts on each side of the entrance!

"Something's wrong," he said as he crouched down in the boat again. "Get me back there quick! After I jump, rendezvous out to sea, like we did before."

"Aye, sir!"

They pushed off the burning pinnace and swing around, heading for the frigate. Brewer looked around the harbor and estimated that six gunboats were answering the recall order. He sighed and set his lips in a grim line, wondering just how high a price they had to pay to keep England's convoys safe.

As the gunboat approached the ship, Brewer took his position in the bows and prepared to jump for the ladder. He timed it well enough that, although it wasn't very graceful, he didn't end up in the harbor. He looked over his shoulder and watched as his gunboat pulled away from the frigate, and, signaling the other boats to follow, turned and led them to a meeting point safely over the horizon.

Brewer scrambled up the ladder and on to the deck, where he was met by Mr. Starling.

"Where's the captain?" he asked.

"Sickbay," Starling replied, "with two large splinters in his chest. Mr. Gerard hasn't reported in yet. William, we must get out of here!"

Brewer's eyes snapped up to the other's face; he read a growing panic that was becoming hard to keep under control. Starling was reaching his limits.

"Get hold of yourself, Jonah," he said. "Report."

Starling closed his eyes and took a deep breath and let it out. "The captain took the ship into the harbor in order to intercept five gunboats that were trying to escape. We were caught between the two forts, and both of them opened up on us. Mr. Trench and the quartermaster are dead, and the captain's in sickbay. I was called up from the gun deck when the captain fell, and I ordered the recall."

Brewer looked around as he listened to the third lieutenant's report. *Lydia* had taken a beating, to be sure, but her masts were intact, so decisive action may yet save the day.

"Sir!" a hand at the larboard rail was calling. "Gunboat approaching! It's one of ours!"

"Tell her to follow the others out of the harbor!"

"Sir! They say they have Mr. Gerard on board, and he's been badly wounded!"

Brewer looked at the deck as he thought furiously. There was no way he could hold the ship still long enough to lower a stretcher to bring Gerard aboard and get him to the surgeon—not without allowing *Lydia* to be blown out of the water. But if he makes Gerard wait, his friend may die. What should he do? Suddenly, he saw the Corsican's face, and it scowled at him. Brewer knew where his priorities belonged.

"Tell them to head out of the harbor with the others!"

"Aye, sir!"

Brewer turned to Starling. "Jonah, you've done a great job. For the moment, you are acting first lieutenant. Stay on deck." He rose and moved toward the wheel, careful to avoid what was left of the sailing master and quartermaster.

"I have the deck!" he cried. He looked to the quartermaster's mates gathered around the wheel. "Who's the senior mate? You, McNally? Fine. You are acting quartermaster for now. Bring us around to port. I want you to swing a little wide; come as close to the eastern fort as you can without putting us aground."

"Aye, Mr. Brewer."

"What's your plan, sir?" Starling asked. Brewer noticed the acting first lieutenant seemed to be in control of himself again.

"I hope that by swinging as close to the eastern fort as possible on the way out, we can actually sail under her guns for a while, at the same time making the western fort fire at long range. Once we swing past the fort and head for the open sea, we shall give her every stitch she'll take. Speed is what we'll need for the getaway."

The sound of shattering wood erupted on them from above, and they looked up in time to see the mizzen topmast fall over. Fortunately, the mast fell to starboard of the mizzen and hung limply over the rail, slowing the ship considerably.

Brewer grabbed Starling by his coat and pointed at the wreckage. "Grab some men and cut that away! Be quick about it!"

Starling ran toward the debris shouting for men and axes.

Brewer turned back to the wheel and saw McNally and his mates struggling to hold the ship on course. He suddenly wondered why they were not firing. Then he remembered; Starling had been called to the deck, so there was probably no-one to tell the men to fire. He went to the waist and saw Mr. Kennedy, a midshipman in Starling's division, helping to get one of the guns back into action.

"Mr. Kennedy!" he called. "You are in command of the gun deck! I want the larboard battery to fire at that fort as long as they're in range!"

"Aye aye, Mr. Brewer!"

Just then he heard a roar as Starling's men cut the last line and the debris slid over the side. The ship squared up immediately and picked up speed. As they neared the eastern fort, the fire from that direction dwindled. Brewer had been right; they couldn't depress their guns enough to fire on the frigate. That would change as they made their escape.

He paused at a thought and glanced out across the harbor, searching for any additional gunboats trying to make their escape. The harbor was covered with a layer of smoke, but Brewer was fairly sure he saw no others making their way out to sea. He sighed, burdened by the cost, but he put it out of his mind and concentrated at the task at hand.

"Mr. McNally," he said, "when we pass the fort, we want to fly hell-bent for the horizon. Our objective is nothing less than to get out of their gun range as fast as humanly possible. I will make changes in our course as necessary, with the object of trying to throw off their aim as we escape. Ready?"

"Aye, sir!" McNally said.

HMS *Lydia* came out from under the shadow of the eastern fort and crossed into the open sea. The western fort opened up on them, but their shot fell short.

"Keep your course as close to north as possible, Mr.

McNally!" Brewer said. "Let's not give that other fort a shot at us."

"Agreed, sir." McNally worked the wheel for fifteen minutes. "Three points east of north is the best we can do, Mr. Brewer."

"Very well."

The problem at the moment was that running as they were left them open to fire from the eastern fort. Two balls went through the upper works, and Brewer felt one impact in the hull on the starboard quarter. Brewer fought the urge to turn, even when the fort put a shot through the stern window. He was betting their speed would get them out of danger, even with the mizzen topmast gone. Finally, he was rewarded when the shots from the fort fell short of the ship. A cheer went up, and Brewer allowed himself to relax for a moment against the rail.

"Mr. Lee!" he called. The midshipman appeared. "My compliments to the lookout in the main top, and does he see any pursuit from Algiers?"

"Aye, sir." The midshipman saluted and went off on his journey.

Brewer pushed off the rail and walked aft to the wheel. He was joined by Mr. Starling and Mr. McNally.

"If there's no pursuit, we can ease back on the sails," Brewer said. "That should make the carpenter happy." He looked to Starling. "Have you talked to him?"

"Yes, sir. He says we've got two holes in the hull, one on the larboard side forward and the other on the starboard side aft. He's pretty much got the one starboard aft plugged. The pumps should be going any minute. He said he'd appreciate it if we slowed down as soon as we could."

Brewer nodded. "Assign all the hands he needs to the pumps. The captain would never forgive us if we let *Lydia* sink now!"

Starling went off to deal with the carpenter, and Brewer turned to observe the deck. The men looked shocked, as if they never expected anything like this to happen. *Who did?* Brewer thought. Still, they needed to be working.

Mr. Lee reappeared. "Lookout says no pursuit, Mr. Brewer."

"Pass word for the bosun," Brewer said. "Quartermaster, reduce sail and put us on a westerly course. We need to find our gunboats."

"Aye, sir," McNally said. He picked up a speaking trumpet and began bellowing orders as though he'd done it for years. Brewer couldn't help but think that Mr. Trench would be proud of him.

The bosun came up and touched his knuckles to his forehead. "You sent for me, Mr. Brewer?"

"Yes, Mr. Hammersmith. Organize your work details; let us get this ship cleaned up. You know the drill."

"Aye, Mr. Brewer."

Brewer looked around again. The crew seemed to be moving like they were in slow motion or something. What was going on? Well, he couldn't worry about that right now. He turned to the acting quartermaster.

"You have the deck. I'll be in sickbay."

"Aye, sir."

Brewer made his way below and forward until he entered the sickbay. The surgeon was working on a patient at the moment, so Brewer walked from sailor to sailor, speaking to each and offering words of encouragement. He prayed with some and for others until the surgeon was able to join him.

"What's the butcher's bill so far?" he asked.

The doctor wiped his hands on his bloody apron. "Including Mr. Trench and the quartermaster, seventeen dead and thirty-nine wounded. That's without the gunboats, of course."

"We're looking for them now," Brewer said. "They say Lieutenant Gerard's in a bad way."

Wallace looked up from his hands. "Why isn't he aboard?"

"No time while we were in that harbor, Doctor," Brewer said, perhaps a little too strongly. "It was him or the ship. Were the places reversed, Gerard would have made the same decision. *Lydia* comes first. Every time. Now, how's the captain?"

The Doctor had sense enough not to pursue the matter of Mr. Gerard. "The captain's going to be all right, but it's going to be a long recovery. Those two splinters were large, and one of them drove in pretty deep. Fortunately, it didn't hit anything important. The other one stayed closer to the skin, but that one nearly hit his spine. Stopped an inch or two short. I was going to come and see someone about moving him out of here when he was able and putting him back in his cabin."

"Not just yet," Brewer said. "I know we took at least one ball through the stern during our escape. I'll look at the damage when I leave and have Mr. Hammersmith make the repairs a priority."

"Aye," Dr. Wallace agreed. "Goodnight can take better care of the captain than I could give him among so many other wounded."

"Also, as soon as the deck is put to rights, see that you get as many as can move well enough up on the deck. I remember the captain telling me that the fresh air did wonders for the wounded when they fought in the wars."

The surgeon nodded. "I'll see to it. Have the bosun let me know when we can begin moving them. Now, you will have to excuse me. I'm needed."

"Of course, Doctor," Brewer said. He made his way out and went aft. As he'd hoped, he found Mr. Franklin, the carpenter, making his way forward.

"What's the situation, Mr. Franklin?" Brewer asked.

"Well," Franklin said as he took a deep breath and let it out slowly, "I've done with the hole in the starboard quarter. I did it first, because I could do it quickly with just a couple of men to help me. All my other men were forward working on the hole in the larboard bow. It was bigger then this one, but I think the water coming in isn't anything the pumps can't handle."

"Very well, Mr. Franklin. Please keep me informed."

"Aye, sir," Franklin said as he saluted and went forward.

Brewer went to the upper deck and spoke to Mr. Kennedy.

"We've got all but two guns back into service, Mr. Brewer," Kennedy said. "Those last two will need the services of the carpenter in order to get them back into action."

"That will have to wait. He's busy with a leak in the larboard bow. I would not be surprised if very soon Mr. Starling is calling for some of your guns crews to man the pumps."

"Aye, sir. In the meantime, I was just about to set the hands to cleaning the decks and putting things back in order here."

"Excellent idea," Brewer said. "Be sure to get the captain's cabin set back to rights as much as possible. Do your best about it; the doctor wants to move him back to his cabin as soon as possible."

"We'll get on it right away."

"Thank you." He turned to the men. "You men conducted yourselves marvelously today. I will see that every man of you gets an extra ration of grog tonight."

Brewer continued aft to survey what was left of the captain's cabin. It wasn't as bad as he thought it would be. The captain's privy had been hit, and one shot came through from the fort took out a good bit of the stern window, but still...

Brewer made his way to the quarterdeck and was pleased to see the hands at work making repairs and cleaning the decks to get rid of the blood. In the midst of it all, Mr. Lee appeared and saluted. He was soaked from head to toe.

"Mr. Lee," Brewer asked, "why are you so wet?"

"I've been working with the carpenter's mates trying to stop the water coming in at the port bow, sir," he said. "Mr. Franklin asks if there is any way you can have a sail fothered under the bottom to help stop the water while he plugs the hole, sir."

"A good idea, Mr. Lee," Brewer said. "I shall speak to the sailmaker."

He called the sailmaker and had him bring a sail suitable for the purpose up on deck. Mr. Hammersmith, the bosun, organized some hands to get the sail in place under the bows of the ship. Within minutes of the sail being lashed in place, Brewer heard the comforting sounds of the pumps going into action. All they needed now was someone to come by and give them a new mast.

His burgeoning good mood was stunted by the realization that they still had not found the gunboats, and the certainty that if he could not do so soon, his friend would die.

Finally, the cry came they had been waiting for.

"Sail ho!"

"Where away?" Brewer called.

"Fine off the larboard bow! Barely over the horizon, sir!"

"Got them, sir!" Mr. Starling said.

"We'll hold this course for the present," Brewer said. "Mr. Starling, have a sling ready to hoist Mr. Gerard up on deck, and have a crew ready to get him down to the sickbay. There will be others who are injured as well, so be ready. Mr.

Hanson, see to it that the gunboats are rigged for towing as soon as their crews come aboard; I don't want to linger in this area."

"Aye, sir. We'll be quick about it," Hanson said.

Two hours later, they ran down the gunboats. Gerard was the first to be lifted onboard, and Starling's crew immediately carried him below to the sickbay. A couple of the surgeon's mates met the rest of the wounded as they came aboard. Many of them with minor wounds were sent to the forecastle where their lacerations were sewn up in the fresh air. Those with worse injuries were sent below to the sickbay.

Brewer sat back and let his men do their jobs. He set extra lookouts to keep watch on any pursuit out of Algiers, but so far there was none. His intention was to make for Gibraltar at best possible speed just as soon as the gunboat crews were aboard and the boats themselves were rigged for towing. Brewer's heart sank when he counted only six gunboats had made it out of the harbor.

Simpkins, another of Wallace's mates, came running up on deck. He looked around to get his bearings, then made straight for Brewer.

"Sir!" he said as he saluted. "Mr. Goodnight sends his respects, and would you please come down to the sickbay at once, sir? Mr. Goodnight says it's an emergency!"

"Goodnight? Where's Dr. Wallace?" Brewer asked.

Simpkins looked exasperated. "I think that's part of the emergency. Sir, please come!"

"Very well," Brewer turned to Mr. Hanson, the senior midshipman. "You have the deck. I shall be in sickbay."

Brewer ran after the surgeon's mate down and forward. As he drew near, he could hear someone shouting hysterically. He entered the sickbay and paused for a moment to allow his eyes to adjust to the dimmer light. Goodnight approached him.

"Mr. Brewer," he said, "I'm so glad you've come, sir. It's Dr. Wallace, sir! I'm afraid he's had some kind of breakdown or something like it!"

"Goodnight, explain yourself!" Brewer said testily.

Goodnight flushed. "Well, sir, after you left, Dr. Wallace began to drink, sir, quite heavily, in fact. He kept announcing to all of us that he needed the 'courage and wisdom of the bottle', whatever that means, sir. Then it seems that he killed old man Tracy, sir."

"Killed him? How?"

"Well, I wasn't at the table, sir, but it seems that he botched an amputation on Tracy's arm and cut the artery, and Tracy died before the surgeon could cauterize the artery to stop the bleeding."

Brewer nodded and looked down at the deck. He closed his eyes for a moment and sighed. "Go on."

"After that, sir, the Doctor drank even more. Then Mr. Gerard came down, and the Doctor cried, 'No, not another one! Get me my saw!' Well, sir, you can court martial me if you like, but I was not about to let him touch Mr. Gerard, not in his state. I saw Captain James here visiting one of his men and appealed to him, and he ordered Wallace tied in a bed. That's him screaming now, sir."

"Thank you, Goodnight," Brewer said, patting the servant on the arm. "You did the right thing. How's the captain coming along?"

"Hard to tell yet, sir. He's sleeping right now. We're watching for infection."

"Right. Can you take a minute to go check on the captain's cabin and see how that's coming along? Mr. Kennedy is trying to put it back together so we can get the captain out of here."

"Aye, sir. I'll be right back."

Brewer moved over to the bedside of the hallucinating surgeon. He stood beside Captain James. Dr. Wallace strained against his restraints and squeezed his eyes shut as he thrashed about. His screams were such as if he were terrified and undergoing torture.

"Doctor!" Brewer cried. "Snap out of it! What's wrong with you?"

The new voice seemed to cut through Wallace's delirium. The surgeon stopped screaming and looked around wide-eyed.

"Mr. Brewer?" he whispered. "Is that you?"

"Yes, Doctor, it's me. What's wrong?"

"Wrong? *Wrong?*" He started to pull against his restraints. "They've found me, that's what's wrong! Now they'll get me for sure! For sure!" The surgeon threw his head back on the pillow and began to laugh hysterically, eventually collapsing and weeping uncontrollably. Brewer looked up and caught Captain James' eye. The marine captain motioned for Brewer to step away with him.

"I've seen this before," James said. "I'm afraid the good doctor has got hold of some bad whiskey."

"That's it?" Brewer asked incredulously.

"It's nothing to take lightly, I assure you. Men have died after going through ravings like the Doctor's."

Brewer sighed. "Great. So what can we do about Mr. Gerard?" He looked around. "Where is he?"

James pointed to a cot laid in the corner of the sickbay, and the two officers made their way over to it. Brewer felt the first lieutenant's head; he definitely was running a fever. His breathing was shallow and fast, and his shirt was soaked with sweat. Brewer looked at James.

"I feel so helpless," he said. "I have absolutely no idea how to help him."

James moved past Brewer to stand at Gerard's head. Tenderly, he slid his hand behind Gerard's injured shoulder and felt around. Gerard gasped in pain, but did not open his eyes. James pulled out his hand and looked at it. It was soaked with sweat. James grunted.

"What?" Brewer asked.

"No blood or exit wound on the back of the shoulder. That means the ball is still in his shoulder." James looked at the makeshift bandages covering the wound, gently lifting the top layers slightly before laying them back on the wound again. He raised his fingers to his nose and sniffed.

"Looks like at least one shirt used as a pressure bandage, maybe two. The trouble with that is that although the bleeding is stopped for the moment, if we take those bandages off it may rip the wound open again and restart the bleeding." James wiped his fingers on his kerchief. "Another thing is infection. Until we can get his clothes off him, we have no idea if the ball carried any of his uniform into the wound. The longer they are in there, they could fester and cause infection or even gangrene, which is a death sentence."

At that moment, Goodnight came back into the sickbay.

"Mr. Brewer," he said, "Mr. Kennedy says the captain's cabin should be ready for him in two or three hours."

"That's good news, Goodnight. Tell me, who's the senior mate down here?"

"In the sickbay, sir? That would be Mullins, sir. Over there, sir, stitching that wounded arm."

"Is he good?"

Goodnight grimaced. "Not really, sir. If you want the best of the lot, that would be Dawson, sir. It's my understanding that he attended medical school for a while before he got in trouble with a young lady in the area and had to go to sea to avoid prosecution. I believe he's tending the wounded up on deck, sir."

Brewer looked at Gerard for a moment before making his decision. "Pass the word for Mr. Dawson."

"Aye, sir."

Dawson appeared a short time later.

"Where have you been?" Brewer chastised him.

"I'm sorry, sir," Dawson replied, "but I was in the middle of sewing a topman's forearm, and I couldn't leave until I finished the job and saw it bandaged, sir."

Brewer clamped his mouth shut and looked at Gerard. *How stupid of me,* he thought. Of course, Dawson was perfectly correct in what he did. He nodded and looked back to Dawson.

"My apologies, Mr. Dawson," he said. "You were quite right to do as you did."

"Thank you, sir."

"I sent for you, because Dr. Wallace appears to have had a breakdown of some sort. Captain James believes he got hold of some bad whiskey and is now delirious." He turned to Gerard again. "Lieutenant Gerard took a ball in his upper chest. According to Captain James, there is no exit wound, so the ball must still be inside his shoulder. Goodnight speaks highly of you, so I want you to do what you can for him."

"I'm not a doctor, sir."

"No, but you went to medical school, at least for a while. That's more than anyone else on this ship can say. Just do your best."

"He may die if I do something wrong, sir."

"He'll die anyway if somebody doesn't do something. Take a look."

"Aye, sir."

Dawson drew a deep breath and let it out slowly as he stepped up and looked Gerard over. He put his ear down to Gerard's nose and mouth while he watched his chest at the same time. He put his finger to the first lieutenant's throat to feel his pulse, then he put the backs of his fingers on the unconscious man's forehead before standing up. He walked away and returned with a stool, a lantern, a forceps, a scissor and more bandages. He handed the lantern to Brewer.

"Hold it here," Dawson said as he positioned the lantern.

"I really can't—"

"Hold it here." Dawson said again. "Everyone else is busy, and I have to see the wound."

Brewer surrendered and held the lantern as instructed while Dawson got to work slowly and carefully peeling the bandages away. The top one came off without too much trouble, but the one underneath—the one directly on the wound—was saturated with dried blood. Now Dawson picked carefully, using the forceps and occasionally the scissor to help lift the makeshift bandage away from the wound. Once he exposed the wound, he pulled the rest of the bloody shirt away, causing a little bleeding at the edge of the wound. He applied pressure with a clean bandage with one hand while he pulled the lantern a bit closer as he examined the wound itself. He felt around the edges of the hole in Gerard's chest as tenderly as possible, but his ministrations still caused Gerard to gasp in pain. He explored the wound with the forceps; Brewer thought they went in slowly for an inch or so but no farther before Dawson carefully withdrew them and covered the wound in clean bandages and tied them down. He stood, wiping his hands on his apron and stood beside Brewer.

"The ball's in there, all right," he said, "but I can't do any more until I can see better. I also think I'd better look through some of the doctor's medical books before I go poking around in there. We have to go in soon, or infection will set in. It may have already, what with the fever he's running, and if it turns to gangrene, well, he's a dead man."

Brewer looked at the surgeon's mate and hoped he wasn't

out of his depth.

He left the sickbay and spent the next several hours supervising repairs to the ship. First, he went forward and found the carpenter to get an update on his repairs. Franklin was supervising two of his mates hammering home a plug in the hole. Brewer likened it to trying to insert a plug in a dike. Franklin stepped away to speak to him.

"Ah, sir," he said. "Thank you for the sail. It really did the trick. It cut down the water flow and allowed us to get the plug put in. We're just hammering it home now. Not the prettiest piece of handiwork, I know, but it should get us back to Gibraltar all right. The pumps are making headway now against the water. As soon as I'm done here, I will go and measure the level in the hold and come report to you."

Brewer nodded. "Good work, Mr. Franklin. I'll be on deck."

He left there and went aft to check on the progress with the captain's cabin. Mr. Kennedy and his crew were nearly ready for the captain to be transported back there. Brewer promised to send Mr. Franklin there at the earliest possible moment to see what he could do about the captain's privy.

He stepped up on deck just as dusk was beginning to fall to find the repairs proceeding apace. Much of the debris had been pushed over the side, and the cook and his mates were almost done sewing up the dead. Brewer counted twenty-seven awaiting burial.

His thoughts were interrupted by the arrival of the bosun.

"We've repaired most of the damage, Mr. Brewer," he said. "Should do well enough to get us to Gibraltar."

"Should?"

"I'm worried about the main topmast, sir. She was hit, but it wasn't enough to bring her down. We've braced it as best we could, but I'm afraid one sharp blow could bring her down."

"Well, keep your eye on it. I'd rather not be hove to long enough to replace it, not with Mr. Gerard the way he is and us with no doctor."

The bosun knuckled his forehead. "Agreed, sir."

Brewer worked through the night helping to set the ship to rights. He performed the ceremony to bury the dead at sea, repeating the words for each time the grate was raised and two comrades slipped into the deep and feeling a little more lost with each. He was everywhere, inspecting and correcting, not wanting to face the world if he should stop long enough to allow it to close in on him.

HMS *Lydia* finally got under way shortly after midnight, making a speed of less than four knots in an attempt to make it to Gibraltar without having to stop to replace any masts. Dawn found Brewer still on the quarterdeck, exhaustion dulling his brain and his body to the point of snapping at everyone who spoke to him.

Mr. Rivkins approached him and saluted.

"I beg your pardon, sir."

"What is it?" Brewer snapped.

"The captain sends his compliments and requests that you join him in his cabin, sir," Rivkins said.

Brewer's eyes narrowed, as though the midshipman may have lied to him. "The captain?"

"Aye, sir."

Brewer closed his eyes and bit his tongue to keep silent. He took a deep breath and let it out slowly to regain some measure of control, then he looked at the midshipman.

"Of course," he said. "My respects to the captain, and please tell him I shall come right away."

Rivkins saluted. "Aye, sir."

Brewer took a moment to walk to the rail and leaned over it to order his thoughts before meeting the captain. He stood up and rubbed his face with both hands and breathed deeply to try to get some life back into his tired brain. Finally, he straightened his uniform as best he could and turned to the midshipman of the watch.

"You have the deck," he said. "I shall be with the captain. Mr. Starling should come on deck at the turn of the watch."

"Aye, aye, sir."

Brewer made his way below and was admitted to the captain's cabin by the sentry. Goodnight met him inside the door with a cup of strong, hot coffee.

"Captain Bush thought you might need it, sir," he said apologetically.

Brewer had the sense to smile and accept the coffee, thanking Goodnight. The first sip was so revivifying that he stood there for several seconds, drinking the nectar as fast as his burnt lips and scalded mouth would allow. Goodnight appeared with another when he was finished.

"Thank you," Brewer said as they traded cups.

"The captain's bunk has been hung in the day cabin," Goodnight explained. "Mr. Kennedy and Mr. Dawson thought the fresh air coming in through the broken windows may be good for him."

Brewer nodded and made his way back to his captain. He found Bush with more color than when he saw him last in the sickbay. His head was propped up on extra pillows, and he smiled when his second lieutenant came in.

"How are you, sir?" Brewer asked.

Brewer waited while his captain's eyes took in his appearance and carriage. Bush frowned.

"Good Lord, Mr. Brewer," he said, barely above a whisper, "you look worse than I feel. When was the last time you slept?"

Brewer shrugged. "I'm not sure, sir. We've all been busy since our return for the raid."

"Give me a report, Mr. Brewer."

Brewer took a deep breath and launched into his report. "We lost the mizzen topmast before we could get out of the harbor, sir, and Mr. Hammersmith's worried that the main topmast may not make it back to Gibraltar. We're currently on course for there, crawling at three or four knots."

Bush frowned. "Why not heave to and let him step a new mast? We have one, haven't we?"

"Aye, sir," Brewer hesitated, closing his eyes and then looked at his feet before meeting his captain's eyes. "But Mr. Gerard's been hit badly, sir. Shot in the upper right chest. We're trying to keep him alive until we can get to port."

"Where's the doctor?"

"Under restraints in sick bay, sir. Captain James speculates he drank a large quantity of bad whiskey. He's delirious, sir; James thinks he may die from it."

Bush allowed his head to drop back on his pillow and closed his eyes. Brewer watched him silently, making sure his chest rose and fell again as he breathed. He took a drink of his coffee; it was nearly tepid now, but it was still warm. He turned when he heard Goodnight appear at the door and shook his head at the servant's offer of a fresh cup. He turned back in time to see Bush's eyes open.

"And the butcher's bill?"

"Twenty-seven dead thus far," Brewer said, trying to sound as matter-of-fact as possible. "Perhaps fifty or sixty injured. With the doctor down, I'm not sure. Sir, only six gunboats made it out of Algiers."

Bush said nothing to the news. He closed his eyes and turned his head away on the pillow. Brewer wasn't sure if he was trying to hide tears but decided not to ask.

"Tell me about Mr. Gerard," the Captain said.

"He was shot in the upper right of his chest when boarding a gunboat. Captain James determined that the ball was still in there. On Goodnight's recommendation, I assigned Dawson to look after him. He went to medical school before shipping out with us. He will be going in to try to get the ball out, along with any of Gerard's uniform that may be in the wound. Captain James pointed out—and Dawson agreed—that if they were left in, they could fester and cause an infection, possibly leading to gangrene."

Bush turned back. "Very well. Please keep me informed." He sighed. "Is there anything else I should know about?"

"We were holed twice below the waterline, one in the port bow and the other in the starboard quarter. Mr. Franklin patched them both. The pumps are keeping up with it easily; we should make Gibraltar with no problems from that quarter."

Bush nodded. "Who has the deck?"

"Mr. McNally, sir. I made him acting quartermaster for the duration. Mr. Starling is to relieve him at the turn of the watch."

"Mr. Brewer, listen to me carefully," Bush said. "I want you to go to the gun room and go to bed. A minimum of four hours' sleep, do you understand me?"

Brewer was suddenly too tired to protest. "Aye, sir."

"Come and see me tomorrow with an update. Now, good night."

"Good night, sir."

Brewer wearily made his way to his cabin. Just before he entered the gun room, he was stopped by Simpkins.

"Sir," he said simply as he knuckled his forehead, "Mr. Dawson's sent me. The surgeon's dead."

Brewer looked to the deck below, part of him glad that Wallace was relieved of his sufferings. He raised his head and nodded.

"Anything else? Mr. Gerard?"

Simpkins shook his head. "Mr. Dawson's not operated

yet, sir. But soon, I think."

"Thank you, Simpkins."

Brewer went to bed, not bothering to take his coat off before falling fast asleep.

It was the sun that brought Lieutenant William Brewer to consciousness. He tried rolling over and shading his face with his hand, but once its rays had pierced the darkness, he knew that sleep would not return. In the distance, he heard the ship's bell going off. *Five, six, seven...?*

His head snapped up from the pillow. Seven bells? What was going on? He sat up quickly and tried to blink his eyes clear of sleep. He leapt to his feet and headed for the door, remembering just before he opened it that he was still in the uniform he had slept in all night. He hurriedly changed and went up on deck.

The sun was high in the sky when he stepped up on *Lydia's* deck. *Good God!* he thought. *That was seven bells in the forenoon watch!* He looked around and found Lieutenant Starling on the quarterdeck.

"Good morning, Mr. Brewer," Starling said when Brewer joined him. I was beginning to wonder if you would sleep all day."

"Why did you let me sleep?" Brewer demanded.

"The captain sent Goodnight up not long after you left him—right after I took over the watch, in fact—with a message that said not to wake you until noon." Starling smiled. "I must say you look better than you did yesterday."

"Thank you," Brewer answered absently. He looked around again. He saw three more corpses sewn up and awaiting burial. He looked up and was pleased to see the main topmast was still there; at least Mr. Hammersmith would be pleased.

"Who relieves you?" he asked Starling.

"Mr. Hanson is to relieve at the turn of the watch," Starling said.

"I'll take the one after that," Brewer said. "That way, you can get eight hours sleep if you wish, and if you will relieve me, Hanson can do the same."

Starling grinned and saluted. "Aye aye, sir."

"Pass the word for a burial detail," Brewer said.

"Aye, sir."

Soon two of the sewn corpses were on a grate while Brewer said the obligatory words before committing their bodies to the deep. He wondered which of them was the doctor but then decided he didn't want to know. He shook his head in disgust when he remembered the way Wallace died. How any man could do that to himself was beyond him, and he vowed that if he had the chance, he would do all in his power to help a friend to avoid it.

"Keep us moving," Brewer said. "I'm going to the sickbay."

He made his way below and found the light dim in the sickbay and the atmosphere foul, even in the middle of the day. He saw Mullins first and went to him.

"How's it going down here, Mr. Mullins?" he asked.

Mullins shrugged. "We lost two more last night, besides Dr. Wallace," he said with a tired voice. "I'm not sure about Mr. Gerard; you'll have to check with Mr. Dawson."

"I shall," Brewer replied. He put his hand on the mate's arm. "You've done well down here, Mr. Mullins. Tell me, when was the last time you slept?"

"I caught a cat nap during the night, sir," Mullins said. "I'm all right, sir."

"If you say so," Brewer gave in, "but as soon as you can, I want you to get at least four hours of sleep. They can call you if you're needed."

"Aye aye, sir," he said with a weak smile. "Thank you, sir."

Brewer patted him on the arm and made his way over toward Mr. Gerard, who was lying on a cot in the far corner. Brewer saw that Gerard's head and shoulders were outside of the blanket that covered the rest of him, and his coat and shirt had been removed. There was a new bandage on the wounded shoulder. He gently touched the first lieutenant's forehead and frowned. It was warm—quite warm, in fact. Gerard's breathing looked to be steadier than when he'd last seen him, and his color was better, even in the dim lamplight. Mr. Dawson was there, asleep against the bulkhead. Brewer hesitated before awaking him, but in the end he had to have the information for his report to the captain.

"Mr. Dawson?" he said gently as he touch the sleeping mate on the shoulder. "Mr. Dawson?"

The mate's eyes fluttered open and took a moment to focus. He leaned forward with his elbows on his knees and rubbed his eyes for a moment before automatically checking his patient's temperature.

"Well?" Brewer prompted.

"It's the same," Dawson said absently. He shook his head to clear it when he realized who was asking. "Sorry, Mr. Brewer. I had him open for over an hour last night, digging around in his shoulder. I got the ball out, and in one piece, too. No fragment issues to deal with. No, the trouble is that his shirt had a hole in it. The coat was torn, but the shirt had a hole."

"And?" Brewer asked.

"I didn't find it. That piece of cloth could still be in his body and causing the fever. It may lead to infection."

"Why don't you go in again and look for it?"

"I'm not good enough, Mr. Brewer," he said, sad but matter-of-fact. "I shiver now when I think of the damage I may have already caused to his shoulder when I went in the first time." He sighed. "We won't really know until he wakes and up tries to use it. I do know one thing; we need to get him to a doctor—a real doctor—and quickly, before his fever brings on something worse."

"I'm working on it," Brewer said. "The trouble is that if we put on too much sail, we could lose the main topmast. If that happens, it may cost us more time than we can afford."

Dawson nodded. "I see."

Brewer looked at the unconscious Gerard with concern. "Look after him, Mr. Dawson."

"Aye, sir," the mate said, but Brewer was already out the door of the sickbay, heading aft.

He went up on deck to check their estimated position before going to report to the captain. When he arrived, the sentry admitted him. Goodnight met him inside the door.

"How is he?" Brewer asked.

"He slept most of the night," the servant replied, "other than a couple time when he moved or was moved wrong by the ship and cried out. I gave him more laudanum when he awoke this morning. He hasn't asked for any more, so I hope that's a good sign."

Brewer nodded and walked into the day cabin. He thought for a moment that Bush might be sleeping, but the captain turned his head to him and smiled, lifting his hand a little off his leg where it had rested.

"Mr. Brewer," he said softly.

Brewer came to his bedside. "How are you this morning, sir?"

"A little better, I think," he said, "but it hurts. What do you have for me, Mr. Brewer?"

"Well, sir, we are crawling along at an average of four knots toward Gibraltar in order not to tax that bad main topmast. We lost three more men last night, including Dr. Wallace."

Bush allowed his head to drop onto his pillow. He closed his eyes and sighed deeply.

"Poor man," he said. "He never could defeat his demons."

"I went to the sickbay and spoke with Mr. Dawson," Brewer continued. "He operated last night and removed the ball from Mr. Gerard's chest. The problem is that Mr. Gerard's running a fever, sir—a good one. Dawson thinks it may be due to the hole in Gerard's shirt." He saw that his captain wasn't following. "Dawson thinks the material from the hole is still in the wound, sir. The problem is that he doesn't want to go in to look for it again. He says he's not good enough. He didn't find it when he was in the first time, and he's afraid that he already may have caused damage to the shoulder area with his probing."

"How long to Gibraltar?"

"At least two more days, at this speed," Brewer said. "I have extra lookouts posted, watching for an Indiaman or something with a doctor on board."

Bush lay back on his pillow and nodded. Brewer could see that even this simple interview exhausted him; beads of sweat were forming on his forehead.

"I should let you rest, sir," Brewer said.

Bush motioned for him to wait a minute.

"You are in command, Mr. Brewer," he said in a voice barely above a whisper. "I have full confidence in you, your abilities and your decisions. Don't question, *command*."

"Aye aye, sir."

The voyage to Gibraltar did not tax Brewer's seamanship as much as it did his patience. Concern for Gerard was foremost in his mind, but no amount of extra lookouts could induce an Indiaman to come over the horizon. John

Company was renowned for the quality of their doctors. Twice while pacing the quarterdeck, Brewer debated with himself the merits of heaving to and replacing the masts. They had acceptable replacements that would get them to their destination, and at a much faster pace than they were now crawling. Both times, he decided against it, reasoning that the time spent hove to may spell doom for the first lieutenant.

The next day, word came from Dawson that Gerard's condition was taking a turn for the worse. His fever was climbing, but Dawson assured the acting-captain that they were doing all they could for him. Brewer stood on the quarterdeck and set his jaw. They would make it in time. They had to.

They finally got within sight of their destination. Brewer called Mr. Starling.

"As soon as we drop anchor," he said quietly, "I want you and to get Mr. Gerard to the hospital ashore. Take Dawson with you; he can answer any questions as to Gerard's care while on board. In fact, have Mr. Gerard brought up on deck now, and have the boat swung out, ready for lowering. I don't want to waste any time."

"Aye aye, sir."

They got Gerard on deck and then lowered him into the boat, Starling and Dawson going down last. The boat pulled away toward the shore, Brewer on the quarterdeck, watching them go and wishing they could move faster. He knew in his heart he had done all he could for his friend; he just hoped it was enough.

He sighed and went below. It was time to report to the captain.

THE END

ABOUT THE AUTHOR
JAMES KEFFER

James Keffer was born September 9, 1963, in Youngstown, Ohio, the son of a city policeman and a nurse. He grew up loving basketball, baseball, tennis, and books. He graduated high school in 1981 and began attending Youngstown State University to study mechanical engineering.

He left college in 1984 to enter the U.S. Air Force. After basic training, he was posted to the 2143rd Communications Squadron at Zweibruecken Air Base, West Germany. While he was stationed there, he met and married his wife, Christine, whose father was also assigned to the base. When the base was closed in 1991, James and Christine were transferred up the road to Sembach Air Base, where he worked in communications for the 2134th Communications Squadron before becoming the LAN manager for HQ 17th Air Force.

James received an honorable discharge in 1995, and he and his wife moved to Jacksonville, Florida, to attend Trinity Baptist College. He graduated with honors in 1998, earning a Bachelor of Arts degree. James and Christine have three children.

Hornblower and the Island is the first novel James wrote, and it is the first to be published by Fireship Press. He has self-published three other novels. He currently lives and works in Jacksonville, Florida, with his wife and three children.

IF YOU ENJOYED THIS BOOK
Please write a review.
This is important to the author and helps to get the
word out to others
Visit

PENMORE PRESS
www.penmorepress.com

All Penmore Press books are available directly
through our website.

BREWER'S LUCK

BY

JAMES KEFFER

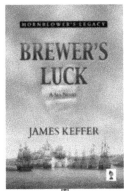

After gaining valuable experience as an aide to Governor Lord Horatio Hornblower, William Brewer is rewarded with a posting as first lieutenant on the frigate HMS *Defiant*, bound for American waters. Early in their travels, it seems as though Brewer's greatest challenge will be evading the wrath of a tyrannical captain who has taken an active dislike to him. But when a hurricane sweeps away the captain, the young lieutenant is forced to assume command of the damaged ship, and a crew suffering from low morale.

Brewer reports their condition to Admiral Hornblower, who orders them into the Caribbean to destroy a nest of pirates hidden among the numerous islands. Luring the pirates out of their coastal lairs will be difficult enough; fighting them at sea could bring disaster to the entire operation. For the *Defiant* to succeed, Brewer must rely on his wits, his training, and his ability to shape a once-ragged crew into a coherent fighting force.

PENMORE PRESS
www.penmorepress.com

The Dragon's Breath

by

James Boschert

Talon stared wide-eyed at the devices, awed that they could make such an overwhelming, head-splitting noise. His ears rang and his eyes were burning from the drifting smoke that carried with it an evil stink. "That will show the bastards," Hsü told him with one of his rare smiles. "The General calls his weapons 'the Dragon's breath.' They certainly stink like it."

Talon, an assassin turned knight turned merchant, is restless. Enticed by tales of lucrative trade, he sets sail for the coasts of Africa and India. Traveling with him are his wife and son, eager to share in this new adventure, as well as Reza, his trusted comrade in arms. Treasures beckon at the ports, but Talon and Reza quickly learn that dangers attend every opportunity, and the chance rescue of a Chinese lord named Hsü changes their destination—and their fates.

Hsü introduces Talon to the intricacies of trading in China and the sophisticated wonders of Guangzhou, China's richest city. Here the companions discover wealth beyond their imagining. But Hsü is drawn into a political competition for the position of governor, and his opponents target everyone associated with him, including the foreign merchants he has welcomed into his home. When Hsü is sent on a dangerous mission to deliver the annual Tribute to the Mongols, no one is safe, not even the women and children of the household. As Talon and Reza are drawn into supporting Hsü's bid for power, their fighting skills are put to the test against new weapons and unfamiliar fighting styles. It will take their combined skills to navigate the treacherous waters of intrigue and violence if they hope to return to home.

PENMORE PRESS
www.penmorepress.com

Historical fiction and nonfiction
Paperback available for order on line
and as Ebook with all major distributers

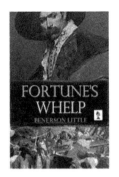

Fortune's Whelp
by
Benerson Little

Privateer, Swordsman, and Rake:

Set in the 17th century during the heyday of privateering and the decline of buccaneering, *Fortune's Whelp* is a brash, swords-out sea-going adventure. Scotsman Edward MacNaughton, a former privateer captain, twice accused and acquitted of piracy and currently seeking a commission, is ensnared in the intrigue associated with the attempt to assassinate King William III in 1696. Who plots to kill the king, who will rise in rebellion—and which of three women in his life, the dangerous smuggler, the wealthy widow with a dark past, or the former lover seeking independence—might kill to further political ends? Variously wooing and defying Fortune, Captain MacNaughton approaches life in the same way he wields a sword or commands a fighting ship: with the heart of a lion and the craft of a fox.

PENMORE PRESS
www.penmorepress.com

MIDSHIPMAN GRAHAM AND THE
BATTLE OF
ABUKIR

BY

JAMES BOSCHERT

It is midsummer of 1799 and the British Navy in the Mediterranean Theater of operations. Napoleon has brought the best soldiers and scientists from France to claim Egypt and replace the Turkish empire with one of his own making, but the debacle at Acre has caused the brilliant general to retreat to Cairo.

Commodore Sir Sidney Smith and the Turkish army land at the strategically critical fortress of Abukir, on the northern coast of Egypt. Here Smith plans to further the reversal of Napoleon's fortunes. Unfortunately, the Turks badly underestimate the speed, strength, and resolve of the French Army, and the ensuing battle becomes one of the worst defeats in Arab history.

Young Midshipman Duncan Graham is anxious to get ahead in the British Navy, but has many hurdles to overcome. Without any familial privileges to smooth his way, he can only advance through merit. The fires of war prove his mettle, but during an expedition to obtain desperately needed fresh water – and an illegal duel – a French patrol drives off the boats, and Graham is left stranded on shore. It now becomes a question of evasion and survival with the help of a British spy. Graham has to become very adaptable in order to avoid detection by the French police, and he must help the spy facilitate a daring escape by sea in order to get back to the British squadron.

"Midshipman Graham and The Battle of Abukir is both a rousing Napoleonic naval yarn and a convincing coming of age story. The battle scenes are riveting and powerful, the exotic Egyptian locales colorfully rendered." – John Danielski, author of *Capital's Punishment*

PENMORE PRESS
www.penmorepress.com

Force 12 in German Bight
by
James Boschert

Considering that oil and gas have been flowing from under the North Sea for the best part of half a century, it is perhaps surprising that more writers have not taken the uncompromising conditions that are experienced in this area – which extends from the north of Scotland to the coasts of Norway and Germany – for the setting of a novel. James Boschert's latest redresses the balance.

The book takes its title from the name of an area regularly referred to in the legendary BBC Shipping Forecast, one which experiences some of the worst weather conditions around the British Isles. It is a fast-paced story which smacks of authenticity in every line. A world of hard men, hard liquor, hard drugs and cold-blooded murder. The reality of the setting and the characters, ex-military men from both sides of the Atlantic, crooked wheeler-dealers, and Danish detectives, male and female, are all in on the action.

This is not story telling akin to a latter day Bulldog Drummond, nor a James Bond, but simply a snortingly good yarn which will jangle the nerve ends, fill your nose with the smell of salt and diesel oil, your ears with the deafening sound of machinery aboard a monster pipe-dredging ship and, above all, make you remember never to underestimate the power of the sea.

–Roger Paine, former Commander, Royal Navy .

PENMORE PRESS
www.penmorepress.com

Penmore Press

Challenging, Intriguing, Adventurous, Historical and Imaginative

www.penmorepress.com

CPSIA information can be obtained
at www.ICGtesting.com
Printed in the USA
BVHW030857210519
548900BV00001B/10/P